VENGEANCE AT THE FALKLANDS

Marcus Baxter Thrillers
Book Five

Tim Chant

SAPERE
BOOKS

VENGEANCE AT THE FALKLANDS

Published by Sapere Books.

, 24 Trafalgar Road, Ilkley, LS29 8HH
United Kingdom

saperebooks.com

ISBN: 978-0-85495-669-2

CHAPTER ONE

His Majesty's Dockyard, Devonport, November 1914

Well, at least it's not bloody Scapa, Marcus Baxter thought to himself. A cold rain lashed his face and the wind tore the launch's plume of smoke to shreds as it slid across the murky waters of the River Tamar. *Though it might as well be.*

Sitting in the stern of the launch, Baxter tried not to brood over his situation. Just a few weeks ago, he'd been on active service, raiding the enemy-held coastline of German East Africa to prevent a planned invasion of Zanzibar. Now, despite the fact that Britain was at war and her Navy heavily engaged around the world, he found himself reduced to a glorified delivery boy in one of the largest naval bases and dockyards along the south coast.

Baxter sighed. *At least it's not Scapa, and at least I'm in uniform.* His cuffs still had the wavy gold lines of the Royal Navy Volunteer Reserve, and they were still only those of a lieutenant. He had hoped for more, given his small but significant victory on the Rufiji River, deep behind enemy lines. Baxter had been given to understand, however, that he was lucky to have maintained even his reserve commission, considering he had overstepped his authority a number of times on that posting. The issue was further complicated by the fact that he'd been on a somewhat sensitive mission for the British Naval Intelligence Division, or 'Room 39' as it was nicknamed, which had required a degree of discretion. Apparently, being employed, and still drawing his pay, would have to be reward enough.

He pulled his scarf tighter around his neck, feeling his mood darken. It didn't help that his head felt thick from a few too many glasses of port the previous night, and he was struggling to adjust to the stark change of temperature, despite years of experience that had taken him all the way from cold northern climes to the equator and then onwards into southern latitudes.

The handful of ratings in the launch eyed him with suspicion. He'd only been at Devonport for a few weeks, hardly enough time to settle in and get to know his fellow officers, let alone the ratings placed under his command. Baxter hadn't felt much like making the effort when he'd arrived, which had perhaps been a mistake.

"Hot cup of tea when we get in, lads," the petty officer in charge of the small crew murmured. "And not long until spirits are up."

That got a laugh and even a small cheer from the crew. Baxter had spent the last week in ostensible command of the launch, running errands for ... well, anyone more senior to him, really. Mostly delivering post, messages and supplies to the guardships and the trawlers tasked with keeping the waters clear of German mines and looking out for U-boats. It was an assignment that probably wouldn't even have warranted a midshipman or sub-lieutenant, let alone someone of his own rank, and he worried at that. Was there someone assigned to the staff here who knew of him, and his somewhat abortive first career in the RN? Or was it just a case of not quite knowing what to do with an officer who'd arrived with orders but no specific assignment?

The dockyard, the largest of its kind in the world, spread up the river ahead of him. The bays were full, old warships slated for the breaker's yard or laid up in reserve being hurriedly brought back into fighting trim. Baxter idly wondered what the current First Sea Lord, Jackie Fisher, thought of the development, given his attempts to rid the establishment of obsolete types. He found himself smiling when he realised the same could be said of him — saved from dereliction by the outbreak of war.

The smile disappeared when he realised some of the sailors were casting suspicious glances his way, and he schooled his expression back into one of professional severity as the helmsman brought them in towards the victualling yard.

"Anything to report, Mr Baxter?" Jones, the elderly lieutenant commander asked as he signed the paperwork to confirm the successful delivery of several sacks of fresh bread, a postbag, and sundry other supplies to one of the minor warships patrolling off Plymouth.

"Nothing, sir," Baxter grunted, then forced himself into a more congenial manner. "Snow on the air, though."

"Well, it is November," Jones said, kindlier than Baxter perhaps deserved. He squinted up at Baxter. "Are you quite well, Lieutenant? You look a little peaky — perhaps you should visit the sickbay?"

"I'm quite all right, sir, but thank you for your concern." He didn't fancy getting a reputation for shirking duty, on top of being antisocial.

"Well, that's us for the day," Jones said. Like Baxter, his insignia was that of the Navy reserve, but unlike Baxter, that was probably as a result of long service in the regular RN followed by retirement into the reserves. "Perhaps I'll see you in the lounge later?"

Baxter hesitated. He tended to take his meals in the mess attached to the officers' quarters, and then retire to his room with a bottle. If he was going to remain posted here for any length of time, he should at least try to get to know some of the other officers. "I might drop by for a gin, sir," he said.

"The tonic will probably do you good. Carry on, Mr Baxter."

Baxter saluted, then beckoned the petty officer over. He realised with a certain amount of chagrin that he'd forgotten the man's name, if he'd ever known it. "Dismiss the men," he said, trying to cover his brief consternation and reaching for something positive to say. "Good work today."

"Good work every day, sir," the bluejacket said as he saluted. "And it'll be good work tomorrow."

Baxter watched him go, standing alone on the windswept concrete of the wharf. The air was bitterly cold and carried with it the smell of rotting seaweed, smoke, and the tang of salt water from the sea. The light was already fading behind heavy clouds that promised snow overnight, but the noise of welding and hammering continued from the big sheds where everything from motor launches to armoured cruisers were being worked on. There were more ships in the harbour and estuary beyond: the long, low shapes of warships and taller merchant vessels and liners. Some would be waiting their turn in the dockyards for repairs, or in the case of some civilian ships for conversion into Armed Merchant Cruisers. Others were just going about their business: tramp steamers plying their trade along the waterways and coasts of England and deepwater freighters keeping the country's lifeblood of international commerce going, despite the new threats of mines and torpedoes. Not that many captains, civil or military, thought the threat would ever become real.

Baxter turned the collar of his peacoat up, shoved his hands into his pockets and turned towards the grey stone buildings that constituted HMS *Vivid*, the shore establishment at

Devonport. A hot cup of tea was as appealing to him as it had been to the bluejackets.

Dinner in the mess hall was the usual stolid affair, and rowdier than it would have been aboard an actual ship, rather than one of the Royal Navy's stone vessels. It was a strange mix in the officers' mess. Some of the men were like Jones, who had come to the end of their active careers and now served in the vital but underrated roles that kept the fighting men and their ships at sea. Others had sailed aboard a shore-based installation for years, finding their niche away from the sea. The majority, though, were young men still undergoing training or assigned to *Vivid* while they awaited postings to ships, and those already assigned to ships currently in the docks.

Baxter ate mostly in silence, managing the occasional short snippet of conversation with his neighbours out of politeness. As was normal in these sorts of situations, officers from different ships and departments tended to eat together at the long tables, although some 'ship visiting' went on, even between the shore officers and those who had seagoing postings.

After the cloth had been drawn and the port drunk, Baxter considered retiring to his small room. Lieutenant Commander Jones, however, caught his eye, and nodded in the general direction of the officers' bar. The silver-haired man was officially his commanding officer as part of the logistics and supply detachment at Devonport, and while social niceties were something of a grey area when it came to the chain of command, it wouldn't do for Baxter to ignore him or pretend he hadn't noticed.

There was an odd energy in the bar as Baxter arrived in Jones' wake. The oak-panelled room, which could have been mistaken for a wardroom afloat in its décor and accoutrements were it not for the roaring fire at one end, was busier than he'd expected. A wall of noise and heat greeted him as a uniformed steward opened the heavy oak door. Baxter paused on the threshold, then shook his head at his own foolishness, in the face of a room crowded with his fellow officers, and plunged in after Jones.

Here, the strictures of military discipline and officers keeping to their own peer groups broke down to an extent. Baxter found himself at one end of a deep, comfortable settee talking to an engineering lieutenant, the third officer from one of the old cruisers in for repair, and another reservist from the pay department.

"We've been told to clear as much space and capacity as we can," the engineer, Eade, said after Jones had introduced everyone and then swerved away to the bar. Baxter had obviously jumped into the middle of a conversation.

"Some sort of rush on?" the young pay officer asked, trying and failing to hide a note of excitement in his voice. Baxter reflected that he probably still cleaved to the notion that a bloody war or sickly season was a good thing; many young men hoped that the war would last long enough that they would have the opportunity to distinguish themselves through action.

"Something big's coming in for repair, sure enough," Eade said, scratching his bearded cheek. "Bigger than anything currently in."

"There have been rumours of an engagement, in the South Atlantic," the cruiser officer, Sitwell, said. He had the look of a man who'd been at sea for a fair proportion of his life, weatherbeaten and steady. "Rumours that it didn't go well for us."

"Poppycock!" the younger man declared. "I'm quite certain we'll sweep all before us from the sea, as and when the Germans deign to come out."

"They have already come out — shelled Hartlepool just yesterday. And we did at least send some of them to the bottom not two weeks ago," Eade said.

Sitwell sniffed. "Heligoland Bight wasn't much of an action — we had them outnumbered and bang to rights. Hardly seemed fair."

"Fair?" Baxter found himself saying. "You don't win battles by being fair. You win them by being faster, stronger, or just more numerous than the enemy."

A slightly uncomfortable silence fell over their corner of the otherwise rowdy bar. "I'd heard a rumour that you were the fighting sort, a Fishpond man," Eade said at last. "What in the Good Lord's name are you doing here?"

Baxter grunted, his mood souring. He tossed back his whisky and felt it burn its way down his throat. "The Good Lord has nothing to do with it, but their Lordships of the Admiralty have made my disposition, just as they have yours."

That was only a partial truth. The gentlemen of Room 39 had seen to his disposition, and it had been more than a few decades since their Lordships had taken any direct interest in the postings of anyone below captain.

"What do you make of the German Navy, then?" Eade asked. "Are we going to sweep them from the sea?"

Baxter shifted, feeling the ache in his right shoulder from the bullet which was still lodged there and which he hadn't had the time or means to deal with. He thought back to the *Kaiserliche Marine* officers he'd met, and often found himself liking, in East Africa. Even when war had been brewing in Europe, the social round between British and German colonies hadn't diminished and he'd spent a fair bit of time in Dar es Salaam. No one had really thought that the war would come to them there, even if the distant homelands were at odds, though all sides had soon been disabused of that naïve notion. "I think they're brave men who know what they're about, even if they don't have our tradition of naval dominance and victory. I'll reserve my opinion on whether we'll sweep the Kaiser's ships from the sea until they actually come out and we have the chance for a decisive engagement."

"That sounds like defeatist talk!" the pay officer burst out. He had the sort of cut-glass accent and self-assurance that came from the right upbringing and the right schooling, that put Baxter's back up. He'd had to deal with altogether too many of his type when he'd been a regular officer, and that hadn't ended well for him.

The two more seasoned officers exchanged a worried glance. The sub-lieutenant was clearly a little tipsy, but even so he should have known better than to say something like that — particularly to a man as large as Baxter and one who had, apparently, a fighting reputation.

"What was your name again?" Baxter asked, keeping his tone urbane and his posture relaxed.

"Smythe," the other man said, a note of uncertainty creeping into his voice.

"Well, Mr Smythe, once you've seen action once or twice you'll realise that it's best not to underestimate the enemy. He's every bit as brave as you, and he builds bloody good ships. The sea is a place for realism, not bluster."

Smythe seemed about to object to Baxter's assessment, then relented when he realised he was on entirely the wrong tack. "Well, we will see, I suppose," he muttered into his gin and tonic.

"We will indeed," Baxter said distractedly, his attention caught by a change in the atmosphere, in the cadence of the chatter in the room. Voices were being raised in consternation, and he heard Jones' voice above them all, coloured by disbelief.

"What the devil's going on?" Eade muttered, starting to pull himself to his feet. Baxter's erstwhile superior joined them at the table, looking so shocked that Smythe jumped to his feet so the older man could sit.

"I say, old chap, you look like you've seen a ghost," the cruiser officer commented, and received a sharp look from Jones.

"It's Rear-Admiral Cradock's squadron," the commander said after a long pull from his drink. "The German Navy have only gone and sunk the whole bloody lot of them."

Those officers with seagoing appointments were already moving towards the door, including Baxter's recent interlocutor. "I think we know why large ships are being sent here," Baxter said, feeling a deep pang of resentment that he was stuck here as a glorified postman when other men were readying to go to sea.

Smythe had obviously sobered up somewhat, but still looked at Baxter in a confused fashion. Baxter sighed. "Battlecruisers, Mr Smythe. If I know the First Sea Lord — and I have served with him — then he'll be sending a battlecruiser to avenge Cradock."

Baxter was wrong in his prediction, but only in terms of the number of battlecruisers being sent. He felt a small measure of satisfaction as the tender he'd been sent out in wallowed across scummy water towards the lean grey shape of HMS *Inflexible*, one of two Invincible-class battlecruisers being despatched to southern waters to hunt down the enemy. Her sister-ship, and the nameship of the class, *Invincible*, was berthed in one of the recently widened drydocks while her engines were serviced.

The dockyard had been working nonstop day and night to prepare the two massive ships for their extended mission. Baxter guessed they would be on their way to the Falkland Islands, Britain's lonely outpost in the bleak and stormy waters of the South Atlantic, from where they would sally forth to hunt Admiral von Spee's cruisers. He derived a certain grim satisfaction from the shock awaiting those crewmembers used to the relative comfort of Rosyth, the Battlecruiser Force's home port.

"The whole squadron?" he heard a seaman exclaim, louder than would normally be expected on the deck of a Royal Navy vessel — even a battered and grimy little tender. The petty officer at the wheel glanced across at him, looking for direction as to whether he should bring down the weight of authority. Baxter shook his head slightly. A lot of men on the base, even those who belonged to the regular service, seemed to be in shock over the British defeat.

"Yes," a grizzled sailor, probably not far from retirement, said. He had the tone of a man who had already explained this at least a few times. "All but *Glasgow*. They say she slipped away in the night."

"Bloody cowards," someone else muttered.

"A little less noise on deck, lads," the PO called out, reading Baxter's expression.

Baxter leant tiredly against the stacked crates of deck cargo they were delivering to *Inflexible*. They'd been working as hard as every other crew on the base to see the battlecruisers resupplied and refitted. While most of the vast quantity of food, ammunition and fuel was going aboard them from big lighters and colliers, even the small tenders were shuttling crates out. He could see a line of men on the battlecruiser's deck, bent double under the sacks of coal being delivered from a collier alongside. He didn't envy them the experience, even if they had the benefit of doing the back-breaking work in the cold. Baxter shivered, remembering the sweltering heat in which the Russian 2nd Pacific Squadron had coaled, back in 1905.

"Well, it's true, ain't it?" someone else said.

Baxter straightened. "*Glasgow* was outnumbered and outgunned," he said, managing to rein in his anger by a very narrow margin. "The rest of the squadron was already sunk. There's no shame in escaping the battle. We're not going to win this bloody war by throwing our ships away, or the lives of the men who sail them."

Silence fell over the tender's deck, everyone shocked by the outburst from their commanding officer. Baxter knew he shouldn't have spoken, that it wasn't his place to educate these men. He should just have given the order for silence on deck.

"Carry on, and do so quietly," he said, his tone icier than he'd intended, and went back to watching *Inflexible* with a hungry expression. He knew there was no way he would ever rise to command such a vessel, though he knew he'd be perfectly capable of taking a vessel that fast and powerful into action.

Managing and commanding a crew of over a thousand men, and being responsible for their lives and deaths... Well, that was something he had less experience of, as he'd just demonstrated.

Glancing back at the petty officer by the helm, Baxter realised it wasn't just himself who disapproved of his own actions. Grizzled old veterans like that always had a view on the officers who were supposed to be in command, though they rarely expressed them.

"What ship?" someone called from *Inflexible*'s deck. It was a traditional challenge, but one that seemed utterly unnecessary in this setting. Baxter was about to call back when the lookout added, "Oy oy, it's the postie!"

The sailor must have felt the force of Baxter's glare even from ten yards away, as he disappeared from the railing and could be heard calling out to an officer to report the approach of a supply boat. A moment later, a lieutenant appeared at the rail.

"Who the bloody hell are you, and what are you carrying?" he demanded in a testy voice.

Baxter took a moment before replying. He didn't like the man's tone, but he knew just how harried the battlecruiser's crew would be. "Post and engineering supplies," he called back.

"Well, you'll have to wait your turn. I've got all hands coaling." There was the slightest pause, then in a slightly more cordial tone, the lieutenant continued, "But do feel free to send up the post."

"Anything we can do to help, sir?" Baxter asked. He couldn't quite make out if the officer was senior to him, but it was a fair bet. As a reservist lieutenant, most regulars who weren't completely wet behind the ears would have seniority.

"Just send up the post and wait your turn," came the response, as the tender bumped up alongside the grey steel behemoth. "But I thank you for the offer. I'll get a party to you as soon as I can."

Baxter leaned against the wheelhouse at the back of the vessel, ignoring the dark looks and muttering of his crew. Nobody liked being volunteered for extra duty, when their own was arduous enough. He wasn't quite sure why he'd made the offer, beyond a general sense of wanting to do more than just deliver the post.

"Cup of tea, sir?" the grizzled petty officer asked. Sikes, that was the man's name.

"Thank you, Sikes," said Baxter, taking the tin mug and cradling it in his gloved hands.

"It's always hard, sir, doing this duty when there's a rush on. Feels like we're not really doing much. But these big beasts can't go to sea without the work we do."

Baxter knew there was a lot of truth in what Sikes said. For every man on a ship at sea, putting his life at risk by enduring enemy action or just the environment, there would be dozens — hundreds even — in dockyards and naval bases, or walking the halls of the Admiralty. All to deliver the Royal Navy's ships to the right place and in the right state to land a crushing blow on the enemy.

"You'll not get disagreement from me," he said. "The lads got tea as well?"

"Yes, sir," the petty officer said smartly.

"Very good. I think we may be here a while — why don't you see if you can stir some life into the stove and get some soup on?"

"Very good, sir," the petty officer said. Baxter, watching him go, thought he could already smell broth on the bitingly cold air.

He looked back to the battlecruiser's comparatively high side. If the ship was destined where he thought she was — where everyone expected, in fact — they were heading to even colder weather than this. At least they were going with the prospect of action, of distinction and advancement.

Baxter snorted. *Never thought I'd be the one hungry for honour and glory*, he thought sourly. If he wanted to keep this uniform, perhaps replace the reservist's braid on his arm with the straight bars of a regular officer, recognition was exactly what he needed, however.

CHAPTER TWO

"Well, there they go!" Jones commented, his voice bright and brittle as they watched the two mighty ships *Inflexible* and *Invincible* — the latter now flying the squadron commander's pennant — churn their way towards the open sea and southern oceans.

"You can almost hear the civvies grumbling from shore," one of the officers gathered on the dockside to watch the battlecruisers get underway commented. "Louder than the bands, even."

Like the rest of the dockyard staff, Baxter felt a certain degree of satisfaction as he watched the ships go, tempered as it was by a slight bitterness that he wasn't aboard one of them. Meanwhile, the work needed on *Invincible* necessitated her sailing with a complement of civilian engineers aboard who would continue their feverish labour.

Despite the late hour, a Royal Marine band was playing the ships out of harbour, and local civilians and personnel lined the dockside to cheer them on towards victory and vengeance for Cradock's squadron. Defeat in battle had brought out the Royal Navy's most aggressive instincts, it seemed. Particularly as its reputation had been tarnished.

"I'm told they went willingly enough," Baxter said. "And they'll be paid well for it."

"Given the mood Fisher is in, I think they would have found it hard to say no. I saw the telegram he sent the dockyard superintendent, threatening all sorts if these ships did not put out to sea within two days."

"What do you make of Sturdee?" the cruiser officer, Sitwell, asked. He was referring to Vice-Admiral Sir Doveton Sturdee, whose pennant flew from *Invincible* and who would command the combined Royal Navy forces in the South Atlantic.

Sitwell's tone was flat and businesslike. He clearly wanted to be going out as well, although his ship was one of the dozens currently awaiting repair or refit in the dockyard.

"Seems odd to send the Chief of Staff of the Admiralty off to sea, particularly as he can't have sailed anything other than a desk for a decade or more."

"Fisher loathes him," Jones said pensively. "But I wouldn't read too much into *that*. The First Sea Lord is known for holding a grudge. Rumour has it he was looking for a chance to get rid of him."

"Cradock's misfortune is Jackie's good fortune," Sitwell said, a note of sourness in his voice. "Never quite knew what to make of Fisher — damn near had a number of good ships sent for scrap at the same time as he got rid of the boarding pikes, and that would have been a shame. Some of them are old, but they've still got teeth."

Baxter felt a scowl start to form on his face and caught Sitwell's eye. "Spit it out, man," Sitwell said.

"I've seen what happens when old ships go up against modern vessels, sir. No matter how much faith their crews have in them, they don't tend to last long."

Sitwell raised an eyebrow. Baxter knew he shouldn't have said anything; Lieutenant Saunders, his contact in Naval Intelligence, had warned him against saying too much about his past — in particular what he'd been doing in East Africa when the war had broken out, which was tied to his activities in the Far East a decade ago. The rogue intelligence agent he'd been hunting for Room 39, George Arbuthnott, had engineered the situation that had landed Baxter on an old Russian cruiser during the Russo-Japanese War.

"I feel that there is more to our Mr Baxter than meets the eye," Jones said mildly, before Sitwell could say anything further, and then sought to change the subject. "Rumour has it that we're going to be graced with Fisher's presence at some point in the next few days — he's coming to inspect the dockyard, and may even thank us for our efforts in getting these beasts to sea on time."

Sitwell sniffed dismissively. "He probably has more important things to do — I can't imagine it's easy having Winston Churchill as the First Lord."

"If anyone's up to the task, it's Jackie," one of the other officers on the dockside offered. Baxter had stopped listening, his mind turning over the possibilities that suddenly presented themselves at this news. He'd served with Fisher when the First Sea Lord had been a captain and Baxter a freshly minted sub-lieutenant, on the North America Station. Jackie, as he was known by those in the service who supported him, had been the sort of commander who had got to know all of the officers under his command. It was probably too much to hope that Fisher would remember him now, though.

Baxter's thoughts were interrupted by someone saying his name. The battlecruisers were still in the steading, having left the dockyard at low speed, but even at this distance he could see the white water starting to froth at their sharp bows as they picked up speed, their White Ensigns snapping at their mastheads in the stiffening breeze.

"What do you say, Mr Baxter?" Jones repeated. "Shall we get back to the job of keeping His Majesty's Navy afloat and supplied with rum?"

Following the frenetic activity getting *Inflexible* and *Invincible* to sea in short order, it was back to the normal routine of the dockyard — even if that routine was a wartime one. The little vessel Baxter was responsible for was a familiar sight to the crews of the warships that now crowded the roadstead. Ships came and went, vessels on active duty coming in for repair and refit or old ships being brought out of reserve and back into service. Squat and grimy it might have been, but he was starting to take a certain amount of pride in the role the little vessel and dozens more like it played in keeping the Royal Navy at sea.

That didn't mean he wouldn't rather have been on one of the battlecruisers that had just sailed out under Sturdee, or even in the Grand Fleet at its cold, lonely station in Scapa Flow, keeping watch for the *Kaiserliche Marine's* High Seas Fleet. The enemy battlecruisers had been out already, shelling coastal cities and slaughtering civilians, and everyone knew the German Imperial Navy would have to sortie its full strength at some point. Hell's teeth, thought Baxter, he would even take a posting on an old cruiser on a far-flung station, if it meant being somewhere warmer and with at least a chance of some action.

So far, there had been no sign of a visit from the First Sea Lord, or anyone else senior for that matter. Baxter had no contact with the dockyard superintendent or anyone on his staff, not that they would do him any good, and he would be damned if he importuned Saunders for a role — the less he had to do with the Naval Intelligence officer the better.

There seemed to be nothing for it but to keep his head down and work hard. And grab any opportunity that came his way with both hands.

Three days after Sturdee's ships had put to sea, Baxter found himself taking a steam launch rather than the usual tender out to deliver post to the ships lying in the steading. While he still resented the occasional cry of 'it's the postie!', he remembered from his own seagoing life how important it was for these men, many of them reservists or recently recruited trainees, to have contact with home and family. The arrival of the postbags would be a welcome break and morale boost for the sailors.

While the launch was by no means fast, not even matching the old torpedo boats Baxter had been aboard in the Black Sea a decade or more ago, it was certainly an improvement on the tender as it cut through the murky waters, with one rating on the tiller and three more preparing the canvas delivery bags. Baxter could probably have left the run to a senior petty officer, but at least here he was closer to the sea and to the grey steel castles that would soon be plying it.

"Destroyer off the port now, sir," the helmsman said. "Should I adjust course?"

Looking up from checking his list of deliveries, Baxter could see the lean, sleek form of a W-class destroyer cutting along at a decent clip. If both vessels maintained their headings, their courses would converge. He ran the numbers, almost unconsciously, and realised that not only would the courses converge in space, but they would also do so in time — a convergence that the destroyer would probably barely notice but would be catastrophic for the launch.

The destroyer's commander seemed to come to the same conclusion, issuing a long blast from the vessel's horn. The signal lamp started clattering, and one didn't need to be a signalman to read the instructions. *Adjust course immediately*, was the peremptory command.

Baxter started to give the relevant orders for a starboard turn and a reduction in speed that would give them plenty of clearance. Despite the alarming speed with which they were closing, he paused for the briefest of moments as he recognised a distinctive figure on the ship's bridge. He was not a big man by any stretch of the imagination, but he was the sort of man who dominated the space he was in, in a way that had little to do with the gold braid on his uniform frock coat and cocked hat.

It seemed the First Sea Lord had come for this 'surprise' inspection after all.

Baxter might have served with Fisher before, but there was nothing to say the Admiral would remember him or be particularly well disposed towards him even if he did. But Baxter couldn't remain on dry land for much longer without losing his mind. This moment might not have the makings of a plum opportunity, but it was still an opportunity for a man willing to seize it.

"Adjust course two points to starboard," he ordered. "And increase speed to full ahead."

"Sir?" the helmsman asked, sounding a little apprehensive. While the course adjustment did take them away from the destroyer slightly, the two lines would still converge inexorably and the increase in speed would probably just see the launch ploughed under even earlier. Anyone with any sense would know it wouldn't manage to cross the destroyer's bows with enough clearance.

The destroyer sounded the horn again, and the signal lamp clattered frenetically. "Proceed as ordered," Baxter said, forcing himself to sound calm.

"Aye, sir, two points starboard and ahead full." Baxter didn't know if it was the calm surety in his tone or just the sailor's ingrained obedience that achieved compliance.

"You men, secure those sacks," Baxter ordered, stepping forward into the bows of the little vessel as it obeyed its tiller and picked up speed. He could see sailors along the destroyer's side trying to wave him off, and furious gesticulation from the bridge. The figure of Jackie Fisher appeared unmoved, glancing between the launch and what was probably a watch in his hand.

Baxter didn't need to look at his own pocket watch, a sturdy and mostly reliable item. There had been moments in his life when he hadn't needed to work things through, carry out careful calculations of the kind he'd been taught at the naval academy at Dartmouth and latterly while learning gunnery on HMS *Excellent*. He just took in the angles, relative speeds and courses of the ships with a sweep of his gaze. The destroyer's captain was giving orders for his own vessel to adjust course and speed — not something the breed of man who gained command of one of those fast, aggressive ships would normally like to do.

Now.

"Hard starboard!" Baxter barked, chopping his hand down as he said it. The vessels were close enough that he could see the grin spread across Fisher's face, as he alone realised what Baxter was doing.

Baxter glanced at the watch in his hand. "And ... boom."

"Boom, sir?" the nonplussed helmsman asked as the launch settled onto its new course, yawing as the wake of the fast-moving destroyer caught them. Fisher raised his hat and Baxter drew himself up to his full height to return the salute.

"Boom indeed."

"Well, carrying out a simulated torpedo attack on a ship carrying the First Sea Lord was one way to express your dissatisfaction with your posting," Lieutenant Commander Jones said. His tone was considerably frostier than Baxter was used to from the old man. He couldn't blame his commanding officer for that.

"Yes, sir," Baxter said, standing to attention in Jones' tiny cubbyhole of an office, tucked away in one of the myriad, last-century buildings that made up the bulk of the installation. While Jones hadn't asked a direct question, a pause had been left for some form of response. Baxter had found that throwing in the occasional 'yes, sir' generally helped things along.

Jones sighed and pushed back his chair, the casters squeaking on uneven floorboards. The office smelt of damp and paper, rapidly lost beneath the odour of tobacco smoke as Jones lit his pipe. Baxter held himself rigidly to attention. He'd taken an enormous gamble by 'showing away' in front of the First Sea Lord. There was no way the wild manoeuvres he'd ordered could be construed as anything other than showing off, except perhaps as rank incompetence and panic, and he knew it would attract a reputation for arrogance and recklessness around the base. If the gambit hadn't paid off, if he hadn't attracted Fisher's attention in the way he'd been hoping, then his life here would probably be more difficult than he needed it to be.

Jones sighed. "As it turns out, of course, the First Sea Lord was amused by your little display. I believe his exact words were 'what bloody idiot assigned him to a supply role?', and a telegram was sent off as soon as he was ashore. You have been reassigned — I can only assume Jackie owes you a favour or you have some interest with him?"

Baxter didn't bother pointing out that if he had any sort of influence within the Royal Navy, let alone with the First Sea Lord, he wouldn't be kicking his heels as a reservist officer at a supply depot. "I have served with Sir John," he said now. "I can only assume, and hope, that I made a favourable impression on him."

"Well then," Jones said, the severity draining from his voice to a degree. He pulled a telegram from a pile of papers on his desk, which he passed across to Baxter. "Orders will follow post-haste, but I'm directed to release you immediately for service on HMS *Astute*, currently undergoing urgent preparations for sea service."

Baxter racked his brain, trying to picture the ship — and he fervently hoped she *was* a ship, not some armed trawler or similar — amongst the vessels that crowded the naval base at Devonport. "She's an Active-class scout cruiser," Jones said, seeing his frown. "The fourth, in fact, and only just finished her sea trials."

"Any notion of which destroyer flotilla she's been assigned to, sir?" Baxter asked. The scout cruisers had mostly come into the service while Baxter was out of it, but he was familiar enough with them — smaller and less heavily armed and armoured than even light cruisers, often only slightly bigger than the destroyers they were designed to lead into battle, but fast enough to keep up with them. That meant he was being assigned to local duties, blockading German trade and keeping an eye out for any attempt of their High Seas Fleet to break out of the Baltic. He would be at sea, at least, and with an opportunity to distinguish himself.

"That's outside my remit, Mr Baxter, as I imagine you well know," Jones said with a touch of asperity. "I can say she's taking on a lot of stores, more than one might think necessary for joining one of the flotillas deployed in the Channel. Perhaps the North Sea?"

"And who has command, sir?"

"Ah, now that *is* within my remit to know," Jones said. "A Captain Gregson."

That wasn't a name Baxter knew, which perhaps wasn't surprising. The Royal Navy was a monumental organisation and was growing every day as new officers were recruited and others were promoted to command ships being brought back into commission. He made a mental note to find out as much as possible about his new commanding officer, discreetly, of course.

"Was there anything else, Mr Baxter?" Jones asked.

"No, sir. Thank you, sir." He couldn't keep the enthusiasm from his voice at the prospect of getting back to sea.

Jones quirked an eyebrow. "Very well, carry on."

As Baxter turned to leave, Jones spoke again, his voice reflective. "There is no shame in supply and logistics work, you know. The fleet couldn't function without us."

"I don't doubt it, sir," Baxter replied, his hand on the doorknob. "And while we all serve at their Lordships' whim, I'm a fighting officer. This isn't where I belong."

Jones looked up from his contemplation of his pipe bowl. "Well, the best of luck to you, Mr Baxter."

CHAPTER THREE

At first glance, HMS *Astute* was exactly the sort of ship where a fighting officer belonged. Long and sleek, she had a fast and dangerous look about her, though Baxter knew that any speed would come at the expense of armour. She packed a reasonable punch, with two 4-inch guns forward, two aft and three along each broadside.

Normally, Baxter would have liked to know a bit more about the ship he was joining, particularly the character of the captain and crew. The telegram that had arrived had been very clear, though, that he was expected aboard *immediately*. That had been backed up by a missive from *Astute*'s first officer, indicating that he was to repair aboard at his earliest opportunity. He'd flung his meagre possessions into his small sea chest and set out for the dockside without any further delay. It helped that he didn't really have anyone to say goodbye to, or any arrangements to be made for possessions remaining behind.

Baxter was pleasantly surprised that Jones had put the steam launch at his disposal to take him out to the scout cruiser. *Astute* was lying in the outer roadstead, the Blue Peter at her masthead — clear in the cold, stiff breeze — indicating that she was ready to depart and any remaining crew ashore should make haste to correct that situation. There were several boats making their way out to her, officers and working parties of bluejackets returning. A collier was alongside, and an oiler waiting in the wings, as well as other supply vessels patiently waiting their turn.

Petty Officer Sikes brought the launch in towards the entry port smoothly, his expression indicating that this was how it was done. There were a few shouts from other waiting vessels as Sikes cut the queue, but Baxter was in no mind to reprimand him. "It's the bloody post — can't wait their turn!" someone bellowed from one of the supply ships.

"Not today, mate," Sikes grumbled under his breath. "Here we go, sir, nice and quick like I was ordered."

Baxter met the petty officer's level gaze until Sikes saluted, then returned the gesture smartly. "Have my chest whipped aboard," he ordered. "Then carry on."

Baxter ascended the boarding ladder, the ditty bag containing his few prized possessions over one shoulder. He put the bag down as soon as his shoes hit the polished wood of the deck, ready to salute an officer who should be overseeing arrivals and request permission to come aboard.

Looking around, though, he saw that *Astute*'s deck was a scene of organised chaos — much as it would be on the other vessels preparing to depart. There was a lot of deck cargo, and he couldn't help noting the number of sacks and crates of coal that were being lashed down. Baxter was no engineer, but he had plenty of experience with long-haul journeys and the vast supply of fuel necessary for them. It looked like the scout cruiser was laying in supplies for an extremely long voyage, much further than an extended patrol in the North Sea. Parties of seamen were carrying more coal below, while others were casting off the collier and preparing to receive the oiler — like many of the newer, smaller warships in the RN, *Astute* had boiler rooms for both fuel types. The deck was noisy, but in a cheerful and busy fashion, and smoke trickled from the triple funnels as the boilers were brought up to pressure.

"Who the devil are you?" a plummy voice demanded. Baxter turned and found himself looking down at a well-built man with the straight bars of a regular lieutenant on his sleeves and the self-assurance of someone born to authority.

"Baxter," he replied, holding out his telegrammed instructions. "I've been ordered to report aboard for duty."

"Well, there wouldn't be any other reason to report aboard, would there?" the other officer responded, glancing at the telegram. "Littleton, third officer."

He looked expectantly at Baxter, who maintained a neutral expression as he saluted. It wasn't necessarily required, but the officer seemed to expect it. "Permission to come aboard, sir?"

"Granted, and welcome!" Littleton exclaimed, his voice warming up somewhat as he returned the gesture. "As you can see, we're a little busy right now. Get your baggage stowed, then report back to me for assignment. The captain wants us at sea before the hands are piped to dinner."

Littleton was away before Baxter could say anything else, bawling at a group of obviously raw sailors who were milling around a hatchway with an array of crates and sacks, clearly arguing about who had priority. His sea chest was up on the deck already, the launch that had delivered him already on its way back to the wharf and no doubt a long day of hard labour.

Another look round the deck told Baxter that his own day was going to be equally long and arduous. A ship was never a quiet thing, particularly when undergoing rapid resupply before a sortie, but there was more noise than he'd expected, and a lot of that was coming from officers — petty and upwards — shouting at the raw recruits who seemed to make up the bulk of the ratings and quite understandably didn't have much of an idea of what was going on.

Baxter sighed, slung his ditty bag over his shoulder and hoisted up his sea chest. He'd spent most of his adult life aboard ships, many of them warships, so he didn't need directions to officer country. While some of the older ships he'd been aboard still situated their officers' cabins in the stern, Baxter knew he'd find the wardroom and his own cubby hole in the conning tower, below the bridge. He ducked through a hatch in the superstructure, and into a narrow passageway lit by flickering electrical lights and headed towards the wardroom. He didn't know which cabin he'd been assigned, but in the wardroom he'd either find the steward or somewhere to leave his dunnage.

"You there!" a voice snapped before he'd gone more than ten feet. "Once you've dropped that off, come and give me a hand with this, will you?"

Baxter paused, rolling his shoulders. Whereas Littleton's tone had been plummy and commanding, this one was trying and failing to achieve something similar.

"Are you deaf?" the young man continued. Then he registered the fact that Baxter was wearing a frockcoat and cap, not the bluejacket of a common sailor, and his eyes went wide as he realised his mistake.

Baxter struggled to check his temper, though his first instinct was to roar at this pimply youth, clearly fresh from the naval academy at Dartmouth. He may never have been quite that idiotic when he was younger, having had a life at sea before he joined the RN, but he did remember how confusing and intimidating an environment a ship could be and how important he'd found it not to give away any sort of apprehension or to appear ignorant.

"What can I help you with, Mr…?"

"Webb, sir," the sub-lieutenant gulped. He started to salute, then obviously remembered that he wasn't wearing his cap and smoothed down his dark hair instead. "It's nothing, sir. Jammed scuttle."

Baxter kept his expression neutral. Now hardly seemed to be the time to be worrying about such things when the ship was in the middle of a hurried resupply and every officer was needed on deck, but he did wonder how useful young Mr Webb would be.

Some of what Baxter was thinking clearly showed on his face. "It's just that … it's rather cold, you see, sir, and a little damp…"

Baxter ducked into the tiny cupboard that served as a junior officer's cabin. Cot, locker and wash stand took up most of the space, and Baxter barely had room to turn. His own cabin would be the same, he knew. He'd coped with worse. The catch on the scuttle — the small, somewhat salt-grimed circular window that provided a little bit of illumination and air that was apparently too fresh for Webb's taste — was indeed jammed open. Thoroughly rusted in place, in fact. With a very slight screech of tortured metal and a shower of rust, Baxter pulled it closed. "There we go, Webb," he said. "I imagine you'll be needed on deck?"

"Yes, sir," the young man said, clearly embarrassed by the whole situation.

Baxter ducked back out of the cabin and paused in the companionway. He took a deep breath and let it out slowly. *You signed up for this — literally fought to get back into uniform*, he reminded himself as Mr Webb clattered around the cabin behind him.

Time to get to work.

The captain may have wanted to get to sea before the hands were piped to dinner, but in the end that meant delaying feeding the men for an hour or more. Baxter, assigned to supervise the stowing of the last consignment of supplies, could see that it wasn't the most popular decision. The men could smell the big pots of plain but hearty fare simmering in the galley, and could no doubt imagine the pleasure of being in their messes away from the biting wind and the snarl of officers, commissioned and petty, determined to see their captain's will enacted.

It was clear that the officers barely knew each other. Baxter wasn't the only one to have reported aboard for the first time this day. The hurry to get an untested crew to sea in a new ship just reinforced his suspicion that they weren't being sent for routine work in the North Sea. That, or the situation at the sharp edge was far more dire than any of them had realised.

He hadn't been introduced to the commanding officer yet, or indeed the first officer. The latter had made himself felt, bellowing orders from the bridge's wings through a loudhailer and no doubt concerned and disappointed as the inexperienced crew fumbled about, trying to get everything stowed.

HMS *Astute* steamed out of Devonport under iron-grey skies, with only the weakest winter sunshine breaking through the heavy clouds and with none of the pomp and circumstance that had accompanied the two battlecruisers on their mission of vengeance. A cold, stiff wind whipped off the Channel, making those on watch even more miserable as their comrades stomped to their dinner with a mix of exhaustion and sullenness. Baxter remained on deck, standing at the stern and watching the countryside around Devonport fade into a dun smudge on the horizon. He'd been back in the country of his birth for mere months in the last year, and before that he'd not set foot on these shores for years.

Well, here he was again. Back where he wanted to be. Baxter walked forward, past the three funnels and the bridge, to stare at the long march of white-crested waves shouldered aside by the scout cruiser. If she *was* ordered to the North Sea, Captain

Gregson was taking them on an odd course, heading south and a touch west. The French coast, perhaps, or the Mediterranean? The East Africa Station certainly needed reinforcement, with at least one German cruiser and who knew how many converted merchant raiders lurking in that waterlogged coastline. He couldn't imagine a relatively modern ship like this one being sent on the thankless task of blockade duty and hunting elusive single raiders, though.

"Now, you have the look of a man who's been at sea a fair bit," Littleton said, coming up beside him. Baxter braced himself for the usual comments about being a reservist, questions about where he might have sailed and why he'd volunteered for the navy. The third officer, however, appeared disinclined to make the usual comments and instead stuck out his hand. "Glad to have you aboard, Baxter. As you might have been able to tell, this crew is fresh from the training establishments and the officers don't really know each other."

"Some seem fresh out of Dartmouth," Baxter said, warming slightly to the officer and accepting the handshake.

"Well, that as well," Littleton commented wryly. "The captain has asked us to gather in the wardroom at five bells so he can brief us and we can all start to get to know each other."

Baxter was surprised at how open Littleton was about the situation, and that the Admiralty had seen fit to send them to sea without a proper shakedown cruise, or even, it seemed, time for the officers to get drunk together. He let none of that show on his face. "I don't suppose anyone has told you what my station is, as yet?" he asked instead.

"I only found out I was third officer yesterday morning!" Littleton said cheerfully. "I'm sure we'll get it all sorted once we're properly underway and know exactly what it is we're doing. Now, I suggest you get cleaned up. Captain Gregson is something of a stickler for his officers being presentable and seamanlike."

Baxter glanced down and realised that this uniform was somewhat rumpled, his hands dirty. He'd managed to avoid doing any heavy lifting of coal, but he'd still needed to pitch in at times. "Wardroom at five bells it is, then," he said, with a nod to Littleton, before heading down to his cabin.

Baxter was on time for the gathering of the cruiser's officers. It wasn't a formal dinner or reception, so while he'd tidied himself up, he hadn't felt the need to change into a dress uniform. The other officers had taken the same approach, and the space was already busy with men in blue frock coats, with white-jacketed stewards moving among them.

Stepping into the wardroom reminded Baxter of his first formal dinner aboard the *Yaroslavich*. The space wasn't quite the same — the old Russian cruiser's wardroom had been grander and more spacious, dripping with gold and luxuries, and overrun with dogs at the start of the voyage. HMS *Astute* was a more modern breed, leaner and faster, with more emphasis on practicality. There was, however, still a long oak table running down the middle of the space, and a drinks cabinet in which the decanters and glasses clinked slightly as the cruiser slid over the long march of the sea.

Littleton raised his gin and tonic in greeting. There was a slight lull in conversation as Baxter entered, but he paid it no heed as he was used to this reaction. He was considerably taller and broader than most of the men present, and, with one or two exceptions, older too.

One of the oldest men present was a steward, who approached him with a slightly arthritic step. "Whisky," Baxter said in response to his enquiring gaze.

"With soda, sir?" the steward asked, his voice a surprisingly rich baritone for such a small and wizened individual.

"No, thank you — just in a glass," Baxter replied. That got the very slightest twitch of an eyebrow from the steward, at which Baxter smiled and emphasised the slight edge of his Scottish accent. "As God intended."

"Very good, sir," the steward said, voice as dry as the desert, and went to fetch his drink.

Baxter glanced around the compartment as he waited for his drink. It was crowded with blue uniforms, though to his eye *Astute* seemed to be a few men short of her full complement. He counted four other men with lieutenant's stripes on their sleeves, all of them the straight bars of a regular officer. There would be both an official and social pecking order amongst these men of the same rank, but he was only interested in what his chain of command would be. A tall, spare man with thinning sandy hair looked to be the most experienced officer, standing slightly apart from the others. He wore commander's stripes, but also engineer's insignia. That would explain his separation from the other officers. Despite Fisher's reforms and the fact that every ship in the fleet was driven by coal or oil rather than the wind, many men still regarded the engineering profession as being 'lesser' than the fighting officers. He didn't see a Royal Marine officer, but then a ship of this size probably didn't warrant much of a Jolly contingent.

Captain Gregson entered just as the old steward returned with a glass of amber liquid for Baxter. Everyone straightened up and the hum of conversation died away. Baxter turned to face the captain, drink in hand, and caught the briefest flash of annoyance in his commander's eyes.

Gregson was a short man, barrel-chested and with grey at his temples and in his beard. Piercing blue eyes glared out from a nest of wrinkles. "Gentlemen," he said, his voice rich with the Welsh valleys. "As some of you may already have surmised, we are not joining the Grand Fleet in its blockade of the North Sea. Nor are we to join the Harwich cruiser force, or any other local formation."

The captain paused, eyeing each of his officers in turn. That beady gaze alighted on Baxter sufficiently long that he started to feel slightly uncomfortable. He was saved from further scrutiny by the late arrival of Sub-Lieutenant Webb, who tried to slip quietly into the wardroom behind the captain but tripped over the hatch coaming.

Gregson stared at the young officer frostily until he wilted visibly.

"When I say 'five bells', I mean it, Mr Webb," he said, his tone even chillier than his glare.

"Yes, sir, my apologies, sir..." Webb was about to try to offer an excuse, but Baxter caught his eye and gave him a tiny shake of the head. The captain would not be interested in the stumbling explanation of a young man who was barely ready to be at sea, let alone in a position of authority over anyone. Thankfully, Webb took the hint.

"Well, we'll say no more of it then," Gregson said, before turning his attention back to the assembled officers. "At ease, gentlemen," he continued, as though it was an afterthought, and with a relieved rustle the officers relaxed. Some sat, sipping at drinks, though the wiser ones remained standing.

"As I was saying, we are ordered to much further flung shores. South America, to be precise. It seems their Lordships feel that the forces despatched to hunt for von Spee are not sufficient, and a fast cruiser is needed to keep an eye out for our opponents if they should get past Sir Doveton."

Baxter raised an eyebrow. In truth, there was little this one cruiser could do, at least without a flock of destroyers following on, and they would be far outside the range of any destroyer that he knew of. *Astute* would need to live up to her name and the very definition of her type, by finding the enemy and reporting his whereabouts while avoiding any sort of engagement.

"Something you want to add, Mr — ah — Baxter?" Gregson demanded.

"Just looking forward to being in warmer climes, sir," Baxter said, meeting Gregson's piercing look without flinching.

"So glad we can accommodate you," Gregson said, his voice remaining even. Baxter didn't rise to the bait. He'd met commanding officers like this more times than he cared to recall. The worst had been Gorchakov, the commander of the Russian cruiser he'd been accidentally imprisoned on in 1904 and a religious zealot who had become more unhinged as the journey progressed. Gregson was clearly a hard horse, but not the worst by a long chalk.

"Very well, gentlemen," Gregson said, when he could get no further rise out of Baxter. "Further details will be provided in due course, along with your assignments."

For a moment, it appeared that this was all they were going to get by way of a greeting from their captain. Then Gregson turned in the hatchway, speaking into the silence he'd left in his wake.

"We all understand, I think, that this is not an ideal situation," he said, a slight note of uncertainty taking the edge off his gruffness. "The crew is a mix of experienced and inexperienced hands, and we are mostly unknown to each other — except, perhaps, by reputation." Gregson's blue eyes rested on Baxter as he said that. The steel returned to the captain's voice as he continued. "But you should know that I intend to weld you and this crew into a fighting machine in the finest traditions of the service. We have a long voyage ahead of us before there is even the possibility of action, and we shall make the most of that time."

His stare swept the room. "Good day, gentlemen."

"Well, that was hardly a rousing welcome speech," Webb said, with a forced attempt at cheerfulness. Baxter winced — the hatch was still open, and Webb clearly had not yet accustomed himself to the notion that voices could carry aboard ship, despite the ever-present rumble of the engines and the wind that whipped around it.

"Oh, do be quiet, Webb," Littleton sighed, and the young man's face coloured. Littleton waited until they could be reasonably certain that the captain was out of earshot, then said, "You're not wrong, though. Our noble captain does not seem like the type one wants to follow into battle."

Baxter took a seat at the long table and sipped his whisky. It wasn't the best malt, but he'd had worse during his lean years after he'd been drummed out of the Royal Navy. A low hum of conversation started up again, but was cut off just as quickly as the first officer strode into the wardroom.

Baxter had only seen him from afar, yelling orders from the bridge wings while he'd been busy aft. He realised, with a start, that he knew the man. Lieutenant Commander Sitwell gave him an affable nod of greeting. "Gentlemen," he said, echoing his captain. "We have a lot of work to do, and as always in the service less time than we might hope. I am sure, though, that we will all rise to the challenge with skill, fortitude and courage."

Baxter sensed the change in atmosphere in the room. This was the sort of address naval officers wanted and expected from their senior officers, not the dry recital of facts and uninspiring attempts at reassurance. He had to credit Sitwell with one thing at least — he knew what he was about. Given where they were going and the hunt they were expected to join, that at least was reassuring.

CHAPTER FOUR

"Warmer climes, you said!" Littleton bellowed cheerfully as he staggered into the wardroom, water sluicing off his oilskin. The stagger almost turned into a headlong plunge into the drinks cabinet as *Astute* began a long slide down a towering wave's reverse slope. Baxter caught the third officer's arm and steered him into a chair before any serious damage to their supply of gin and whisky could be done.

Hancock, the elderly steward, could not hide his annoyance with the amount of water that had been deposited on the deck that he'd just finished mopping. Baxter was certain the old man should have retired long since to the sort of establishment that would appreciate his precise standards; however, he seemed to cling to the sea even though it was clearly his nemesis.

"I said I was looking forward to them, not that we would steam out of Devonport straight into the Caribbean," Baxter replied. "That's the way the sea works, you know."

Littleton bellowed with laughter, causing Webb to look up from his untouched corned beef sandwich with a look of misery. The young lieutenant had at least been able to emerge from his cabin after more than a week of heavy seas and storms that had battered the cruiser. "Are you eating those, Webb?" Littleton asked, reaching out and snagging one half of the sandwich before the other man could reply.

Webb pushed the tin plate across to Littleton. "About time for my watch," he mumbled, heading off to find his own wet weather gear.

"He'll get his sea legs soon enough," Littleton commented after the young man had half-staggered, half-slid from the room.

"He'd better," Baxter said. "Not much future for him in the service if he can't keep his food down or stay upright in a bit of bad weather."

He caught Littleton eyeing him thoughtfully. "Bit of bad weather? This is the foulest I've seen it, old chap! Lifelines fore and aft and nobody on deck unless they can help it. The messes are properly swimming in bilge and vomit."

Baxter rose, moving easily with the ship's roll as she started to climb the next wave. Littleton was a professional and experienced officer, certainly, not a reservist like himself or a recent recruit like Webb. Most of his service, it seemed, had been in coastal waters or in shore establishments, gathering the sort of experience that a man on his way to high rank required.

"This? It's rough, I'll grant you," he said, peering out through a salt- and water-smeared scuttle to watch the wave they'd just crested slide away into the distance, a steep wall of blue-grey water that towered away to a torn white crest.

"But you've seen rougher?" the other lieutenant asked.

"You spend as much time at sea as I have, Littleton, and you'll see worse."

While Littleton, as the third officer, was technically superior in the ship's chain of command, they were the same rank and over the past week or so had fallen into a sort of easy familiarity. Baxter occasionally found himself missing the camaraderie of a tightly knit crew like the one he'd had on the Turkish blockade runner *Resadiye*, at least until their supposed commanding officer had drawn a gun on him. But at least aboard a Royal Navy ship he was alongside men who wore the same uniform and were all working towards the same goal.

"As a merchant seaman?" Lieutenant Taylor, the navigation officer, asked as he entered the wardroom. He gave Baxter a wan smile, almost lost in the pale expanse of his face. "I thought you chaps all stayed tucked up in port if the weather got a bit hairy."

Taylor seemed like a decent enough sort. His skills as a navigator were yet to be determined, as they hadn't seen the sun for days and visibility was such that they'd only know if they were near a landmass when they were on the verge of running into it.

"Well, that only makes sense if you don't have an urgent cargo," Baxter said mildly. There'd been a bit of this ribbing, good-natured enough, as the regular officers aboard had assumed that he was solely a merchant seaman who had joined the reserves, as so many had. Baxter didn't feel particularly inclined to disabuse them of the notion. "And, of course, a typhoon can come down on you in the Pacific with barely any warning."

Taylor nodded sagely, but Littleton guffawed. "Don't try to pretend you know what he's talking about, old chap — you've barely left home waters in your entire career."

"Not unlike you," Taylor said, his expression cooling somewhat. Before the exchange could develop into open unpleasantness, though, the ship gave a great lurch and lay over on her starboard side. Baxter reached out to steady himself as the foaming sea raced up to cover the scuttle he was standing by. For a moment, the ship's side was suddenly the deck. Baxter crouched instinctively, somehow keeping his footing as the tin plate carrying the sodden remain of Webb's sandwich crashed next to his head.

For a terrible moment, the cruiser hung in that position, rolled almost on her beam ends. Every fibre of Baxter's being screamed at him to move, to get to the bridge or the wheelhouse to find out what was going on, but his rational mind knew that moving now and trying to get on deck would be suicide. And, as he'd told the other two men, this wasn't anything new to him.

"Are we broaching?" Taylor yelled, a note of real terror in his voice. The ever-present roar of the winter gale was strangely muted, but from elsewhere Baxter could hear panicked shouts. They were doomed if the ship was caught side-on by a wave and turned all the way over. *Astute* would never right herself, and instead plunge to the bottom. The lucky ones at that point would be those in any open compartment or on deck — they would drown quickly.

The moment stretched. Baxter could feel the ship's life through his hands on her metal, feel the thrum of her engines and the strain her hull was under. Instinct more than anything else told him when the crisis moment came and went. "We'll be fine!" he said, raising his voice above the tumult. The cruiser started to right herself a second later, almost jerking free of the water. She had been over on her side for mere seconds, but the watery light that filtered through the foamy water running down the small scuttle felt like a blessing.

Astute snapped upright with cries of relief and pain and the sound of loose items and bodies crashing around. The helmsmen managed to bring her bows round and for another stomach-churning moment Baxter looked back down the slope of the enormous wave that had almost overwhelmed them. The view swooped as the cruiser crested, smashing through the torn waters, and then began her slide down the far side.

Baxter straightened. Experienced sailors would probably have come through relatively unscathed, but there were many amongst the crew who had barely been through training and had never experienced a blow like this. Gear would be strewn all about, and given the violence of the ship's motion there would be more than a few injuries.

The storm battered them for another two days. Two days of hammering through the great waves, of rolling and pitching in a way that made even some seasoned hands vomit, not caring about where they vented or who they did it in front of. Captain Gregson spent most of those two days on the bridge, spelled occasionally by Sitwell, and drove his crew and in particular his officers hard to keep the ship afloat and in as good a condition as possible.

The sickbay was full of men with broken bones and contusions. The ship's surgeon, Dr Martin, and his mates were run off their feet trying to keep on top of the steady trickle of minor injuries and keep the severely injured comfortable until such time as the fury of the seas abated enough to allow for surgery.

Mercifully, the storm blew itself out sometime during the night of the second day. The Atlantic was not a placid ocean at any time, but the great mountainous peaks that had rolled at the ship as she gamely ploughed onwards had settled into long rollers that stretched away towards the horizon under scudding broken cloud and a low winter sun that crept ever higher in the sky as they inched towards the equator and summer.

Order and tidiness were re-established throughout the ship, though not with the alacrity expected in the Royal Navy. *Astute* had been carrying extra coal stowed as deck cargo, and a lot of that had been lost as the ship had been flung about during the storm. Crates and sacks had caused damage on their way over the side, and more of the heavy blocks of Welsh coal had been found in the most unusual places, including the galley and the captain's cabin, having been washed down companionways.

More problematic was the amount of coal dust that clogged the pumps, requiring considerable maintenance and not a little swearing from the artificers.

"If that blow had continued much longer, we may have been in a lot of trouble," Sitwell said as those officers not on watch gradually accumulated in the wardroom after a hard day trying to put the ship back into order. "As it is, with a few licks of paint and some polish on the brightwork, you'd never have known that we'd just been through it."

"It has meant we've not been able to drill as much as we'd like," Baxter pointed out.

The cruiser's first officer gave him a cool look. "We'll have plenty of time for that once we're in the calmer waters of the Caribbean. I think you'll have your work cut out for you at your station."

Baxter nodded. He'd been assigned to command the two forward 4-inch guns in action, along with his normal watch-keeping duties. While Lieutenant Simons, the gunnery officer, was nominally in charge of all *Astute*'s batteries, there was no centralised fire control system on a ship like this and each officer would be responsible for directing fire if it came to it. *When* it came to it.

"I'm looking forward to starting on Simons' training programme," Baxter said, keeping his tone light. The last thing he needed was bad blood between himself and a brother officer, particularly the ship's first officer, and Sitwell seemed to have somewhat taken against him after their exchange in Devonport. Baxter wouldn't have been surprised if some of his sourness stemmed from his transfer, from one of the old but still powerful armoured cruisers that would have the opportunity to participate in the fleet action everyone was expecting. Not only was the more modern scout cruiser nowhere near as potent, she was on detached service with little chance of a glorious action and therefore promotion for all those involved.

The lieutenant commander nodded, just as Henry Simons drifted into the wardroom. He was, as far as Baxter knew, a recent graduate of HMS *Vernon*, the Royal Navy's gunnery school in Portsmouth. He'd attended it himself, around the start of the century, but that was one of many things he'd chosen not to share with his new colleagues.

"How about it, Guns?" Littleton asked cheerfully. "Ready to start licking the men into shape so we can sweep the Kaiser's chaps from the sea?"

Simons was a somewhat lugubrious individual, but the expression he turned on his colleagues was positively mournful. "Oh, training. Yes. Indeed."

Baxter stared at him curiously for a moment. Simons seemed to be at a loss as to what was now required of him.

"I've got a bit of training in that area," he said at last. "I'd be happy to assist — it'll be a big task with such a raw crew."

"Thank you, Mr Baxter, that would be appreciated," Sitwell said drily, while Simons struggled to hide his relief.

HMS *Astute* steamed on across seas that were, if not placid, then considerably less violent than they had been for the first few days of her passage. Taylor, the navigator, had somehow managed to keep them broadly on course, though this feat was easier in a steam vessel than it would have been in the sort of square-rigger Baxter had first gone to sea in, under his father's tutelage. The storm had delayed them somewhat as they had battled slowly over the marching mountains of water, which would be a source of concern for the captain when considered with the amount of coal lost overboard during the blow. The cruiser at least had the advantage of both coal and oil boilers, so it was unlikely that she would be left adrift anytime soon. The Admiralty's orders, as communicated by Sitwell to the officers, had been very clear, however — they were to make best speed to the east coast of South America to guard the rich shipping lanes there from raiders, and that would involve burning a prodigious amount of coal.

Knowing how much had been lost was, therefore, a pressing concern. Littleton drew that particularly unpleasant duty — as the chief engineer was busy doing what he could to service engines that were the cruiser's beating heart — and made no secret of his displeasure, even if he didn't have to go crawling through the bunkers himself.

"I've figured you out, old chap!" Littleton told Baxter when they ran into each other on deck. It was a blustery day, the wind driving cold spray across the deck, but the air temperature was already noticeably warmer than the chill they had left behind in winter-bound Devonport.

Baxter glanced at him, suspecting that the other man was very far from having figured him out. "Do tell," he said in response.

"I first thought you volunteered to help Simons because you were toadying up to Sitwell," Littleton went on, a somewhat smug expression on his face. "Then I had it! You could see what was coming along for all of us, so you got in on helping Guns so you wouldn't get assigned the coal."

Baxter glanced out to sea. "You've got me there. Terrible stuff, coal. A shame we stopped using sails, really."

"Well, there we are, then," Littleton said, a little nonplussed. He blinked up at Baxter, as though he was realising for the first time just how big he was, and nodded decisively. "Well, we'd best be about this — wouldn't want old Sitwell to get angry."

"Just so," Baxter said, already moving on towards the ship's superstructure to find Simons and try to chivvy him into actually putting a proposal in front of the captain for gunnery drill. His expression caused a number of bluejackets to step quickly out of the way and throw parade ground-worthy salutes.

Over the next couple of days, it became clear that their stores were not in a good state. Ironically, despite the loss of deck cargo during the storm, HMS *Astute*'s fuel situation was of least concern. She'd been loaded with extra to allow for a rapid passage across the Atlantic, so even with the losses she was carrying enough coal and oil to complete the journey, though she would be later than anticipated.

"The food stores will last us, but the fresh meat has been spoiled," Webb reported. Baxter had the afternoon watch as the cruiser ploughed ever onwards, her prow pointed almost due west towards the pale disk of the sun, still high in the sky at this longitude.

Baxter was tired after a long day of running 'dry drills' with the gun crews. For some reason best known to himself, Gregson had yet to approve any live firing practice, which was the only true way to get a gun crew gelled together. Baxter had come straight from practice to his watch, and was not in much of a mood for casual conversation. "Well, we've got nothing to worry about on that account," he said, in a tone that he hoped would put an end to the exchange.

"The men won't be happy, sir," Webb said.

"The men are no more content when they have something to complain about."

Baxter stepped up to the bridge railing. Although, as officer of the watch, he was responsible for the ship, the captain's chair was sacrosanct and he instead moved around on the open bridge, occasionally raising his field glasses to scan the horizon. It was chilly and the air smelt like rain. Soon enough they would be changing into their white tropical uniforms, but not just yet.

The array of speaking tubes near the captain's chair emitted a sharp whistle, cutting across the noise of the wind. A bridge messenger listened briefly before turning to Baxter. "Masthead reports smoke two points off the starboard bow, sir."

Baxter swung his glasses to the indicated bearing. The lookout, on a platform high up the cruiser's only mast, had a much better view, but it only took him a few moments to pick out the plume of smoke for himself.

It could only mean one thing. They weren't alone on this stretch of sea.

CHAPTER FIVE

Baxter held the thin plume of smoke in the magnified view for a few moments. He wanted to run up to the lookout post to make a better assessment, as he might have done in previous years, but his position was here on the bridge until he was relieved. Which left him with the question of whether he should summon Gregson or Sitwell.

Although they had been steaming for some time without seeing another vessel, it didn't come as a surprise to encounter one. The seas may have been swept clear of enemy merchant shipping, either taken or holed up in neutral ports, but there were plenty of friendly or neutral ships abroad.

"Two stacks, I'd say," Webb said, referring to the number of funnels on the distant ship. "Maybe three."

"Good eyes," Baxter replied, not lowering his field glasses and conscious of the tense silence on the rest of the bridge. This was probably nothing, almost certainly a friendly or a neutral, but for many of the men this could be their first contact with an enemy vessel.

"Should I send for the captain, sir?" Webb asked, a note of nervous excitement in his voice.

Baxter paused, trying to determine what was in front of them. Whatever she was, she appeared to be lying to under a thick cloak of her own smoke that moved sluggishly in the wind. He was able to make out some details, at least. Too tall to be a warship, but that didn't mean she wasn't an enemy merchantman that had somehow managed to avoid the RN cruisers whose business it was to close the seas to the Kaiser.

"Why don't you do that, Mr Webb?" he said at last. Even if the vessel ahead of them was friendly, intercepting it would at least break the tedium of the voyage and give the untested sailors some experience of an engagement.

Gregson arrived on the bridge within moments of Webb stepping away to call him. The captain looked drawn and tired, but then he had a lot on his plate. Passing through the storm had been hard on all of them, and the captain had been on the bridge for a lot of the time. Baxter made his report and Gregson spent a few minutes staring at the ship himself. "Probably just a merchantman," he said at last, his tone suggesting he really shouldn't have been disturbed for this. "Any signal or other sign they've seen us?"

"No, sir," Baxter said. He knew that supported the notion that the ship was indeed a civilian one, and probably a neutral. "She seems to be remaining stationary, in fact."

"Probably maintaining her machinery or recovering someone who's gone overboard. We're not in the business of harassing passing merchantmen," Gregson said wearily. He walked across the gently rolling deck to his tall wooden chair and pulled himself up into it. "We'll pass within a few miles on this course — we'll signal and find out if she needs assistance, but I see no need to interfere with her beyond that."

Baxter bit down his response. His gut told him that there were reasons to investigate a ship behaving suspiciously and well off the beaten track. He was, however, not the captain nor even the first officer, who might have sufficient leeway to nudge his commander. "Aye, sir," was all he said, before turning to instruct the signals rating to prepare the necessary hoist of flags.

Although the captain was on the bridge and showed no inclination to return to his cabin, Baxter still had the watch until Gregson stated otherwise. He prowled around, keeping an eye on the crew and the worsening state of the weather as the day drew on. Thickening clouds scudded overhead, and while there was only the occasional raindrop he had no doubt there was a downpour due.

Baxter checked occasionally on the mysterious ship and was now convinced she was one of the high-speed passenger liners that had plied these waters in happier times. She remained stationary, showing no sign of alarm or even having noticed the Royal Navy cruiser steaming past her. She wasn't flying any colours, but that wasn't entirely unusual. The more he watched her, though, the more Baxter thought there was something odd about her.

Gregson shifted on the wooden chair. "I think we can make our enquiries," he said, raising his old-fashioned telescope to scrutinise the ship again.

Baxter nodded to the signalman, and a moment later the bundled flags jerked up to the starboard yardarm then broke out in the prescribed signal. *Do you require assistance?*

Baxter raised his glasses to watch the liner, now a little more than three miles away. Painfully short range for an engagement, if it came to it — *Astute*'s main guns could throw a four-inch shell six or seven miles.

"We could try the wireless, sir?" suggested Webb, when there was no response from the other ship.

"That would broadcast our presence to the entire Atlantic," Baxter replied, keeping his voice low. If the captain wanted to use wireless telegraphy to try to stir the other ship, that was his prerogative, but Baxter had a feeling that Gregson was an old Navy man who had little truck with such innovations. He'd met a few in his time, including a number who still decried the loss of sailing rigs from their ships.

The view was obscured momentarily by a squall of cold rain that hammered the cruiser as she sliced across the waves. When the grey sheet of rain parted, as suddenly as it had come on, the liner was still there, but had broken out the Stars and Stripes, snapping proudly from her gaff, and a signal hoist to indicate that she was the liner *San Francisco* and that she didn't need assistance.

"Well, there we are then," Gregson said, apparently satisfied by the exchange. "And we certainly don't want to repeat the mistakes of the last century and board an American. Touchy bunch, the Americans, particularly when it comes to us Brits."

Baxter hadn't taken his eyes off the liner as HMS *Astute* continued to steam past her. Although she clearly had steam up herself, the civilian ship was showing no sign that she was planning on moving on and was just using her engines to keep station. "What the devil is so interesting about that patch of water?" he wondered aloud.

"Well, you know these mercantile types, sir," Webb said, his slightly nasal, brassy voice carrying clear across the bridge. "All sorts of strange whims can take them — maybe he just doesn't like the look of the weather."

Baxter lowered his glasses and looked across at Webb. He'd learned the sea aboard merchant ships — sail and latterly steam — under his father's tutelage. He may not have liked his father and wasn't even entirely sure if the old Bible-thumper was still alive, but he wouldn't brook any suggestion that merchant sailors were incompetent or adverse to foul weather.

"Mr Webb," Gregson said, voice flat and hard. "I would encourage you to remember that you are serving alongside reserve officers who have joined us from the Merchant Navy. You might recognise them from the slightly different insignia, as Mr Baxter wears, and should consider that they are every bit as capable as any regular officer. Even you."

Baxter was surprised by the interjection. After only a few days' association with the captain, it had become clear the other man didn't think much of him, and Baxter had put that down to his status as a reserve officer. There were some regular officers who didn't have much time for the 'Wavy Navy', though in his experience they were few and far between. Most acknowledged them for what they were: seasoned professionals who gave up their time to train in peacetime so that they would be ready to serve when the need arose.

Webb looked suitably chastened, and Gregson swung his angry glare on Baxter. "And, Mr Baxter, as officer of the watch, it would behove you to maintain discipline."

"Yes, sir," Baxter said, smarting at the rebuke despite his best effort not to. Webb and every bluejacket on the bridge maintained the rigid lack of expression common to sailors when someone else was catching hell. It would disguise their satisfaction that an officer was getting ticked off.

Gregson strode towards the companionway, and Baxter looked back to the liner, bringing his glasses back up. The cruiser continued on her steady way past the liner, the helmsmen and engine room ignorant of the brief drama that had played out on the bridge, but despite the change in the two ships' relative positions, the liner was still presenting her port side. If she had been holding position, Baxter would have expected to see her stern, or at least be on her quarter.

San Francisco was turning slowly on the spot. Baxter's mind raced, taking in the particularly thick, dark cloud of coal smoke that hung around the ship. Far more than even an old furnace should be producing, unless it was burning particularly poor coal. Or if there were two ships…

"Cup of tea, sir?" a raspy voice said by his elbow, startling him slightly. Baxter turned to see the steward Hancock looking up at him, proffering a tray with a number of steaming tin mugs. Baxter took one and gratefully inhaled the scent of Navy-fashion tea. "Anything the matter, sir?"

Baxter took a sip of the hot, sweet tea and felt it warm his gullet. "I don't like the look of the *San Francisco* over there," he said at last, deciding that he may as well confide in someone. It was not something he would say to an ordinary rating, but the steward occupied a strange space within their little steel-bound world.

"The *San Francisco*, sir? That's not her, which might go some way towards explaining your discomfort."

Baxter stared down at the older man. "Are you quite sure?" he asked. "She is still some distance away."

"Well, I did spend a few months working for the Red Star Line and often saw her in harbour. You get to know the shape of a ship, even when she's at some distance."

Baxter handed the steward his glasses. "Make certain, if you please."

It didn't take Hancock long to reach a conclusion. "Quite certain, sir," he said firmly. "Most certainly not the *San Francisco*."

Baxter managed to bite off a curse. "Mr Webb, if you would be so good as to ask the captain to return to the bridge," he said, bracing himself for the inevitable recriminations that would come — particularly if Hancock was wrong. Webb swallowed, obviously coming to the same conclusion, but did as he was ordered.

Gregson returned to the bridge with surprising alacrity, his professionalism overcoming any annoyance or doubt about the officers he'd been lumbered with. "What is it now, Baxter?" he demanded.

"Hancock reports that he's fairly certain that the liner isn't who she claims to be," he replied calmly.

"Well, I've been around long enough to trust the judgement of old salts like Hancock," Gregson said in a surprisingly mild tone. "German, do you think?"

"I can't think of any other reason to pretend to be a neutral, unless she's actually British or French and thinks *we're* the enemy." Baxter paused, assessing whether the captain would be receptive to what he had to say next. "I also think there's a second, lower ship to leeward of that liner. They've been manoeuvring to keep her out of our sight since we spotted them."

"Preposterous," Gregson said. "You'd need a fine touch indeed to keep station like that at sea."

Baxter didn't argue with that. He'd seen the effects of two ships crashing into each other when alongside, back in 1905, in calmer waters than these. It didn't change his assessment of the situation, though.

He expected Gregson to order him to carry on, but after a moment's reflection the captain took his telescope from under his arm and snapped it open so briskly it almost sounded like a gunshot. He trained it on the suspicious vessel once again. Baxter mirrored his posture and the two of them stood like that for a few moments. The fading light made it increasingly difficult to make much out.

"She is making a lot of smoke — enough for two ships, unless she's burning really foul coal," Gregson said at last, a suspicious note entering his voice. "By God, Baxter, I do believe you may be right."

Gregson marched over to the speaking tubes and stood next to them for some minutes, drumming his fingers on the brass cap that kept water out of the system. Baxter could feel the tension on the bridge. Then the captain flipped open the speaking tube and blew into it to get the attention of the men in the wheelhouse, buried beneath their feet in a considerably more armoured location than the bridge.

"Quartermaster, adjust course five points to starboard and increase to full revolutions," he ordered. As the cruiser began to cut a long curve through the Atlantic, Gregson pulled himself back into his chair. Sitwell appeared on deck just as the turn began, but was a seasoned enough sailor that he didn't lose his footing as the deck heeled.

Baxter felt a surge of adrenalin as the cruiser picked up speed. *Astute* was still a relatively new vessel, and her machinery was in good order after some time in the dockyard. She didn't respond like a destroyer or torpedo boat, but the increase in speed was noticeable after a few minutes. She surged forward, smoke whipping from her stacks and the White Ensign snapping at the flagstaff. She wasn't closing with the other ship, but the comparatively sharp turn and increase in speed would allow her to cross the liner's bows and see what, if anything, she was trying to hide.

"Should I order battle stations, sir?" Sitwell asked, after Webb had brought him up to speed with remarkable brevity.

"Yes, why not?" Gregson grunted as he settled himself into his chair. "But pass the word not to load the guns without express orders. We don't want to risk shooting at an American by accident."

It took a couple of minutes to find the Marine bugler and have him sound battle stations, which didn't bode well for the rest of the exercise. The cascade of notes, normally enough to stir the blood, sounded thin and weak in the cold wind, the young Marine going even redder in the face as he struggled to force the call out. Aside from the hapless bugler, the Royal Marines seemed to know their business, running to their combat stations with little fuss. The bluejackets, and not a few of the officers, seemed to be milling around in some confusion as to what they were supposed to do next.

Baxter clattered down the companionway from the bridge onto the foredeck and his own action station with the forward 4-inch guns. He'd had time to speak with the petty officers in charge of each piece, Hiscock and Evans, both of them experienced seamen. They were busy marshalling their mostly inexperienced crews, shouting and shoving none too gently to get them into position around the long guns. The seamen all looked nervous, as well they should — in common with most ships of her ilk, *Astute*'s main guns weren't turreted, they didn't even have a gun shield, and they would be horribly exposed if rounds did start flying.

It took them too long to clear away and prepare for action. Baxter didn't need to glance down at his pocket watch to know that was the case. He also knew that standing there staring at his watch and looking generally displeased would help neither the gun captains do their jobs nor the morale of the harried ratings.

He split his attention between his guns — which would likely be the first to shoot if this turned into an engagement — and the other ship. She steadfastly wore American colours, though Baxter was now sure that she was trying to brazen it out.

"She'd better swap colours if she does turn out to be German," Webb said beside him, his voice excited. Baxter knew that a lot of the younger sailors, men who hadn't seen action, would be feeling the same thing. They were doing something other than just battening down the hatches to survive a storm or steaming along under an iron-grey sky, with the possibility of some sort of action.

Baxter ignored the young man. *Astute* must have been doing at least twenty knots by now, fast enough that the liner couldn't continue circling to keep her port side towards the British cruiser. "There!" he said, catching a glimpse of a lower ship tucked up against the liner's side. He thought he saw lines between the two ships being cast off, then lost sight of them in another squall that tore up the intervening two miles of sea.

He lowered the glasses and glanced up at the bridge. The order to load the guns should have been given by now — surely the lookout would have spotted the other ship.

"Don't you have a duty station to be at?" he asked Webb irritably.

He blanched slightly. "Sorry, sir," he mumbled, turning away.

"Mr Webb," Baxter said, then stepped closer and lowered his voice. "If shells do start flying, keep your wits about you and don't let the men see your nerves."

"I'm not shy, sir!" the young man objected, voice rising. A couple of nearby bluejackets glanced across with amused expressions.

"I didn't say you were, lad. It's probably about to get very loud, and very dangerous, though."

His tone finally got through to Webb, who swallowed hard and nodded. "I understand," he said.

Further discussion was forestalled by a shout from the bridge. "All guns, load high explosive!" came Sitwell's bellow. A moment later the same message was relayed by speaking tube to the gun crews. Looking back out to sea, Baxter saw that the situation had changed dramatically.

A warship was tearing away from the shelter of the liner's tall side, the ensign of the *Kaiserliche Marine* flying proudly from her gaff. For a moment, Baxter thought it was the *Königsberg*, the cruiser that had proved to be such a menace on the east coast of Africa. That was an impossibility, as that ship was on the far side of the world and would never have made it here intact. Their newly discovered opponent was clearly of the same or similar class. Three funnels spewed black smoke as the German ship picked up speed, turning hard to starboard to bring a broadside of five guns to bear. Baxter had seen these weapons at work, and knew they were more than capable of inflicting serious damage on *Astute*. Of course, the Royal Navy cruiser's battery was just as capable of returning the compliment, albeit at a shorter range. Not that it mattered, as the enemy cruiser's long turn had brought her into dangerously close range.

"Load high explosive!" Baxter ordered as targeting and range information flowed from the gunnery officer, Simons, perched above the bridge in the dangerously exposed observation platform. "Full charge!"

"Why aren't they bloody letting us have it?" one of the gunners muttered as the men worked the mechanisms to swing the long gun to bear. Tension was palpable across the deck.

Baxter remained by the speaking tube, feeling the familiar anticipation before action. Not excitement exactly, or fear. The last time he'd been in this situation, he'd been in command, albeit of a much smaller vessel. Not being on the bridge and deciding when to unleash *Astute*'s arsenal was frustrating, particularly as the battle was about to be engaged at such short range and hitting the target would not be a challenge.

"Why aren't we giving them the good news?" someone else shot back.

"Blighters on the bridge probably think it's polite to let them fire first."

"Silence there," Baxter ordered, putting no real sharpness into the order.

The German captain had clearly decided that the stand-off had gone on long enough. Baxter saw the flash of the enemy cruiser's guns firing almost simultaneously.

"Our father, who art…" someone began to say, though the rest of the prayer was lost in a tumult of noise as the German shells howled overhead and crashed into the sea a hundred yards or more off their port side, five plumes of water appearing in a relatively neat group. A moment later the sharp cracks of the high-velocity guns' firing reached their ears.

"Long, by God!" someone exclaimed.

Baxter glanced up to the bridge. From this angle, he couldn't see much, just telescopes and the ends of field glasses aimed unwaveringly at the German cruiser. He itched to be up there, to be the one giving the orders.

Looking back out to sea, he thought he could see the reason for the captain's hesitation. The liner, still flying the American flag, was making steam away from the developing engagement, but was still dangerously close to the German cruiser. Deliberately so, in Baxter's estimation.

Simons, up on the observation platform, was continuing to feed information to the gun crews, though there wasn't much change as the cruisers were sailing on parallel courses. His fire control task would be next to impossible once the battle really kicked off, but he was doing his best right now.

The German cruiser fired again, the same disciplined ripple of flashes along her broadside. Short this time, but well grouped, plumes rising between the two ships but rather too close to *Astute* for comfort. "Come on, you blighter," a gunner muttered, casting a dark glance towards the bridge.

"Silence there!" the gun captain snapped, taking his cue from Baxter. They could all agree with the sentiment, though.

The word came through a moment later. "Starboard guns, commence!" Sitwell bellowed from the bridge, followed a moment later by Simons' voice from the speaking tube.

"Shoot!" Baxter barked. The gun fired, the noise tremendous as it crashed back in its mounting. The racket seemed to go on forever, but it could only have been a matter of seconds as *Astute* fired a slightly ragged broadside. She was firing six guns to the German's five, as the two rear guns were mounted fore and aft rather than side by side as they were on the enemy ship, but the British crews' practice was lamentable compared to the tight firing of their opponent. The shots were well over, aside from one stern gun that was short.

"Reload!" Baxter ordered, then turned on his heel when he didn't hear the clang of the breechblock opening. The firing of their own guns seemed to have stunned the crew more than the German shells dropping ever closer to them. "Reload!" he repeated, more forcefully than should have been necessary.

His command stirred them into action. Gunners swung the still-hot breechblock open, releasing cordite fumes. There was no cartridge case to extract, allowing the gun crew to load the shell and then bags of propellant. "Come on, lads!" the gun captain called. "Faster if we're going to sink that bastard."

They closed and locked the breech with a *clunk*. Baxter realised there hadn't been any indication of whether the order to commence meant fire at will, or whether they would be firing broadsides. There seemed to be some confusion along the line of guns, and he saw Littleton, who had the broadside guns, glance towards him with a quizzical expression. Simons hadn't ordered any correction to the guns' laying either.

The German fired again, managing a third broadside in the time it had taken the Royal Navy men to reload. *Astute* was bracketed this time, water plumes rising on either side close enough to deluge the decks. Shrapnel from a surface burst rang off her unarmoured sides, and the ship seemed to shudder slightly. "Damn it," Baxter growled, his professional pride smarting at the better German practice and his frustration with the gunnery officer growing. "Reduce elevation three degrees."

He waited impatiently as a sailor fumbled with the wheel that managed the gun's elevation, and therefore range. "Shoot!" he snapped as soon as the bluejacket indicated compliance.

The forward gun firing set off another ragged thumping volley that spat flame into the gathering darkness. Baxter was up at the rail, field glasses on the German cruiser as he counted the seconds of the shells' short flight. He made out the splash of the first shell, just off the enemy's port quarter, close enough to wet her, but once again the other guns shot over. "Reload! Don't wait for my bloody orders! Anything from Guns?" he asked the messenger waiting next to the speaking tube. The sailor shook his head.

Baxter looked up at the bridge, knowing that even if he could see anything it wouldn't avail him much. Webb was coming down the companionway, shouting something to Baxter, when the Germans found their mark. A single shell hit *Astute*, detonating against the superstructure a foot above Webb's head.

CHAPTER SIX

Baxter staggered back, ducking as shrapnel whistled past his head. He heard men shouting, the thud of bodies hitting the deck. Someone was screaming, a high-pitched keening, but it wasn't Webb. He was ... gone. A pool of blood was spread around the detonation, evidence of his previous existence, the shell having ripped him apart from the waist up. The stench of blood and guts mixed with the smell of cordite.

Baxter shook his head, trying to clear the ringing in his ears and shake that image from his head. He'd been looking directly at the young man when he'd died, and despite all the terrible things he'd seen in the wars he'd fought, he knew that was one sight that would stay with him.

He turned back to his men. The screaming man was one of the starboard gun crew, lying on his back and clutching his right leg with trembling hands, his trousers stained with blood that pulsed out around a long piece of shrapnel lodged in his thigh. The other men were ducked into whatever cover they could find, all of them no doubt acutely conscious of their lack of protection. Only Hiscock, the petty officer in command of the crew, was holding his position.

Baxter pointed to two men and then gestured to the injured man. "Get him to the sickbay," he said, forcing himself to sound calm and measured. He realised he didn't yet know what each man was trained on, so couldn't identify someone to replace the injured man. "Stand to your duties."

The starboard gun crew went back to their hesitant loading of the weapon, while the commander of the port gun pushed a man forward to fill in for the injured gunlayer. Baxter glanced at Webb's remains, and the torn and twisted metal of the companionway. The shell seemed to have detonated on contact with the steps rather than against the superstructure itself. That was lucky, though not for the young man who had died.

"You two, get him over the side," Baxter said, his voice sounding flat and hard even to his own ears. The sailors he'd detailed blanched, but they edged forward from their station at the unengaged gun to go about their grisly duty. One of them vomited as he took hold of Webbs' ankles and what was left of his trunk, leaving the sailor holding entirely separate limbs. Baxter didn't have any more time to pay attention to them, though.

Astute's guns were banging away now, ragged broadsides sent hurtling towards the German cruiser seemingly without any input from the bridge or the gunnery officer perched above it. The enemy was returning two salvos for every one of theirs, though, disciplined ripples of fire down her sides. The German wasn't firing with quite the same speed as Baxter had seen from the *Königsberg* a few months ago, both when she had caught HMS *Pegasus* in Zanzibar's harbour and when she had attempted to prevent his own escape from the Rufiji River. Nonetheless, the German crews were obviously more highly trained and seasoned than *Astute*'s men.

The British cruiser shook as another German shell found its mark, towards the stern this time. Fire blossomed as the round detonated, but the aft guns were still blazing away. Visibility was getting worse. While the stiff breeze was whipping both ships' smoke away, it was almost nightfall and heavy racing clouds blocked whatever light there was. *Astute* could only find her target by watching for muzzle flashes, and shell splashes were barely visible against the lowering sky, making correcting fire almost impossible.

With no changes being ordered from either the ship's commander or gunnery officer, the officers in charge of each battery were having to make their own adjustments with little or no information. No matter what corrections they made, however, they still couldn't land a hit while the German consistently bracketed them, deluging *Astute* with water and shell splinters. Fire flashed higher up on the superstructure, and again in the stern, as more shells found their mark. Even over the thunder of guns and the ringing in his ears, Baxter could make out the sounds of men shouting and screaming.

It was dark enough now that the men were dim shapes as they worked their gun, briefly illuminated by the dazzling muzzle flash as the weapon fired. Baxter felt the concussion as much as heard it, a sensation he was well used to after so many years spent around naval artillery. There was something not right about the shot, though. Something in the noise or the brief cloud of smoke that accompanied the discharge. Watching for the shell fall, he thought he saw the splash of it landing well short, despite his correction to the gun's elevation.

The sea was getting up, rolling both the cruiser and her target, the white crests of the waves ghostly in the darkness. Baxter could hear rain over the sea and wind, and as he watched, the bright flicker of the enemy's guns was swallowed by darkness as another squall rolled across the seascape. A moment later, they were deluged by rain, its hammering loud even in comparison to the thump of the guns.

"A spot of rain shouldn't stop you loading, gentlemen," he said to the half-seen gun crew, who were finding what shelter they could against the deluge.

The gun captain emerged from the darkness. "It's not the rain, sir — there's nothing coming up the hoist!" he shouted above the noise.

Baxter turned, feeling a rising tide of fury. The shell hoist, situated between the two guns and abaft, was supposed to provide a steady stream of shells and propellant from the heart of the ship. Down in the shell room and magazines, sweating bluejackets should have been loading ammunition onto a platform that would then have been rattled up to the deck to feed the guns once the ready ammunition supply had been used. The sailors were clustered around the hoist, though, as nothing was coming up from below.

He strode across to the speaking tubes and selected the one that linked his position to the magazine and shell room that should have been feeding him. "Where's my ammunition?" he demanded once he was sure there was someone at the other end of the tube, then bent his ear to hear the response.

"The hoist is jammed, sir!" came back the tinny response. "We're working on it!"

Baxter closed his eyes briefly and ran a hand over his face. The rain was tapering off as the squall moved on, but visibility had barely improved. The RN cruiser at least had a respite from German gunnery, though he didn't doubt the enemy was still out there somewhere, glasses and telescopes sweeping the sea for any sign of *Astute*.

"Well, bloody well get on with it!" he snapped into the tube. "And detail some men to start bringing shells and ammunition up by hand — we have to be ready to shoot back."

Astute was steaming on into the night, maintaining a steady course despite the presence of a now unseen enemy vessel. Baxter realised that the ship's course hadn't been adjusted at all in the last few minutes, which was unusual in even the most straightforward engagement. He flipped open the tube to the bridge, but got no response when he spoke into it, and when he craned his neck to look he couldn't make out any activity.

Baxter hesitated, then called Hiscock and Evans over. "I'm going up to the bridge to find out what's going on," he said. It was a risk, leaving his post when they were at battle stations, but the two petty officers seemed steady enough. "Hold your fire unless specifically ordered."

"Nothing to fire with, sir," Evans pointed out.

"*When* the supply is renewed, do not fire unless ordered," Baxter snapped.

"Aye, sir," both men said in unison, perhaps picking up on his strained nerves.

Baxter turned away without another word. The companionway up to the bridge on the starboard side was gone, torn away by the shell burst that had killed Webb, so he went up the port side, each firm boot on the wet metal step seeming to tighten the ratchet of his anger.

His fury drained away when he arrived on the bridge and found a scene of devastation, caused by the shell that had exploded in the cruiser's upperworks. The captain was slumped in his chair, blood streaming down his face from a head wound, and there was no sign of Sitwell. Webb, assigned as the signals officer and to general duties on the bridge, should have been there. Bluejackets were trying to tend to the injured, but right now Baxter was the most senior officer on the bridge.

A rush of adrenalin hit Baxter, but he didn't have time to relish the feeling, or to berate the obviously unsteady sailors for not immediately passing word for the first officer to report to the bridge. He jabbed a finger at a messenger, a lad whose eyes were wide with a mix of fear and excitement. "You — find Lieutenant Commander Sitwell and let him know the captain is injured. Pass the word to sickbay that we have injured men on the bridge.' Baxter turned to the bluejackets. 'You four, get these injured men below. Start with the captain. The rest of you, back to your stations!"

That at least got the men moving. As soon as someone more senior arrived, Baxter would be able to hand the conn over to him, but until then, he needed to get the situation in hand.

"Anyone able to make out the enemy ship?" he asked, moving over to starboard and raising his own glasses. It was now pitch black out there, the sort of darkness that only a cloudy night at sea could offer. The German would be running with all external lights doused, just as they were. It would take one of them deciding they had a target and opening fire, or some idiot switching on a searchlight, for the target to be fixed again. Baxter wasn't sure that continuing the engagement would be a good idea, but he'd be damned if the enemy was to get the edge on them again.

"No, sir," a nervous young sailor responded.

"Keep a sharp eye out, lads." Baxter turned, examining the full sweep forward as best he could while he wondered where the hell Sitwell was.

Astute continued on her steady course through the night, maintaining fifteen knots, her engines thumping away below. Baxter ordered a slight change of course and a reduction in speed, to reduce the noise of their passage and to throw off any particularly canny German officer who might be trying to predict where she would be.

A tense silence fell over the bridge. Baxter was aware of the glances being exchanged by the men around him, all of them unsure about what to make of a reserve officer being in brief command of their cruiser — an officer who had been on board barely a week. He kept his back straight and chin up as he scanned the darkness as best he could, searching in vain for a patch of deeper darkness that might denote the enemy cruiser. The sea was getting up and the rain squalls were becoming more frequent, hovering on the cusp of becoming another storm. Normally he would have cursed the weather preventing them from seeking out and destroying the enemy ship, but it was clear to anyone with an ounce of sense that *Astute* was in no state to continue the engagement.

In truth, the ship and her crew hadn't even been in the right state to go *into* the fight.

The sailor he'd despatched to find Sitwell reported back to the bridge. "Beg your pardon, sir," he rushed out breathlessly. "Jimmy the … I mean Mr Sitwell has been taken to the sickbay. He was hit while organising a firefighting party."

Baxter wasn't a superstitious man — no more than any other sailor, in truth — but he was starting to believe that the ship was cursed, that there was a Jonah aboard. But then, the first officer's duties included damage control, so it made sense that he would have been in harm's way.

He stepped quickly to the speaking tubes. "Guns, this is the bridge."

"Gunnery here," Simons said, sounding both distracted and irritated despite the tinny distortion of the brass tube. "Who is this?"

"This is Baxter — the captain and first officer have both been injured. I suggest you nip down and take command."

There was a brief pause. Baxter could picture the gunnery officer in his armoured cupola, rangefinder in front of him and glasses to hand, chewing his lip as he considered his options. Not that there was more than one correct option at this point.

Simons went for the incorrect choice. "I can't nip down just now, old chap — rather busy with gunnery, as I'm sure you can imagine. You were officer of the watch — you have the conn. Get Mr Littleton up there to relieve you, soon as you can." There was a strained pause. "Do you understand, Baxter?"

"Perfectly," he growled, before snapping the speaking tube shut so sharply he caused the messenger to jump.

Baxter had never heard anything like it. While it was true that the officer of the watch had the conn — was formally responsible for the ship — until relieved, Captain Gregson had clearly and formally taken the bridge when the ship had gone to action stations. Simons was being rather derelict in his duty, in refusing to come down.

Baxter's stormy expression caused the hovering messenger to take half a step back. "Kindly find Mr Littleton and ask him to report to the bridge," he ordered. "Let him know he's now in command."

He wondered exactly what gunnery Simons was busy with, given how poor their shooting had been so far and the fact that they had no idea where the enemy was anyway. It wouldn't do to say that out loud, of course.

With a clunk and hum audible now that the gunnery had ceased, the searchlight mounted just abaft the three funnels came to life, sending out a questing beam of light in the hopes of picking up the German cruiser once again. Unless they got very lucky, or the gunnery officer was better than Baxter thought, all the searchlight would do was mark their own position.

Baxter turned to look out to sea, hoping that Simons had a rough notion of where the enemy cruiser was rather than just starting a sweep of the sea. There was no sign of the sleek German vessel in the bright circle of light. A moment later, the enemy gave his position away by opening fire, the five guns firing almost as one. While the Germans now had an aiming point, *Astute* was mainly saved by the fact that the ships' relative positions had changed significantly since they'd lost sight of each other. The enemy gunners still managed to raise a tight group of splashes a hundred yards to port.

Baxter cursed under his breath. *Astute* opened fire again, far more sporadically now, and Baxter's impression that there was something wrong with the guns was reinforced now he could see the full broadside fire from this vantage point.

The enemy ship fired again in the time it took the Royal Navy gunners to reload, and a third time barely seconds after *Astute's* next salvo. The forward gun was firing at least, suggesting that either the hoist had been repaired or the ready lockers had been refilled by men bringing shells and propellant up by hand.

The harried-looking messenger reappeared on the bridge, but had to stop and gulp for breath before he could report. "Found Mr Littleton, sir," he gasped out. "He says she's all yours, old chap. Sir."

It was preposterous that both the second and third officers hadn't leaped at the chance to take command. Baxter didn't have time to worry about it, though, or even reflect that he was now fully responsible for a far larger vessel than anything he'd commanded before. "All right — what's your name?"

"Briggs, sir." The sailor flinched as another German salvo came in, creeping closer to *Astute* as her own fire went wild into the night. Baxter remained standing straight, the men around him taking their cue from his apparent disregard for danger.

"Very well, Briggs. Get on the speaking tube and pass the word to the searchlights to cease operations immediately. Don't take no for an answer."

He didn't need to worry about ordering the guns to cease fire, as that seemed to be happening naturally. It was a problem for after they survived — assuming they did.

Briggs seemed to be in something of a heated argument with whoever oversaw the searchlights. Baxter tapped on his shoulder and indicated that he should step aside. "This is the officer of the watch," he said into the tube. "If that light isn't off in the next ten seconds, I'll come back there and smash it myself."

There was a pause. "Aye, sir — switching the searchlight off."

Baxter switched speaking tube to talk to the armoured wheelhouse, almost directly below his feet. "On my mark, hard to port and full-steam ahead," he ordered sharply, expecting a repeat of the argument he'd had with the searchlight crew. Instead, he got a crisp acknowledgement and a sense that the quartermaster was just happy someone was still in command.

Baxter glanced up, and saw the searchlight flicker out. "Hard to port, now!" he snapped down the speaking pipe. The wheelhouse obeyed immediately, the cruiser starting a much tighter turn than she'd employed to get round the merchant raider. "Take two men and pass the word to all stations — no lights, and no firing," he ordered Briggs.

As the harried messenger dashed off again, calling to others to join him, Baxter reassured himself that the bridge was now organised and under control. The German ship fired another salvo, light flickering miles away, but the sharp manoeuvre he'd ordered had foxed the enemy. For now.

Baxter had no real notion of where they were, the ships having run on for some time as they traded blows. He knew that an officer more senior to him would appear shortly and start giving new orders, and he had every intention of ensuring that they wouldn't be able to find the enemy to continue the engagement. He'd just ordered another course change, to bring their bows pointing just south of west, when Littleton appeared on the bridge.

"What the devil do you mean, turning tail like that?" the third officer demanded furiously. There was a note in his voice that suggested something other than anger, though Baxter couldn't put his finger on it. "Turn this bloody ship around so we can finish off that German."

Surely he's not idiotic enough to think we were winning that fight? Baxter wondered. He had his anger well under control now, which was just as well. He thought of confrontations he'd had in the past, and smiled to think of how he'd resolved some of them. Cleasby, going into the Mediterranean. Arbuthnott, going over the side of a Japanese armed merchant cruiser's bridge. All the way back to the officer whose jaw he'd broken in a fight over a woman. That was the only one he felt a stir of guilt over, given the woman happened to be the other officer's wife.

"I don't know if you noticed, Littleton, but we weren't getting the best of that engagement," he said carefully. "There's something wrong with our bloody guns, for a start, and the ammunition hoists are clearly faulty."

"Nothing that a bit of pluck and ingenuity couldn't have sorted out," Littleton said with a snort. "Just a pity a reservist got to the bridge first."

That was it. The whole thing was a performance. The third officer knew as well as Baxter that they needed to evade the German cruiser until they could find out what could be done about the guns and ammunition supply, but he also had a reputation to maintain. In the finest tradition of the service, and all that.

Baxter stepped closer to Littleton, and had the satisfaction of seeing the other officer swallow and try to take a half step back before he realised he was still at the top of the companionway. Littleton was tall and well built, but Baxter still loomed over him. "Well, you've got the bridge now, Mr Littleton, so thank God you're here. I'll return to my station."

The officer flushed slightly. "Yes, do that," he said.

"You might want to stand the men down soon and feed them, though," Baxter added, keeping his voice low to avoid giving the impression he was trying to curry favour with the men.

Littleton, thankfully, kept his own voice down as they conferred. Now that he had made his display for the sake of keeping up appearances, he seemed willing to be a more collaborative officer. "With that German still out there?"

"We'll need to keep a sharp watch, but this night's just going to get dirtier and I can't imagine he'll find us. The men are cold, wet and hungry — it's been a long day."

Littleton nodded hesitantly. "We'll see what Simons says, if he ever comes down from his perch."

"In that case, I'll see to my crews. You might want to suggest to Simons that we change course occasionally, just in case that German captain is a sly one."

Shortly after Baxter returned to the foredeck, the crew was indeed stood down from action stations. He winced as the plaintive bugle notes sounded, but as he'd predicted, the night was getting increasingly rough and stormy, and the enemy cruiser would have to be dangerously close for the sound to be heard.

"Good work today, men," he said, as the bedraggled bluejackets finished securing their guns. "Go and get some food and rest."

"Did we even hit anything, sir?" a voice asked anonymously from the darkness.

"Honestly, I don't know — but we'll bloody well thump it into them next time we meet."

That raised a half-hearted cheer. It was the first taste of combat for many of them, and only the most naïve could claim that this hadn't been a defeat. Many would have seen Webb, who seemed to have been well-liked, being annihilated. Baxter didn't feel much better himself: getting away, even if it meant they would live to fight another day, didn't feel like victory. *Astute* had been hit at least three times, though it had been hard to keep track of in the chaos of the engagement. Despite what he had told the men, he was reasonably certain that they hadn't landed a single shell on their enemy in return.

Baxter waited on the deck as another squall passed over them. The guns were secured, cold enough that the rain merely sluiced off them rather than steaming away, the barrels pointing forward with impotent menace. He realised he was bone-tired and hungry, but something told him that he needed to investigate the magazines before he did anything else.

CHAPTER SEVEN

It was well into the third watch and Baxter had been up since first light, consuming only bully beef and hard tack, and enough coffee to float the cruiser. The after-effects of the engagement, with all its tension and adrenalin, dragged at his limbs. His gut, however, told him that he needed to find out what the devil was going on belowdecks.

He found the engineering commander already supervising a crew of artificers working on the hoist for the forward guns. The normally laconic engineer, Larkin, looked both tired and angry, his features stained with grease and coal dust. "It wasn't a maintenance issue," he told Baxter, his expression darkening. "Or it was, after a fashion. The damn thing hadn't been installed properly, which is the dockyard's fault, but none of my crew had spotted the problem. I take full responsibility, of course."

And you're probably the only officer aboard who would admit that. "Well, it was dashed inconvenient, sir," Baxter said instead. "But we got through it."

"I can assure you, Mr Baxter, it won't happen again. From now on, the supply of ammunition to your guns will be smooth."

"What about the rest of the ship? We took a few hits."

"I've not had a chance to have a proper look, but the engines at least are in full working order and the fires are out." Larkin peered more closely at Baxter. "You look done in. You should get some rest and perhaps clean that blood off yourself."

"I want to check something first," Baxter said, and continued down rattling companionways into the warm heart of the ship.

He could tell, from the occasional heel in the deck under his feet, that Simons or Littleton, who now constituted the commander and executive officer, had followed his advice about changing course on occasion.

Down in the magazines, where the propellant was handled, he found a group of exhausted bluejackets. "Did we win, sir?" one of the sailors who had laboured through the two-hour engagement asked. Of course, they would know nothing of what had gone on above, just labouring away to send up the bagged propellant.

"No," Baxter replied bluntly. "Have you men not been stood down?"

"Nobody passed the word to us, sir."

"Well, you're dismissed," he said. "Go and get some food and some rest."

They filed out gratefully, leaving Baxter standing in the low compartment surrounded by the chests of bagged propellant. He hadn't officially been a gunnery officer, with responsibility for spaces like this, for a very long time. The last time he'd been in a magazine, in fact, was when he'd helped suppress a mutiny on the Russian cruiser *Yaroslavich*, back in 1905. Although this was a newer ship than he was used to, the layout remained familiar to him.

Astute certainly seemed to have a good supply of bagged cordite charges, testament in part to how slowly they had been firing, but something in the space didn't feel right. He went to the nearest open case, from which the sailors had been pulling bags to send up to the shell room and then onwards to the gun position above. As soon as he laid hands on the top bag, he knew what the problem was. He picked the heavy tube up, feeling the weight of it, the coarseness of the shalloon fabric.

He checked the rest of that case, then opened two more at random to confirm his suspicions. His anger rose from a simmer to boiling point as he left the magazine and headed up to the bridge. He carried one of the heavy charges, in contravention of a lot of rules, but his stormy expression and the fact he carried the weight one-handed cleared the way in front of him.

Simons was on the bridge. "Ah, Mr Baxter, there you are," the gunnery officer said cheerfully. "You'll be pleased to know that both the captain and first officer are alive, and Sitwell at least will make a... Why the devil have you brought a charge up here?"

"Because it's bloody wet," Baxter ground out. "Which goes at least some way towards explaining why we couldn't hit the broadside of a barn even at that range."

Baxter had been expecting anger or denial, a reprimand for the way he'd spoken to a senior officer. But the gunnery officer merely looked at him with cold disdain. "And what the devil do you mean by poking around in the magazines?" he demanded. "That is not your duty station or your business."

"It's my bloody business if my guns aren't smashing up German ships because the cordite's duff," Baxter responded, keeping his voice low. They'd attracted the attention of everyone on the bridge, though the enlisted men were all staring out to sea or otherwise busying themselves in that way sailors did when they knew they shouldn't be listening. "It was pretty clear that we should have had that German bang to rights at the third or fourth salvo, but the shells were behaving very erratically."

Simons nodded to the hatch into the chartroom at the back of the bridge. "Mr Yates, you have the conn."

Yates was the cruiser's fifth officer, a young man barely older than Webb had been, but with just enough time in the service to be a full lieutenant. Unlike the now departed sub-lieutenant, he at least seemed confident and capable.

Simons clanged the hatch closed behind them, dogged it, then turned and glared at Baxter. The electric lighting made him look even more sallow than usual. Taylor looked up from the charts he'd been puzzling over. "I think we're…"

"Give us a moment, Taylor, would you?" Simons said, his voice so tight that the other officer didn't hesitate in going back out onto the bridge.

As soon as they were alone, the ships' gunnery officer turned to Baxter. "Cordite isn't the black powder you were used to," he said abruptly. "It still fires when it's wet, as you well know. We threw plenty of shells at the enemy."

Baxter took a deep breath. Simons had all but admitted that he knew the magazines had got soaked, but clearly didn't seem to think it was much of an issue. He knew he shouldn't have confronted the gunnery officer openly on the bridge. It would do no good for the men to know they had faulty ammunition, or that the officers were at each other's throats.

"Was it during the storm?" he asked.

"That, and because we have a raw and untrained crew who do not know proper procedures."

And a gunnery officer who didn't think to train them. "All the magazines?"

"No," Simons said. "And, as I said, the cordite still detonated. I expect the fact we couldn't hit that bloody cruiser even at that range is down to the gunlayers and the officers commanding the batteries. You clearly couldn't follow simple directions."

Baxter realised he was still holding the heavy bag of explosives. He fought down the urge to throw it at Simons and instead handed it to him. The gunnery officer took it automatically, holding it in both hands and looking at him quizzically. "It's not just damp, Simons, it's sodden, and all of that water turned into steam when the propellant burned."

Simons looked down at the sullen mass in his hands, as though seeing it for the first time and realising the destructive potential he was holding. Not for the first time, Baxter wondered how in hell this man had passed the course at HMS *Vernon*, the RN's gunnery school. Perhaps standards had slipped since his own time there.

"That would have affected the ballistics," Simons admitted after a moment.

"And we're bloody lucky we didn't have a gun burst."

Simons rubbed wearily at his forehead. "Littleton is keen to run that German blighter down and give him what for," he said. "It's a little hard to see how we can continue the engagement, though."

"You're in command, Simons. It's your decision."

"Until Sitwell is back on his feet — the doctor said he was knocked out, but did not sustain serious injury."

Baxter kept his peace, waiting to see what conclusion Simons would jump to. The gunnery officer stared at the map with a brooding expression, then glanced at Baxter. "Thoughts?"

"We've lost the German for now, and that's a good thing — we're not in a fit state to fight, even without damage that needs to be made good. The forward shell hoist needs to be repaired, and the others checked. We need to make sure there's an even distribution of cordite that isn't wet. Ideally, we need time to train the gun crews properly."

Simons traced his finger across a chart. "The storm had taken us off course to the south, and we hadn't made that up when you saw that liner. We can turn around and steam like hell for Bermuda, and hope that German isn't actually looking for us."

"His orders will be to raid commerce," Baxter said. "Unless I miss my guess, he was arming the liner to do the same thing."

Simons scowled. "There's nothing to say that she wasn't exactly what she appeared, an American liner that had been stopped by a combatant vessel for inspection. Just as we were considering doing. Now, the question is, Baxter, would you turn down an engagement with an enemy warship when all evidence points to you having superiority?"

"I'd follow my orders, Mr Simons," Baxter said formally. "Though if I had the chance to send an enemy cruiser to the bottom without too much risk to my own ship, I'd take it. Everyone in the *Kaiserliche Marine* will know about Coronel by now — they'll want to keep pressing the advantage."

"So he may have gone about his business, or he may be patrolling along our potential route to Bermuda and refit. There's no way of knowing."

"He'll be in those waters either way, as it's a rich shipping lane," Baxter said, voice hardening as he tried to nudge Simons towards the only obvious conclusion. "There are neutral ports nearby, which would allow us time to repair and resupply, as well as making a full report to a British consul."

Simons glanced up from the chart. "I haven't even made a brief report by wireless — didn't want to give away our position."

"Might I suggest we make the briefest of reports? It's entirely possible that we're the only ones who know they're in these waters," Baxter said evenly. "All we'd be doing is letting them know we're in the area — they wouldn't be able to find us."

"How the devil would you know? You're a signals officer now as well?" There was fresh anger in Simons' voice, and Baxter knew he had to step carefully. Whether he liked it or not, the gunnery officer was his superior, indeed his commanding officer right now.

"I've spent some time with officers who understand these things," he said, thinking of East Africa, and a signals officer whose understanding of radio telegraphy had been invaluable in defeating a German plan to invade Zanzibar. Baxter had recommended him to Naval Intelligence. "Enough to get the rudiments."

Simons stared at Baxter. Then he raised his voice and shouted, "Taylor!"

The hatch swung open with enough alacrity to make it clear the navigation officer had been lurking outside, no doubt trying to make out what was being said.

"At Mr Baxter's suggestion, we're going to try to put into a neutral port on the east coast of South America to make emergency repairs and assess our readiness before we continue. Kindly find us somewhere suitable to put in."

"You mean we're going to run and hide?" Littleton exploded, coming in after Taylor. "Having already ceded the sea? How will this look?"

"Less bad than it would if we went to the bottom, without even making a report," Simons retorted, apparently now completely comfortable with Baxter's reasoning.

"Mr Littleton does make a good point in one way, though," Baxter said, then punctured the pleased expression on the officer's face before it could fully form. "There will almost certainly be German merchantmen in many of the ports along this coast, not to mention consuls and agents. We should try to avoid giving away our position and current state."

Taylor frowned at the charts, shuffling them around the plotting table. "I put us about here," he said, pointing, "to the south of our intended course. The nearest major port is Montevideo, in Uruguay. We can probably find a sheltered cove there to make repairs, without drawing too much attention."

Simons rubbed his eyes. He looked as exhausted as the rest of them. "We won't have a lot of time if we're discovered, as Uruguay is both neutral and, I gather, relatively friendly to the Kaiser."

"I shouldn't worry too much about it," Littleton said blithely. "Once we make contact with the consul, the full might of His Britannic Majesty will be brought to bear on the locals to allow an exception for us, I'm sure."

Baxter couldn't help but smile. He'd felt this weight being brought to bear in the past, though in that instance he'd been on the receiving end of it by dint of being aboard Russian warships on their doomed journey to the Far East.

"What do you want to do, Mr Simons?" he asked.

"We'll make for Uruguay and find somewhere quiet to lick our wounds," Simons said, after a long pause.

"Then we find that German blighter and finish him off," Littleton said hotly. "We have been ordered to patrol these waters."

"That will be up to Mr Sitwell, or the captain," the gunnery officer said sharply. "Right, gentlemen, you have your orders. Carry on."

Baxter's watch was long finished, and he hadn't been assigned to any damage control parties or any other duties. What he needed was a stiff drink and some sleep, so he didn't point out to Simons that he had not, in fact, given him any orders.

CHAPTER EIGHT

Littleton had found them a pleasant enough bay on the coast of Uruguay, somewhat to the east of the main harbour and capital, Montevideo.

"It's called Piriápolis, apparently," Simons said. "It's a new city. Bloody strange concept, that. New city."

Baxter looked away from the broad, sandy beach against which clear blue waters broke in gentle waves. They were on the western side of a spit of land that projected into the Atlantic, providing a remarkably sheltered anchorage. Beyond the beach, a relatively small collection of pleasant-looking whitewashed buildings nestled in the sheltered bay, backed by the occasional jungle-covered hill. "It is the new world, old chap," he pointed out mildly.

Simons sniffed. "That promenade looks like something you'd see in Italy."

The arrival of a warship in this out-of-the-way spot seemed to have caused a bit of a stir, not least among the labourers who, despite the early hour, were already working on a partially completed promenade that would one day run along the entire sweep of the bay. The work had been disrupted by *Astute*'s arrival, and now small figures could be seen on the beach staring out at this apparition visiting from another, more violent world. Those crewmembers not actively engaged in damage control or other duties lined the cruiser's landward railing, staring towards the land beyond and all the exotic promise it held.

"Well, we've only got twenty-four hours here, technically," Simons said, voice brisker. "And a lot to do."

HMS *Astute* had made good time here, running through the night with all external lights doused just in case the German cruiser's commander was preternaturally capable. Daylight had allowed them to examine the damage they had sustained. As well as the hit that had killed young Webb and the detonation in the upperworks that had briefly put the cruiser out of command, she had received two hits aft and a number of near misses that had peppered the hull with shrapnel. Given how exposed the gun crews were, the butcher's bill was remarkably light, with only Webb killed and a score injured. Dr Martin was doubtful that three of them would last the day, and he'd carried out one amputation.

"Gentlemen."

Both Baxter and Simons came to attention as Lieutenant Commander Sitwell stepped onto the bridge. He was wearing a fresh uniform and walked unaided, but his gait was painful and stiff. Martin had informed the other officers that the first officer had been burned and 'somewhat knocked around'. The doctor hadn't been expecting him to be up and returning to duty any time soon.

Sitwell had clearly decided to put the lie to that. He returned their salutes crisply. "Mr Simons, make your report."

Baxter eased to one side as unobtrusively as he could while Simons filled the first officer in on the battle and their race for neutral waters. In the finest tradition of the Royal Navy, his language was official and dry, sucking any of the drama out of the fight and then the conflict of wills in the chartroom as they had run through the night. "I conferred with Mr Littleton and Mr Baxter, and we determined the best course of action was to find a sheltered spot to assess damage and, ah, the condition of our ammunition."

Sitwell's eyes flicked to Baxter and then back to Simons, his expression unreadable. "Is there a problem with the ammunition?" he asked.

Simons seemed to misread the danger hiding beneath the deceptively mild tone. "Just some water ingress in the forward magazines, sir. The cordite got a bit moist."

"A bit ... moist?" Sitwell said, an acid edge creeping into his tone.

"Yes, sir." The gunnery officer's voice began to falter towards the end of the sentence as he caught Sitwell's steely glare.

"I see. Well, we'd better make use of the time we have here."

"I already have work parties dealing with the damage..." Simons started.

"Are we resupplying with fresh provender?"

"No, sir," Simons said meekly.

"And have arrangements been made to contact the consulate in Montevideo?"

"No, sir."

"See to the former, if you please, Simons, and for God's sake do something about the ammunition. Mr Baxter, a word."

Sitwell glanced into the chartroom, and saw that Taylor was busy with his courses and plots. The two officers instead went down into the captain's day cabin, one deck below.

"I understand that you had the bridge after the captain was incapacitated?" Sitwell said without preamble.

"That's correct, sir," Baxter said.

Sitwell sighed. "And I also understand that it was you who decided to break off the action, threatening to destroy the searchlight being used to try to find the enemy vessel. You then gave a series of orders that appear calculated to ensure a more senior officer wouldn't be able to continue the battle once they were on the bridge?"

Baxter straightened slightly. "I took steps to ensure the German ship could not find us again, sir," he said. "She clearly had the better of us in that engagement, and I felt it wise to ensure our continued survival."

Sitwell moved round the desk and sat down heavily. "It's been suggested to me that you demonstrated cowardice in the face of the enemy."

Baxter felt a hot surge of anger and took a moment to steady himself. "Every man's entitled to his own opinion," he said at last. "Though they should be examined and altered when demonstrably wrong. Sir."

"So, in your professional opinion, we were not going to get the better of the engagement and it was better to prevent the ship being lost than to fight a glorious last stand?"

"That's correct, sir. And given that the two more senior officers I did hear from were … otherwise engaged, it fell to me to make that decision and act on it."

"Well, as far as I can tell, it was exactly the right decision."

That was good to hear, but Baxter didn't relax. While he was used to having a bad reputation follow him around, one that he'd earned thanks to his somewhat reckless behaviour as a younger officer, he wouldn't brook the suggestion that he was shy. "I'd welcome a court-martial, sir, if it would clear the matter up officially."

Sitwell looked at him sharply. "You're not afraid of anything, are you, Mr Baxter?"

Baxter allowed himself a small smile. "Aside from one or two women who could scare anyone, sir, no."

"Well, I don't think a court-martial will be necessary," Sitwell said with sufficient finality to indicate the matter was closed. "We do need to make a report to the minister here and gather any new intelligence or instructions, and I'm loath to trust the telegraph — if there's even a line to this town. Take five men and the launch and make best speed to Montevideo. Report to the legation, inform them of our situation and that we may require more than the allowed day to make our repairs, and gather any further information as you see fit. I shall expect you back within the day."

"Very good, sir. And if you've had to move on before then?"

"Speak to Mr Taylor to arrange a rendezvous. If we can't manage that, make your way to the Falkland Islands by whatever means you can."

There was a polite knock at the hatch and a messenger popped his head in at Sitwell's curt order. "Mr Yates reports that there is a gentleman calling himself Signor Piria alongside, demanding to know what we are doing in his bay and to speak to the captain."

Sitwell nodded. "I'll be up directly," he said, then turned to Baxter once the messenger had gone. "Carry on, Mr Baxter. And do try to keep a low profile."

The run across to Montevideo had been pleasant enough, barely sixty miles across relatively placid waters where the River Uruguay's estuary started to run into the South Atlantic. The easterly breeze kept it from becoming swelteringly hot, and the men in their crisp tropical white uniforms were in good spirits despite the recent unsatisfactory brush with the enemy. Steward Hancock had received permission to come along in order to acquire supplies for the officers' mess.

Montevideo, the capital of a still relatively young country, was a bustling and busy port with broad, clean avenues and a large, well-situated harbour. While the city seemed welcoming, buzzing with the energy of a transport hub that was benefitting from being a neutral port as the old world descended into war, some of the ships docked there did arouse some angry chatter from the men.

"Bloody Germans, sir," the petty officer at the tiller, Pearson, commented as he steered the little steam launch through the busy harbour.

Baxter glanced up. They were relatively close to a freighter that wore the German Imperial ensign at her flagstaff. "There'll be a lot of them hiding in neutral ports," he said.

"Do you want me to steer clear, sir?"

"We're the Royal Navy, Pearson. We're not worried about a few German merchant sailors."

While Sitwell had ordered him to keep a low profile, there was no real way to hide who they were, and Baxter had no qualms about flying the White Ensign at the launch's stern. A German sailor at the rail of the merchantman noticed them and called something to his shipmates. Within moments, the railing was lined with German sailors, all staring in sullen silence as the British launch puttered past.

Then one of them launched a gob of yellow phlegm towards the launch, falling well short. A pail of slops followed, splashing into the murky water. Whistles and jeers accompanied the impromptu bombardment.

Baxter could see the sailors under his command tensing up, and was glad that, while there were small arms aboard including his trusty Smith and Wesson, the launch didn't mount anything approaching artillery. Opening fire on an unarmed merchantman in a neutral report wouldn't go down well with his superiors or the international press. One of the bluejackets leaned forward, clearly preparing to bellow something back.

"Steady there. Remember who we are," Baxter said. A murmur ran along the length of the boat, rising in volume as something landed close enough that the neat paintwork was splashed with oily water. "Not quite up to the same standard as the cruiser we faced down," he went on, knowing that reminding the men of the recent engagement could cut both ways.

He relaxed slightly as that got a laugh out of them. "And you know why they're hiding in here?"

"Because of us, sir?" one of the men asked. He had their attention now; the men moved away from the polished railing to look aft to where he sat by the tiller.

"Just so. They know if they stick their noses out of his harbour, we'll have 'em. Send them to the bottom or take them as a lawful prize. All across the world, every neutral harbour you could think of will be stuffed with German freighters."

"Shame they won't come out so we can get some of that prize money!"

Baxter didn't know if the prize laws that had made many sailors of all ranks wealthy in previous conflicts still applied. That was no reason to dampen their enthusiasm, however, particularly as the cheerfulness of the British sailors seemed to be annoying the Germans. The bombardment petered out as the launch moved past them, and the Germans hadn't got the rise they were clearly hoping for.

"Bet that lot are up to no good," Pearson muttered, casting a dark glance at the merchantman. "Like that liner who was lurking about."

Baxter felt his own mood darken at the mention of the ship that had been masquerading as SS *San Francisco*. There had been something deeply wrong about her commander's behaviour. The last Baxter had seen of the ship in the fading light, she had still been flying the Stars and Stripes. A neutral civilian ship should have been running like smoke and oakum away from an engagement like that. While his attention had mostly been on the enemy vessel, he was certain that she had been remaining in the combat area deliberately, either to provide a distraction or because she had in fact been armed and had been contemplating joining the engagement.

And that meant she was, in fact, a German ship — almost certainly an armed merchant cruiser — who had broken with the forms and laws of war to fly false colours in an engagement.

"Here we go, sir," said Pearson as he brought the launch round in a smooth arc towards a landing jetty.

"Look out to port!" a sailor in the bows shouted. Baxter spun in time to see a German launch racing towards them, smoke pouring from its short funnel. It was already close enough that Baxter could see the crew's faces, some with the idiot grins of young men doing something stupid and others with grim determination in their expressions.

The situation reminded him briefly of his simulated torpedo attack on the destroyer carrying the First Sea Lord, and his very real run in an ancient Russian torpedo boat against a gunboat preparing to bombard Odessa. The stakes weren't as high here, as a collision or deliberate ramming between two small boats in a neutral harbour was hardly the stuff of diplomatic incidents, even in peacetime. It would just be considered high jinks.

"Hold steady," Baxter ordered. He would be damned if they would sheer off first, not so much for his own pride but for the pride of the service and the men under his command. Pearson, to his credit, held his course.

The Germans were shouting now, and one of them was brandishing a mop in a somewhat incongruous manner. "'E thinks 'e's going to clean the seas of us," one the sailors said in a broad Brummie accent.

"What a ruddy idiot," Pearson growled. "Want me to ram him, sir?"

Baxter could almost laugh. The German sailors, most of them young men, probably had no real notion of what the war was about. In all likelihood, they had been at sea or in some far-flung harbour when it had broken out, just as he had been. All they knew was that their country was at war, and they were trapped here by the marauding Royal Navy, unable to carry on with their trade or get home so they could join up and fight for their fatherland. This display was nothing more than frustrated venting, by men who didn't have the first notion of what war was really like.

"Hold your course, Pearson," Baxter said calmly. A collision would be nothing more than embarrassing, particularly as these were small vessels and not travelling at any great speed. Their little drama wasn't even attracting much attention on the busy docks, though a few sailors on the ships that crowded the harbour were taking a lazy interest.

"Stand by to repel boarders, sir?" the Brummie sailor asked, getting a laugh from the other bluejackets.

"Not one German boot on this deck, lads," Baxter replied, eyeing the approaching vessel and trying to decide if that was their intent. He briefly considered breaking out the small arms the launch carried, but decided against it. If the German merchant sailors were really that stupid, they would be dealt with in the old-fashioned way.

"Come on, you bastards, just try it," one of the sailors growled. They were spoiling for a fight as much as the Germans were, and with more reason. The engagement with the German cruiser had been a blow to morale, particularly with the loss of an officer, and it had got the bluejackets' blood up.

Baxter watched the rapidly closing boat, and made eye contact with the man at the wheel. The moment was fleeting, Baxter's irritation at these boys showing away obviously communicating itself. The oncoming launch held its course for a few seconds more, then the helmsman spun the wheel until they were running on parallel courses a dozen yards apart. The German sailors hollered and hooted at their British counterparts. They, on the other hand, kept their discipline without Baxter needing to remind them, and their stoic silence seemed to deflate the merchant sailors. With a final few insults and comments about British courage, the launch turned away, and the moment of drama passed.

"Put us ashore there, Pearson," Baxter said drily, indicating a nearby pier that was already crowded with small boats. "I'm going to make my report at the consulate. While I'm doing that, see to Hancock and make sure he keeps out of trouble while he's victualling."

"Very good, sir. And the men, sir?"

"Boat watch of two men, and rotate after two hours," Baxter said, knowing that it would be cruel to deny two sailors the opportunity of a run ashore after a trying time at sea, even if it hadn't been a long journey. "Nobody gets too drunk."

"Aye, sir. I'll keep 'em out of trouble. Well, out of too much trouble, anyway."

Baxter glanced at him. "Remember, we're just here for a few hours. I don't want to be bailing you out of gaol."

"Very good, sir."

Pearson had brought them neatly alongside a set of steps in the stone pier while they spoke, and the crew tied the launch off with practised ease. Baxter glanced around, making sure the boatload of angry Germans had returned to their ship. Satisfied that the petty officer would keep the men in his charge within acceptable limits, he straightened his cap and ran up the steps onto the solid ground of Uruguay.

CHAPTER NINE

It felt strange being on land again, even after a short stint at sea. The surface under his feet remained resolutely firm and steady, rather than exhibiting a comforting roll, and the smells and sounds of human habitation were widespread rather than being confined to a steel and wood hull surrounded by the vast grey expanse of the ocean. Even the sky was wrong, sliced between buildings rather than being an endless dome, stained by a myriad of chimneys rather than the black cloak of the cruiser's triple stack.

It was even stranger to be in a country not caught up in the war. It had been mere months since Britain had become embroiled in the conflict. For the first few weeks, it had seemed to exist in a sort of surprised confusion — doubly so in the protectorate of Zanzibar, where Baxter had happened to be stationed on that fateful day in August, 1914. Even though the Royal Navy contingent there had almost immediately gone to work, in seizing a German tug in the harbour, it had still been a long time before people had really understood what was happening.

Here in Montevideo, basking in a pleasantly warm summer, the war seemed a distant thing despite the presence of ships from the combatant nations. Baxter felt strangely conspicuous in his white tropical uniform, while on the streets of London and Devonport his uniform would have been unremarkable as the country began its mobilisation.

As a minor South American nation, at least to Whitehall's mind, Uruguay did not merit a full ambassador but rather a minister plenipotentiary with a small staff. Baxter had hoped to deliver his report to a functionary, with any luck a naval attaché, rather than having to wait for the minister to become available. Having handed over Sitwell's hastily written report to a confidential secretary, he was required to wait in case the minister had any questions. Thankfully, it was barely half an hour before he was ushered into a cool inner office, sparsely decorated beyond the obligatory portrait of King George V glowering down on all comers from behind his bristling moustache. Baxter wasn't quite sure whether to come to attention or how to address the representative of his government in this country.

His Excellency Alfred Mitchell-Innes, a sturdy man with a neat dark moustache, high forehead and intelligent eyes, saved him from any awkwardness. "Lieutenant Baxter, I believe?" he said, coming round his heavy mahogany desk and extending a hand. His voice had the smooth intonation one expected from a diplomat, with perhaps just the slightest touch of Edinburgh about it.

"Yes, sir," Baxter said, returning the firm handshake.

Mitchell-Innes gestured to a slightly incongruous incidental table and comfortable armchairs off to one side of the office, and the steaming teapot that sat upon it. Baxter noted that there were three delicate porcelain cups.

"My apologies for keeping you waiting," the minister went on after he'd poured. "And I must ask you to indulge me a moment longer, as I've asked one of my colleagues to —" He broke off at a discreet knock, which was followed by the entry of an affable-looking older man in a white linen suit. He had a walrus moustache and was holding a cane. Despite his lack of uniform, it was immediately clear that he was RN, or at least ex-RN, and Baxter got a sinking feeling in his stomach as he guessed the newcomer's role. "Ah, Lewisham, impeccable timing as always!"

Baxter sipped his tea, relishing it despite the heat, and tried to contain his impatience.

"Yes, as I was saying, Mr Baxter, I'm sure you're keen to be back aboard and about your business, but I thought it best if Lewisham here heard what you had to say firsthand."

"Yes, sir," Baxter said blandly. "Though I'm not sure I'll have much to add to Lieutenant Commander Sitwell's report. We engaged a German light cruiser, found in company with a civilian vessel that claimed to be American, and fought an inconclusive battle. We're now anchored off Piriápolis effecting repairs."

"A German cruiser, operating in these waters — this is troubling," Lewisham said, bushy eyebrows lowering. He had the look of a cheerful blunderer, but Baxter got the distinct impression that there was a lot more to him than that.

"Yes, sir," Baxter said. "Certainly a light cruiser, not dissimilar to *Königsberg* and the cruisers believed to be in von Spee's force."

"And he had the gall to stop an American liner?" Mitchell-Innes said.

Baxter hesitated before replying, just long enough that both men noticed. "Speak frankly, Lieutenant," the minister said. "We're all friends here."

He very much doubted that, but spoke his mind anyway. "I don't believe that the liner was in fact an American, though she continued to fly those colours for the duration of the engagement. Frankly, sir, I think she was a German liner taking on stores, personnel and possibly weaponry, to operate as a commerce raider."

"Seems bloody fortuitous that you stumbled across them, then," Lewisham said. "But stranger things happen at sea. Do you have any proof of this?"

Baxter eyed him coolly. If his guess was right, Lewisham was almost certainly a retired Royal Navy officer working for Naval Intelligence — it would make sense for Room 39 to have people stationed throughout the neutral world, keeping an eye out for enemy ships and tracking merchantmen. "Very little, sir. The wardroom steward did indicate that he had seen the SS *San Francisco*, which she was claiming to be, several times. He was adamant that she was not that ship."

"Well, without proof, there is little we can do," Mitchell-Innes said decisively. "I will, of course, promulgate a warning to our merchant vessels in these shipping lanes, though I am sure they are all acutely aware of the presence of German raiders somewhere off this continent."

"Is there any news of von Spee, sir?" Baxter asked.

"Very little, I'm afraid, though we have guessed he's coming this way," the minister said. "If he does, of course, he'll run straight into Sturdee, who was last reported at the Abrolhos Rocks some days ago."

Baxter nodded judiciously, racking his memory for where that land was. It had been many years since he'd last sailed these waters.

The minister appeared to realise he was in danger of saying too much to a relatively junior officer. "I will make representations to the government here that *Astute* be allowed to remain in these waters for more than the allotted time, given her apparent damage. And please give my compliments to her captain — if he should decide to bring her into Montevideo, I would be happy to entertain him."

Baxter took that as a dismissal, rising as he drained the last of his tea. "Very good, sir," he said. "Can I also report that you will be informing the Admiralty?"

"Of course, of course."

"I'll walk you out, Mr Baxter," Lewisham said, levering himself to his feet with the aid of the cane.

After a final exchange of pleasantries with Mitchell-Innes, Baxter followed Lewisham out of the office. He wasn't in any way surprised when the older man guided him into a much smaller, plainer office for a quiet word. "I assume you've already surmised that I report to Naval Intelligence?" he asked with a directness that took Baxter slightly aback. Lewisham had seated himself behind a much smaller desk than the minister's and began writing as he spoke.

"It had crossed my mind, Mr Lewisham."

"Sharp, but then you wavy navy chaps often are — despite what our brother officers might say. Now listen, old chap, because we don't have a lot of time. The reason we think von Spee is coming this way is that there's been a lot of activity among some of the German merchantmen here, taking on coal and other provender. More than they could possibly need for their own purposes, and they clearly aren't going to be running any blockades into Germany."

"They're going to resupply von Spee? I'm no sea lawyer, Mr Lewisham, but it seems to me that would breach the neutrality of this harbour."

"Well, indeed, but no more than His Excellency putting pressure on the government of Uruguay to allow a belligerent vessel to remain in harbour long enough to make good her damage. The blighters will sneak out at night, no doubt, and make for some hidden anchorage to await the *Kaiserliche*

Marine's finest. There is very little I can do about it, alas, without jeopardising my assignment here."

Baxter nodded. "I can certainly inform Sitwell, or Captain Gregson if he's recovered, and we can do our best to intercept them. We have orders to join Sturdee's squadron, but orders are contingent on reality."

"Indeed they are," Lewisham said, signing the letter with a flourish and sealing it into an envelope that he addressed to the captain of HMS *Astute* before passing it to Baxter. "This is for your captain, and has everything I know. Obviously, I can't give him orders, but hopefully he will act on it."

Baxter tucked the missive into his jacket pocket, then looked enquiringly at Lewisham. The intelligence officer was staring at him, clearly trying to make his mind up about something. "Was there anything else, sir?"

Lewisham put the lid on his pen with a decisive snap. "No, I think that covers everything."

It clearly wasn't everything, but the intelligence agent was obviously loath to say too much to someone who, as far as he knew, wasn't indoctrinated into intelligence work. This need for secrecy, the institutional paranoia, was something that had made Baxter uncomfortable about being dragged into this shadowy world. His own experience of it, starting all the way back in 1905 when the rogue Naval Intelligence agent Arbuthnott had roped him into a mad scheme that had almost got him killed on a number of occasions, had left him with a somewhat dim view of the whole profession.

He was aware of the irony that he could put Lewisham's mind at ease, as he was associated with, if not officially assigned to, Room 39. Saunders had been clear, however, in his instruction not to divulge too much, and Baxter wasn't particularly inclined to get wrapped up in intelligence work of his own volition.

"Very good, sir. Well, I'd best go and find my shore party and see how much damage they've done."

Lewisham, clearly someone who knew what bluejackets could be like on a run ashore, winced. "Hopefully not too much — we are trying to stay on good terms with as many neutral powers as possible. This is, I think, going to be a long war, and we are going to have to make some difficult decisions that will make a lot of people unhappy."

Baxter shifted, unsure whether Lewisham was trying to communicate something further. The older man seemed to pick up on his discomfort. "Be wary out there, Baxter — this may be a neutral port, but just as we have people here, so do the enemy. We watch each other, terribly politely, but that doesn't mean they won't start anything."

"If anyone is going to start anything, Mr Lewisham, it won't be the Germans," Baxter said as he rose, his tone grim.

The intelligence agent smiled. "Good man. I do envy you, being out there. It's a lot … simpler than this work, in its way."

Baxter nodded, but didn't say anything about his own experience within Lewisham's sphere. As hard and dangerous as warfare on the high seas was, he could understand the point. While there was subterfuge, as the German cruiser that was still lurking out there had demonstrated, at some point it came down to the honest exchange of blows and, usually, clarity over who was the victor.

"I'll pass on what you've said as soon as possible. If there is a way to take these freighters and prevent them from resupplying von Spee, we'll find it."

Lewisham nodded. "If I learn anything more, I'll get word to you one way or the other."

Baxter walked back towards the harbour under a high midday sun. The air was humid, like a damp blanket lying over the estuary of the River Plate on which the city sat. The novelty of being ashore had well and truly worn off, and he was almost relieved when he was hailed by a sailor from his party. Despite the gentle slope in the mainly flat city, the man was sweating and making heavy work of trotting towards him. "Mr Baxter, sir!" he shouted along the length of the street, drawing the attention of a number of well-dressed locals. The legation was in one of the better areas of the city, and one unused to Birmingham-accented bellows.

Baxter raised a hand in acknowledgement, hoping that would perhaps lead to some restraint. Thankfully, the fellow lowered his voice as he approached.

"PO Pearson sent me, sir," the seaman said through gulps of warm, humid air, before remembering protocol and offering a relatively crisp salute.

"I should hope so," Baxter said. The last thing anyone wanted was RN personnel running loose and unsupervised in a foreign port, not without a damn good reason. "What is it?"

"It's Hancock, sir — he swears that he just saw the liner, the one claiming to be an American, coming into harbour. Said he got a good look at it before it all kicked off and it's the same damn ship. Begging your pardon, sir."

Baxter nodded. He was inclined to trust Hancock, as the old steward still seemed to have sharp eyesight and judgement that was just as keen. Montevideo was a large and busy port that seemed to have a significant and active German presence, so it made sense that the ersatz *San Francisco* should have put in here.

"Did you see where she berthed?"

The sailor grinned. "That we did, sir. We've been watching her like a hawk since she put in."

"Well then, why don't you show me?"

Pearson had done a surprisingly good job of keeping the enemy ship under watch without being too obvious about it. It did help that the Royal Navy sailor's uniforms, even the tropical white, didn't stand out too much in a harbour crowded with seagoing men from a dozen different nations. The thing that surprised Baxter most was that the men were all still stone-cold sober — either Pearson had taken his orders seriously, or the suspicious liner had been sighted before they'd had a chance to find a suitable watering hole.

The ship certainly gave no impression of being anything other than what she claimed to be, a civilian vessel belonging to a neutral power. She flew the American flag and, as a courtesy to the host nation, that of Uruguay. Though she was anchored a little further out in the sheltered harbour, she was still close enough for Baxter to see that the sailors moving about on deck were in neat white uniforms, as first-class passengers would no doubt expect.

"Notice what's missing, sir?" Pearson asked. They were watching the liner from the end of a long, wedge-shaped mole that jutted out into the estuary.

"Passengers," Baxter said. Even if they might have been battened down belowdecks then, given what was about to occur, he couldn't imagine they would be out of sight now. "No one's come ashore?"

"Just crew, sir, since we've been watching. Might have landed in a hurry, in the time it took for Hancock to get us along."

"Or she might just be travelling without them," Baxter mused. "I imagine a lot of people wouldn't be on the seas voluntarily."

Pearson snorted. "Plenty of posh folk wouldn't think twice, begging your pardon, sir. Never occur to them to worry about it. And would she even be at sea if someone wasn't paying passage?"

Baxter couldn't argue with that. There was very little he could do about it right now — even if the liner was German, she was in a neutral port, just as *Astute* was. He could send word to the cruiser, but there was no way she would risk moving into Montevideo harbour to investigate the ship and confront her even if she *was* German. Maintaining the pretence of being an American in a neutral harbour was perhaps in breach of the rules and customs of neutrality, particularly as the government of Uruguay seemed perfectly content to allow German merchantmen to remain as long as they desired. But how could it be proven?

Raised voices behind them distracted him from the problem. The docks were noisy, as such places were in every part of the world, with the shouts of stevedores, the chug of engines and the metal-on-metal grind of machinery, interspersed with the occasional horn or whistle and the deeper thud of mighty ships' machinery. The racket was coming closer, and when he glanced back, Baxter saw a small crowd of people milling about where the broad stone sweep of the quayside bumped up against commercial premises. They were the ones doing the shouting, and had more of the character of a mob than a crowd.

"Pearson!" Baxter snapped, heading away from the waterfront as he spotted some white uniforms in amongst the increasingly angry people. For a moment he thought his men had somehow got involved in some sort of local dispute, but as his rapid pace brought him closer, he saw that they were the focus of the mob rather than being part of it.

"If they've gone and got in a fight..." he heard Pearson grind out.

Baxter recognised the steward, Hancock, and the two men who'd been sent to carry the victuals for him. The mob was yelling at them as they struggled to get clear, obviously heading for the launch. While the mob hadn't turned violent, Baxter could see several younger men getting worked up enough to throw a punch. They were all, as far as he could see, local men being encouraged from the sides by shawled women.

"We can work out whether they provoked this or not later," Baxter said. "Right now, we need to get them out of here."

His grim tone communicated itself to Pearson. The petty officer wasn't a big man, but solidly built, and no man achieved his rank without being ready to get stuck in when he needed to.

Baxter knew there was no point trying to cow the entire crowd; large as he was, and loud when he needed to be, large groups of people had a particular force of their own. A man could be intimidated by another man, and Baxter had been known to send small gangs running for their lives, but it would take a file of Marines to disperse this mob.

Instead, he used his bulk and strength to wade into the crowd. A young man with the look of a student was shouting something about traitors and pirates, his back turned to Baxter. His words choked off as he found himself moved inexorably out of the way and he turned wild eyes to see who it was.

When he saw Baxter, his expression changed to one of mild panic as he backed away.

Baxter's Spanish wasn't bad, and he had a vague appreciation of the differences between the language as it was spoken in South America and in Spain itself, but even so it was hard to make out what the crowd was shouting about and what had got them so enraged. He thought he could hear German mixed in as well, which would make sense from what Lewisham had told him about the local German community.

Not that it mattered. The crowd was turning violent, perhaps because he and Pearson had forced their way into it or perhaps because that was its trajectory anyway. Someone swung a broken piece of packing crate at his head, and Baxter blocked it without thinking, getting a grip on the cheap wood. He made sure to make full eye contact with the man who had swung at him and then closed his fist, crushing the flimsy material before yanking the improvised weapon out of his hands. The man fell back, but others were coming forward with makeshift weapons.

Mindful of Lewisham's orders, Baxter did his best to restrain himself and the other Royal Navy sailors. Hancock was bleeding from a gash in his forehead, being supported by one of his mates while the other did his best to fend off someone swinging a stool. "Try not to hurt any of these blighters!" Baxter shouted over the tumult, before ducking to avoid a brick and backhanding the burly dockworker who had thrown it and made the mistake of coming within his reach.

"That's all very well, sir, but they're doing their best to kill us!" Pearson shouted as he and another sailor piled in from the side, kicking and shoving as they tried to get the steward out.

Baxter caught the semi-conscious Hancock's collar with one hand and lifted him clear of the scuffle, passing him back towards more of his men who had appeared. They may not have been Marines, and boarding drills might have been a thing of the past, but at least some of these men were seasoned bar brawlers and they knew what they were about. They formed a tight knot around their injured comrade. As Baxter and the others struggled free of the crowd, he was pleased to see they were fighting to protect themselves, shoving and blocking rather than throwing punches.

"Back!" Baxter snapped to his men, knowing they wouldn't like the order now that their blood was up. An international incident was the last thing they needed now. "Back to the launch!"

They obeyed, because obedience was the first thing every Royal Navy sailor had hammered into them, and Baxter was not the sort of officer you ignored. They fell back, and this time the locals didn't follow them. A few more missiles came their way, but once they were away from the close confines of the streets that led up from the dockside, the civilians seemed less inclined to press their point, whatever it was.

"Where the bloody hell are the bobbies?" the Brummie sailor muttered.

"Last thing we want is the local polis," Pearson shot back. "They'll just decide we started it."

Baxter raised an eyebrow at the implicit suggestion that the bluejackets *hadn't* started something. That could be sorted later. "Keep moving, lads," he said, as the little band trotted across the harbour towards the small pier where the launch was tied up.

As the mob dispersed with a few last jeers, Baxter caught sight of someone who looked considerably more European — possibly German — at the back of the crowd. For a moment, he thought the fellow was wearing a Royal Navy uniform, then realised it was more akin to the smart uniform of a civilian shipping line.

Baxter had a notion of what that meant, and what had precipitated the angry mob, but now wasn't the time to stop and investigate.

His first order of business, when they got back to the launch, was to see Hancock hustled into the little covered cabin and patched up. "Looks like a nasty gash from a thrown bottle, sir," Pearson said, as he did his best to clean and bandage the wound. "Going to need stitches, Hancock. Sorry."

The older man groaned. "Twenty years in the Navy, on and off, and never once injured until today," he said, voice shaky despite his attempt at a smile.

"Hard to get injured in the pantry," Pearson told him, not unkindly.

"Have you ever been around knives and such, during a storm?" came the plaintive rejoinder. "A pantry is a dangerous place indeed, young man."

"What happened?" Baxter asked, cutting across the banter. He took a seat on the wooden bench across from Hancock, mostly because he was too tall to stand up in the cramped space.

One of the men who had been escorting Hancock spoke up. "It was them bloody Yanks, sir. Going around telling anyone who would listen that we'd tried to stop them at sea and then opened fire on them."

"Americans? Are you sure?" Baxter asked sharply.

"Claimed to be, sir," the sailor replied. "Sounded like one, and all."

Baxter drummed his fingers on the bench as he thought. Could he have been wrong about the liner? While they hadn't opened fire on her — indeed, Gregson had put *Astute* at a disadvantage by holding fire until he was sure there was no chance of hitting the civilian ship — it wasn't beyond the bounds of possibility that a civilian crew might make the mistake of thinking they were under fire, even if no shells were landing anywhere near them.

Her behaviour had seemed suspicious; that could also be ascribed to panic or just some misguided attempt to be a neutral observer to an engagement. Had the German cruiser just been stopping a civilian ship to determine if she was in fact British, or carrying war materiel for Britain?

But why would a neutral collude in attempting to hide the German? Threats to her own safety, perhaps. Baxter could feel a headache starting to build behind his eyes.

"Just one?" he asked, remembering the sailor's phrase.

"Beg pardon, sir?"

"Just one American sailor? On shore by himself?"

"No, sir, a party of them, victualling same as us. Only one did the talking, though — isn't that right, Jack?"

Another sailor standing in the hatchway nodded thoughtfully. "Aye, Harry, that's right. Just the one."

"The others were suspiciously quiet, come to think of it," Harry said thoughtfully. "Think he was an officer as well."

Baxter scowled as he thought. "Stitches, you say, Pearson?"

"Reckon so, sir."

Baxter rubbed his jaw, the rasp of stubble reminding him that he'd been on the go for more than a day, with just a snatched hour of sleep here and there. He was well used to this life, to ignoring the grind of fatigue, but just for a moment he contemplated ordering everyone back aboard the launch. He could find a way to alert Lewisham about the suspect ship once he'd got the men under his command back into the relative safety of the cruiser.

He lowered his head slightly to peer out of the porthole opposite him. He could see the liner, the red, blue and white flying proudly from her flagstaff. Maybe she was exactly what she claimed to be, but his gut told him it was a lie. That the young man who had tried to get his men hurt or even killed by a mob was lying when he claimed they were American, and spinning a falsehood about coming under fire. And he'd be damned if he was going to let it go until he knew for sure.

CHAPTER TEN

Baxter might have been determined to get to the bottom of the mystery liner, and whether she was in fact the innocent *San Francisco*, but he also had his orders and the men under his command to think about.

The first order of business was to get Hancock back to *Astute*. This was achieved by using some of the local currency he'd drawn from the legation to hire a local boat to convey the steward and three of the shore party back to Piriápolis. The sailors, sensing that their commander was up to something, were reluctant to leave, but accepted their orders despite knowing they were about to miss out on a caper.

Baxter sent them back with a brief note outlining what had occurred and how Hancock had come by his injury, and laying out his intention to keep the liner under observation as best he could. He knew Sitwell wouldn't like it, and if Captain Gregson had recovered, he would be apoplectic. He didn't see that he had much choice, though, and officers separated from their commands sometimes had to make decisions that conflicted with their orders when the situation demanded it.

They were sufficiently far from the liner, lying as she was in the deeper harbour some distance from the docks, that Baxter felt comfortable watching her without needing to take too many measures to camouflage their presence. He still didn't want to be too obvious about it, giving orders that the men detailed to keep watch shouldn't just stand and stare at her through glasses.

After that, it was a question of settling down to wait and see if the liner did anything suspicious before someone arrived from *Astute* or got in touch with him via the legation. While Baxter was well used to exercising a necessary patience at sea, where days or weeks could pass by in pure monotony, now he found himself prowling the cramped interior of the launch's small cabin or pacing the vessel's length.

"Activity on deck, sir," Pearson commented. It was getting on towards evening, the sun threatening to disappear behind the mountain range that backed the peaceful city. "Looks like they've got passengers after all."

Baxter cursed under his breath and took the field glasses from the bo'sun. Sure enough, a number of people in civilian clothes — including a few women — were taking the air on the fo'c'sle. It was hard to tell at this distance, even with glasses, but they appeared to be well dressed — first-class passengers, then.

"Why the bloody hell did they hang around a naval battle if they had civilians onboard?" Baxter muttered. None of it made any sense.

"Can't help you there, sir," Pearson replied. "They do have a lot of crew around to help 'em. Taking their health seriously."

That was true. There were a lot of sailors dotted around the fo'c'sle, apparently idling but probably there to serve the passengers' requirements. And to stop them doing damn fool things like leaning too far out over the railing or trying to climb onto the bowsprit.

Looking into the liner's waist, Baxter could see a lot more sailors. While he wasn't too familiar with travelling in the relative luxury of a passenger ship, beyond a brief time on a Royal Mail ship on his way to East Africa, he couldn't imagine even a vessel designed to cater to every whim of wealthy passengers would need quite that many men. The men were stripped to the waist, as though they were ready for hard labour in the heat and humidity of the bay, and despite the presence of ladies forward of them. Looking beyond the liner, Baxter focused the glasses on a somewhat grimy collier that was just putting off from the quay. She was low in the water, obviously heavily laden, and he could see another similar dirty vessel taking on coal from a nearby warehouse. He knew, without a shadow of a doubt, what the stripped men on the liner were doing — preparing to take on coal, and take on far more that the liner could possibly need for herself, unless she was planning to steam all the way round the Cape and to the west coast of the United States without resupply.

"We need to get a look at what's going on aboard that ship," Baxter said, lowering his glasses.

"How do your propose we do that, sir? Swim across?"

Baxter chose to ignore the slightly impertinent question. "No. We're going to need some civilian clothes. Labourers' clothes, preferably, and some of them big enough to fit me."

"That's a tall order, sir, but I'll see what I can do," Pearson said dubiously, obviously seeing where Baxter was going with this. "This a volunteer-only sort of caper, sir?"

Baxter smiled grimly. "Yes — pick out three good volunteers, please."

The rough working man's clothes that Pearson had managed to acquire — and Baxter had no intention of finding out how he'd done so at short notice — barely fit his large frame, and he knew the cotton shirt would tear if he had to exert himself too much. The other three men looked considerably more natural, though it transpired none of them had even the broken Spanish he could muster.

"Just know enough to order a beer, sir," Harry, one of the two men who had pulled Hancock out of trouble, said with a rotten-toothed grin. Jack nodded agreement. It seemed the two of them came as a unit.

"Well, just keep your mouths shut and let me do any talking that's needed," Baxter said as he fidgeted with the waistband of his trousers.

"Yes, sir," they chorused.

"And what talking will be needed?" a drawling voice asked behind them. "And what in blazes is going on here anyway?"

Baxter winced, knowing the moment he had dreaded was upon them — Littleton had arrived with fresh orders.

The officer ducked into the cabin. "Sitwell is furious, you know," he said urbanely, but Baxter cut him off before he could say any more.

"Give us the cabin, lads," he told the sailors, who had been busy neatly folding and stowing their uniforms. It wasn't as though they wouldn't be able to overhear the conversation outside on the deck of the launch, particularly as Littleton's plummy tones had a strangely penetrating quality. But there were forms to be obeyed, particularly when officers were about to argue. It gave the men the opportunity to pretend that they hadn't heard anything.

"What's happening, Littleton, is that I'm using my initiative to investigate suspicious activity, and possible abuse of local neutrality."

"You're going to board an American ship in a neutral harbour?" Littleton spluttered.

"No, I'm going to sneak aboard what's claiming to be an American ship to find the truth of the matter. They won't even know I'm there."

"I find that hard to believe," Littleton scoffed. "Look, Sitwell's orders are clear. Report back to *Astute* on the double and explain yourself. I mean, what the devil did you think you were going to do if you did pull this off and proved she is a German raider?"

"Return to *Astute* and make a report," Baxter said smoothly. That was the truth as far as it went — he wasn't entirely sure what his plan would be, but it would certainly involve a return to his ship at some point, assuming he was still alive and at liberty, of course.

"Well, that's all very well, but I'm ordering you to abandon this damn fool enterprise and return to the cruiser, as per Commander Sitwell's orders."

Baxter straightened as much as the cabin allowed, looming over the third officer and staring unblinkingly at him. "No, you're not," he said quietly. He reckoned he had the measure of the man now. Littleton wasn't a bad person, but nor was he a good officer and he was, at heart, a weak man. "You're going to agree with my assessment of the situation, and you are in fact going to order me to progress with the operation."

"I am?" Littleton glared defiantly at Baxter, and then swallowed. "I'm listening."

"I assume you came here in one of the ship's boats?"

"Just as soon as Hancock returned. He's fine, by the way. Dr Martin stitched him neat as you like."

"I need you to remain here with both boats and monitor the situation. Once we know what's going on, and hopefully have some proof that liner isn't *San Francisco*, then we'll need to inform Sitwell immediately in the hopes of intercepting her when she leaves."

"You think that's imminent?"

Baxter had been turning this over in his mind. "They're taking on a lot of coal and other supplies," he said. "Far more than they need. I think they're going to resupply that cruiser we tangled with, and given how quickly they're loading the coal aboard, I think they're planning on leaving tonight."

Littleton nodded, still uncertain. Baxter clapped him on the shoulder. "This is what we signed up for, old chap. Cutting out enemy ships from harbours they think are safe, in the old way."

"Not that you're *actually* going to cut her out."

"Nowhere near enough men for that, even if she wasn't in a safe harbour. All we're going to do is sneak aboard, see if we can find out what they're up to, and then sneak off. That's why I need you and the launch to keep watch from here, follow her at a distance if she does weigh anchor, and get us off."

As Baxter said it out loud, he knew it sounded like a madcap notion, but he'd engaged in wilder escapades with less preparation.

Littleton sighed and rubbed the bridge of his nose. "*If* I'm going to permit this, I should really go along," he said wearily.

Baxter looked him up and down. "No offence, Littleton, but you don't look the type to be hauling bags of coal," he said. "And I would think your Spanish isn't up to much."

"Good job you're one of those wavy navy types, not a proper officer," Littleton said, with a wan smile that was intended to take the sting out of the jibe.

"Something like that," Baxter said. He knew he was in danger of crossing a line, of refusing to obey a direct order that could get him unceremoniously kicked out of the Royal Navy, or worse. But he also knew it was the right course of action, that they needed to know what the suspect ship was up to.

"Are you quite sure about this?" Littleton asked. "That this isn't just a need to prove that you were right all along?"

Baxter knew there was at least a grain of truth in what the third officer said. "I'm sure this is the right thing to do," he said.

The other man nodded reluctantly. "Very well. I won't stop you."

Baxter released the breath he hadn't realised he'd been holding. So far, in his still brief return to service, he had managed to navigate his way through some sticky situations through creative interpretation of his orders where necessary. He was glad he didn't have to find out whether he was prepared to disobey orders now.

"And you'll shadow the liner if she does leave before we manage to get off?"

Littleton looked uncertain. "I have orders to return immediately."

Baxter didn't point out that Littleton had orders to return with Baxter. "With any luck, I'll be on and off in a jiff and an hour behind you getting back to *Astute*," he said. "Right now, I'd best be about it, though. This is only going to work if they're still loading the colliers."

Littleton straightened and nodded decisively, as though he was the one who had made the decision. "Very well — carry on as you see fit, Mr Baxter. I'll return to *Astute* and let Sitwell know what your intentions are. *If* you determine she is an enemy vessel, we'll need to be ready to intercept her as soon as she's out of Uruguay's territorial waters."

Baxter nodded, knowing that was the best he was going to get. He ducked out of the cabin and glanced across at Pearson. He knew the petty officer wanted to be on the mission, but Baxter needed a steady man in charge of the launch. "You understand your orders?" he asked quietly.

"Yes, sir — follow on if she hauls anchor while you're still aboard, and look for any splashes."

Baxter snorted. He'd been careful to check that the men who had been volunteered by Pearson were able to swim, as he knew they might have to make a swift and undignified exit from the vessel. "Very good — carry on."

The three bluejackets, now in their rough workmen's clothes, were waiting on the quay. Hicks, the sailor from Birmingham, looked nervous, as did Harry. The laconic Jack just looked bored. Baxter had considered going alone on the mission — cloak and dagger wasn't necessarily the RN's forte. The liner was a big ship, however, and if they were going to find anything incriminating in what little time they had aboard, he would need numbers. He also knew there was at least a chance that they would be caught out and would have to fight their way free, or risk being shot as spies.

"All right, lads, last chance," he said to the three sailors. "Any man who doesn't want to risk this can step away now."

"Already changed, sir — doesn't seem much point in backing out now," Harry said.

"Never hear the end of it, if we don't go," Jack agreed.

Baxter nodded. "Right then. Let's be about it."

They were cutting it fine by the time they'd worked their way round to the quay where the second collier was still loading. The time taken to prepare, and then to argue with Littleton, meant the collier was almost full, lying low in the water, as crates and sacks of coal were dumped into her hold and increasingly onto her decks. It was late in the afternoon, the harbour bathed in a glorious golden light as the sun dropped towards the hills beyond the city.

"How much bloody coal do they need?" Harry demanded as the four of them paused in the cover of a narrow alley that ran between two warehouses.

"Got to keep the cabins nice and warm for the rich folks," Hicks said.

"Keep it down, lads," Baxter murmured without taking his eyes off the chain of sweating men moving between the warehouse and the collier. Everything depended on what they did next. The liner's captain seemed to be in a hurry to depart, as his own crew was being supplemented by civilian workers who had gone out with the first collier. He'd been working on the assumption the same approach would be taken with the second load. He allowed himself a small smile — it would be the height of irony if all they managed to do was help an enemy vessel take on coal but were prevented from following up.

Nothing else for it, though.

"Remember, act like you belong there," he told his sailors.

"We're the bloody Royal Navy, sir — we belong anywhere we want to be."

Baxter raised an eyebrow at Hicks' familiar tone, but he couldn't disagree with the sentiment. "Follow me."

He stepped out of the alley and walked along to the warehouse that seemed to be emptying its entire stock out. There were dozens of men working, and while most of them would probably know each other, he was banking on there being enough of a casual workforce that they would blend in. A foreman was supervising the loading at the quayside, while a second man ensured the coal was moving in a steady stream from the stockpiles on the backs of sweating labourers. Baxter waited until the foreman's back was turned and walked calmly across the flagstone floor to the queue of men waiting to take their turn at the coal pile. The dockworker in front of him didn't even glance round, and within a few moments there were already five or six men behind them.

As they'd been at sea, the four interlopers were sufficiently tanned and weatherbeaten that they didn't stand out too much from the predominantly Spanish workforce, although Baxter had to slouch to disguise his height at least a bit. He realised one thing did mark them all out, though — they were altogether too clean. Coal dust was vile stuff, and it got everywhere. During his time on a Russian cruiser, where he'd been forced to take part in the coaling, he had never really felt entirely clean. Even in the wardroom, everything they had eaten had been slightly gritty and left an aftertaste of carbon.

Their state of cleanliness was about to change anyway, as they reached the front of the line. Baxter kept his eyes forward and cast down, and without hesitation grabbed a rough hessian sack and hoisted it onto his shoulder without any effort. The smell of the coal, acrid and cloying, filled his nostrils, but he focused on the task as he turned and followed the man in front. He didn't risk looking back at his sailors, but guessed from the grunts of effort that they had followed suit.

They trudged across the broad expanse of the dockside to the collier. Her engines were idling, a dull grumble almost below hearing, and a trickle of dirty black smoke emanated from her single smoke stack. Montevideo was a deep-water harbour, and Baxter was reasonably certain the liner could have tied up alongside without issue. That suggested an abundance of caution on the part of her captain; that or he didn't want the risk of someone getting aboard without his knowledge.

Baxter went up the gangplank and tossed his burden into the overflowing hold. He glanced around from under the brim of his soft cap, quickly assessing the situation. As he'd suspected, the collier was almost ready to depart for the half-mile journey to the erstwhile American lying out in the harbour. He had to find a way to get his party aboard without drawing attention to themselves.

The men sweated in the heat as they continued their labours. "'Ow much longer, sir?" Harry rasped in a low voice after the third trip.

Baxter glanced over his shoulder. The dockers were all clearly exhausted, having laboured for most of the day with only the occasional break to load the colliers. At the end of it, he guessed, they would receive a few *pesos* and the promise of more work in future. He knew from personal experience that working civilian shipping was a hard life, and the dockers were often the most undervalued part of the machine.

The foreman was talking with the master of the collier and an officer from the liner. Judging from the hard chopping motion the collier's master was making with his hand, Baxter guessed he was stating in no uncertain terms that he couldn't risk more in this load. "This run, lads, carry as much as you can," he murmured back. He didn't want to risk saying more, as the more they spoke the more chance there was of being overheard. The men were schooled to obedience, though, and set to with only the barest grumbling. Baxter led by example, lifting a sack one-handed and putting it over his shoulder before bending at the knees to lift a second with his free hand, ducking his shoulder to get it onto his back with a grunt of exertion. He was ten years older than the last time he'd had to do this, and he realised now how much those years counted.

He didn't let any of that show on his face as he led his small party back up onto the collier. This was the moment of decision, he knew. As he'd surmised, this would be the last load, and the foreman was detailing workers to remain on the collier to help with the offloading. The selected men were gathering in colliers' bows, availing themselves of a butt of water and a sack of hard tack that had been provided.

Baxter dumped his load on top of the massive heap of coal already sprawling from the colliers' open holds, trying to make as much noise as he could without looking like he wanted the attention. The bluejackets — their civilian clothes now grimy with coal dust — followed suit.

The foreman looked across at them, his expression darkening. The officer from the liner murmured something to him and, while his scowl didn't disappear, it did lighten somewhat. He called across to Baxter's group. "Extra money if you stay aboard for the offloading!" he called out.

Baxter made a show of considering that. He didn't want to seem too keen, particularly as no amount of extra money had been specified. There were plenty of other men who would happily take the offer, though. "All right, we'll do it!" he shouted back, the pause giving him enough time to remember the right phrase, and he was gestured to join the men milling in the bows.

"So far, so good," Hicks said. He was the youngest member of the party, and his nerves were starting to show. Harry and Jack had both clearly been around long enough to keep their cool.

Harry opened his mouth to tell Hicks to shut the hell up, then closed it again when he caught the dark look Baxter gave them all.

They had a tense few minutes, keeping to themselves as much as possible except to avail themselves of the now somewhat warm, gritty water in the butt and what little biscuit there was left. Baxter mopped his forehead with a square of handkerchief, and saw it come away black. He was aware of some of the dockworkers casting angry glances their way and guessed they had trespassed on some territorial issue — he idly wondered whether the unions had made it to South America yet.

Finally, just as the sun was starting to touch the horizon, the collier cast off from the quayside and started labouring its way across to the liner. The failing light picked out the bigger ship's clean lines, etching her tall sides in sharp detail. She was a handsome vessel, Baxter had to admit, built for speed as well as the comfort of her passengers. A lot of that comfort would disappear, as the outsized load of coal would have to be stored in cabins and storerooms, and the extra weight would certainly eat into her speed.

The little vessel bumped up alongside her more elegant cousin, crunching into the fenders. Voices shouted from above, in English and Spanish, and once again Baxter thought he caught German in the background.

Here we go, Baxter thought, rising from where he'd stretched out against the ship's side. The strenuous labour of coaling had taken more out of him than he'd expected, and he'd need all his energy for what lay ahead.

CHAPTER ELEVEN

Cargo nets on winches were coming down from the liner, and for a moment Baxter thought his mission had failed at the first real hurdle. As he watched, dockers started loading sacks of coal into the nets. Then rope ladders came down the side and more men started up them, some of them hauling sacks, and he could see gangplanks being readied for when enough weight had been transferred to bring the decks of the two ships closer together.

Baxter started for one of the rope ladders. The foreman saw him and shook his head, pointing to the cluster of men around the nets. Baxter thought about protesting, but the more interactions he had with these people, the greater the chance of them being found out. They would just have to bide their time.

They worked in the flickering glow of electric lighting, joining the labourers in shifting sacks and crates into the cargo nets. The encroaching night brought a slight drop in the temperature, but the cloying humidity didn't let up. Insects flickered in the glow of the two ships' lights and buzzed around the workers' heads. A lot of the men had stripped to the waist and the bluejackets had followed suit. Baxter wished he could follow suit, but he was sufficiently scarred from a life around violence that it would risk drawing attention.

Baxter noticed there was no sign of the passengers they'd seen on deck during the day, not even a couple of curious bystanders. The night was sticky enough that he was surprised they weren't taking the air on deck, or even going ashore. He couldn't imagine that genuine passengers would allow themselves to be confined belowdecks by the crew, even if it was for their own safety.

The cranes swung the nets full of coal up onto the liner's deck with mechanical regularity. The men who had gone up the rope ladders joined the liner's exhausted crewmen in offloading them, and slowly the difference in the ships' heights started to reduce. They would never be even, but after an hour of hard labour the gradient was sufficiently manageable that they were able to run gangplanks from the liners' waist down into the collier.

"Now's our chance," Baxter murmured. His men, who had managed to remain close to him, merely gave him looks that ranged from hangdog to sullen. He guessed they were all beginning to regret volunteering for this assignment, and in truth he was beginning to regret putting them in this position.

Too late now — the collier would remain here until it was empty, and while the three sailors had got away with grunting in response to the occasional comment or question, he couldn't be sure they would be safe if he left them to their own devices.

"Come on, lads," he said, grabbing a crate. "On me."

They each grabbed a sack and followed Baxter as he strode confidently towards the still steep gangplank. His pulse had increased — it was now or never, he realised.

The foreman glanced their way just as Baxter was approaching the somewhat precarious bridge between the two vessels. For a heartbeat, he thought they would be redirected on to other work, but the foreman was clearly tired and just wanted this tedious day to be done with. He didn't even acknowledge them as they started up the gangplank.

The liner's deck was every bit as busy as the collier's. Local labourers worked alongside the seamen, and seeing the latter went a long way to confirming Baxter's suspicions about the ship. As soon as he saw the liner's crew, he knew exactly who these men were. They were German, and not only that — they were the Kaiser's men.

In the weeks before war was declared, he'd spent some time in German East Africa, and had found himself in the company of *Kaiserliche Marine* sailors on more than one occasion. He'd fought some of them in the surf, hand to hand, after war was declared. There was the same snap of discipline in how they moved, how they responded to quiet commands from men who were clearly officers and petty officers, even if they weren't in uniform. A merchant crew could be a tight-knit, efficient machine, but the hierarchies were less formal and the discipline looser.

Baxter took all of this in, then kept his eyes down as they bore their burdens up onto the once-pristine deck. He was relieved to see that men were being directed belowdecks to deliver the fuel — the liner's bunkers, accessible from the deck, would long since have been filled. A lot of the available space on deck was already covered by lashed-down cargo, what looked like crates of tinned goods as well as coal, and now they were cramming the excess into whatever space could be found belowdecks. Which would, of course, be rather more than on a warship or an average-sized merchantman.

He didn't break stride as he headed across the deck, weaving around what appeared to be crates of cabbages and other fresh vegetables that would need a thorough wash before they were consumed, and joined a line of men going down through a midships hatch. He just had to trust that Harry, Jack and Hicks were behind him. Someone stationed by the hatch and looking suspiciously like a sentry barely glanced at him as he went below.

It was noisy belowdecks, the sounds of shouted commands and the thud of burdens being gratefully deposited magnified by the more confined space. Baxter was briefly taken aback by the surprising opulence, but then this was a passenger ship. Even second-class passengers, of the sort who would be berthed in this part of the ship, would expect a certain amount of comfort. Things would get more spartan further down in the third-class and steerage areas, but here the decks were carpeted, the fittings were all polished mahogany and brass, and the electric lights had shades. It was all beginning to look a bit shabby, of course, as the dock workers and sailors tramped through with their filthy burdens and deposited them in cabins. Baxter half smiled as he guessed that somewhere aboard there was a steward in paroxysms of grief as his beautifully maintained interior was destroyed.

That did beg the question of who the civilians he'd seen on deck had been, and where they were quartered. This was looking more and more like a ship in the process of becoming an armed merchant cruiser and a military supply ship, which was no place for anyone not bent on martial matters.

Glancing back, he was relieved he still had his train of miserable-looking sailors. They followed the men in front as they were directed deeper into the ship. All he needed now was an opportunity.

That came not long after they'd been directed down a companionway by a crewman who spoke badly broken Spanish with what sounded suspiciously like a German accent to Baxter's ear. The human chain was starting to break up and thin out as they were sent to different parts of the ship, keeping her on an even keel as the weight was added.

"Stand by," Baxter murmured. They were now in the more basic areas, perhaps not the crew quarters but not far from them. There were only a couple of dockers in front of them and none behind. There was a side corridor ahead with no obvious sentry. Baxter tried to orient himself — while he had never been aboard this vessel, most followed the same internal logic and he'd always had a good grasp of where he was inside a ship. There should be cabins along here, hopefully somewhere they could lay low before working out how exactly they were going to go about proving that this *was* a German ship.

Another sentry appeared at the end of the corridor. He didn't speak, but held up four fingers and pointed right, then two and left. Baxter could have cursed — that would break up his little party. He and Hicks would have to go right with the two men in front, while Harry and Jack would be directed left and would then be left to their own devices. He just had to trust that they would know how to comport themselves.

Baxter went right with Hicks behind him, alert for any opportunity to drop out of sight. The sentry hadn't given them instructions, but the men in front seemed to know what was expected and turned into one of the third-class cabins to deposit their loads, before coming out and squeezing past Baxter and Hicks.

Baxter went on a bit further. It was eerily deserted, with a lot of the crew on deck and no passengers in evidence. Baxter took a second turn, making sure they were well away from the sentry, before selecting a cabin that was half-filled with sacks to drop their own. It wasn't unlike his own cabin on *Astute*, the compact space filled with a cot, wash basin and clothes stand — most of it now buried under sacks.

"What now, sir?" Hicks asked as he followed suit. "Do we find Harry and Jack?"

Baxter had been thinking about that. "No, they're better just trying to hide. We need to get into the crew quarters to try to find hard evidence that this is an enemy combatant running under false colours."

"Without being seen, sir?"

"It's a tall order, I know," Baxter said, sticking his head back out of the door. "We'll go down into steerage, work our way aft and then try to get up to the officers' quarters."

He led the way, moving as quietly as he could away from the previous intersection. The deep pile carpet was apparently reserved for first-class passengers — here, those who had barely scraped together their passage had to make do with bare deck, which did make creeping along it harder.

Luckily, the crew didn't seem to think they needed to post sentries further into the ship. But then, why would they? It was madness to expect someone to try to sneak on board. The little doubting voice in Baxter's head began to question again whether this was because it was just an innocent American merchant vessel, but he'd seen sufficient evidence that the doubts were fairly muted.

"What are we looking for, sir?" Hicks whispered.

"Anything that proves this blighter's a German," he replied. "Log books, bills of lading, any official documentation."

"Got it, sir," Hicks responded, then asked, "D'you hear that?"

"Hear what?"

"Sounds like someone calling out. In English."

Baxter paused, listening hard. It was only a matter of time before the ship had its fill of coal and the collier would cast off. Baxter had to achieve what he'd come here for, find his two errant bluejackets, and then sneak back onto the deck as though they had never been away before that happened.

"Over here, sir," Hicks said, breaking into his deliberations. The bluejacket moved along the passageway and stopped at one of the plain doors, pressing his ear to the wood. "There are English people in there!"

His voice had risen in his excitement, but Baxter ignored that as he moved to the door. Now he was closer, he could make out the voice calling from inside. Not only was it English, it was a woman, and apparently she was in some distress.

"Good ears," he told Hicks, trying the handle and finding the door locked. He glanced left and right along the passageway, making sure that they were alone, then rapped lightly on the wood. "Whoever is in there, step back from the door."

Baxter took a couple of steps back himself and braced to shoulder-barge the door. Hicks stopped him with a hand on his arm. "If I may, sir, I've got a quieter way to do it," he said, producing a short piece of wire from his pocket.

It was the work of a few moments for Hicks to open the lock with a small *snick* rather than the crash and tear of splintering wood that Baxter would have produced. He stepped back with a slightly apologetic look, muttering something about not always having been a sailor. Baxter merely shrugged — he'd worked with men with worse backgrounds, and being able to open a lock quickly and quietly was a useful skill to have.

He ducked through into a relatively large compartment. It looked like it was intended for stores, except now it had been turned into a makeshift brig. Looking around, Baxter made out a number of men who were clearly merchant seamen, and a clutch of unhappy-looking people in clothes more appropriate for passengers rather than sailors.

"And who the devil do you think you are?" a somewhat pompous man with curling moustaches demanded, standing from his seat on an upturned crate and straightening his tweed shooting jacket. "Some sort of local stevedore intent on a bit of robbery, eh?"

"On the contrary, sir — Baxter, Royal Navy."

Another civilian bounced to his feet, declaring, "See, Henrietta dear, I told you the Navy would be along soon enough!" He was a trim young man with a thin moustache who spoke with a clipped upper-class accent. Baxter immediately pegged him as an Army type, or someone who very much wanted to be. The woman he addressed was dainty, freckled and red-headed, and stared up at Baxter from under her practical cloche hat.

"Are you, Mr Baxter? Are you here to rescue us?"

"Well, of course he is!" a second woman said. She was older, plumper, and wearing a tweed travelling dress. From the facial resemblance and age difference, Baxter guessed that they were mother and daughter, which made the man with the moustache the husband and the would-be soldier Henrietta's betrothed.

"Don't be absurd, Henry," a new voice came in. "The navy can't do anything while we're in a neutral port, and this chap's clearly here for a snoop."

The woman who spoke was sitting a little apart from the other civilians, though she was dressed as well as they were. She rose, smoothing her travelling skirt and observing Baxter coolly with pale blue eyes that matched her light blonde hair.

"Don't call your sister that," the older woman snapped.

The woman opened her mouth to speak, but Baxter had already had more than enough of this. At any other time, he would have obeyed the usual social niceties. Well, more or less, anyway. Right now, though, was not the time for familial bickering.

He closed the door, making sure it clicked closed audibly. "That will be quite enough, thank you," he said, thinking fast. He'd come in with a half-formed plan that had relied on him getting in and out with the proof he needed, but that had changed into a rescue mission. Now that he knew British citizens were being held prisoner aboard the ship, he couldn't leave them in German hands or risk them being killed if and when *Astute* managed to intercept the liner. "I may not have come aboard to rescue you, but that's exactly what I plan to do. But first, would somebody mind telling me how you came to be here?"

CHAPTER TWELVE

The merchant seamen, who had been sitting or lying slightly further back in the compartment, came forward, eager to know what was going on. Baxter got the story more effectively from the master of the ship the civilians had previously been travelling on, the SS *St Auburn*. She had come out of Liverpool and had been on her way back to her home port with a cargo of timber, coffee and rubber as well as a handful of paying passengers keen to get back to the home country. Or at least she had been, until she'd encountered SMS *Kassel* and, unarmed and relatively slow as she was, had been forced to surrender.

"The German navy boys were decent enough," the grizzled merchant captain, Nielsen, said. Despite his name, he spoke with a broad Aberdonian accent that Baxter guessed would have been impenetrable to many of his brother officers. "Allowed us to pack our dunnage and transfer across before they sent her to the bottom. No looting or any other funny business."

Baxter glanced towards the door, where Hicks was listening intently and keeping an eye out. He didn't know what he was going to do yet, although he'd already discounted trying to sneak the prisoners off the liner. He was keenly aware that every moment spent gathering this intelligence, however useful it might be, was eating into the window he had to find Harry and Jack, get any concrete proof they could, and then get off the ship. It was looking more and more likely that they would have to use the backup option of going over the side, at this rate.

"And how have they been treating you aboard this vessel?"

"Most of the officers are proper gents, some of them even seem a bit ashamed of the whole thing, and the civilian crew aren't so bad. They keep us down here but fed and watered, and we're allowed on deck under guard." He gestured to the five civilians — Mr and Mrs Sears, their daughters Henrietta and Pippa, and Henrietta's husband Charles Finlay. "The Germans are decent enough to give the gentlefolk their own cabins."

"There is that one fellow, Leiter; calls himself a German American," Mr Sears, who seemed to be of imperturbable stock, put in.

"Aye, he can be a bit —"

"A bit of a rotter, really," Charles Finlay finished, before the old sailor could say something saltier. He was a solicitor, apparently, and an officer in the Territorial Forces trying to get home to report for duty, having being on a grand tour with his new wife and her family. "Said some positively ghastly things to Henrietta."

"We were being transferred, along with some crew and supplies, when we were spotted by a Royal Navy cruiser." That was the older Sears sister, Pippa, who seemed to regard the situation as a minor inconvenience. "We didn't see much of the fight, as we were locked up down here before we started, but *Herr* Leiter did claim that the *Kassel* got the better of it, and it proved why the US should stay out of the war or come in on the Kaiser's side."

Baxter rubbed at his jaw. "Well, let's just say that neither side won that fight," he said at last. "And I think I'd like to meet this Leiter."

"Well, if you are going to rescue us, one imagines you will," Pippa commented pointedly, giving him a cool and assessing stare down an impressively aquiline nose. Mr and Mrs Sears made the right middle-class murmurs of agreement to that sentiment.

Baxter looked around the dim compartment, suddenly exasperated. He didn't have the men to cut this vessel out, even if she *wasn't* lying in a neutral port. No one had been able to tell him how many of the crew were civilian employees of the liner company, and how many were *Kaiserliche Marine* men transferred from *Kassel*. He could try to get ashore, get a message to Lewisham or the authorities to let them know that the liner — the name of which he had yet to determine — was flying under false colours and actively imprisoning British citizens. He had no proof of it, however, and every second he lingered here reduced the chances of finding any proof and getting off the ship. He knew the civilians wouldn't like it, though he suspected the merchant seamen would understand at least.

"I need to get —" he began, but Hicks broke in.

"Germans coming, sir!" he hissed, hurrying back from his post at the door. "Sounds like a bunch of them."

Baxter's indecision fell away at the threat of imminent danger. "Lock the door, Hicks, then act like you're a merchant sailor." He glanced around at the civilians, whose previously hopeful expressions had started to slide into anxiety. "I am afraid I must ask you all to do me a great service and pretend that nothing out of the ordinary has happened."

"I'm yet to be convinced that anything *has* happened," Pippa commented coolly, before returning to her crate, which sat directly under one of the only bare lightbulbs, and picking up her book.

Hicks had already managed to secure the door with his trusty twist of wire, and he hurried to follow Baxter's orders and mingle with the merchant sailors. Some of them seemed enormously entertained by this turn of events, grinning and jostling him in a mostly friendly manner.

Baxter ignored the older Sears daughter's comment, and went to the back of the compartment. His intention was to blend in with the captives in the hope there wouldn't be a headcount. He crouched down with his back to the bulkhead, resting his arms across his knees and putting his head back. He didn't need to pretend to be tired, after his day's labour.

The clatter of approaching boots stopped at the door to the compartment, as he'd feared it would, and he heard the rattle of a key in the mechanism. There was a muffled curse in German, and he exchanged glances with Hicks, who just shrugged as though to say 'nothing to do with me, gov'nor'. Baxter relaxed when he heard the key being withdrawn and the door was swung open.

Baxter couldn't see the man who came in clearly, as the merchant sailors had clustered around to provide him and Hicks with some cover. He certainly sounded American, though different to the mercenaries and sailors from the United States that Baxter had run into in the past. He seemed smoother and more cultured, and spoke with slightly clipped tones that hinted at time spent in Germany as well.

"Ladies and gentlemen," he said in English. "The captain apologises for our unexpectedly long delay in beautiful Montevideo — such a shame none of you were able to make it ashore to enjoy the delights of South America. You are now requested to return to your cabins, and please excuse any mess, as we prepare to get underway."

Well, that's bloody torn it, Baxter thought as the officer stepped back. Now was the dangerous time, of course, if one of them managed to give the game away.

Charles Finlay spoke. "Once again, Mr Leiter, I must protest at our detention aboard your vessel. Whether or not our countries are currently locked in a state of belligerence, we are civilians — as are these men — and all the laws of man and decency demand that you put ashore in this neutral port."

"You, and some of these men, are of fighting age — and some even of fighting temperament. I apologise, but our orders are clear — to Germany, and internment."

Finlay took a deep breath, as though he was about to argue that point, and Baxter closed his eyes. He guessed this was a routine for the solicitor, but if he pushed it and angered Leiter, it would keep the Germans here and risk his discovery.

"Oh, do leave it, Charlie," Pippa said, sounding tired and bored. "I really rather fancy having done with today, and listening to the posturing of men."

Leiter actually laughed at that, a hearty sound that still somehow came across as hollow and humourless. Thankfully, that seemed to be the end of the matter, and with some grumbling and a slightly strained attempt at good humour from Mrs Sears, the civilians — or rather, the wealthy civilians — were escorted out of the compartment.

Baxter got one clear look at Leiter, a tall and well-built man, dark-haired and with somewhat bland good looks. He was peering at the sailors, a somewhat suspicious look on his face. While most of the seamen had relapsed into sullen silence, one or two of them were clearly not able to hide their newly returned good spirits. The German obviously decided it was just sailors being sailors, and swung the door shut with a clang. "Dinner in one hour!" he shouted through it, the false humour that he had demonstrated with the Sears party fully evaporated.

"You'd best be on your way by then," Nielsen said, turning to Baxter. "We're on better terms with the common sailors who bring us food, and they'll know you don't belong."

"What are we going to do, sir?" asked Hicks.

Baxter rose, stretched, and tried to ease the knots of tension between his shoulders. He could feel the beat of the ship's mighty heart starting to pick up speed as they got steam up. It would be some time before they would be ready to go, particularly with the extra weight of the cargo brought aboard, but that probably also meant that the collier had cast off, or would do so soon.

"We're going to capture this bloody ship," he said, with more confidence than he felt.

"Just us two, and some spit, sir?" Hicks responded, sounding incredulous.

"There are four of us aboard, and as soon as this barky gets underway, Pearson will be in her wake. More than enough, with surprise on our side."

"And us, sir, them that want to fight, anyway," Captain Nielsen put in.

Baxter's mind went back to the civilian ship he and a handful of others had pulled out of German hands off the coast of East Africa. No one had died then, but one of the merchant seamen had come damn close, and he didn't want that on his conscience. "I appreciate the offer, Captain, but this is a job for professionals — we'll try and keep you out of it until we've got the ship secure, when we'll need your help managing her."

"I'm a bloody professional now, am I?" he heard Hicks mutter. "Not at taking bloody ships, I'm not."

Baxter glanced sharply at the bluejacket. "What is your station, anyway, lad?"

"Me, sir? Canteen assistant, sir."

"Well, Hicks, that doesn't mean you're not in the business of sinking, taking or burning the enemy's vessels. You *are* in the Navy, after all."

As Baxter had anticipated, it took some time for the liner to come up to steam. It was stifling belowdecks and reeked of unwashed bodies and coal. The discomfort worked in their favour, though, as any man who didn't have business down below was up on deck avoiding the heat and humidity, the grit of the coal underfoot and under clothes and nails. Letting themselves out of the compartment, Baxter and Hicks moved quietly through the guts of the ship, avoiding the engine room as stokers and engineers would be working in the sweltering heat. They were both hungry and thirsty, but trying to acquire supplies would risk discovery.

Baxter's mind worked furiously as they moved. He had virtually no resources or assets, aside from the element of surprise. Admittedly, from what he had gleaned from the imprisoned sailors, most of the German crew were civilian seamen, though no doubt they had a smattering of veterans and reservists among them. Some of the men were almost certainly not German, either. That still didn't even the odds. He was loath to involve Nielsen and his men, and even Finlay — who seemed keen and as a Territorial felt an obligation to be involved — would hardly swing things further in their favour.

"I don't know much about these things, sir, but I do know we're not supposed to go attacking ships in neutral waters," Hicks said after they found a quiet corner to rest and recover themselves. "Think I've heard you say something to that effect before."

Baxter had already thought of that, but dismissed it. "They're going to abuse everyone's territorial waters and creep down South America's coast," he said. "It would be almost impossible for the countries along the way, even those with any kind of navy, to monitor the activity of a single liner."

"What are these blighters even trying to do, sir?"

"The amount of coal they've taken on, and the other supplies, can mean only one thing — they're going to try to resupply von Spee. And maybe link up with the cruiser we fought yesterday."

"That doesn't sound good, sir."

"It's a desperate effort for them, and even with the amount they've taken on it would be a drop in the squadron's requirements, but it would give them a little bit more time. I intend to put a stop to that."

Baxter knew making an attempt on this ship was crossing a line legally. Morally, however, the Germans had already crossed the line — there was no way for them to claim they weren't undertaking military activity in neutral waters and under the cover of a false identity. It would be something for the courts to decide, long after the fact and when men felt safe to give opinions and cast judgements on the actions of those who were there in the moment.

"And how are we planning on doing that, sir?" Hicks asked.

It was a good question. He was about to answer when he became aware of a slight pitch and roll that told him that the liner was underway and picking up speed, ploughing her way through placid waters. With any luck, Pearson would obey his orders and follow the liner at a discreet distance.

A lot could have gone wrong in the hours since Baxter had led his volunteers on the mission, though. There had been more than enough time for Littleton to have returned from *Astute* with fresh orders. The launch could have been overrun by the same people the Germans had been riling up with stories of the Royal Navy attacking neutral shipping.

Baxter had no way of knowing, however, and no other way forward than to trust in the petty officer and the men under his command. He'd left his pocket watch in the launch, along with his revolver — both of which might have been a bit of a giveaway — so he had no way of knowing exactly what time it was, but it must have been fully dark by now. There was nothing else for it.

"Eyes and ears open, Hicks, and mouth shut," Baxter ordered, as he pulled himself up. "We head aft and up."

"Very good, sir," Hicks replied.

They moved aft through the liner, on the alert for German sailors moving around, which limited how quickly they could progress. Twice Hicks had to get Baxter's attention and draw him into empty cabins or other compartments piled with coal, hearing the approach of enemy seamen before Baxter did. The lad had good ears, it seemed.

All the time, Baxter kept an eye out for the two errant bluejackets. He'd heard no alarm being raised or the sounds of running men, so he could only assume that they had found somewhere out of the way to lie low. Harry and Jack were both experienced RN seamen, so if there was one thing they knew it was how to keep a low profile. Usually that talent would be handy in avoiding petty officers looking for someone to give a rough detail to, but it was equally applicable to avoiding the notice of enemy forces.

As they went up ladders and along passageways, they started to hear more and more people talking in German. Their voices were muffled by bulkheads and closed doors, so Baxter couldn't make out what they were saying, but he could well imagine the satisfaction of the officers at least. They'd taken on coal remarkably quickly, somehow maintaining their false flag throughout, and had once again put one in the enemy's eye.

At least, they thought they had.

CHAPTER THIRTEEN

"I think they're all in the first-class lounge, sir," Hicks commented, as they crouched by a door that would lead out onto the cruiser's main deck. "I can hear 'em from here."

Baxter briefly considered what the seaman had said. It would make sense for the officers to avail themselves of facilities usually reserved for the most privileged passengers. They had worked hard and done well, Baxter reflected, and no doubt thought they deserved a little luxury. There would be men on watch, of course, and the stokers would be sweating in the ship's boiler rooms, but most of the sailors who had actually done the work would either be sleeping or eating, far from the rarefied air of officer country.

A liner engaged in her normal peacetime activities would have an enormous crew, he knew, but many of their duties would revolve around the comfort and safety of the passengers — stewards, cooks, pursers, entertainment and the like. Between the captured merchant seamen and Mr Finlay, he had a rough idea of how many men were actually aboard, and it did sound as though most of those supernumeraries had already been put ashore, not to mention men being drafted onto the German cruiser. Some sailors and officers had come across as well — the men Baxter had identified as professionals earlier — but that would have been to stiffen the crew rather than to increase it.

The more Baxter thought about it, the more he began to suspect that he actually held the balance of power here — as long as he moved with speed and determination.

Without further hesitation, he opened the hatch and looked around. There didn't even seem to be anyone keeping watch on the main deck, so he led Hicks out and across to the railing. It was good to be out in the clean air, but they didn't have time to enjoy it.

"Shirt and shoes off, Hicks, then we swim for the launch."

"What if it's not there, sir?" Hicks asked, swallowing nervously.

"It'll be there," Baxter replied, as he stripped off his own shirt. Pearson was a good, steady hand who followed orders but was also capable of thinking for himself. Hicks, however, looked positively terrified.

"Well, the thing of it is, sir, while I wasn't exactly lying when I said I could swim, I'm not really the strongest. More of a doggy paddle than anything, sir, and as for diving..."

Baxter stared at him incredulously. Before he could say anything, though, Hicks' head snapped round. Baxter moved quickly back towards the hatch they had exited the superstructure through just as two figures emerged around the corner. He was about to lunge forward, ready to surprise and battle the German sailors, when he realised he was about to launch himself at two young ladies.

Henrietta actually squealed when she saw him in his half-dressed state, and recoiled, shielding her eyes with one gloved hand. Baxter drew himself up, knowing there was no dignified way out of this. "Mrs Finlay, Miss Sears," he said drily. "Lovely evening for a promenade."

Pippa smiled, while doing her best to pretend that she wasn't staring. "Ah, Mr Baxter," she said. While he'd only met her an hour ago, he'd already pegged her as someone it would be hard to fluster. "Going for a swim, I presume?"

Enough pleasantries, Baxter decided, and stooped to kick off his boots. "Indeed. Are you unescorted?"

"We have the run of the ship now we're away from land, with obvious limitations."

Baxter thrust his somewhat grimy boots into Pippa's hands. They were well worn and patched, but had been on his feet for many miles and had mostly held together — it would be a shame to lose them. "Good — you can look after a couple of things for me, then."

"These, and...?"

"Hicks over there," he said, jerking a thumb at the somewhat sheepish sailor. "If you can sneak him back to your suites, that would be ideal."

"I'm not sure..." Pippa began, but Baxter was already moving. He'd tarried long enough on deck. He ran straight at the rail, threw one bare foot onto it, and then launched himself into the depths of the night that had come on while they'd been creeping around belowdecks. He enjoyed a brief moment of absolute freedom as he fell through the cool air. There was no light, beyond the small pool of orange illumination that the liner cast about herself and the phosphorescence of the wake, stretching out behind. Then he hit the water, a clean dive that took him deep under the surface.

He clamped down on the urge to suck in air as he plunged deep, the cool crisp water scouring at least some of the day's filth from his body. For a moment, he almost lost his orientation; the moon may have been bright but he was deep enough that it took him a moment to see its glimmer through the water as he stared about with stinging eyes. Then he struck upwards, chest burning, following the little bubbles trickling from his nose as the last of his lungful of air was forced out of him.

He broke the surface with a great gasp, savouring the sensation of the wind on his face. He took a moment to orientate himself. He'd ordered Pearson to follow the liner out of Montevideo as close as he could without being seen, and he was reasonably certain that the German ship had followed a pretty steady course. Looking left and right, and then back at the harbour, he took a rough position that seemed to confirm that. His best option, he decided, was to swim parallel to the slowly dissipating wake and hope Pearson's crew spotted him. The sky was clear at least, the moon bright, but he couldn't see a vessel following. That didn't mean it wasn't there, of course — it was a small vessel and he'd ordered Pearson to run without lights and with a minimum of noise.

Baxter trod water for a moment, watching the liner. Somehow, no one had noticed his dramatic dive from the ship. With a reduced crew, and all of them exhausted, it was perhaps unsurprising. When he was certain the vessel wasn't stopping or putting a boat in the water, he turned and set off with a strong, even stroke.

He was acutely conscious that he'd left men aboard the liner, and while they had shown themselves to be tough, capable seamen, they were still his responsibility. And now he'd implicated two young Englishwomen in the situation. He remained alert, listening out for the sounds of gunshots or raised voices, but heard nothing.

Baxter settled into an easy rhythm. It was strange, out here the middle of a vast estuary in the darkness. Even though the liner was still nearby, close enough that he could feel the throb of her engines through the water, he began to feel truly alone, isolated in a way that he had rarely felt during a life spent mostly at sea. It was almost peaceful, just him and the effort of swimming, the cold of the water starting to creep into his limbs despite his exertions. A sense of deep calm came over him then, a detachment from the world and its troubles that would help keep him going, driving through the water towards the glowing lights of the city. Distances were hard to judge in the darkness, but he had no intention of swimming all the way there.

The launch would be out here somewhere. They might have seen him go over the side, if someone had been keeping watch in the little boat's bows with a set of glasses. Even though it was dark, the vessel sailing in neutral waters was properly and fully illuminated.

He slowed slightly, his limbs already feeling tired and leaden, and switched to a breaststroke so he could keep his head above water, staying alert for the launch. He knew some of his brother officers, men like Littleton, would be shaking their heads at the way he had thrown himself into this self-appointed mission without any real planning. And he would be due a thorough carpeting from Sitwell, or Captain Gregson if he had recovered. Baxter almost smiled as he reflected on what Ekaterina Juneau would say — no doubt something about the follies of going off half-cocked. He hadn't seen the wild Russian countess for a decade, not since his time aboard a Russian cruiser, but he could still picture her perfectly, hear her voice as he imagined what she would say.

The truth was that Baxter had taken a calculated risk to do his duty. His life, and that of anyone who spent their life at sea, was a dangerous one even in peacetime. More than anything else, he relied on the fact that Pearson was a capable petty officer who would follow orders. And if something *had* gone wrong, Baxter would find another way to deal with the situation. Assuming that the exertions of the day didn't overcome him and he drowned out here.

The water was colder than he'd banked on, and it belatedly occurred to him that there might be sharks in the area. He paused and trod water as he took stock of the situation. It might be safer to strike for the nearer shore after all, even if that would leave him alone, on foot, and without documentation.

He smiled ruefully. Even without Arbuthnott, or the Naval Intelligence Division, or Ekaterina's machinations, he'd somehow *still* managed to find himself in a sticky situation.

Baxter caught a glimpse of something out of the corner of his eye, and turned back in that direction, staring into the darkness. His vision at least had remained keen, even if his hearing wasn't as sharp as it might once have been, and he caught it again, a flicker of movement. A smudge of black against the bright stars, and below it a gleam of white.

Baxter struck out with a reinvigorated stroke, thrashing forward to intercept what had to be the launch. They clearly hadn't seen him, puttering along on a course that followed the liner a hundred yards or more to the south of Baxter's own course. If he'd spotted it just a few minutes later, it would have been well past him rather than still in front of him, and he now swam as hard as he could to meet it while he still had the opportunity.

As he got closer, Baxter began to wonder who had trained the bluejackets on board — he wasn't exactly being quiet as he swam towards the boat, and yet there was no alarm raised, no order to heave to or turn towards him. He caught a glimpse of men in the bows, all of them staring intently at the liner, which was now a little over a mile away.

The launch was making good speed given how small its engine was, water foaming around its bow as it slowly gained on the passenger vessel. Baxter realised that he was in danger of being left behind, but didn't want to break his stroke in order to call out — that would lose time and he couldn't guarantee that they would hear him. Instead, he struck out harder, forcing his aching limbs beyond the limits of his endurance as he struggled to reach the tantalisingly close gunwale. He broke his stroke in order to reach for it, missed, and was forced back by the water creaming along the boat's side. He thrashed forward, trying to gasp out a shout to the oblivious bluejackets and instead sputtering on water.

Adrenaline surged through him, galvanising his limbs. He was *not* going to die in such a ridiculous way. He lunged forward, managing to get one hand on the polished wooden side rail. The water pulled at him, trying to keep what it had claimed, but he got a second hand on and with a grunt managed to pull himself onto the launch's deck.

Gasping and shivering, he pulled himself up. He heard the man at the wheel in the stern exclaim, "Bloody hell!" as he rose into view.

"Mr Pearson," Baxter said with more calm than he felt, "cabin, now!"

He ducked through the low hatch into the cramped cabin that took up about a third of the launch's stern, stripping off his sodden underclothes and grabbing the uniform he had left on board earlier. The petty officer stepped through and saluted smartly.

Baxter blew out a breath as he pulled on his white trousers and forced himself to relax. The men had been following his orders and watching the liner, and he couldn't really hold their failure to spot him against them.

"Nice to see you back, sir," Pearson said after an uncomfortable pause. Baxter kept his silence while he shrugged into his jacket. He didn't ask about Hicks and the other two sailors, but then it was clear they were absent. "Did you ... find much success?"

We found all sorts of things. "Some. Break out the small arms, Pearson."

The PO didn't even blink, just went to the small chest under one of the bench seats, pulling a key from his pocket. "May I ask what our orders are, sir?" he asked, as he unlocked the case and started pulling rifles and boxes of ammunition out. Baxter was surprised to see lever action Winchester rifles, of the kind he'd seen American mercenaries use during his involvement in the Italo-Ottoman War, rather than the more familiar Lee Enfields.

"We're going to board and take that German ship, Pearson, and rescue our shipmates," Baxter said evenly as he retrieved his revolver and checked it was loaded. "Are the men trained with those rifles?"

"Not really, sir."

"Well, not to worry," he said, taking one and examining it. He pulled the lever forward, opening the breech, then shook fat .44 rounds from the box Pearson had opened and started slotting them into the weapon. "Distribute these to the most steady men, revolvers for the others."

Baxter stepped back out onto the deck. The wind was coming up and the waves were growing taller and longer as they inched towards the open sea. He took a deep breath, relishing the tang of salt now he was out of the water. He had work to do this night, work that suited him better than creeping around an enemy ship trying to avoid notice.

CHAPTER FOURTEEN

It didn't take them long to catch up with the liner. While passenger ships were designed to make fast, luxurious crossings and would normally be able to show the little steam-powered launch a clean pair of heels, the captain was either husbanding the machinery or she was so overburdened she couldn't achieve her potential.

Baxter watched the pool of light coming closer, a knot of tension in his guts. He was conscious that what he was about to do could be considered against the laws of war and the sea. By all rights, he should abandon the operation now and — armed with his knowledge of the ship's provenance and the fact British citizens were being held aboard — steam for HMS *Astute* as fast as he could in order to make a report.

And then hope Sitwell or Gregson believed him, and that the cruiser was in a fit state to sortie, and that they were able to find the suspect vessel...

No. The liner was carrying British citizens into harm's way, and critical supplies to a German squadron that could continue to cause havoc in shipping lanes if it was not brought to heel. Given the situation, and the resources he had, there was no other option. The law be damned.

Behind him, Pearson was quietly taking the other bluejackets through the operation of the Winchester rifles, the sort of basics that a Royal Marine would have down pat but a seaman very rarely had to worry about. The weapons had all been well maintained and stored correctly, at least. Baxter guessed they were an emergency wartime purchase, so only recently delivered. They gave him no cause for concern, and what worries he had were more about the men handling them. Pearson and one or two others aside, the men were fairly raw and all of them understandably nervous.

He turned to them now, putting one foot up on the gunwale to steady himself as the launch's pitch and roll became more pronounced. He waited until Pearson had finished showing one of the seamen how the safety catch worked, ordering him to keep it on no matter what. The petty officer nodded to indicate that the men were as ready as they could be.

"Remember, lads, most of the men on that ship aren't fighting men — they're merchant crew who won't want anything to do with a scrap." *Probably*. It was likely the men who had remained aboard when the liner had become an auxiliary cruiser had been sworn into the *Kaiserliche Marine*, but he doubted they would have much stomach for a fight. "They'll also be tired after the day's exertion. Some of them are proper fighting sailors, though, so stay alert. We hit them hard and fast, don't give them time to work out what's going on, and carry the ship before they even know we're there. Nobody shoots unless they have to, and *nobody* loots. Remember, there are British seamen and civilians aboard, and they're relying on us to rescue them."

"Not to mention Harry and Jack, and Hicks," one of the more grizzled sailors said with a grin.

Baxter smiled. "Them too. Now —" he glanced over his shoulder, and saw they were closing fast with the liner's starboard quarter — "you all know your assignments?"

The men nodded, hands tightening on their weapons.

It seemed, for a moment, that they had not been spotted. The liner, small in comparison to newer vessels but still intimidatingly large, continued on her way, surrounded by a halo of electric light. The little gnat of the launch continued arrowing towards her side, filled with tense and now silent sailors.

"*What boat?*" a voice called from the afterdeck of the liner, pitched to be heard above the wind and engine noise. Whoever it was, they were shouting in English and he thought they might have an American accent.

"Keep on course," Baxter said over his shoulder, before cupping his hands over his mouth to reply.

"*Servicio de Aduanas!*" he called back, trying to pitch his voice to carry to the sentry but not wake the whole damn ship. His grasp of Spanish might have been lacking, but any sailor knew what the Customs Service was called in many languages.

"What's that? Customs?"

"*Sí*, Customs!" Baxter called back. They were close to the liner's side now, the men standing by with lines and grappling hooks.

"Whaddya want?"

"Contraband inspection!" It was an absurdity, of course — a Customs boat wouldn't pursue an American liner through the night for an inspection, but it was the best he could do in that moment and all he really had to do was keep the man talking for a few seconds longer...

In fact, he didn't have to keep him talking any longer at all — the liner's side loomed above them. "Grappling hook!" he snapped.

The sailor detailed to the task took up his line and started whirling it over his head. He let go, sending the grappling hook arcing up into the night towards the liner's rail. Baxter winced as it clanged off the side and fell back down into the launch.

"Sorry, sir," the sailor said as he hurriedly wound the line in.

"Give it here, lad," Baxter replied, holding out his hand. He didn't bother swinging it for any length of time; he just gave it a couple of whirls then launched it up and over. The line snaked over the railing and he quickly pulled it back, drawing the line taut as the grapnel hooked onto the railing. Without hesitating, Baxter swung himself off the launch and hit the side of the liner feet-first, hauling himself up the ship's side.

"*Gott im Himmel*," he heard someone mutter above, but there was no way to know if it was his interlocutor from before. He didn't let himself worry about that, or consider what would happen if the German managed to remove the grapnel — he just had to get to the top and silence the sailor before it occurred to him to raise the alarm. The rope shifted under his hands, and Baxter realised the German was trying to dislodge the grapnel.

Baxter climbed up the last few feet as he heard the *click* of a clasp knife being opened. That was bad, but it still hadn't occurred to the sailor to seek help. He got his head above the gunwale, and the German's eyes widened when he saw the cap that bore the RN insignia.

Baxter lunged forward, grabbing a handful of the sailor's tunic, and then used his weight to haul him over the railing. The fellow was too surprised to call out as he went flailing into the sea beyond the launch.

Baxter didn't have time to worry about him. He jumped up onto the deck and pulled out his revolver. He left the hammer down; the last thing he needed was the damn thing going off by accident.

Pearson was up next, followed by the rest of the small boarding party, some of them grunting and puffing up the rope with their slung rifles hanging against their legs.

"Right lads — quiet as we can," he said. "Follow me."

Baxter led them back the way he had come an hour or so ago, slipping quietly across the afterdeck and then onto the companionways that led up the superstructure's exterior towards the boat deck. As with everything else on board this vessel, the staircases were designed to be pleasing as well as functional, with polished wood rather than the bare metal one might find on a warship.

It was eerily quiet, with no sign that anyone had taken notice of their arrival, which reinforced Baxter's conviction that the ship was undermanned. There should have been lookouts at the very least, even if they were still in neutral waters. With the crew worked to exhaustion, the captain had probably taken the opportunity of being in peaceful waters to give them as much rest as possible.

A mistake that Baxter planned to exploit to the fullest.

He paused as they reached the second deck of the superstructure. The boat deck was above, the white-painted lifeboats creaking on their davits. Light and sound flooded from the portholes of one of the compartments, which Baxter guessed was the first-class lounge. Someone was playing music hall tunes on a piano, with more enthusiasm than skill, and they could hear a hubbub of German voices and laughter. A door opened, and a second later there was the sound of a match being struck and a flare of light. A cigar's rich smell reached them. No conversation, though, just the contented sigh of a man taking the night air and a little peace and quiet.

Baxter considered waiting, and seeing whether the fellow would do the decent thing and go back into the lounge. When it became apparent that he was staying put, no doubt enjoying the view of Montevideo as it receded into the night, he had no other option. Holding his hand up to keep the other men in place, Baxter casually continued up the companionway, hands shoved in his pockets.

The German was a plump, middle-aged man with a fine moustache, holding a brandy balloon in one hand and a fat cigar in the other. Baxter guessed he wasn't a regular officer, although he was wearing a *Kaiserliche Marine* uniform. He blinked at Baxter, obviously drunk and slightly nonplussed — it helped that in the flickering orange light, their tropical uniforms didn't look familiar. *"Guten Abend, mein Herr,"* the fellow said, before proceeding to ask something that Baxter couldn't follow — perhaps asking him if he'd joined the ship in port.

"Ja, ja," Baxter replied confidently, nodding and smiling as he closed the range on the smaller man, who now blinked up at him with dawning realisation and horror.

Baxter got a hand over his mouth, then turned him bodily until he had his back to Baxter. Reaching a forearm around the man's neck, Baxter pulled him back out of the line of sight from the lounge, using his other hand to grab the brandy balloon before it was dropped. The chap started to struggle, clawing at Baxter's arm and kicking backwards into his shins, so he increased the pressure around his neck until the officer went limp.

Baxter carefully lowered him to the deck, before gesturing the sailors forward and holding a finger to his lips. "You two, watch that door," he whispered. "Club anyone who comes out — only shoot if you have to."

The two rifle-armed sailors nodded and grinned, obviously relishing the chance to do harm to the enemy — and officers, no less. Baxter led the others up to the boat deck. It was quieter up here, though light oozed around a blind pulled down over one porthole and, looking up the last companionway, he could see the glow of a binnacle light on the bridge.

There was sweat on his back despite the cool night air, as they approached what would be the most dangerous phase of this operation. Baxter took a breath and went quietly forward, the sailors padding after him. He took the steps of the companionway two at a time, past what was probably the captain's stateroom, silent and dark, the chartroom and wheelhouse above that, and then onto the bridge which surmounted the superstructure.

This at least was familiar to him, even if was broader than the bridge of even larger warships. It was open to the sky and the elements, with a captain's chair sitting empty and the officer of the watch standing at the forward railings. There were lookouts port and starboard, staring into the darkness as the ship approached the open sea.

Baxter kept moving, clearing the entryway. The sailors went past him silently, a flow of men moving with tight discipline to their assigned tasks. There would be no gentlemanly offer to let the men surrender, and instead the bridge crew were overpowered swiftly and ruthlessly. His orders had been clear — no alarm should be raised, no warning shouted down a speaking tube. Only shoot if you have to.

Baxter took the officer of the watch, placing the Smith and Wesson's muzzle against the side of his head and thumbing the hammer back. "*Stille*," Baxter hissed. "*Kapitän?*"

The man started to shake his head, but found the movement curtailed by the cold steel at his temple. "*Nein. Leutnant.*"

"Where is he?" Baxter risked a glance over his shoulder, and was pleased the see that Pearson was leading two of the party back down to secure the wheelhouse and chartroom.

"Lounge, with the other officers." The man gave Baxter an almost reproachful look. "This is piracy, you know. We are a civilian vessel in —"

"You are hardly a civilian vessel," Baxter cut in, suddenly in no mood to argue. It would be for the courts to determine the legality of what had been done here. He gestured the officer over to where the rest of the bridge crew had already been tied up and gagged in the middle of the broad deck. "Keep these men under guard," he ordered a bluejacket. "The rest of you, with me."

As Baxter started back down the steps, he heard a thump and a muffled cry from the wheelhouse, and increased his pace. A German sailor, the sort of big steady man often promoted to the role of quartermaster, burst from the wheelhouse and darted for the companionway, a bloody knife in one hand. Pearson, bleeding from a gash in his cheek, staggered from the hatch, a murderous look in his eye as he raised his Winchester.

Baxter jumped the last few steps, tripping the big man just before he reached the companionway and then catching his collar before he could go down it headfirst. He yanked the sailor back, punched him in the guts, and then followed with a cross to the jaw that sent him sprawling. Pearson cracked him on the bridge of the nose with his rifle's brass butt plate, then raised the weapon for a second strike. Baxter put a hand out and Pearson subsided, and instead fumbled for a kerchief to stem the bleeding. The other two men emerged from the wheelhouse, nodding as Baxter shot an inquisitive glance their way.

"Are you able to continue?" he asked Pearson, who nodded. "Take the wheel, then."

Heading back down towards the boat deck, Baxter realised that the commotion had caught the attention of the officers in the lounge.

"*Willy, bist du das?*" a slurred voice demanded. The speaker was relatively steady on his feet as he emerged through the door, then yelped as he was jumped and dragged down by one of the sailors Baxter had left to guard the entrance. There were cries of confusion and consternation from inside the brightly lit lounge, and the jaunty piano music cut off mid-flow.

Baxter kept going forward, as there was no other option now. He ducked through the door and straightened up, bringing a cold gust of menace into the cheerfully opulent space. Everyone turned to stare at him as he took the room in at a glance. The officers were mostly lounging around mahogany tables polished to a mirror shine, or sitting on deep leather couches. Charles Finlay was at the piano, his wife Henrietta beside him. Pippa Sears was sitting nearby, looking perfectly bored by everything.

"Gentlemen," Baxter announced into the stunned silence. "You are now prisoners of the Royal Navy. Please conduct yourselves accordingly."

He heard one of the men mutter something about them outnumbering him. He levelled the revolver with a steady look and advanced into the space, trying not to blink in the bright lighting, almost painful after so long moving around in the dark. "Try me."

Bluejackets with Winchesters filed in after him and Baxter heard the distinctive noise of oiled gunmetal moving as one of them levered a round into the chamber. A *Kaiserliche Marine* officer started to rise from his seat next to the piano, but Finlay moved quickly, grabbing a bottle of schnapps from a tray on the piano and smashing it over the man's head.

The fight went out of them at that point. A few of them put their hands up, while others signalled their surrender by sinking back into their seats. "Which of you is the captain?" Baxter demanded. "*Kapitän?*"

Silence greeted his question, along with surly glares or feigned indifference. Then an older man, with salt and pepper hair and a moustache, sighed and rose. "I am Klaus Meisner, the master of this vessel," he said in unaccented English, inclining his head slightly. While he was in a naval uniform, like some others Baxter had encountered it looked new and didn't fit properly.

"*Herr* Meisner *was* the captain of this ship," Pippa said mildly, glancing up from what appeared to be a journal and putting a fountain pen down. She didn't give any indication that she knew who Baxter was. "However, he has been superseded by a *Kapitänleutnant* Fleiss, who was assigned from the *Kassel*. He has the last stateroom in the first-class section, one storey down."

Baxter swore, turning towards the door. "Keep them here," he told the three sailors who had come in after him. "Shoot anyone who gets out of line. Aside from the civilians, of course."

"How thoughtful of you," Pippa murmured, as he turned and strode from the lounge.

Although he wanted to secure the captain, and any documents he might have, himself, Baxter's responsibility was for the whole operation. They had the bridge and wheelhouse, and most of the officers, which went a long way to controlling the ship. The crew, which vastly outnumbered his party, were not secured yet, nor were the engine and boiler rooms, but he was less concerned about them as long as they remained ignorant of what was occurring. Baxter sent two men to secure the captain, and make sure no documents were destroyed or otherwise disposed of, and other men to make sure the officers didn't get out of hand despite the rifles pointed at them. He knew how much being captured like that would smart. Men who had been raised and trained to be proud of their service could be careless with their lives, and the lives of others, in those situations.

Hicks ambled up after Baxter had sent off two more sailors to sweep the upper decks and round up any watchmen. The sailor was slightly cleaner; no doubt Mrs Sears had objected to him tramping coaldust into the family's quarters. The lad saluted smartly. "Where do you need me, sir?" he asked without preamble.

"Good to see you're still with us, Hicks. Take these two and go and release Nielsen and his people. Quietly, mind you. No shooting, no shouting."

"Very good, sir."

"And keep an eye out for Harry and Jack," Baxter added, as the trio set off. The fact that the two sailors, separated from the party hours ago, were still lying low was an indication of how quiet the boarding party was. That, or the two errant bluejackets were aware of what was going on and were seasoned enough to know when they had an excuse to take it easy. There was no man who would work or fight harder, in Baxter's estimation, than the British bluejacket. But there was also no man more willing to slack off when he thought he could get away with it.

Baxter leant over the boat deck's railing and looked aft. He saw a German sailor, up in the bows, meekly surrendering to the sailors who had come out of nowhere. His control was spreading through the ship like floodwater, but he needed reinforcements.

He went back up to the bridge, checking in on Pearson as he went. The petty officer still looked angry, but the wound to his face had been dressed and appeared to have stopped bleeding at least. Baxter continued up to the bridge, and gave orders for the bound men to be moved belowdecks. The merchant seamen released by Hicks had started to appear on deck, some of them having armed themselves along the way, which gave Baxter more resources. Even if they weren't trained RN personnel, it meant more manpower.

Baxter took up a pair of glasses and scanned the area to port and starboard. He needed to know where they were, but the night was sufficiently dark that he couldn't make out any landmarks beyond a vague notion that they were still in the estuary, though not far from the ill-defined line where fresh water became the ocean. He glanced up at the night sky — navigation had never been his strong suit — then flipped open the speaking tube to order a course change, bringing the liner into a long turn to the north and back towards Piriápolis. At least, that was his hope.

Deep below them, the German stokers and engineering staff would still be labouring away in their private hell of heat and noise, hopefully unaware that their labours were now carrying them into captivity. The common seamen, those who hadn't been rounded up as Baxter's sailors, went about their work or were asleep in their bunks or hammocks, the companionways up from their messes covered by his men. At least, he hoped that was the case.

The speaking tube array next to the captain's chair emitted a sharp whistle, indicating someone wanted to speak to the officer of the watch. Baxter hesitated, but only momentarily — not answering would be more suspicious than muddling through. He would just have to hope that the distortion that came with the speaking tubes would help disguise his voice. He flipped the cover open. *"Ja?"*

It was the engine room, that much he could tell, the accent guttural and almost lost through the pounding of the massive pistons that drove the big ship through the water. Baxter paused, trying to work out what had been said. He told his interlocutor that everything was fine, that they had made a minor course change.

There was no response from the other end, then a hesitant confirmation.

"He didn't sound very convinced, old chap," Charles Finlay commented, arriving on the bridge with an older German officer in front of him. Finlay had a Luger automatic pointed at the small of his back, but Baxter didn't ask where he'd acquired it.

This officer — who wore the rank symbols of the *Kaiserliche Marine's* equivalent of a lieutenant commander — offered Baxter a courteous bow. His uniform was rumpled, as though he'd pulled it on in a hurry, and he had huge bags under his eyes. "I am acting *Kapitän sur Zee* Fleiss. May I congratulate you on the dash of your operation," he said in flawless English.

Baxter was slightly taken aback, as he'd been expecting more bluster and attempts to capture the moral high ground. He didn't let that show, and instead offered the officer a sharp salute. "Thank you, sir," he said. "Can I assume that you are content to offer the formal surrender of your crew and vessel?"

"I was under the impression you already had control of the ship?" Fleiss asked diffidently.

"We do, sir, but it's best to observe the formalities, don't you think?" Baxter replied, channelling every irritatingly upper-class officer he had ever encountered.

"Quite so, quite so," Fleiss said. "I would offer you my pistol, but one of my passengers has … commandeered it. But I formally surrender."

Finlay was grinning behind the German, obviously pleased to have had at least a small part in this adventure. He would no doubt dine out on this for years, whether in the restaurants of London or the mess halls of France. Assuming he lived that long, of course.

Baxter nodded, assessing the man. There were some German officers he'd met, most recently in East Africa, who would not hesitate to change their position once they realised just how precarious Baxter's control of the ship really was. Fleiss didn't strike him as being that sort. "In that case, sir, I'd ask you to address your men and inform them of their new situation, and that they would be best served co-operating — I'd like to avoid any more unpleasantness."

"Further unpleasantness, as you say, would not be desirable. I will instruct my crew to follow your orders from here onwards."

The solemnity of the occasion, and the strange mix of relief and satisfaction that Baxter felt, was shattered by the appearance of Mrs Sears, still in her tweed travelling dress. She bustled onto the bridge, tutting at Mr Sears who followed in her wake, and jabbed an accusatory finger at Baxter.

"And what exactly do you mean, Mr Baxter, by appearing in front of my daughters — *both of them* — in an undressed state?"

CHAPTER FIFTEEN

"I'd give anything to see the looks on the lads' faces when they wake up to us off their port quarter," Baxter overheard Hicks saying just after they had dropped anchor about a mile from HMS *Astute*. They were still inside Uruguay's territorial waters, but far enough from shore that he hoped they could avoid too much attention from any observers.

"Those lazy blighters won't believe their eyes," Harry said. Jack just nodded sagely. The two errant members of the original boarding party had been found fast asleep in a supply locker. Baxter suspected they had been sleeping off a drunken evening and had been kept well away from him by their comrades until they'd fully recovered. He couldn't fault them, in truth — they'd followed his orders and kept out of sight.

"Won't believe what they missed," Hicks went on cheerfully. "And what old —"

"Silence there, lads," Pearson said, his gashed cheek red and swollen. Baxter was thankful the petty officer had intervened so he didn't have to. He guessed what the seaman had been about to say, as he'd already heard similar from others. *Brassneck Baxter swam ten miles then stormed a German warship by himself.* It was nonsense, of course, but it should die off of its own accord relatively soon.

Baxter feigned not hearing what was being said as he swept the sea to port. It was still dark, but soon the rising sun would flood the bay with light and, he hoped, pick out HMS *Astute* still lying at anchor. Piriápolis was a scattering of light to the northeast. As far as he'd been able to tell, the resort town didn't have much in the way of a fishing industry, and this was borne out by the lack of any activity along its beach. It was about the time that men who earned their living from the sea would have been getting ready to put out, particularly on such a beautifully calm day. They'd be safe from close inspection, then. Anyone staring out into the gleaming morning would just be able to make out a medium-sized liner flying a Union Jack that Baxter's crew had found in the ship's flag locker, along with a range of other belligerent and neutral nations' and Imperial German and *Kaiserliche Marine* ensigns.

They had also recovered a trove of other information that confirmed that, while she may have claimed to be SS *San Francisco*, she in fact had been the SS *Ludovic* of the Hamburg-Amerika Line and was now SMS *Ludovic*, an armed merchant cruiser of the Kaiser's fleet. Baxter had felt a profound sense of relief when they found her original papers, the orders attaching her to the Navy, and sundry other documents that he suspected contained her orders. He hadn't seen anything that looked like a codebook, which the Naval Intelligence Division would kill for.

"I'll be bloody glad to get some of these German lads off the barky, sir," Pearson said quietly as the liner was secured in her anchorage. "Captain seems all right, but some of them are right hard cases."

Baxter couldn't help but agree. Fleiss had been as good as his word, requiring his officers to submit their surrender and informing the crew that they were now prisoners. Baxter had kept armed RN bluejackets and Nielsen's crew moving around the ship as much as possible, to keep an eye on things, but also to convince the prisoners that he had a lot more men at his disposal than he actually did. It seemed to have worked. After some consideration, Baxter had decided not to inform the engineering room crew or the stokers, given they were in a position to do some real damage, and operated in a place far removed from the bridge crew. Thankfully, there wasn't a change of watch during the short journey to *Astute*'s anchorage, and any man who did stick his head out was quietly taken into custody. As he'd suspected, most of the seamen were actually employees of the passenger line, and while they may have volunteered to remain aboard as the ship adopted a more martial aspect, they were not fighting men.

Despite these precautions and assurances, it had been a nervous couple of hours as they made their way back north, and it was only as Baxter made out the much lower, leaner shape of the scout cruiser against the dun landscape that he really began to relax. "Make to *Astute*, Pearson," he said. "Report ship in our hands, and request immediate reinforcement."

"Very good, sir," Pearson said.

"And have the launch brought alongside — I suspect I'm about to be summoned."

Baxter leant against the bridge railing as the signal lamp clattered. He'd snatched some sleep, in between trying to avoid Mrs Sears (who had been convinced but barely mollified that there had been exigent circumstances when her daughters had stumbled across him in a state of undress) and dealing with the sundry problems of having taken a prize. There wasn't an immediate response from *Astute*. The crew seemed to be asleep, no doubt only maintaining a harbour watch while the men got some well-earned rest, but those men on watch should have been more alert. As Baxter and his men had just taught the *Kaiserliche Marine*, being in neutral waters was not a guarantee of safety.

Baxter raised his glasses and swept them over the cruiser and the coastline beyond, mostly to disguise his scowl of irritation.

Finally, he saw a stir of activity on the bridge and then along the deck as bluejackets came out to stare at this strange apparition emerging from the light morning mist.

He saw the cruiser's signal lamp clatter. The signal was supplemented by a hoist of signal flags, which Baxter understood better. Surprisingly, he wasn't being summoned back aboard *Astute* with immediate effect.

As he watched, a file of Marines hurried onto the cruiser's boat deck, hastily buckling on belts and slinging rifles over their shoulders. He watched the boats being lowered and crewed with a certain amount of trepidation, given what he'd seen of the crew's capabilities so far, but was pleasantly surprised that the process was completed with only a modicum of confusion. More than would have been tolerated on a ship in the Grand Fleet, but better than he'd expected. At least no one ended up in the water.

The boats put off and were pulled across the gentle waves towards the liner. Baxter's heart sank as he recognised Simons in the lead whaler. The day had started out so well, but would likely take a turn for the worse.

He didn't let his annoyance show as he turned away from the view and straightened his cap. "Pearson, as soon as the relief arrives, I want you to muster our party. All weapons and ammunition to be accounted for, and every man reported sober, correct, and with their pockets empty. Am I clear?"

"Very clear, sir."

"Carry on."

Baxter waited on the bridge. He knew that it could be viewed as being petty, not greeting the new arrival as he came aboard, but he also didn't want to leave the bridge without an officer on duty. From his vantage point at the ship's apex he heard the whalers coming alongside, one of them crunching into the liner's side and no doubt scraping her already abused paintwork, and a moment later the rumble of boots as the Marines came aboard, accompanied by staccato orders from the sergeant in command of the section and then the slightly less disciplined movements of bluejackets swarming aboard. He heard Simons demand to know where 'the officer commanding' was and Pearson directing him to the bridge.

Baxter came to attention and offered a formal salute as Simons came up onto the bridge. The lieutenant, on the other hand, took a moment to glance around. "Well, I have to say, this is a lot nicer than our bridge," he said nonchalantly as he flicked a return salute. "I can see why you didn't want to come down."

Simons walked to the polished brass railing and rested his hands on it, clearly trying to emulate the stance and attitude he'd seen other officers adopt, then looked again at the well-made fittings, everything more comfortable and made to a higher standard than the plain naval fittings. "Bit of a glance at how the other side live, eh?"

Baxter kept his peace. He'd served on warships that had prized luxury — well, the officers' comfort, anyway — above practicality of construction. But then, he'd been in the service longer than Simons, and he'd also been on Russian warships that dated from the last century.

"Well, what do I need to sort out here then, eh?" Simons asked.

"We have most of the crew in custody, but until you arrived we were certainly outnumbered if not outgunned. The captain has given us his formal surrender, but the engine room crew remain unaware of this fact. They should probably be taken into custody as quickly as possible."

"Yes, yes," Simons said, his tone testy. "Well, we have more than enough men to take care of that. Take your men and return to *Astute*. Lieutenant Commander Sitwell expects a report from you immediately."

Who was in command had been weighing on Baxter's mind. Gregson was old-school, inflexible, and a stickler for the way things should be done. He would not take kindly to Baxter's somewhat cavalier approach to Uruguay's neutrality. Sitwell was a different kettle of fish, younger, and with the aggressive mindset that was better suited to the command of a fast hunter like the scout cruiser.

"Understood, Mr Simons," Baxter said, unable to bring himself to call the lieutenant 'sir' despite his temporary elevation to first officer. He headed for the companionway, but paused at the top. "Word of advice? Try not to antagonise Mrs Sears."

With that, he clattered down the steps and away, ignoring Simons' startled exclamation and demands for more information.

There was a palpable change in mood aboard *Astute* as Baxter and his tired but triumphant sailors returned. There was a jauntiness in the bluejackets' step that hadn't been there before, and there was even a rapidly silenced cheer when the boarding party reported back aboard.

The party mustered on the main deck, all doing their best to look sober and correct, and all barely suppressing tired grins as Pearson took the roll call before turning to Baxter. "All present and correct, sir."

Baxter nodded, surveying the line of men. "Good work, lads. I'll see if I can organise an extra tot of rum."

The grins weren't suppressed at all now. Baxter straightened up. "Carry on, men," he said, and felt a certain amount of pride as the men fell out. They would return to their messes and their normal duties, hopefully after some rest, but they would be known from today onwards as the men who, outnumbered by far, had taken a German ship almost entirely by stealth, without a single shot being fired. Even if the capture was quietly forgotten about, brushed under the carpet to avoid international embarrassment, the lower decks would remember. Even when the fleets finally clashed on the open seas and if the war dragged on long enough for grander legends to be forged, some men would remember this moment.

Baxter watched them go, then turned on his heel and went to make his report. He found Lieutenant Commander Sitwell in the wardroom, sitting at the long dining table in front of a stack of books and ledgers. The ship's acting commander looked as tired as Baxter felt, though their trials were different. Baxter came to attention in front of the table, peaked cap tucked under his arm.

"Take a seat, Mr Baxter," Sitwell said, not looking up from the sheaf of messages he was reading but at least doing him the courtesy of not ignoring him until he was finished. Baxter pulled out a chair and sat, and a moment later Hancock appeared at his shoulder with a steaming mug that smelled wonderfully of freshly ground coffee.

"One of the benefits of a stop on the South America coast," Sitwell said as he finally looked up and saw Baxter taking a gulp. "Though you've found a way to make our stay ... uncomfortable, shall we say?"

"Yes, sir," Baxter said. "I felt that it was justified, given British citizens were being held prisoner aboard."

Sitwell sat back, toying with a pencil as he regarded Baxter. "Tell me everything."

Baxter followed that order as best he could, though he did leave out some of the detail that wasn't really pertinent to the outcome of the operation (such as his suspicion that Harry and Jack had been found stone-drunk long after it had concluded). Sitwell remained impassive throughout, beyond leaning forward and steepling his fingers as he listened.

"And your assessment of German intentions?" he asked, once Baxter had concluded his report with the formal surrender.

"Given the amount of coal and other supplies, I think it likely that they were going to try to resupply von Speer's squadron. There was far too much aboard even for an attempt to run the blockade back to Germany." Baxter briefly considered leaving it there, as he knew he needed to be circumspect about how much he knew of such matters, but he decided it was important Sitwell had the full picture. "I also understand, from what I heard in Montevideo, that German merchants had been engaged by German agents here to procure such supplies."

"By Mr Lewisham, yes — his letter reached me, and he said the same thing when he visited me last night."

Baxter didn't let his relief at that show. As the official arm of NID in Montevideo, Lewisham's involvement would give at least some cover to Baxter's actions, and it was helpful to know he had carried through on keeping *Astute* informed.

"We did also recover a lot of papers, sir, which I have had sealed ready to be transferred to Mr Lewisham."

"No codebooks?" Sitwell asked, almost wistfully. While wireless telegraphy was a relatively new phenomenon, the desire to know the enemy's secret signals was an old one. It would be quite a coup for any ship, although not one that could ever be formally recognised.

"Alas, no, sir."

Sitwell sat back again, not quite masking his disappointment, then his tone became very careful. "And Mr Littleton ordered the operation?"

Baxter experienced brief indecision. He had no way of knowing what Littleton had told the commander, or indeed anyone else, about their exchange in the launch's little cabin. He could very well have been claiming credit for the whole thing, or he could have been hedging his bets in case it had become a disaster. Either way, Baxter had no desire to get into a war of words and exchanged accusations with a brother officer, even if he had little time for the man personally or professionally. He had more than enough bitter experience of that sort of thing from his younger days. "We conferred and agreed a course of action, sir," he said after a moment.

Sitwell nodded, apparently satisfied. "I'm inclined to agree with your assessment," he said, his voice suddenly brisk. "I'll want a full written report at your earliest convenience."

"Very good, sir."

"If I might interject," said Lewisham from the doorway, after coughing to announce his presence, "I think it would be better if there was no written record of this operation."

Sitwell looked up, glowering at the intelligence officer. Lewisham looked fresher than any of them, despite the fact he had clearly been active through the night and was old enough to be a retired naval officer. He was dressed in civilian clothes, though there was enough of a military cut to them that he didn't look out of place in the wardroom. "If I may, sir?" he asked, gesturing to a chair and then sinking into it gratefully. Although he was a guest aboard and had no legal authority over anyone, his manner made it clear that he was a man who should be listened to, and if not obeyed, then his advice taken.

"I think it better that this whole matter is quietly forgotten about," Lewisham went on, putting his stout cane between his knees and resting his crossed hands on it. "Officially, anyway. The legalities of the matter aside, it has the potential to embarrass His Majesty's government at a time when relations with neutral neighbours are being strained by the necessities of blockading Germany's imports."

"What would you suggest then, Mr Lewisham? We send her to the bottom?"

Sitwell's question had been sharp with sarcasm, but the intelligence officer appeared to give it serious consideration before shaking his head. "No, no. I think there might still be some use to be had out of her, and there might yet be secrets for her to give up. I do want her out of these waters, and swiftly. Mr Baxter chose his anchorage well, but it's only a matter of time before someone notices her and puts everything together."

"I would like some of that excess coal Mr Baxter mentioned — our bunkers are low, and it would save buying some here."

"I would advise making all haste to make the transfer so we can get her on her way," Lewisham said. While he was careful to couch it as advice, it was clear that this should be considered an instruction. "I would further suggest she goes somewhere out of the way, at least to begin with — down to the Falklands, perhaps?"

"There is the matter of the civilians aboard — I imagine they would prefer to be ashore as soon as possible so they can make arrangements for onwards travel," Baxter said. He wasn't a man who was afraid of much, but the thought of further interaction with an aggravated Mrs Sears filled him with dread.

Lewisham smoothed his moustache. "I think it best that there is no sign that SMS *Ludovic* was ever here — we don't know how much the crew told the legation about their prisoners, and if they were to appear on shore there may be some concerns raised. By all means, put them ashore in Argentina. Your prisoners will need to be transported to the Falklands."

Sitwell rubbed his forehead. "We can accommodate some prisoners aboard *Astute* — best not to have them all on one vessel."

"Will the two ships travel in company, sir?" Baxter asked. It was an impertinent question, he knew, but Sitwell didn't seem to mind.

"Not if we want the incriminating evidence away from here — we sustained more damage than previously thought. Not enough to require proper harbour facilities, but Larkin wants to spend more time in sheltered waters to make sure we are shipshape and watertight. He asked for five days, the blackguard, and I gave him four."

Baxter kept a straight face. He didn't doubt that the engineering commander actually only wanted three days, and the amused glint in the commander's eyes indicated he knew this as well.

"That will mean *Ludovic* running unescorted down to the Falklands," Lewisham said.

"Not really," Baxter said, inspiration coming to him. "SS *San Francisco* will be making the journey unescorted, but as she's a neutral that shouldn't be a problem."

"Well, the Imperial German Navy did put a lot of work into preparing *Ludovic*'s disguise — it would be a shame not to use it," Lewisham said, a slow smile warping his walrus moustache. "Almost rude, really."

"*Kassel* at least will know that's just a disguise," Sitwell pointed out gravely, threatening to throw cold water on the idea.

"Assuming she's still in the area, it will take them a while to realise the ship has been taken," Lewisham pointed out.

Sitwell still didn't look convinced, then shrugged. "You'll have to stick to coastal waters; unless they've got Germany's answer to you aboard, Baxter, they won't want to risk being seen trying anything in international waters."

Baxter nodded, though he was surprised at how pleased he felt that he'd been confirmed as having charge of the prize — or would at least be along for the journey, he reminded himself.

"Well, gentlemen, as usual in the service, we have a lot to do and very little time in which to do it. Mr Baxter, you've had a long night and look dead on your feet — are you fit to return to *Ludovic* and take command?"

Despite the restorative cup of coffee, Baxter knew he was exhausted. His body ached from the exertions of the previous day — the feast of coal and then his swim to the launch — not to mention the release of tension when they had finally pulled off the capture. He wouldn't admit to that, though — he'd pushed through longer, harder days.

"I'm fit for duty, sir," he said calmly.

"Very good — return aboard at once and relieve Mr Simons. We'll need as much coal as we can transfer, not to mention fresh provender, and we'll transfer half the prisoners."

"If I may ask, sir, how many men will be assigned?"

Sitwell grinned. "Not as many as you'll need, though I will give you as many Jollies as possible to keep your prisoners in check."

Baxter had expected that answer. It had been a long time since a Royal Navy ship had had to man a prize, probably not since the struggle against the slavers in the last century. *Astute* would need as many of her crew as possible in order to remain an effective fighting machine, which meant Baxter would only get a handful of men. He'd deal with any problems from that when they came.

Lewisham gestured to the valise case of papers Baxter had brought across. "If I might beg your indulgence a while longer, Commander, I will go through this treasure trove and see if there is anything we need to communicate to Admiral Sturdee — I'll want to send some dispatches with Mr Baxter, with your permission."

Baxter didn't let his weariness show as he got up and came to attention. "With your permission, sir, I'll return and make preparations for offloading."

"Carry on, Mr Baxter."

CHAPTER SIXTEEN

A day later, SS *San Francisco* — as she was disguised — was seen making her way south along Argentina's coast, riding through a moderate swell at a brisk pace, her three funnels leaving behind a pall of black smoke. Her sides and decks were clean and she went unencumbered by deck cargo.

Baxter took a certain amount of satisfaction at the state of his command. She may not have been armed in any way, beyond the Marines' rifles and a small stock of small-arms provided for the bluejackets in case of emergency, but she was a beautiful vessel in her way, and remarkably fast now that she had shed so much of her unaccustomed cargo. It had taken a lot to get her shipshape — much of the coal had disappeared into *Astute*'s bunkers or had been used to top up the liner's fuel. Some of the fresh food had also gone to the cruiser, denuded as she was after the journey across the Atlantic and the spoilage of much of her supplies along the way. The crew had worked like champions, including the men who had been with him for the boarding. They at least had had some rest before the work began in earnest.

"The men certainly seemed delighted when we put the coal over the side," Lieutenant Yates commented. It was almost as though the young officer, Baxter's second-in-command aboard *Ludovic*, had read his mind. Yates was the fifth officer, which also meant that he was *Astute*'s torpedo officer. That made him available for general duties, as it was commonly felt that the two submerged tubes would rarely, if ever, be used.

Baxter smiled. "Trust me when I tell you this, Yates — once you've carried enough of that bloody stuff, you get to hate it.

Getting rid of the surplus like that will have been quite a tonic for the men."

They'd thrown a few hundredweight over the side once the liner was underway. The transfer of coal and prisoners had gone on well into the evening, the men sweating even as the temperature dropped. Lewisham, who seemed to be a good-natured man normally, had become increasingly irascible until he had all but threatened Sitwell with the full weight of the Naval Intelligence Division and whatever influence they might have with the Admiralty in order to get him to discontinue the operation and get *Ludovic* on her way, and whatever was left that wasn't needed went over the side. Although nobody wanted to admit it, none of them wanted to risk resupplying the German cruiser or any raider if the liner fell into enemy hands again.

"I will take your word for it, sir." Yates, while almost as new to the service as the late Mr Webb, was urbane and self-confident, and Baxter found himself warming to the man — mostly because he actually seemed to be competent, and took his duties seriously.

"Are we shipshape and Bristol fashion, Mr Yates?" Baxter asked formally. The lieutenant had been put in charge of the parties organised to clean the ship, ensuring the prisoners who had remained aboard were both properly secured and provided for, and seeing to the comfort of the Sears family and the merchant seamen.

"We are, sir. Captain Nielsen and his men all volunteered, as you'd expect, to help run the ship. I have supplemented the engine room and stoker watches, and if I might be so bold, Captain Nielsen seems like a capable and seamanlike officer — he could stand a watch. It will mean long watches for us, obviously — though I for one am up to the challenge."

Baxter fought down the urge to yawn massively at the mention of the need to keep long watches. "I'll think on it. The other civilians?"

"Safely and happily ensconced in first-class accommodation," Yates said, then coughed into his hand. "Mrs Sears is ... formidable, and was most insistent on both the cabins having the necessary state of cleanliness. Every admiral's steward in the fleet would be proud of the job Hancock did. We've also prepared a cabin for you, sir, also in first class. Hancock is waiting there to show you to your accommodation."

He almost protested that he would be quite content in the captain's quarters or one of the other officer's cabins, but the last two days of hard work was finally catching up to him. "Wake me in four hours."

"Very good, sir."

Baxter headed down, past the boat deck that scant hours ago he had been fighting German officers on. He knew there was much he still needed to do. For a start, he wanted to interview those enemy officers who had remained aboard, and arrangements would need to be made to ensure the package of dispatches addressed to Vice-Admiral Sturdee from Lewisham were delivered. He reflected on his last meeting with the intelligence officer, a quick exchange when he'd come aboard *Ludovic* to hand over the wax-sealed package in person.

Baxter had only met the man a few times but thought he had a sense of the sort of person he was. Steady. Imperturbable. The sort of man an enemy operative would find impossible to read. Lewisham had been bright-eyed with excitement yesterday, as they met in the liner's first-class lounge. He didn't say what he had found in his examination of Fleiss's papers, but his teeth had gleamed below his moustache as he grinned broadly. "By God, Baxter, we may have got him!" he'd exclaimed. "This gives us what we need to run von Spee down! You must get this message to Sturdee as quickly as possible."

Baxter had promised to make good time — he didn't want to be cooped up on an unarmed passenger ship and responsible for the lives of British civilians any longer than he had to be.

He paused once he was on the first-class deck, raising a hand to Hancock who was hovering by a hatch at the far end, then leant on the rail and looked out to sea. He was on the port side, facing the open Atlantic and the cool breeze that came off it.

"The war must seem very far away," Pippa Sears commented as she joined him at the rail. He glanced over and saw her settling a remarkably sensible hat over her golden hair. As before, she was dressed in travelling clothes, a long tweed skirt and close-fitting jacket over a frilled blouse. Baxter, never having mixed much with high or even moderate society beyond his association with the Count and Countess Juneau, had no real sense of civilian fashion but could only assume that this was all in the current style.

Pippa assessed him with cool blue eyes, in a way that suggested she knew what he was thinking. "Do you find me terribly forward, Mr Baxter?" she said after a moment.

"The war *is* very far away, aside from our little part in it," he said, rather than answering her second question. He wasn't much in the mood to discuss the women he'd known, several of whom would make Miss Sears seem like something of a wilting violet.

She nodded, some of the challenge leaving her expression. "We know little, beyond what we have been able to glean from the papers and gossip along the way. Many people seem to think the war is not going well for us. Others say it will all be over by —"

"I wouldn't listen to gossip," he cut in. He was tired of hearing that the war would be over by Christmas. "Or trust the newspapers."

"So you think we'll win?" she asked.

"I can only speak for the Navy, Miss Sears. For all our faults, we're more than a match for the *Kaiserliche Marine*."

She nodded, contemplating his words. "How far away is the war, Mr Baxter? Aside from our corner of it — I must seem presumptuous, taking a little bit of ownership like that. But you must admit, we are a part of it."

"I can't argue with that, although the sooner we can get you ashore, the happier we will all be."

"Are we such an inconvenience?"

"You are at risk," he said flatly, then glanced up at the sun and did his best to estimate where they were in relation to Africa. He pointed out to sea, a little north of east. "The closest action I know about is three thousand miles or so that way, in East Africa. If you go north from there, fighting rages in France, and the Mediterranean will soon become a battleground. Particularly if Italy comes in, or the Ottoman Empire."

Baxter paused, realising just how little he knew about what was going on. At least when he'd been a glorified postman in the dockyards, he'd had a good idea of what was happening, through official channels but also by listening to and occasionally talking with the officers of the ships in for refit before going on to active service. Current newspapers had also been readily available.

"And do you relish this war, Mr Baxter?" Pippa asked. Her tone was serious, and her earnestness made him smile.

"Now, that *is* forward, Miss Sears," he said. "If you'll excuse me, I've had a busy few days and even us doughty men of the navy need our rest."

She gave him a slight smile. "Of course, my apologies for detaining you."

"No apologies needed," he said, pushing away from the rail and heading to his cabin.

That evening, Baxter allowed Hancock to put on 'a little bit of a spread' in the first-class dining lounge. While *Astute* had procured much of the fresh provender the liner had so recently loaded, the canny old steward had managed to ensure enough was kept aside that the officers, crew and passengers of SS *Ludovic* wouldn't be subsisting on dried and tinned goods for the few days it would take them to reach another neutral port.

Baxter, more used to a warship's wardroom, found the experience slightly surreal. *Ludovic* didn't offer quite the same level of luxury as the big Blue Riband ships, like the still-lamented *Titanic*, but her first-class lounge was still beyond the sort of comfort he'd seen afloat or ashore, with the possible exception of *Yaroslavich*'s wardroom. They dined under chandeliers that swayed slightly in the gentle roll. The table was set immaculately, the food prepared by the liner's chef and served by her stewards (overseen by the ever-watchful Hancock).

Baxter wasn't used to hosting this sort of dinner, as the commands he'd held in the past few years had been brief and altogether too busy for such matters. In addition, he was the only RN officer present. Yates had the bridge — as an officer needed to be on watch at all times — and Sitwell hadn't been able to spare him any more commissioned men. The extended Sears family, who had been given the courtesy of bringing their dunnage along when their previous ship, the SS *St Auburn*, had been taken and scuttled, were surprisingly resplendent, and the German officers he had invited were determined to make a display in their full dress uniforms. Klaus Meisner, the former captain in more peaceful days and now technically an *Oberleutnant sur zee*, headed this group of four men. Two were unremarkable, one a portly former merchant sailor who kept glancing nervously at his fellows and occasionally at Baxter, and a sallow youth assigned from *Kassel* who kept his eyes down throughout.

Unfortunately, the group also included *Leutnant* Leiter, who Baxter would rather have left with *Astute* and who maintained a simmering silence throughout the first two courses of a delicately fried local fish he couldn't identify and then a consommé.

"I must extend my compliments to your chef, *Herr* Meisner," Mr Sears declared as he finished the thin soup with every sign of relish. "Particularly given the limited ingredients available to him."

Meisner inclined his head politely. His chosen profession was one that required civility at all times, and that habit seemed to linger even now. Before he could say anything, though, Leiter interjected.

"And particularly given that he is being held prisoner unjustly, and forced to work in the galley!" the man snapped. His face was flushed, though Baxter suspected that was at least partially to do with the number of glasses of champagne that he'd seen away.

Meisner started to say something in German, maintaining the same diffident tone Baxter had heard from him before. The sailor seemed like a decent sort, but the fact he rather than Fleiss had been left aboard was another problem for Baxter.

Meisner might have been Leiter's commander when the ship had been operating as a liner, but Fleiss had shown the sort of steel naval officers sometimes needed to keep young hotheads in line. Leiter opened his mouth to interrupt, but subsided when Baxter cleared his throat.

"*Herr* Leiter," he said, "you were invited as a courtesy, and in the hope that we could enjoy a cordial meal as fellow officers and sailors. While our nations are indeed at war, I hope that we can still offer each other that courtesy."

Leiter glared angrily at him, but then subsided. "My apologies, Mr Baxter," he said to the half-finished bowl of soup.

A silence settled over the table after that, though in truth the meal had hardly begun as a cheerful affair. The quiet was only broken by the clink of cutlery and the occasional murmured request to pass the salt. The soup was followed by a roast leg of Argentine beef, a dish altogether more to Baxter's liking.

"It is a shame that our two nations have to be at war," Henrietta Finlay said suddenly, her clear voice cutting through the tense silence. "We have so much in common, and war seems to be such a horrible thing to pit men against each other."

Leiter glanced up, fury in his eyes, and Baxter also caught the pimply German midshipman looking at the young Englishwoman, with an altogether different expression. He suppressed a smile, but was glad Finlay didn't catch the way the officer looked at his wife — that was the sort of complication he didn't need aboard.

"I will drink to that," Meisner said with surprising feeling as he raised his glass of red wine Hancock had told him was a pinot noir. "I have had the pleasure of sailing with, indeed fighting alongside, many men of both England and France over the years, and rarely regretted it."

Baxter raised his own glass, thinking as he did about the men of the Imperial German Navy that he'd known and liked over the years. It hadn't stopped him prosecuting this new war against them to the fullest of his ability, but he would be the first to admit that he didn't relish it.

"A strange notion, for one of His Imperial Majesty's officers," Finlay said, though his tone was curious rather than accusatory.

"And one, unless I miss my guess, that Mr Baxter shares," Meisner said. Baxter kept his peace, watching to see if he would need to bring the meal to an abrupt close or not. The older German was rising in his estimation, revealing a thoughtfulness somewhat at odds with his bluff presentation. "We do not hate each other, Mr Finlay, despite the vitriol being thrown around by those in both our home countries. We are, after all, professionals, and I truly hope that this war can come to an end."

"With a German victory, of course," Baxter said, smiling slightly as he sipped his wine. He didn't have much of a taste for the stuff, despite the time he'd spent with Russian officers who'd seemed to operate on a cocktail of vodka and champagne, but even he could tell that this was an expensive vintage.

"Oh, indeed," Meisner said, the grave words undermined by his own grin. "Just as, I am sure, you are hoping for an English victory!"

Baxter thought about that for a moment. He had to admit, he didn't know much of what this war was really about. He'd been in Zanzibar in the months during which Europe had seemed to stagger without much volition towards the conflict.

"I certainly hope that Britain and her allies come out of it unscathed," he said, mostly for form's sake. "And who doesn't like to win?"

"You navy chaps really are peculiar," Finlay said. He was clearly slightly discomfited that he was the only man of fighting age not in uniform, even if he had been on his way home to do his duty.

"You said you fought alongside British and French sailors, *Herr* Meisner," Baxter said, reaching for any conversation gambit that would distract the other diners — his guests, technically, though it was hard to see himself as the ship's captain, given how short his tenure would be. "The Boxer Rebellion?"

Meisner inclined his head again, a sort of seated bow that would have marked him out as being from an older generation if the silver in his beard and hair hadn't. "And yourself, Mr Baxter?"

"A bit before my time," he said. "But not *long* before my time."

"Ah, I remember that well!" Sears put in cheerfully, then had the good grace to blush slightly as he added, "I had business interests in the area, which were quite alarmingly affected."

The conversation, to Baxter's relief, flowed from there. Mrs Sears didn't say much, and both younger women only interjected occasionally — Henrietta, he suspected, because she felt slightly embarrassed by her outburst, and Pippa because she seemed to find the whole thing quite dull.

Pippa caught his look, eyes unreadable except for a flash of amused disdain. Rather than look away, he held her gaze and raised his glass to her along the length of the table.

While the evening — they were dining at a time more suitable to the civilian day rather than mid-afternoon as was customary in the service — flowed on and became more convivial, Baxter kept his peace and drank as little as possible. Leiter's mood didn't improve and he remained stubbornly silent.

The chef had managed to scrape together six courses, and had already offered his abject apologies for not having the inventiveness to do more with the ingredients. While several of the dishes were quite familiar, others were improvisations with local ingredients, and they finished on a jelly concoction with a range of fruits.

The conversation showed no signs of drying up, though Mrs Sears was making pointed comments about the ladies withdrawing that both daughters duly ignored. Leiter did excuse himself after a little while, glaring pointedly at the two younger German officers until they both followed him. Meisner, Finlay and Mr Sears had fallen into something approaching a friendly discussion about commerce and the law that held little interest for Baxter. This also seemed to be the case for Pippa and Henrietta, who finally allowed their mother to chivvy them back towards the relative luxury of their cabin.

"Gentlemen," Baxter said to the three men reclining comfortably around the long dining table. "If you'll excuse me, it's about time that I relieve Mr Yates."

There was a murmur of approbation as Baxter rose, signalling to Hancock that he should follow. The steward detached himself from the wall, where he had waited silently in case he was needed, and followed his commander out of the first-class lounge. "Sir?"

"Has the crew's dinner been seen to as well?" Baxter asked. As he didn't have a quartermaster aboard, Hancock was acting in that capacity as well as looking after the officers.

"Indeed, sir. They have enjoyed *Ludovic*'s largesse — though there were some complaints that the rum ration was cognac."

"Sailors don't like change, Hancock."

"No, sir, they do not. And they do like their rum."

The steward withdrew as Sears emerged on deck, a balloon of brandy in one hand and a lit cigar in the other. "I do like to take the evening air and an excellent repast," he declared airily. "Cigar, Mr Baxter?"

"I don't indulge — thank you, though."

"I imagine you're looking forward to being shot of us civilians being under your feet?" Sears went on before Baxter could move away.

He paused and thought about that. "I'm looking forward to you and your family being out of harm's way, Mr Sears," he said truthfully. "A war is no place for civilians."

Sears glanced at him in surprise. "We seem quite safe just now — I rather thought that was the point of running under American colours."

Baxter rested his hands on the railing as he stared out to sea. "That is the intention, and there's a good chance the ruse will work. But out there is a German cruiser, and she's almost certainly heading south as well to try to link up with von Spee."

"And stranger things happen at sea," Sears said placidly. "Mr Lewisham did explain why we didn't go ashore in Montevideo or Buenos Aires, but it all sounded very cloak-and-dagger to me. In truth, my lady wife will not be content until we are on British soil again."

"I'm afraid I won't be able to arrange that, sir, but we should be able to touch somewhere with a shipping link to Britain. Bahía Blanca, perhaps."

Sears sipped pensively at his brandy. "If I had my way, Mr Baxter, we'd stay there until this has all blown over — the sea doesn't seem terribly safe just now, despite the best efforts of you chaps. But Mrs Sears pines for England's green fields, and young Charles is keen to taste war before it's all over."

"He'll have his chance, Mr Sears," Baxter said.

"You think it will go on for some time? Henrietta is quite distressed at the notion of her husband going off to war."

"I merely mean to say that we will not be a cause for further delay to your journey, Mr Sears," Baxter said diplomatically.

"Are you a family man, Mr Baxter? Children?"

"Not to the best of my knowledge." He thought back to the women he had known, had become entangled with. Connie, the American mercenary he'd shared more than just danger and excitement with in the Italo-Ottoman War. There'd been the woman when he was on the North America Station, not long after the turn of the century, who he barely remembered but who was the root cause of his dismissal from the Royal Navy, through no fault of her own. He felt an old familiar stab of pain, dulled by time and distance, when he thought about Ekaterina, about the letter that still lay unopened at the bottom of his ditty bag. He'd never really thought about having a family before, given his life — but she was the only woman he could possibly imagine such a thing with, and the idea was beyond preposterous.

Sears barked a laugh. "Quite right, man in your profession. I dote on my two, of course. Couldn't be more different, but they're the apples of my eye."

Baxter realised what Sears was trying to say to him. "I'll see them safely ashore in one, maybe two days from now, Mr Sears. And I intend to see the oceans swept clean of the enemy."

It was an idiotic thing to say, of course. Perhaps he'd had a bit too much of the fine wine. Sears seemed to appreciate the sentiment, at least.

"Well, I really should stop distracting you from your duties, Captain," he said, reaching out to shake Baxter's hand. His grip was surprisingly firm. "Good evening to you."

CHAPTER SEVENTEEN

The following morning brought a plume of smoke on the northern horizon. Baxter and Yates observed it from the bridge's starboard wing, looking back along the liner's length.

"Is it *Astute*, sir?" Yates asked, lowering his glasses and rubbing his eyes.

Baxter's own eyes felt gritty. His whole body did — he and the lieutenant had been standing watch for about four hours each, and while the liner had been swabbed and polished to a military level of precision, somehow there was still coal dust on the air. He was well used to the privations of a maritime life, sometimes going days without sleep and living with a minimum level of comfort. It was ironic, therefore, that the comfort of his accommodations — a full suite of rooms — somehow made the task he was undertaking harder. Getting up for this watch was a struggle when it involved pulling himself out of a comfortable bed rather than from a cot in a cramped cabin.

"Hard to say," he replied after staring at the distant ship for a couple more moments. It was still little more than a fleck of grey beneath its canopy of smoke. It didn't help that the two cruisers he knew to be in these waters were of a similar size and class. "If she is, Larkin managed the repairs far faster than expected."

The smoke, though... *Astute* used a combination of coal and oil, a combination that some officers felt was the future while others still pined for the days of sail. *Kassel*, unless she varied from her sister ships, would be coal-fired, making for a darker plume. "I think it's the bloody German," he said.

"Some of our prisoners seem to think the same," Yates noted, pointing aft towards the quarterdeck where Leiter and the other German officers were excitedly pointing astern and slapping each other on the back. "A definite case of counting their chickens before they're hatched."

Baxter scowled, regretting giving the German prisoners liberty to move about certain parts of the ship and take the air on deck. Leaning over the railing, he spotted Pearson on the boat deck. "Pearson! Round up some Jollies and invite the German gentlemen to return to their quarters!" he called out, then turned his attention back to the following ship. He didn't want to think of it as 'pursuing', not yet anyway. Not until he had confirmed his suspicion.

The cruiser remained steadfastly behind them for the rest of the morning, gaining very slightly as Baxter didn't order an increase in speed. While his fuel supplies were still plentiful, there was no point burning through them or taxing the machinery unless he absolutely had to, and he wanted to see what the unidentified vessel would do. He passed the word to the wireless telegraphy office to keep a sharp ear out for any signals.

Pearson came onto the bridge towards midday, saluting smartly. "Beggin' your pardon, sir, but the German gentlemen are demanding to speak with you."

Baxter returned the salute. "Which ones, Pearson?" he asked, though he could guess who it would be.

"Mr Leiter, sir, and his — well — his followers, I suppose you'd call them."

"Very well, Pearson. Mr Yates, you have the bridge."

The German officers had been lodged in the second-class cabins, under unobtrusive but visible Royal Marine guard. Baxter found them in the second-class lounge, which unfortunately looked aft towards the only other ship to share this surprisingly lonely stretch of sea. The smoke cloud was little more than a smudge, closer than the horizon now and an ever-present reminder that *Kassel* might come on them at any moment.

"Now look here, Baxter," Leiter said as soon as he stepped into the lounge. The space wasn't quite as luxurious as its counterpart on the deck above, but still nicely appointed, and the younger German officers lounged around in deep red leather armchairs, most of them with a drink in hand or close by. "We demand —"

"You demand nothing, *Herr* Leiter," Baxter said mildly. His previous encounters with the German-American had taught him what to expect and he didn't let the man's brusque, contemptuous manner get under his skin. He held Leiter's stare until the prisoner looked away, obviously discomfited and somewhat taken aback that his accustomed bluster had been punctured. "Now, what can I do for you?"

Leiter took a breath and with a visible effort mastered himself. His tone when he spoke again was slightly strangled, but he at least tried to match Baxter's evenness. "Sir. It's pretty clear to everyone — and any neutral observer would agree — that you seized this vessel illegally, while it was in neutral waters. While it's a well-known fact that you Brits don't like to give up anything when you've got your hands on it, we dem… we would *like* to petition that we and the crew at least are released as being illegally detained."

The whole thing came out in a rush, clearly rehearsed in advance. Leiter's square, strong-jawed face had a slight look of distaste as he finished speaking, as though he'd bitten into a lime, and Baxter guessed he knew he'd rushed it and sounded somewhat pompous and desperate at the same time.

It was disconcerting, hearing an enemy speak fluent English and with more of an American accent than a German one. That didn't put Baxter off his own pace. "I'll leave the matter of legality to lawyers and judges, *mein Herr*. Though it doesn't escape me that, despite the fact this ship had clearly been commissioned as a naval vessel, you were masquerading as a neutral and keeping undeclared prisoners in your holds. No one's coming out of this smelling of roses." He held his hand up to forestall an angry interjection, guessing that Leiter was about to berate him for using the exact same tactics. "I have my orders, Mr Leiter, and I intend to follow them."

Baxter's gaze swept the room. He guessed not all of the officers spoke English, but enough of them did to be able to follow at least some of what was being said, and those who did not were clearly picking up on the mood.

"Well, sir, if you will not see reason, perhaps you'd honour the custom of parole?" Leiter said.

Baxter raised an eyebrow. The idea of officers being released, on their word that they would not fight again until an enemy officer of a similar rank had been released, had been the subject of much discussion in messes and clubs since the war had broken out. No one quite seemed to have worked out how to approach this modern, technological conflict. "This is not our grandfathers' war, Mr Leiter, and I doubt any of us can expect anything other than a prison camp when captured."

"You would deny us the opportunity of honour and glory in the service of the *Reich*!" one of the other officers burst out. "Unjustly so!"

Baxter gave him a contemptuous look but didn't bother to say what he thought of that particular notion. The young officer subsided back into his chair, and Baxter turned his attention back to Leiter. He briefly considered asking why a man who had obviously lived in the US for some time — may even have been born there — would be so interested in the internecine squabbles of the old world. He wasn't one to pry, though, and he could guess at the range of motives. Leiter no doubt still thought of himself as a German, and clearly had the martial enthusiasm of a man who had never been to war.

"Will that be all, gentlemen?" he asked.

"You know damn well that's *Kassel* behind us!" Leiter snapped, dropping his attempt to be conciliatory. "Pretty soon the boot will be on the other foot, my friend!"

Baxter just glanced at him, then settled his cap back on his head. "Well, as I'm sure you can appreciate, I'm quite a busy man — good day to you."

He stepped back out on deck. It was still fairly warm at this latitude, the men still going about their duties in tropical whites. They were still within Argentina's territorial waters, close enough that they could make a quick dash into a neutral port if *Kassel* or another of the Kaiser's raiders did intercept them. It reminded Baxter somewhat of the long, dreary journey down the west coast of Africa, round the Cape and then up to Madagascar; here at least it wasn't as swelteringly hot or humid. The land was a low, dun smudge to starboard, with a hint of blue mountains in the hazy distance.

He stepped away from the lounge and spotted Pearson hovering nearby. He was the senior petty officer aboard, and like the rest of the ship's command structure was acting above his rank as the direct link between Baxter and the enlisted men, both sailors and Marines. While Yates seemed capable enough, he was still an unknown quantity for Baxter, which made him doubly glad for a PO he knew to be steady. "I want a careful watch on the German officers," he said quietly. "There's a good chance that some of them at least are going to try something rash in the next few days."

"Understood, sir. I'll add some of our boys to the Jollies."

Baxter didn't know where the feeling had come from. There wouldn't be much that the imprisoned officers could do. They were too far from shore for them to swim to land with any real chance of success, and the following ship was too far astern to make swimming to her a realistic prospect. Sabotage, perhaps, or an attempt to steal a boat? The manner in which he had seized the vessel with a handful of men might have given them the idea they could try something similar. He was fully aware that he'd only achieved what he had through complete surprise and the enemy's false sense of security — neither of those were advantages Leiter and his followers had.

What they were, though, was desperate — to do their duty, if nothing else, and to go home as heroes rather than men who had been taken prisoner in the first months of the war. He couldn't blame them for that, but he was going to do his best to see them delivered into captivity at a British harbour, just as he had promised Mr Sears that he would see his family safe ashore in a neutral harbour. He resisted the urge to rub his temples or quietly curse Sitwell for not taking at least one of these problems off his hands.

The latter problem intercepted him as he made his way back towards the bridge. The Sears sisters were taking the air, promenading up and down the deck, while Mrs Sears occupied a deck chair and kept a close eye on them — or rather, on the bluejackets who had found an excuse to be somewhere nearby. She reserved a particularly haughty scowl for him. "Mr Sears tells me, Mr Baxter, that you are planning on abandoning us in some … foreign port."

Baxter sighed inwardly, but Pippa spoke up before he could reply. "You really should refer to him as Captain, Mother," she said, with exaggerated patience.

"Have you been promoted, Mr Baxter?" Henrietta asked excitedly. "You didn't say anything."

He gave both women a small smile, unaccountably grateful for Pippa's interjection. "It's a matter of custom and courtesy, Mrs Finlay. While I remain a lowly lieutenant, I am in command of this vessel. That means that, by custom, I am referred to as 'Captain'."

"A reservist lieutenant, at that," Mrs Sears muttered. It seemed she still hadn't quite forgiven him for the partial nudity he had inadvertently subjected her daughters to.

"As to your question, madam," he said, mustering as much politeness as he could, "my orders are to put you and your dunnage ashore at the earliest convenience, somewhere where you will be able to take ship for Britain."

"And how long before we are ashore in whatever flea-infested fishing village you settle upon, do you anticipate?"

Baxter's jaw muscles tightened. While Mrs Sears had been tolerable company the night before, she had clearly woken and chosen to be as uncivil as possible today. "I anticipate being able to look into Bahía Blanca tomorrow, madam, to see if there are suitable vessels to convey you home."

"Tomorrow!" Henrietta squeaked, and Pippa put an arm around her sister's shoulder. "I had hoped for a few more days at least. I had hoped we could keep sailing forever, well away from that beastly war."

Baxter was slightly taken aback by the display. He had heard of men who had been handed white feathers, sometimes by complete strangers, if they hadn't obviously already signed up.

He guessed Henrietta's attitude had more to do with not wanting to see her husband go off to war.

"Forever sailing like the *Flying Dutchman* would become tedious after a while, Henry dear," Pippa said, then glanced at Baxter. "Though there would be *some* diversions, I'm sure."

Baxter didn't know what to make of that. "Oh, Pip, you do read too much," Henrietta said, then burst into tears.

He was saved from any further engagement by Yates calling down to him from the bridge. With some relief, he took the steps of the companionway two at a time, given there seemed to be some urgency in his second-in-command's shout.

"She's broken out the White Ensign, sir!" Yates declared excitedly when he arrived.

Baxter gave him a cool look. "And you think that means she's *Astute*?" he said, not for the first time wondering about the standards at the Dartmouth naval academy.

Yates opened his mouth, then shut it again. "That was my first thought, sir, but of course it's just as likely to be a *ruse de guerre* on the part of an enemy vessel."

"An astute observation, Mr Yates," Baxter said, more sharply than he'd intended judging from the way the young officer's face coloured slightly.

"Should I make the recognition signal, sir?"

"No," Baxter replied. It occurred to him that *Kassel*'s captain may not yet know that *Ludovic* had been taken, though Baxter guessed the two ships had been due to rendezvous and his opposite number would therefore be suspicious. A hoist of flags or a coded wireless signal might give the game away. "Order an increase in speed to fifteen knots."

"Sir," said Yates, sending the order down to the engine room.

It would take a little while for *Ludovic* to pick up speed, but it was surprising just how quickly the slight increase in the ship's pitch and roll became noticeable as the big engines started to thrust the liner through the waves at a higher speed. Deep below their feet, sweating stokers would be hurling coal into the furnaces to keep the steam pressure up. Theoretically, the liner could go at least five knots faster, but Baxter didn't have a full crew of stokers and didn't want to wear them or the machinery out unnecessarily.

Baxter watched the cruiser through his field glasses, waiting for the corresponding increase in speed. It came sooner than he expected.

"She seems to be keeping pace with us," Yates observed, as he joined Baxter on the bridge wing again. "This ship may have some legs, but whoever that cruiser is, she should be able to outpace us."

Baxter nodded, his mind worrying at why the cruiser wasn't trying to overhaul them. There could be any number of perfectly reasonable answers to that, of course. It could quite easily be Sitwell, trying to keep them in sight and get Baxter to slow to meet him and not wanting to overtax his own machinery. Or indeed it could be *Kassel* trying to run them down but not able to make her top speed if her machinery was worn out and her fuel supplies low. He couldn't help feeling, though, that something else was going on.

"Keep a sharp eye out, men," he ordered the lookouts. There was a real risk, in situations like this, that all attention would be fixed on one vessel, allowing enemy ships to get dangerously close from another direction.

Baxter remained in the wing for a while, staring north through his glasses. The ship behind them was close enough now that he was starting to make out some details. "That's *Kassel*, all right."

"Ship off the starboard quarter!" barked the nearby lookout suddenly, his voice overly loud given both the ship's officers were close at hand. Baxter snapped round and Yates looked like he was about to order action stations.

"Looks like a pleasure boat," Baxter said, as he found the offending vessel in his glasses. She was clearly no threat, a sleek clipper-rigged sailing yacht that seemed to skip over the water with her big sails bellied out. She was a beauty, all right, the sort of vessel he would delight in sailing, and Baxter felt a brief surge of joy at seeing her. She was within a thousand yards or so of the liner, and wasn't making an attempt to close beyond that. He could make out people on her polished foredeck, watching them.

Looking beyond the yacht, Baxter could make out other vessels on the water now. None of them were particularly close, but he guessed they were moving into a more populated section of the coastline and there would by nature be more in the way of sea traffic. Some of them seemed to be interested in the foreign ships transiting their waters, which was natural enough, but could be dangerous. He thought briefly of the confused night in the North Sea, more than a decade ago, when Russian sailors had mistaken British trawlers for Japanese torpedo boats.

That wouldn't happen here, and not just because *Ludovic* was essentially unarmed.

Baxter suddenly realised why the cruiser was trailing behind rather than overhauling them. Why she was resolutely flying a British flag despite the fact her captain must have realised by now that his ruse had failed. She was clearly a combatant vessel abusing neutral waters, and at least giving the appearance of being in pursuit of a vessel flying the flag of a neutral country.

All of this while sailing into waters where they were being watched by any number of Argentine citizens.

"Mr Yates — course adjustments, five points to port and as much speed as the engine room can muster," he said, his voice measured, despite the tension suddenly roiling in his guts.

"Sir?" the lieutenant asked, looking nonplussed. "It's not —"

"Follow your orders, Mr Yates," Baxter said, his voice tight and controlled. The more he thought about it, the more he was convinced of the German captain's intentions, and with that certainty came the strange calm that he often felt when battle was about to be joined — though the key thing now was to avoid any sort of engagement.

Yates clearly wasn't convinced, but he had his orders. "Yes, sir," he said with a salute, and hurried away.

Baxter checked his watch, and looked up at the sky. The sun's position, relative to the ship, was changing as her bows came round onto the new course he had ordered, taking her away from Argentina's coast. He needed distance or darkness, and most of all to be out of sight of any civilian vessels.

The German captain had shown himself to be capable of a deep level of subterfuge, but it was a new low for him to launch an attack while flying a British flag. Would this display be enough for him? Would he chase them until night, and then attack under his own colours? That seemed more likely.

"Mr Yates, you have the bridge. Maintain this course until I order otherwise."

Yates acknowledged his orders as Baxter turned on his heel and went in search of Klaus Meisner.

He found *Ludovic*'s former master taking his ease in the second-class lounge. Baxter had contemplated having him brought up to his own cabin, but the situation required delicate handling — the sort of handling, in fact, that he was not well suited to. But he knew that a peremptory summons into what had once been the preserve of Meisner's passengers would not be a good way to start.

"It seems we have changed course," Meisner said cheerfully. "And picked up speed — I must caution you, *mein Herr*, that these engines are due for an overhaul soon."

"Thank you for your advice," Baxter said politely, as he settled into a chair and accepted a cup of tea from Hancock.

"The regular officers all seem very excited as well. I gather they think it is *Kassel* behind us."

"She is," Baxter said. He'd warmed to the old German officer during the dinner the night before, and had at least some understanding of him. He was a veteran, a man used to command and to combat. No doubt loyal to his *Kaiser* and his *Reich*, but a fundamentally decent man cut from old-fashioned cloth.

"I hope you are not expecting me to inform on my subordinates, were I aware of any escape attempt, or indeed to order them to desist? It is their duty to try to escape, as you refused them parole."

Baxter nodded. "I understand, nor would I ask you to do anything that would go against your conscience and your own duty. I would, however, like to ask what you know of *Kassel*'s captain."

A flicker of distaste passed across the older man's face, almost lost in the whiskers and crow's feet. "*Fregattenkapitän* Neidermeyer? I only met him a few times. He seemed … capable."

Damned with faint praise, Baxter thought. He took a breath and then plunged on, following his instinct that Meisner was an upright man. "I think that *Kapitän* Neidermeyer suspects that *Ludovic* has been taken, and intends to run us down to recapture her, and to achieve this in Argentine waters by flying a British flag."

"What a preposterous notion!" Meisner snapped, anger flaring in his eyes. "You and he have both danced around the edges of what is both legal and decent, but why would anyone undertake such a vile act?"

"He wants everyone to see a ship flying a British flag, looking a lot like a cruiser known to be in these waters. When people become aware that what appears to be an American vessel has been stopped and boarded, then taken away as a prize, they will put it together."

Meisner's angry expression faded as he thought through the consequences of that. He muttered something in German, about the chances of it bringing the US into the war on Germany's side. "It would be a deeply dishonourable act," Meisner said after a moment. "Though I can assure you, Captain, that no man of the German Empire would open fire under false colours, particularly on an unarmed ship. Stop and board you, perhaps. But not that."

Baxter nodded. "It could backfire on the German Empire, should the US find out about the ruse," he pointed out.

Meisner's face crumpled. "It would be a great boon to the *Reich* if they were to succeed, but it is a foolishness, and beyond that would bring terrible dishonour upon our navy and our nation. There is nothing I can do to stop it, if that is what Neidermeyer truly plans, and I cannot in good conscience help you."

Baxter resisted the urge to press the old sailor further. While Meisner hadn't directly admitted his belief that Neidermeyer was capable of such a ploy, he'd said enough to convince Baxter that his suspicions had at least a grounding in reality. It could be, of course, that Meisner was lying to him in order to provoke some form of mistake, but he didn't think so.

As Baxter rose and headed for the door, Meisner spoke again. "None of this would be possible, of course, if you had flown your own colours. Then it would clearly have been a case of a German ship attacking a British one."

Baxter's jaw tightened. "Well, I can't disagree with you, and I intend to fix my blunder in that regard."

CHAPTER EIGHTEEN

Leaving Meisner to his contemplations, Baxter made his way back to the bridge. He didn't hurry, as he didn't want to convey a false impression of panic. The change in course and sudden increase in speed had attracted some attention, and the sailors and Marines on duty were all looking more alert, despite the fact that, being shorthanded, they had been standing double watches.

Back on the bridge, Baxter quickly apprised himself of the situation. "Course sou'sou'east, sir, and seventeen knots," Yates reported. "Engine room reports we should get her up to twenty, but can't promise how long we can sustain it."

"Thank you, Mr Yates," Baxter said briskly. He felt more energised and alert than he had since ... well, since he'd come back from East Africa, in truth. He assessed their position relative to the pursuing ship, checking the time and the height of the sun again. Still very high, but he knew how quickly it would start to disappear.

"If I may, sir..." Yates said quietly, stepping alongside him at the rail. "I'm not entirely certain..."

"Do you not understand your orders, Mr Yates?" Baxter asked, feeling a flare of temper but trying not to let it show. Something obviously came through in his tone or the look he directed at Yates, who took a half step back.

"Well, sir, I do, but they are a bit confusing. Even if that fellow back there is the German, it's not like he can do anything anyway, and it does look like we might be fleeing unnecessarily..."

Baxter knew that if the lieutenant said 'again', there was a good chance that he would be going over the railing. Thankfully, for Baxter's career and Yates's health and wellbeing, the younger officer trailed off.

"Are you questioning my judgement, or my courage, Mr Yates?" he asked, his voice quiet and icy.

"Of course not, sir!" came the swift reply, slightly louder than Baxter would have liked.

Baxter had no intention of explaining his reasoning or justifying the course he had chosen. "A point south, Mr Yates," he said, affably enough, then turned his attention back to the pursuing ship.

The key, he knew, was to keep ahead of *Kassel* while also taking themselves well away from land, preferably out of territorial waters and certainly away from prying eyes. Getting to a safe harbour before the enemy ship caught up with them and sent them to the bottom was crucial, and that meant reaching the Falkland Islands. He couldn't risk running directly away from South America, as it would be altogether too easy for the Germans to cut them off — they needed to steam at a shallow angle away from the coast to maintain their lead while also pulling away.

Baxter took a last look at the cruiser. She had adjusted course, and he couldn't shake the feeling that she was picking up speed as well. She still showed the white and red at her flagstaff and no hostile intent. The Argentine clipper was running parallel to their course as best she could in the prevailing wind, demonstrating an admirable ability to sail close-hauled.

He went to the front of the bridge, slinging a pair of glasses around his neck. "Mr Yates," he said, without looking round.

"It's not your watch. I suggest you go below and get some rest — we've got a long day and a longer night ahead of us."

"Yes, sir," Yates said. He heard his second-in-command head for the companionway, then exclaim, "Miss Sears, I'm afraid that this is no place —"

"No place for what, sir?" he heard Pippa's clear voice demand.

"Well, no place for a civilian," the lieutenant said, his voice softening.

"She's a civilian ship!"

Baxter turned on his heel, scowling. "Technically, Miss Sears, she is an armed merchant cruiser commissioned into the Imperial German Navy and captured by the Royal Navy. However, I am sure we can make an exception for you. Let her up, Mr Yates."

Pippa stepped onto the bridge, her sensible heels clicking on the bright polished wood of the deck as she looked about curiously. "So, this is what the bridge looks like," she said airily, nodding polite greetings at any sailor whose eye she caught. "You must get dreadfully cold up here without a roof or windows."

Baxter felt his scowl ease and he smiled slightly. "It's not so bad, Miss Sears, as long as there's a steady supply of hot drinks. We don't like to shut ourselves away from the weather on the bridge as rain and spray can make windows opaque, and they can be something of a menace when they shatter."

"Do you find they shatter frequently?"

"In certain circumstances," he replied. "Bullets and shell splinters can have that effect, or indeed a direct hit from a shell. What can I do for you, Miss Sears? Or is this more of a social call?"

"Oh, a bit of both, I'm quite sure. I have been despatched to enquire about what is afoot? We seem to have shot straight past your intended port of call without looking in to see if there was a ship to take us home."

Baxter rubbed his forehead. In the hurry to put them on a new course, he'd forgotten about the civilians aboard. Not just the Sears party, but Nielsen and his crew. They had volunteered to help man the ship, but he doubted many of them would be willing to stay aboard on what could very well be a suicide run.

"I apologise, Miss Sears, but plans have had to change." He didn't want to leave the bridge unattended, so he gestured towards the small chartroom that opened onto the back of the bridge. Hicks, who had reverted to his previous role of bridge messenger, swung it open obligingly.

The space was cramped and dim, lit by small scuttles and dominated by the chart table. Pippa stood a little closer to him than was necessitated by the space, looking up at him with her head cocked to one side. In this light, her eyes were slightly more pale green than blue, he noticed, flecked with hazel. "We're in a bit of a bind, Miss Sears," he said, forcing himself to keep his mind on the business at hand. "There's a German cruiser behind us, masquerading as a British ship."

He paused, waiting to see if Pippa would protest that warships should not operate under false colours. Of all the civilians, she at least seemed to grasp the need for deception in naval war, or at least took his word for it. He decided he needed to be as direct with her as she was with everyone else.

She listened quietly as he explained the situation, drifting away from him to look with real interest at the charts spread across the heavy mahogany table bolted to the deck. "Could you not run down your American colours and reveal us to be a

British ship? That would force your enemy to reveal his own colours and may discourage him from attacking us in Argentine waters."

"I have strict orders to avoid risking any more of a diplomatic incident than I already have, and the Argentine authorities may want to intern the ship if I run up British colours," he said frankly. "I'm afraid we were all too confident in establishing this as an American vessel, and the government in Buenos Aires could very well take exception to the deception. Running into a neutral harbour now also wouldn't help — my opposite number may have the gall to demand our surrender, and we would risk discovery."

Pippa nodded. "So you intend to run for the Falkland Islands?"

"As though the Devil himself is on our heels. Begging your pardon."

"Mother warned me about sailors and their language," she said, dismissing the matter with a wave of her hand. "There is no opportunity to put us ashore, then? This ship appears to have many substantial boats, and the weather appears quite clement. That rather pretty yacht might also take us off."

Baxter considered that for a moment. He'd like nothing more than to have the civilians off his ship, but they'd feel the loss of Nielsen and his men. "We'd have to slow to put the boats in the water, and come to a full stop to transfer you to another vessel. I'm afraid I don't have the luxury of doing that."

Pippa didn't seem too disappointed, despite the apparent danger she was in. He guessed that her father would be less pleased. "Mrs Sears will no doubt be happy that our next port of call will be British soil."

Pippa actually smiled at that. "Well, we were trying to do a grand tour before this war got in the way," she said, then turned towards the hatch. "New experiences and so forth. Have you been to these islands, Mr Baxter?"

"Once, when I was very young. I've sailed past them more recently."

"What an interesting life you have led," Pippa said thoughtfully, then moved to the hatch. "I have distracted you from your duty for too long already."

"Please reassure your family that I have every intention of getting them to the Falkland Islands in one piece."

She smiled fully this time. "I must confess, I did wonder. Our German ... guests talk a lot about honour and glory, but very little about survival. Charles can be a bit tedious on the subject as well."

Baxter returned the smile. "With the greatest of respect to your brother-in-law, that sort of attitude doesn't last long when you've actually seen the face of battle."

"I like you, Mr Baxter," Pippa said as he undogged the hatch and swung it open. "You're refreshingly direct."

"The feeling is mutual, Miss Sears," he responded, and caught a smirk on Hicks' face before the sailor could fully suppress it.

"I shall reassure Mother that we are safe and that everything is in hand, then."

Baxter watched her go — she moved with efficiency rather than grace, apparently unbothered by the movement of the deck under her half-boots or getting about a ship despite her relatively voluminous skirts.

He shook his head, realising he was at risk of becoming distracted by her. He gave Hicks a hard look for good measure, then moved forward and pulled himself into the tall wooden chair in the centre of the deck. He deliberately didn't look back towards the pursuing vessel and only glanced once at the yacht. It was important that the men on the bridge saw their commander calm and collected, particularly after the unexpected change in course and the new urgency of the speed they were working up towards. Much of the gossip that spread through a ship started with the bridge crew. Baxter was sure that word of the situation would spread, but so would the fact that the captain wasn't concerned and was confident they would outrun the enemy ship.

At least, that was his hope.

The day dragged on, long and bright, with just enough of a cool breeze that it didn't become stiflingly hot. Perfect sailing weather, as demonstrated by the clipper that showed an irritating stubbornness in remaining in the area, even if *Ludovic* did start to outpace her — there was only so fast a sailing vessel could go, after all.

Lieutenant Yates relieved Baxter after four hours, and they went through the time-honoured ritual of handing over the watch. Course and speed, sea conditions, anything particularly noteworthy, and orders. Argentina was barely visible in the distance, the mountains far to the west entirely lost in a haze.

"That one's a persistent blighter, sir," Yates said. "Ah, there she goes!"

Baxter was briefly confused about which ship Yates was talking about, and felt a flicker of hope that he meant the cruiser was breaking off her pursuit. Then he saw the yacht, by now some little distance behind *Ludovic*, putting about to race away across her slightly curved wake. From the look of it, the wind was in her sweet spot and she flew along with every scrap of sail set.

"I do love a tall ship," Yates went on. "Used to race in my father's East Coast One, absolute beauty. What about you, sir?"

"Yachts? No. I more or less grew up on sailing brigs, though," he said, raising his glasses to observe the yacht's handling in more detail. "Vessels my father commanded."

Baxter looked beyond the yacht and focused on the far more martial vessel. "I do believe she's gaining on us," Yates said, having matched his posture and the direction he was looking.

"Yes — slowly, but measurably. What do you think she's doing — twenty-four, twenty-five knots?"

Yates pursed his lips, obviously gratified at being consulted. "Well, if the wheelhouse is right and we're making twenty-three — I'd say she's doing a shade over twenty-four. Can't be more than that."

"Agreed. It's a question now of who can maintain the speed," Baxter said. "We've got a plentiful supply of coal, but less of a crew. Our stokers are going to tire out sooner."

"Is that going to make much of a difference, sir?"

"I've seen it happen before," Baxter said, remembering being pursued across the Mediterranean by an Italian auxiliary cruiser. That time, the ship he'd been aboard, *Resadiye*, had been oil-fired and therefore tireless. The bigger Italian ship had lost ground on them over the course of the day and night as her stokers had flagged and the furious rate at which they must have been throwing fuel into the furnaces had dropped off.

That hadn't saved the Ottoman vessel, of course — she'd ended up run aground, shelled to a hulk and then burned to the waterline. But that was a different story, and he didn't intend for *Ludovic* to end up in the same state.

"We'll need to supplement the stokers with as many men as possible," he said after a moment's consideration. "And come nightfall, lighten the ship's load as much as we can."

"Very good, sir. I'll ask for volunteers, and when that doesn't work start assigning men."

"Carry on, Mr Yates. I'm going to give Hancock the good news about lightening the load."

The steward took that news about as well as could be expected — with a look of grim resignation. Baxter gave orders to be woken in two hours, then retired to his cabin. Instead of dropping into the relatively large, comfortable bed, he stretched out on a chaise longue that was barely long enough for him, his feet propped up against the bulkhead. While he usually slept solidly, no matter the sea conditions, he found himself lying awake and staring at the bulkhead, his mind working through the issues he faced but also, occasionally, filled with images of Pippa Sears' eyes.

He therefore knew that it was definitely less than two hours before he was roused again by Hancock tapping at the door. "Sir, you're needed in second class, as a matter of urgency," he said hurriedly, before disappearing just as quickly.

Baxter dragged himself to his feet and pulled on his white tunic and cap. Something in the steward's tone made him stop just long enough to retrieve his revolver and make sure it was loaded. He hadn't heard anything untoward, testament to how well built the liner was. It wouldn't do for first-class passengers to hear each other, let alone be made aware of the existence of the other classes.

Stepping out onto the deck, however, he could hear shouting and the rumble of boots running on the deck below. He went down the steps two at a time.

"Do you need me, sir?" Yates called down from the bridge entryway.

"Stay on watch!" he shouted back, before heading in the direction of the commotion. He clattered down the steps to be met by Pearson, who had a Winchester rifle in his hands. "It's the German officers, sir," he reported. "They've got out."

Baxter's jaw clenched. He'd given specific orders that the watch on the prisoners should be tightened, but now wasn't the time to argue about what had gone wrong. "Where are they?"

"Looks like they're trying to free the rest of the crew, some of them anyway."

"Right." Baxter thought fast as he led the way towards the lower decks, where thirty German enlisted men were being kept prisoner. "Break out the small arms. I want extra men on the bridge, and guarding the boiler and engine rooms."

"Boat deck as well, sir?"

He paused at the foot of the companionway. Having experienced captivity at the hands of the Russians, Baxter was determined never to be taken prisoner again — he'd always find a way to fight his way out. "Good idea, but least priority," he said, conscious of just how stretched his small crew already was.

Pearson jogged away to distribute the weapons and organise extra guards, and Baxter was met by the corporal in charge of the Marine detachment, a burly, red-faced man who saluted with the sharpness of someone expecting a carpeting. "We'll worry about how they got out later, Corporal," Baxter said. "Where are they?"

"One blighter's already been cornered and surrendered, sir," the Marine NCO reported crisply. "He's under guard in his cabin. "We think two of them are down in steerage, trying to find a way to get their lads out. Not sure about the captain or that Leiter rotter."

Baxter was oddly disappointed that Meisner had taken part in the escape, but he was an officer of the Imperial German Navy whose parole had been denied — it was his duty to try to escape.

"Let's make sure they don't get any more of their men out."

Baxter led the way further into the superstructure and then down belowdecks. He knew his duty was to be on the bridge and sending Yates to co-ordinate the hunt for the escapees. He was here, though, he was armed, and he probably had more experience of this sort of thing than anyone else aboard.

He moved quickly, but knew he couldn't rush. There would be bluejackets and Jollies running around down here, all of them alert and spoiling for trouble. The last thing he needed was to shoot one of his own men, or meet his own end by friendly fire.

The last time he'd been below, he reflected wryly, it had been deathly quiet, just the ever-present thump of the ship's heartbeat. Now it was chaos, men shouting in both English and German and boots thundering up and down the corridors. Baxter heard the crack of a rifle shot and then someone screaming in pain. He moved towards the noise, and found a group of Royal Marines gathered around a sailor lying in the corridor, clutching his guts. From the expanding pool of blood beneath him, Baxter guessed a bullet had gone straight through him.

"Where are they?" Baxter asked, his voice grim.

"We've got 'em trapped in a cabin two doors along," one of the Marines said, then looked up and realised he was speaking to his commander.

Baxter waved him down as he started to come to attention, and moved to the corner in the passageway. They were in the honeycomb of cramped cabins that would have housed the third-class passengers. His shoulder was to a solid steel bulkhead, part of the ship's internal skeleton. "Armed, I assume?"

"At least one gun, sir."

"You men down there," Baxter called out, his voice sounding flat and hard. "You have ten seconds to surrender. I assure you, no harm will come to you if you give up peacefully."

He was still trying to work out how to repeat that in German when a response came in heavily accented English. "Come and get us!"

The speaker sounded desperate and on the verge of panic, a young man whose pride and sense of honour convinced him that surrender wasn't an option. In other circumstances, Baxter might have felt some sympathy for him, but the wounded bluejacket was moaning piteously, and gasping out his last breaths. He turned to Pearson and held out his hand. "Rifle."

Pearson handed it over. "It's loaded, sir."

Baxter glanced around the corner. He caught a flash of movement, and ducked back as someone fired, the round ricocheting down the corridor to bury itself into a bulkhead. Baxter crouched, ducked round the corner and fired, working the lever to eject the spent cartridge as he went forward. He fired again, not really worrying about hitting anyone, just keeping them away from the doorway.

He kicked in the door of the first cabin he came to, sweeping it with the still-smoking muzzle, then brought the rifle into his shoulder as he turned to the partition between the two cabins, levelling the muzzle. For a moment he considered what would happen if the partitions weren't quite as flimsy as he assumed, then pulled the trigger.

The noise was deafening in the small space, but not as punishing as a 4-inch gun being fired next to his ear. He worked the action as quickly as he could, firing in a line across the partition; the clatter of the fat brass cartridge cases hitting the uncarpeted deck punctuated the rifle's bark. Dust and splinters flew from the wooden partition as he emptied the full fourteen rounds through it, then dropped the rifle and dragged his Smith and Wesson out and, using his enormous strength and bulk, crashed through the weakened wood into the next cabin.

The fusillade through the wall was enough for the Germans, however. "*Bitte! Bitte!*" one of them was shouting, hands raised and a look of sheer terror on his face.

Baxter released the pressure on the trigger. Despite the fact he'd been firing blind, the cabin was small enough that one of the four men packed into it was dead, sprawled across a lower bunk with an ugly wound in his face. Two of the other men, both of them enlisted sailors, were injured. Somehow, the young officer was unharmed and still standing, crammed into the far corner of the tiny space as though he'd been trying to open the porthole to squeeze out.

The Marines boiled into the cabin, their eyes widening when they saw the damage he'd done. Pearson had retrieved the discarded rifle, and looked up from feeding rounds through the magazine gate. "Where to next, sir?" he asked.

"Engine room," Baxter growled. He was angry, though the rage was tamped down. Angry with himself for allowing this to happen, and angry with the prisoners who had thought they could achieve anything beyond getting his and their own people killed.

It became clear, as they moved through the rest of the ship, that the German officers' attempt at an escape had been a futile gesture. They'd managed to release a few of the enlisted men, but not enough to overwhelm the armed Marines and sailors. The RN bluejackets had gone about subduing and rounding up the unarmed escapees with a will. Baxter and the men following him twice had to break up what had almost become dockside brawls. A round discharged into the ceiling brought the enthusiastic fighting to an abrupt end, battered and bloody combatants on both sides looking around wildly to determine whose side had fired the shot — the German sailors, who had at least been holding their own, resubmitted to captivity with sullen glares and muttered comments about the English cheating by bringing guns.

"Good job they didn't manage to overpower many of my men and take their weapons," the Marine corporal commented after they'd subdued what, as far as they knew, was the last group of escapees. Led by Meisner himself, they had been trying to fight their way into the number one furnace in order to no doubt sabotage the ship's power plant, stopping her or at the very least slowing her down.

"I imagine it's quite hard to prise a rifle out of a Jolly's hands, Corporal," Baxter said.

"Even when we're dead, sir."

Baxter smiled at the grim humour, then felt the expression slip as he surveyed the battered prisoners. "*Herr* Meisner, where's Leiter?" he asked.

The German shrugged. He seemed tired, and resigned to a return to captivity. "With one of the other parties, I assume — I was not privy to the planning of this escapade."

Baxter turned to Pearson and the Marine corporal. "I want a full headcount and every German accounted for. Particularly Leiter. I'll be on the bridge."

He worked his way back up through the ship, passing Marines herding enemy sailors back into captivity, and less cheerful ones trying to deal with the wounded. They had a surgeon's mate assigned from *Astute*, who would have his work cut out for him after even a relatively brief skirmish such as this. Baxter forced himself to greet them all, smiling with the bluejackets who were revelling in the victory, and stopping to lend a hand with the wounded as needed. All the while, he tried to recall if Leiter had been among the recaptured Germans he'd seen, perhaps trying to keep his head down, and came to the conclusion that he hadn't seen the insufferable young officer.

What are you up to, Leiter? he wondered as he finally made it above deck and into the rapidly fading twilight.

The guard he had put on the first-class cabins was still there, but looked uncomfortable even as he saluted. Baxter returned the salute and continued past him, then stopped and looked back sharply. "What is it?"

The Marine snapped to attention. "I've been standing here and keeping watch, just like you said, sir. But Miss Sears, see, she didn't take too kindly…"

"Damnation," Baxter growled, not needing the guard to finish the sentence. A premonition of danger made him pick up his pace as he went up the last flight of the companionway to the boat deck.

This was a slightly more open space than the rest of the superstructure. The three yellow-painted funnels pierced the deck. Benches, facing out to sea, were set at intervals, and he could make out deck chairs stacked against one bulwark, looking strangely incongruous. In happier times, this would be the preserve of first-class passengers as a space to promenade and take the air. The officers' quarters were located in a deckhouse between the first and second funnels, forward of his position, and a short stretch of deck led to the next companionway up to the bridge. Along with the large air intake funnels that alternated with the lifeboats, there were altogether too many places for someone to hide from view.

It was eerily quiet after the noise belowdecks. The lifeboats shifted slightly in their cradles as the liner rolled in the long swell that indicated they were well out into the South Atlantic now. Baxter moved quietly to the foot of the steps up to the bridge. "Yates?" he called out softly, and something in the tightness of his tone brought his second-in-command to the railing quickly.

"Sir?" he replied, matching Baxter's volume.

"Everything all right up there?"

"In order, sir. *Kassel* was still behind us when we lost the light, and I have been maintaining the ordered course."

"Good man." Baxter paused, tapping the barrel of his revolver on his leg as he looked back along the boat deck. "Did you post guards on this deck?"

Yates nodded. "Yes, sir. Two men on the companionways."

"Blast!" That was what was missing.

"Shall I come down and assist, sir?"

"Absolutely not," Baxter said. "Hold the bridge at all costs."

"Sir, it might be better if you —"

"Hold the bridge, Mr Yates," he cut in. He knew Yates was about to suggest he take the bridge, and he knew by rights that he should. But he was determined to see this through.

He paced back along the deck, carefully checking every spot he could think of to hide. He lifted the covers on each lifeboat to peer inside, cursing at how long this would take, until he reflected that there weren't many places for Leiter to go.

When he reached the steps down to the first-class deck, he descended just far enough to get the Marine's attention and beckon him up on deck, holding his finger to his lips as the Jolly clattered forward. The man nodded, taking exaggerated care to move quietly as he joined Baxter.

"There are Germans still loose on this deck," Baxter whispered. "Pass the word — I want men on every companionway that leads down from the boat deck and more men up here helping me search. And make everyone aware that they might have hostages."

Baxter went back up as the Marine saluted and hurried away. The sensible thing to do would be to wait for reinforcements, but at the same time he wanted Leiter and whoever was with him to be under pressure. He started moving forward again, moving as quietly as he could. His eyes were adjusting to the dimness on deck, at least — there was a bit of starlight and the moon was a quarter full, but the smokestacks went some way towards blocking the light.

There was, as always, the thrum of background noise that came on every ship — the engines, the whisper of wind around the rigging of the radio mast forward and the lap and hiss of water as the great steel hull was thrust through it. Added to that was the banging of doors as the prisoners were resecured. Baxter closed his eyes, trying to block out that background noise and ignore the ringing in his ears that came from spending more than half of his life around artillery being fired.

He shook his head, frustrated, and crouched, staring along the deck as far as he could see. If there weren't the civilians to be considered — and while he had no way of knowing if they were in fact being held hostage by Leiter, he couldn't take the risk — he'd probably start putting rounds into the lifeboats and anything else that could harbour a particularly irritating enemy prisoner.

Then he heard it: a light tapping noise coming from one of the lifeboats nearby that was followed by a slight thud and a squeak. Baxter moved carefully in that direction, crouching in the cover of one of the air vents. "Leiter, there really is nowhere for you to go. Just give up now and there won't be any repercussions."

He was conscious, as he spoke, that he'd tried the same tack belowdecks with little result.

Leiter didn't disappoint him. "We have Miss Sears and Mrs Finlay. You may have Miss Sears back, as she's more trouble than she's worth. We will release Mrs Finlay once we have got this boat in the water."

"You know I can't let you do that, Leiter," Baxter said, voice hard.

The boat creaked as a German sailor pushed back the canvas covering, revealing seven occupants — Leiter, the young German *leutnant*, and three German sailors, along with the two women. Henrietta looked petrified, and Pippa furious. The younger German officer, whose name Baxter couldn't remember, held a small revolver that he kept pointed at the two women. Leiter snapped something at the enlisted men, who started to clamber out of the boat and move to the pulley system to swing the boat out and over the water.

"Do you really expect me to believe that you'll shoot two women if you don't get what you want?" Baxter asked reasonably, raising his revolver but being careful not to point it at the Germans. The officer was sitting very close to Pippa, and Baxter did not want to risk hitting the women. "None of you are monsters."

Leiter looked momentarily uncertain, then his resolve hardened. "You give us no choice!"

Boots thumped on the deck behind Baxter, Marines fanning out on side of him.

"Stay back!" Leiter yelled, spittle flying. He had a pistol as well, a little pearl-handled thing that Baxter couldn't help but think was a lady's weapon. Not the sort Ekaterina or Connie would have used, of course, but the latter would have scoffed at the very notion of being a lady anyway.

"There's nowhere for you to go, and if you hurt either of those women I will hang you myself."

Leiter's resistance seemed to be on the verge of crumbling. His eyes darted left and right at the rifle-armed Marines. Before anyone could do or say anything, though, Charles Finlay stepped past Baxter with his appropriated Luger in his hand. "Hold a gun on my wife, will you?" he snapped as he adopted a classic shooter's posture. He pulled the trigger and shot the young man holding a gun on Henrietta clean through the left eye.

As the dead man crumpled, his blood and brains splashing the normally pristine deck, Leiter swung his automatic onto Finlay. Baxter, recovering swiftly from his surprise, shot him, the revolver kicking in his hand and the noise of the shot almost drowned out by Henrietta's piercing scream.

Leiter went down, clutching his shoulder. "Hold your fire!" Baxter roared, using the voice that had made itself heard over a Pacific typhoon. "Enough," he said. The German sailors had their hands up and were shouting that they'd surrendered. The Jollies looked about ready to gun them down where they stood.

"Good shot, Charlie," Pippa said into the stunned silence, trying for nonchalance but clearly shaken.

"I did say I was the regimental pistol champion," Finlay said, looking pale and shaky as he crossed to his wife and gathered her up so that she sobbed into his shoulder rather than her hands.

Baxter was done with this wretched episode. "Corporal, get these men back into their rooms and —" he pointed at Leiter — "this officer to the surgeon's mate. Mr Finlay, I'll thank you to see your wife and Miss Sears back to your cabins, and further to remain there until instructed that it is safe to leave."

"And the body, sir?" the Marine corporal asked.

"Funeral service tomorrow morning," Baxter said. A lot of mistakes had been made this night, and in the previous days. Some by him, some by others. He wasn't about to compound his own errors by having the enemy dead unceremoniously thrown overboard.

He glanced around the scene one last time. "And have someone up to mop and holystone this deck," he said sharply, before turning and stalking towards the bridge.

CHAPTER NINETEEN

Lieutenant Yates reported their heading, speed and position crisply. "We did lose some revolutions there for a little while, I assume because the stokers were fighting the Germans, but they're labouring like champions to get us up to speed."

"How much speed?" Baxter asked. They'd dealt with the attempt to take over the ship, but the Germans might have got what they wanted anyway if the lost speed allowed SMS *Kassel* to overhaul them in the dark.

"We'd reached twenty-three knots, sir, and were perhaps going to make twenty-four, but dropped to twenty-one for about half an hour. It's going to take a little while to reach that speed again, and the enemy did seem to be gaining on us while we could still make her out."

Baxter nodded without speaking, and took two turns across the width of the bridge. He paused briefly on the port bridge wing to stare astern, eyes straining into the darkness to the north as he tried to make out where the German cruiser was. She would be running without lights, of course, as she was on the hunt. His only chance of picking her out would be from the plume of smoke, but she was still far enough away that it wasn't visible in the dark.

He looked along the liner's deck. They hadn't doused exterior lights yet, as that would have looked suspicious while they might still be observed, and had otherwise been occupied. That would make it easier for *Kassel* to trail them, and also perhaps confuse her captain somewhat. He might guess that they were running for Port Stanley, in which case it didn't matter if he could fix their position ahead of him. He couldn't discount the possibility that his quarry would run for a neutral harbour in the safety of darkness.

That course would make a lot of sense, Baxter realised. Run dark into an Argentine port, or even tuck into a sheltered cove on the coast, and hope *Kassel* overshot them so completely that they could escape north. In the best case, the German cruiser would run far enough south she would encounter superior RN forces and that would be the end of the matter, or be forced to break off and run into the deep ocean.

In Baxter's experience, however, it was best not to rely on hope and a low opinion of your enemy's capabilities. Particularly in situations where the enemy had shown himself to be perfectly capable. It did give him the germ of an idea, though.

Feeling energised, Baxter stepped into the chartroom briefly to check the position Yates had plotted, then took up the dividers and plotted a number of possible courses. Here was a problem he could solve, or at least have a damn good crack at. He grinned broadly at his second-in-command as he stepped back out onto the bridge, glancing down at his sturdy pocket watch. "Mr Yates, I make it eight twelve — do you agree?"

Yates drew back his sleeve to look at his newfangled wrist watch. "Eight twelve exactly, sir."

"At nine fifteen, I want a three-point turn to starboard and a reduction in speed to fifteen knots."

Yates blinked. "Very good, sir," he said, though he was clearly trying to work out which neutral harbour they were going to run for. "Should I stand down the extra crew assigned to the boiler rooms?"

"No, but they can rest and eat for now — they're going to have their work cut out for them after that. I will need every available man assembled on the boat deck, though. We have a lot of work to do in the next hour."

Pearson scoured the ship for anyone who wasn't a stoker or engaged on other key duties, such as guarding the prisoners or tending to the wounded. Even Hancock was there, and when he heard the tramp of feet heading past his cabin, Charles Finlay had volunteered. The deck was already scrubbed clean of the blood and other reminders that a life had ended there, and the men who listened carefully as Baxter told them what needed to be done seemed unfazed by the events of the previous hours.

They set to with a will and worked furiously, making their way along *Ludovic*'s starboard, putting out lights and closing porthole covers in what Baxter hoped would appear to be a haphazard fashion, giving the impression of a ship gradually going to sleep for the short South Atlantic night, cabin lights blinking out one by one. They were aided in this, of course, by the fact that many of the cabins were unoccupied, but they also had to seal the portholes in any cabin being used by the sullen German prisoners and instruct the wary Marine guards to keep a very close eye on them for the next few hours.

"We found out how the blighters got out, sir," Pearson said, as Baxter met him while touring the ship to inspect the work. "Mr Leiter had managed to bring up a plank or two in his room. Must have worked through the nights to do it, and quiet like. Allowed him to come back around and sneak up on one of the guards and get his mates out."

Baxter grunted. He had to acknowledge the man's ingenuity, and there was no doubting his courage, even if it was wasted. "And their weapons?"

"Mostly taken from the guards, though one or two had managed to hide their sidearms. The Marines searched their quarters thoroughly, of course, but a bluejacket has more of an eye for these things. From hunting for contraband and the like, sir."

Baxter smiled grimly. What he really meant, of course, was that sailors were more experienced pilferers — certainly any man who'd been with the service any length of time. It was not a habit Baxter could approve of, but it could come in handy. "Very well. Next time I'll set the sailors to the task."

"Really hope there isn't a next time, sir."

Baxter's smile turned into a grin. That was a sentiment he could appreciate — he'd settle for a nice, normal duty posting. But that was unlikely to happen at sea during wartime. "Carry on, Pearson," he said.

Pearson ordered the course change at the specified time, bringing the liner's bows swinging ponderously round onto a new heading that would take *Ludovic* towards any number of the smaller ports and harbour towns along Argentina's coast. Her speed dropped at the same time, giving the engineering crews and her overtaxed machinery a brief respite.

It had been many years since Baxter had been in these waters, and he assumed that a lot of what had been sleepy little coastal villages were now thriving towns. Not that they would have a chance to find out this night.

Baxter walked the length of the liner, getting reports from the work crews that everything was in order. He bumped into Pippa Sears in one of the upper deck cabins, diligently making her own checks. She looked somewhat incongruous, pushing her feathered hat back in order to bend and make sure a porthole was properly sealed. "I know you ordered us back to the cabins, but poor Henry is inconsolable and I couldn't abide remaining there," she told Baxter in a brittle voice. "It's rather my fault, you see, that we were in that position. I was so desperately keen to know what was going on. I do hope those sailors who were on guard were unhurt."

"I'm aware," he said, voice harder than he'd intended, then forced himself to relax. "The men were knocked cold but not otherwise harmed. It couldn't have been an easy experience for you either, Miss Sears. I appreciate you helping out in this way despite that."

"Better to keep busy and all that," she said, briefly forcing some lightness into her tone that faded as quickly as it had come. "While I'm glad Charlie made sure Henrietta wasn't harmed, I don't think that poor man deserved to die that way."

"Few men do, Miss Sears," Baxter said. He could think of any number of men who fit that description, not least Webb, or the men who had died under his command in East Africa. It was the way of things in his life, but she didn't need to hear any of that and he wasn't in the mood to try to explain it. "He did choose to point a pistol at your sister."

Pippa's eyes flashed with anger. "That bastard Leiter talked him into it," she spat with sudden vehemence, then coloured slightly. "Does my language shock you, Mr Baxter?"

"I'm a sailor, Miss Sears. Very little shocks me," he responded gently, realising just how close she was to breaking down. "Now, you'd best be getting back to your family."

She nodded without argument, which surprised him, and he touched his cap. "Good evening to you, Miss Sears."

She smiled at his formality, which he hoped would re-establish normality for her. "Good evening, Captain."

Baxter's strides were long but not hurried as he headed back to the bridge, having assured himself that everything was as it should be. Right now, assuming the cruiser hadn't changed course dramatically, *Ludovic* would be running at a sharp angle to the line drawn by *Kassel*. They would be losing ground faster than they already were, but Baxter was confident that the German would have brought them into range long before they could look for any help from the squadron that had assembled at Port Stanley. Assuming they were even there and not already out on the hunt.

"Heading as you ordered, sir, and speed is currently fifteen knots," Yates reported.

Baxter nodded, an uncharacteristic coil of tension in his guts. He'd been in a fair number of battles, not to mention fights ashore, including the first major fleet action of this century. This was different, however, because they had nothing to throw back at the enemy, and their escape and survival rested entirely on him getting this ruse just so.

"The trick of it, Yates, is to make sure he sees us on this heading, but that it doesn't look like we're trying to deceive him."

"That's usually the trick to a deception, sir," the lieutenant said. "That, or make your man so desperate to fall for it that he doesn't believe the evidence of his own eyes."

Baxter relaxed slightly. There was no judgement in Yates's urbane tone. "Remind me never to play cards with you."

He let the moment stretch before speaking again. "The thing of it is, our opponent has shown himself to be a canny player."

Yates appeared to give this genuine consideration. "Well, he's got two options, doesn't he, sir? He'll either think we carried on this course and ran for the cover of the Argentine coast, or we've doubled back and made for open water in the hopes of losing him."

"That's my assessment as well," Baxter said, pleased that Yates hadn't tried to offer an opinion or otherwise tried to influence his decision. There wouldn't have been an argument if Littleton or Simons had been here, as they were senior and would be in command. But the liner would already have surrendered or been sunk in that circumstance — this was a conclusion he could come to without any sort of hubris.

"What are your orders, sir?"

Well, that is the question. Baxter didn't answer, instead turning to Pearson, who was waiting by the starboard entryway with a whistle in his hand and a blandly expectant look.

Baxter nodded, and the petty officer blew a long, shrill note on the whistle. Within seconds, every light on the starboard side of the ship — and those on the port side they'd been able to get to — went out, plunging the liner into darkness. If the Germans had eyes on her and hadn't already given up, she would have seemed to have disappeared.

"Pearson, see to the rest of the port lights, quick as you can."

"Yes, sir."

Yates turned to Baxter. "I could take a boat out once it's done, to make sure we aren't showing a glimmer?"

"We wouldn't be able to stop for you, and I'd hate to lose you," Baxter said, allowing himself a slight smile. "Inspect the whole ship as thoroughly as you can — I don't want even a glint of light. You have my permission to shoot anyone who disobeys."

"I doubt it would work with Mrs Sears. I'll just ask her politely."

Baxter grinned. "Carry on, Mr Yates."

Baxter moved to the bridge's front rail, enjoying the feeling of isolation as the ship went on her way. He felt the wind on his face and saw nothing but darkness ahead, aside from the faint luminescence of the waves as they swept past the vessel towards the South American coast. All the while he turned over the problem, trying to second-guess the man who was trying to outfox him. Did he have the same low opinion of RN officers that Leiter and some of the other younger officers he'd met had, or was he an older hand who might have served alongside some of Baxter's colleagues or known them on far-flung colonial postings?

Never assume your enemy is less capable than you, unless they've already proven it, Jackie Fisher had told the collection of young officers he'd gathered around himself on the North America Station, when Baxter had worn the uniform of a regular officer.

Yates reported back to the bridge. "We are running completely dark, sir," he said. "Not even a binnacle light."

Baxter nodded, staring head. He wasn't sure, but he thought he could make out a slight glimmer of light as they steamed towards the dark bulk of the land. He held his peace for another twenty minutes, during which time Yates quietly and efficiently went about his duties.

Now was the time for a decision. For a moment, he contemplated holding this course and running into harbour. He could get himself and his men ashore and into internment, from which His Majesty's government would no doubt swiftly see them released — assuming it wasn't too much of an embarrassment. It would certainly see the passengers and Nielsen's men out of danger, and he could probably scuttle the liner in deeper water and transfer everyone by boat.

"Mr Yates — four points to port, if you please, and every knot the engine room can give me."

"Yes, sir!" came his first officer's crisp response out of the dimness. There was a sense of relief evident in his tone — he may not have known what Baxter had decided, but a decision had been made.

The ship's motion changed as her bows came round, rolling more and pitching less as the waves came in from her port side rather than from astern. The motion became less noticeable as *Ludovic*'s speed started to come up again and she began to cut through the water properly. The waves became a bit longer again as she came away from the coastline at a shallow angle, and Baxter was struck once again by the power of the well-maintained machinery. Her engines may not have set her flying from the off, but they were powerful enough to send the big ship forward as fast as any modern cruiser, and faster than some older destroyers.

The night's work wasn't done, but they were heading in the right direction again, and picking up speed. Their survival in the next few hours depended on two things — that he'd read his opponent correctly, and they could drive the ship as fast as she could go for as long as humanly possible.

Baxter kept himself and the crew running through the short southern night, labouring purely by the stars and the newborn moon. "Everything that isn't bolted down and can't be burned goes over the side," he ordered Yates, Pearson and Hancock. "Keep enough food and water for the next two days, and the rifles and ammunition."

"We going to get close enough to fight that blighter with Winchesters, sir?" Pearson asked.

"Hopefully not, but I don't intend to surrender without a fight."

"And the wine, sir? The liquor?" Hancock asked, his voice plaintive. "There are some lovely vintages, and a particularly fine selection of Scotch whisky."

"Everything." Baxter hesitated. "Maybe keep one or two of the particularly good whiskies, and enough brandy for the men's ration."

"I assumed that came under the food and water command, sir," Hancock said with that officious blandness that was the weapon of stewards everywhere.

"And this is the most important bit — everything that might identify this ship as a German merchant vessel or armed merchant cruiser goes over the side or into the furnaces. Similarly, anything related to her disguise as an American liner. Sink it, or burn it."

Baxter's various course changes — and what some of the men called his 'mad Scottish japes' when they thought he couldn't hear — had created a sense of anticipation with the crew. They knew something was afoot, and Baxter had already heard Hicks groaning that he was planning on trying to take the German cruiser with the same dangerous tactics he'd used for cutting out *Ludovic*. That was far from the truth, of course, but he needed to maintain momentum and not let the men slide into speculation. He was relieved to see the crew set to with the sort of will they'd shown getting rid of the coal two days ago. Pearson had organised them into parties with particular tasks — some shifting the food and drink that had been left aboard, others discharging the water, and others ripping out furnishings, decorations and anything not directly related to the operation of the vessel. It became something of a competition between them, to see who was fastest and could also raise the biggest splashes off the side of the vessel.

"The enemy could make out the splashes, sir," Yates pointed out as the two of them watched an upright piano being manoeuvred out of the second-class lounge and launched over the side with a great whoop and a fountain of water. "Or indeed hear the men enjoying themselves."

Baxter watched as the piano was followed by crates of expensive wine. He very much doubted they were as full as they were when the men first picked them up, and made a mental note to watch for drunkenness in the next few hours. "She's still five miles away, at least, and unless I've misread her captain, on a heading out into the Atlantic. If anyone does see, they'll mistake the splashes for waves."

Yates nodded, then somewhat hesitantly asked the question that was on his mind. "Assuming you're right, sir..." he began.

"Spit it out, man," Baxter said.

"Well, you seem to have settled on the notion that *Kassel*'s captain will think we've run for the open sea. I believe your reading of his intentions was he wanted to board us within sight of neutrals in the hope of provoking a crisis. Why wouldn't he just continue on his previous course and forget about us? I'm quite sure he has orders to join up with von Spee, with or without *Ludovic*, sir."

It all came out in a bit of a rush, rather than in the young officer's more measured tones. He clearly expected to be reprimanded for speaking out of turn, but also wanted to get this off his chest.

Baxter took his time responding, as it was hard to put into words. He'd fought men like this German captain before, knew their ways, and more to the point, he knew in his gut that he was right about the situation. "He may have wanted us where it would damage Britain's cause, Mr Yates, but more than that, he just wants this ship taken. He'll want his people back, and the supplies we may still be carrying. If he thinks we're trying to break out, that's the way he'd go. He may have his orders to join up with their East Asia Squadron, but he won't want to let this ship stay in our hands too long. No, Mr Yates, he's out there somewhere, running in the direction he thinks we've gone."

There was a crash from aft, in the region of the first-class quarters, and a female voice raised in distinctly unladylike anger. Baxter sighed. "Mr Yates…" he began.

"I have the bridge, sir," the lieutenant responded, before Baxter could dispatch him aft to tackle the problem that seemed to be brewing with the Sears family.

Well, Baxter would give him this one. He headed back along the ship, following the sound of Mrs Sears giving some sailors a dressing-down that a drill instructor would have been proud of. "I am quite sure that Mr Baxter, when he said that 'everything must go overboard', didn't mean our baggage and the fittings!"

"I'm afraid I did, madam," Baxter said, as evenly as he could. "This is a somewhat large and heavy vessel, so if we're going to lighten the load in any appreciable way, everything must go."

The heavyset woman turned on him, furious. "Do you mean to say there will be no dinner either?" she demanded in a slightly strangled voice.

"There will be dinner, madam, though not quite of the same quality as last night," he said calmly, though he could feel his anger starting to bubble to the surface. The bluejackets were all watching, waiting to see which way he would jump and elbowing each other in the ribs when they thought no one was watching. Thankfully, Mr Sears came to the rescue.

"Oh, do be reasonable, my dear," he said, with exaggerated patience. "There's a war on, don't you know, and we must all do our bit. Besides, I'm sure the navy will reimburse us."

"I will even provide a receipt," Baxter said, hiding his amusement at Sears' apparent concern for financial loss at this time. "But by all means, do retain your necessities and valuables," he added hastily, with a sidelong look at the bluejackets.

"I will see that they do reimburse us!" Mrs Sears declared haughtily, before retiring to her cabin. There followed the sound of cases being flung open and her calling for her daughters.

"These cabins last, lads," Baxter said, before nodding cordially to Mr Sears and making his way back to the bridge. He desperately needed sleep, but then so did most of the men under his command. At least they wouldn't be expected to fight an action, he reflected ruefully, because if it came to it their only options were to abandon ship or surrender — there would be no fighting if *Kassel* did catch up with them.

CHAPTER TWENTY

Baxter remained on the bridge for another hour while the liner was stripped and lightened, very gradually sitting higher and higher in the water, so there was less of the hull being dragged on by the Atlantic's cold waters. Yates steadily reported an increase in speed that slowed as it approached her theoretical maximum of twenty-two knots.

"Good lord," Yates breathed, having checked their speed. He disappeared into the chartroom to note their dead-reckoning position. "Twenty-four and a half knots. At this rate, we'll take the Blue Riband."

Baxter glanced across at him. "I think that's only awarded to passenger liners on their normal courses, Lieutenant," he said, then had to stifle a yawn. The occasional item was still going over the side, though it had reached the point of scullery items and chamber pots from the lower decks. "Stand the men down in watches, Mr Yates, and then get some rest. We may need to step lively tomorrow morning."

"I'm feeling quite spry, sir. I'd be happy to take the first watch."

Baxter almost argued, then nodded gratefully. While Yates had been on watch for as long as he'd been awake, he perhaps had not had quite the same active days that Baxter had.

"You may want to put your nose into purgatory first, sir," Yates went on. "Warrant Officer Murphy is quite unhappy."

Baxter nodded. The last place he wanted to go right now was the engine room, but they were all reliant on the smooth functioning of that department. He didn't know Artificer Engineer Murphy, beyond a brief meeting as the prize crew was drawn together and rowed across to *Ludovic*, but a man generally didn't attain the King's warrant without being at least competent, particularly in a technical branch. "Very well — I'll see what I can do about that."

He found Murphy right in the heart of his domain, in the crowded engine room. This was the sort of territory a deck officer rarely found himself in, and even more rarely welcomed into, and Baxter had forgotten just how infernally loud the engine room could be. *Ludovic*'s quadruple expansion engines were easily twenty feet tall and stretched the entire length of the engine room, filling it with the sound of machinery and thumping pistons turning the twin crank shafts. Men had to yell to make themselves heard above the noise, and the engineering staff were busy around the vast machine, oiling moving parts and adjusting wheels and levers.

Murphy, a young and energetic man for his rank, saw Baxter come in and came up from the lower deck onto the gantry that ran around the upper level of the engine room. He shouted something as soon as he was close by, but all Baxter caught was 'sir' and 'you'll have to'. Baxter tapped his ear and shook his head. Exasperated, Murphy swung open a heavy watertight hatch and beckoned Baxter through into one of the adjoining boiler rooms.

The terrible noise of the engine room was cut off as soon as the warrant engineer closed the hatch, but the heat, if anything, increased. It wasn't exactly quiet here, either, between the scrape and rattle of shovels moving coal and the roar of the furnaces, but it was quieter in comparison. They were overlooking one of the three enormous boilers that provided steam to the engine room. Below them, men stripped down to their trousers laboured in front of open fireboxes that emitted a fierce heat and an orange glow. The whole place stank of coal smoke, wafting out every time a heavy shovel-load of the stuff went in.

"I was within a few miles of a battleship exploding, Murphy, and I swear that was quieter than your engine room."

Murphy gave him a gap-toothed grin, before taking a salt pill from the dispenser by the hatch and popping it into his mouth. He was one of the more senior members of the non-commissioned staff of *Astute*'s engine room, and the only one who could be spared from the cruiser's maintenance and repair. While he would normally be in charge of maintaining the machinery, and fabricating replacement parts as needed, now he was in command of the whole engine room, and seemed to be thriving on it. "It's not so bad, once you get used to it!" he shouted, his volume that of a man who was so used to raising his voice he forgot to bring the volume down when he didn't have to. A few stokers glanced up, then went back to their back-breaking labour.

"What can I do for you, Mr Murphy?"

"As I was saying in there, sir, you'll have to reduce the revolutions soon. The machinery's in good enough nick, so it is, but if we go on like this something *is* going to give. Not to mention my stokers need a break."

Baxter glanced down into the interior of the boiler room. "I can send more people down," he said.

"Well, sir, we're grateful for the help and all, particularly Mr Nielsen's lads, but not everyone's a stoker and there's more to it than just shovelling. You have to be careful, do you see, sir? You take too much from one bunker, or even just a corner of a bunker, and you unbalance the whole bloody ship. And how would the officers feel, if their nice trim was disturbed?"

Baxter nodded. "What's the coal situation?"

"We're fair flying through it, sir."

Baxter closed his eyes, trying to visualise their position on the chart and then rough in where he thought *Kassel* would be. Would her captain have reduced speed at all? Likely, as he wouldn't want to risk overshooting *Ludovic* in the darkness. "Will the engines stand up to another hour like this?"

Murphy didn't look happy. "They will, sir, though it's a shame to treat such a lovely piece of kit like that. The men'll manage, too."

"I never doubted it. One more hour, Murphy. We'll reduce to fifteen knots until tomorrow morning — then we may need everything she's got."

"You'll have it, sir," Murphy said.

"Good man." Baxter glanced again at the sweating stokers, both the trained and skilled men and the others labouring alongside them. "The sooner the whole fleet can switch to oil, the better."

"Well, that would be a sight, sir. But where would we get the stuff?"

"Where indeed, Mr Murphy?" he said, then turned and headed back to the more civilised realms of the ship. He gave Yates his orders about the speed change, made one last check on their position, and then made his way back towards his cabin. Somehow, he wasn't surprised to see Pippa Sears leaning nonchalantly against the railing outside his cabin door in the pale moonlight.

"You naval gentlemen keep such unsociable hours," she said with an arch look.

"The service demands it, Miss Sears," he said, pausing at the door. He had to admit, she was a fine-looking woman. "Was there something I can do for you?" he asked, forcing himself to sound gruff.

"Dearest Mama is filled with concern that we are all about to die or, worse, be captured by the beastly Germans. She is, I am afraid, quite shaken by the events of the last few days, more so than she likes to appear, though in truth I think the loss of her luggage has troubled her more than anything."

"So ... she's sent you to seek my reassurance?" he asked.

"It's turning chilly out here — are you going to invite me in?" There was a slight quaver in her voice as she said that.

"That may not be appropriate, Miss Sears," he said, meeting her challenging gaze. "Would you like me to invite you in?"

Pippa held his look for a moment longer. Baxter wasn't sure whether he wanted her to come in or not, and she was clearly thinking the same. After a moment she glanced out to sea. "Well, I'd best be getting back before they start to wonder where I am. I did come of my own accord to ... to, yes, seek reassurance that we are not all, in fact, going to die."

"I can reassure you that I — we — will do everything in our power to make sure you get safely to dry land. Even if that land is the Falklands."

She smiled, slightly sadly. "Then I imagine we will go our separate ways, Mr Baxter?"

He shrugged. "I go where the Navy requires me to go, just as you go where your parents require."

"I wonder which is the harder taskmaster," she mused, then started back up the promenade to her own quarters. She paused and looked back at him over her shoulder. "You interest me, Mr Baxter. I shall write to you, if that would be agreeable? I assume the Navy will have some way of finding you?"

Assuming they don't drum me out again after this latest escapade. "They will, and yes, that will be agreeable."

Pippa offered a real smile, rather than the usual sardonic smirk. "Well then. Good evening to you, Mr Baxter."

"Good night, Miss Sears."

Baxter went into his cabin. He'd been clear that nothing should be spared, and the large comfortable bed had been removed along with the rest of the furniture and fittings. The mattress, at least, had been left behind for him. Baxter went to his meagre belongings, little more than the ditty bag that had been with him since his time working the tramp freighters that crept along Britain's coasts, connecting the islands and harbour towns together. Right at the bottom, under the blue winter uniform that he'd put on tomorrow as they edged ever southwards, was a crumpled and somewhat water-stained envelope, still sealed and with just his name written on it in an elegant copperplate. It had been with him on every voyage and through every battle, the letter written by Ekaterina Juneau but handed to him by another on a cold dockside in Vladivostok. He'd almost thrown it away, at the time angry at having been taken into captivity by the Tsar's secret police when Ekaterina was nowhere to be seen. That anger had long since passed, and the worn correspondence had become something of a good luck charm to him.

He folded the letter along its well-worn crease, tucked it into his shirt pocket and stretched out on the mattress. Sleep, this time, came quickly.

Baxter was on watch for first light. It was chilly on deck, cool enough that there was a hint of steam on his breath, and he was glad of the wool frock coat and trousers of the blue winter uniform.

He wanted to pace around, partially to keep warm but also to check for ships, or their telltale plumes of smoke. That wouldn't do, though. The men on watch with him, the lookouts at each wing and in the centre, Hicks standing dutifully by the speaking tubes, all looked tense.

Petty Officer Pearson arrived just as the sun started its laborious climb into a clear blue sky. "Lovely weather today, sir," he murmured, not wanting to break the hush.

"Remarkably clear for these latitudes," Baxter replied as he watched sunlight slowly creep across the scene, turning everything first a silvery grey than bringing out the colour sharply and vividly — the brightly polished decks, the yellow paintwork of the funnel behind him, the crisp whiteness of the few strands of cloud in the sky, and the depthless blue-grey of the sea through which they ploughed.

Glancing to starboard, Baxter could see nothing but the ocean and a single lonely seabird that turned lazily on the wind. No sign of Argentina's ironbound coast, somewhere below their horizon.

Lieutenant Yates appeared on the bridge, bleary-eyed and unshaven, shivering slightly in his tropical whites. It wasn't his watch yet, but Baxter couldn't begrudge his presence. "Any sign of the blighter yet, sir?" he asked.

Hancock had arrived on his heel with steaming mugs. "Coffee, sir?" the steward enquired, and Baxter took the proffered mug.

"Nothing yet, Mr Yates," he said placidly. "You may want to consider changing into winter uniform, old chap — it's just going to get colder as we head south."

Yates looked around, as though noticing for the first time that he was the only one still in white. "Yes, I might just do that, sir."

"And while you're heading aft, make sure the lookouts are all awake," Baxter added in a quieter tone.

Yates headed back the way he'd come, but before he left the bridge the speaking tubes emitted a shrill whistle. Hicks bent to it, listened intently, then stepped smartly to Baxter's side.

"After masthead reports smoke directly to the north."

Baxter felt his stomach clench, but didn't let it show on his face. He was certain *Kassel* would be well to the northeast by now, hunting for the liner in deeper water. If she *was* directly behind them, it meant *Kapitän* Neidermeyer had spent the night idling south, perhaps looking into any ports along the way.

"Confirm that, if you please, Yates, and see if you can get the range," Baxter said. "In person."

"Aye, sir." The young officer almost ran from the bridge, mug of coffee still in hand, and Hancock tutted as he went to mop up the slopped beverage.

"Sir, smoke off the port quarter, below the horizon!" one of the bridge lookouts called.

Baxter put down his coffee and moved onto the port wing, raising his field glasses as the lookout gave him the exact bearing. He found the smoke, and perhaps the top of a ship's funnels rolling in slightly heavier seas than they were experiencing.

"Well spotted," Baxter said, running rough calculations in his head. Whoever that was, they were about to come over the horizon, which meant the ship was maybe seven or eight miles away. He silently cursed the lack of a proper rangefinder on this civilian vessel — one of the many things that would have been transferred along with weapons and ammunition if her mid-ocean rendezvous with *Kassel* hadn't been interrupted by *Astute*.

He watched as the ship came up over the horizon, which meant she was currently going faster than *Ludovic*. The same low, dangerous shape that had been dogging them halfway down South America.

He was still on the bridge wing when Yates came back. "Definitely a cruiser, sir," he reported. "On the same heading, ten miles or so astern and gaining."

"Colours?"

"Nothing I could make out, sir."

"What do you make of that one?" Baxter asked, pointing to the vessel further out to the east. It didn't take Yates long to come to the same conclusion he had.

"Cruiser as well, sir. Couldn't be anything else. I can't see her colours either. On a course to intercept us, and also making more knots than we are."

"Well. It's clear that one is *Astute* and one is *Kassel.*"

"But which is which?"

"That's the question, isn't it, Mr Yates?" Baxter said cheerfully. In his mind's eye he could almost see the triangle the three ships would make if seen from above — *Ludovic* at the sharp south point, the stern chase almost directly behind her. But was this a neat right-angle triangle, with the two cruisers more or less on an even latitude? And would they come within range of each other before they caught up with the undefended liner?

"I would suggest action stations, sir, but I'm not sure what they would be."

Baxter grinned. "Certainly get the men to breakfast and then send as many as possible to the engine room — we're going to need more speed, and soon. And inform our passengers that they'll need to move belowdecks. They'll be safer there if we do come under fire."

It wouldn't make much difference if they started taking direct hits, as the hull wasn't armoured, but they'd be safer from flying shell fragments.

They ran on like that as the sun climbed higher in the sky and the only blemish on the clear air were the three columns of smoke as the three ships raced south. Baxter went to the afterdeck and spent some time watching both the pursuing cruisers. They were both sufficiently far away that he couldn't make out many details, or see what flags they flew.

"I make us less than fifty miles to the Falklands, sir," Yates reported, having spent a little time in the chartroom. "We should raise them by mid-morning."

Baxter checked his watch. "Today is what, the sixth of December?"

"Seventh, sir."

He nodded. Unless something had gone horribly awry, Sturdee's squadron would either be at anchor there, or already out on the hunt for the German East Asia Squadron. With any luck, they had already run into and destroyed von Spee's ships. A battle at the edge of the world could go unreported for days, even with the invention of wireless telegraphy.

Hancock appeared on deck, holding what looked suspiciously like the Book of Common Prayer in his hands.

"Yes, Hancock?"

"I believe you wanted to give the men killed yesterday a proper burial, sir?" the steward said, a slightly chiding note in his voice.

Baxter nodded. "Of course."

"I took the liberty of having the men sewn into shrouds and laid out on the quarterdeck. I'm afraid it won't be a very formal occasion, sir. Nobody has their dress uniforms."

If there was going to be a time to be away from the bridge, seeing to this solemn duty, it was now, while both cruisers were still so distant they couldn't tell which was which. Baxter nodded. "We'll do what we can, with what we have."

After a last check on their position relative to the pursuing vessels, Baxter went aft. He met Pearson along the way. "Order the men not otherwise engaged to muster on the afterdeck, and pass the word that our prisoners are to be brought aft as well. Invite the Sears party to join us, if they so choose."

It took a little while to muster the funeral party. Baxter stood on the aft deck, his back resolutely to the following ships, and looked at the bodies. Three bluejackets and a Royal Marine had been killed in the escape attempt, along with five Germans. He'd only seen two of them die, and had killed at least one of the Germans himself, the others falling in the mad, vicious close-quarters fighting in other parts of the ship. They were bundled in the time-honoured tradition, but instead of being sewn into hammocks or sailcloth, they were in the liner's fine bedlinen, each of them lying on a stretcher.

It occurred to Baxter that this would be the first time he'd officiated a funeral at sea. He'd been to a number, of course, particularly during his time as a captive-cum-compatriot of the Imperial Russian Navy. Men had been killed under his command, during the borders skirmishes and clashes of Empires that he'd managed to involve himself in, and in the weeks following the outbreak of war. But he himself had never stood on the deck of a ship he commanded and spoken the words over shrouded corpses. They lay in a neat row, with nothing to identify whether they were British or German, or who they had been.

The British personnel filed onto the deck and adopted a neat parade formation under Pearson's command, well away from the Germans, who did their best to parade despite the fact many were walking wounded. Captain Nielsen and a representation from his crew stood between them. Mr and Mrs Sears, Charles Finlay, and Pippa all attended, standing a little apart and looking suitably solemn. Everyone did their best to ignore the rifle-armed Marines keeping watch on the prisoners — Baxter didn't think they would try anything at a funeral, but he wasn't about to take the risk.

He noted Leiter wasn't present. The sickbay attendant who had charge of the wounded had already informed Baxter that those still alive were likely to remain so, and Leiter was well enough to be up and about. That was a problem for another time.

Baxter stepped forward, and opened the Book of Common Prayer. Hancock had marked the relevant passage, and he started without any preamble. It had been many years since he'd opened a book of religious character, as he'd had more than enough of such things while sailing with his father, the dyed-in-the-wool Presbyterian that he was. His voice carried across the deck, and he hoped the familiar words would be a comfort to the men at least.

He didn't rush the solemn verse, but he didn't hang around either. They all had too much to do. He came to the final verse. "We therefore commit their bodies to the deep, in sure and certain hope of the resurrection of the body, when the Sea shall give up her dead."

He closed the book with a snap, raising his eyes from the text to look around sternly. Only Meisner met his gaze from amongst the Germans, and he was relieved to see the civilians were taking this as seriously as the other men.

"Off hats," he ordered, removing his own cap. There was a rustle as everyone but Pippa Sears removed theirs. He nodded to Pearson, who had charge of the party. A German Navy ensign had been preserved from the cull, along with a White Ensign. The men were buried one after the other, the correct flag placed over each stretcher as it was lifted and the mortal remains slid over the side, the weighted bundles splashing as they hit the water.

Finally, it was done, and Baxter dismissed the parade. Pippa nodded to him seriously, but made no approach. He turned to see Meisner approaching him. Baxter noted he was in his civilian uniform.

"Mr Baxter, I wanted to thank you for giving our men the dignity of a proper burial," he said, offering his hand. "I also wanted to apologise for my part in the ... events last night. I had no part in the planning of them, but I felt duty-bound to fight with my men."

Baxter paused, then shook his hand firmly. "I expected nothing less, sir," he said. "We all must do our duty."

"May I keep the flag?" Meisner asked, noting that Pearson was folding it up and then binding it to a weight.

"I'm afraid not," Baxter said.

"What a foolish thing this war is," Meisner said, a great weight of sadness in his voice; then he seemed to collect himself and gestured to the following vessels. They were both much closer now, not quite in long gunnery range yet, but not far from it. The cruiser that had been further out to sea, which Baxter fervently hoped was *Kassel*, was now clearly further away than the one directly astern. "This day promises to be an interesting one. Much will depend on which of those ships is ours, and which is yours."

"Indeed it will," Baxter said, without giving any indication as to which he thought was which. "If you'll excuse me, I must be about my duties."

Meisner nodded. Drawing himself up to his full height — barely up to Baxter's chin — he offered a smart salute, which Baxter returned.

Nielsen was up next on his list. He intercepted the merchant captain as he and his small party of sailors made their way back belowdecks. "I wanted to apologise for not inviting you to stand watch," Baxter said.

Nielsen grinned, showing tobacco-stained teeth. "With what happened, sir, I can't say as I'm sorry. Was there anything else you wanted from us?"

Baxter knew that a lot of Nielsen's men, not just the trained stokers on his crew, had been working in Murphy's domain. "You've already done a great deal, but when the time comes there's one more thing you can do for us."

"Anything, Captain."

"When — if — the time comes that we come under fire, I intend to keep this ship afloat for as long as I can in the hope that help will arrive."

The Aberdonian's eyes blazed fiercely. "And we'll be happy to help you, sir, if it means putting one in the eye of yon blackguard chasing us!"

"What I'll need from you, Captain, is for you to get your men, the Sears family and the prisoners into boats and towards the Falklands. Only do so when I order it; but when I do order it, it must be done swiftly and without argument. We should be close enough that you'll be able to sail in within hours. I'll detail a Marine per boat to keep the prisoners in order."

"I wouldn't worry about it — when it's you and the deep ocean in a wee boat, friend and foe don't matter anymore."

That wasn't necessarily why Baxter wanted an armed guard along, but he didn't voice his suspicions about how some of Nielsen's crew might behave towards the prisoners. "Well, I'll let you get on with your arrangements."

"You'll tell the land folk?"

"They'll be informed if it becomes an issue." Another argument with Mrs Sears was the last thing he needed.

Hicks appeared at his elbow. "You're wanted on the bridge, sir," he murmured, keeping his voice low, as there were still civilians and prisoners around. "As a matter of urgency."

CHAPTER TWENTY-ONE

"Foremast lookout reports smoke to the south, sir," Yates reported. "A lot of it."

Baxter raised his glasses and stared south. There was no sign of the rocky, isolated islands they were making for yet — just the South Atlantic that appeared to go on forever, grey and cold. After a moment, Baxter spotted what the lookout had seen, a number of smoke trails rising straight up and then dispersing in the wind. "I count seven, sir," Yates reported.

"Eight," Baxter said. The foremast watchman, some forty feet above the deck in an armoured box, would be able to see further. "Order the foremast to confirm my count."

"Is it von Spee?" Yates asked, his voice betraying only the slightest note of concern.

"Too many ships — at the last report, the East Asia Squadron only had five. They might have been reinforced with lone cruisers, like our friend back there, but I don't think so. I think that's Sturdee's squadron."

"They've not made good time, have they, sir?"

"They've come a long way without the benefit of refuelling, unlike us," Baxter pointed out. "But, no, they've not made good time at all."

He walked to the port bridge wing and watched what he suspected was the German cruiser. She was sufficiently far back that she wouldn't be able to make out the squadron ahead, though that situation would change rapidly. Would Neidermeyer continue his pursuit at that point, trying to bring them to action and sink them before the Royal Navy ships could respond? That was assuming they had the fuel to respond, if it came to that.

Baxter realised there was another problem. As far as he knew, von Spee was operating without detailed information on the strength or position of the powerful British squadron sent to destroy him. *Ludovic* had been carrying that message south, or had orders to link up with *Kassel* once she was out of harbour and pass the message along — Lewisham hadn't been entirely clear on that. That could change if the German cruiser chasing them sighted the British ships and warned von Spee. The German admiral would have limited options at that point, far as he was from a friendly harbour. But he could give the Falklands a wider berth and therefore remain at large that bit longer, denying the Royal Navy a swift and decisive victory here and tying up powerful units on far-flung stations.

"Mr Yates, we will reduce speed," he said. "Let's try to make that German think our machinery is playing up." At the speed they'd been steaming, that probably wasn't far from the truth.

"Yes, sir. What speed?"

"Twelve knots," Baxter said. "Let's let *Astute* catch us up — it's time we blackened that German's eye."

That went down well with the men on deck, despite the fact a German cruiser that had demonstrated excellent gunnery practice would soon be catching up with them. While Baxter was confident the ship astern was their own cruiser and that she would catch up with them before the German, there was the question of how much time they had — assuming neither ship adjusted speed to keep up the pursuit while not taxing their machinery and fuel supplies.

"Should I have the wireless room signal *Astute* and let them know our intention, sir?" asked Yates. "It would have to be in plain language."

Baxter mulled that over. While Sitwell had assigned a wireless telegraphist to the prize crew, and the liner had a remarkably modern and powerful set according to that specialist, they had been ordered not to broadcast unless absolutely necessary, and had not been given a copy of the latest naval codes in case the ship did fall into enemy hands. "No, best not to," he said at last, thinking of a discussion he'd had with Andrews, a signals officer and telegraphy specialist he'd met on Zanzibar. Saved from a sinking ship in Zanzibar Harbour, to be precise. A lot of what the young officer had talked about had gone completely over his head, but there was something — not the theory, but a practical application of it...

"Both ships are gaining on us, sir," Yates reported, breaking into Baxter's train of thought. "I don't believe either have reduced knots."

Baxter turned his attention back out to sea. Having spent so long watching the ship chasing them, he was very familiar with her appearance. As she crept closer, at a more rapid rate now, he was convinced. "That is most certainly *Kassel*," he declared. "Which means that the ship astern is *Astute*."

"We'll know for sure when she sees the squadron ahead of us and adjusts course," Yates said confidently, then he frowned. "Unless he thinks that's von Spee out there, or that he can nab us before they can turn around."

"That is the question. About another half hour before he raises the squadron's smoke?"

"Something like that," Yates agreed. "I'm just glad she's not anything larger — we'd be in extreme range not long after that if she had anything bigger than four-inchers."

Baxter nodded. There had to be some way for them to prevent *Kassel* from seeing the squadron and alerting von Spee, assuming he was even near the area. Try to ram the cruiser? It would never work. *Ludovic* would be pounded to scrap before then, and if she wasn't, the other ship was faster and more nimble. Neidermeyer would likely stand at least some distance off to shell them, so he'd be delayed for at least a little while, finishing them off. That, perhaps, was the best they could do, unless *Astute* did come up and engage the enemy. He didn't doubt that Sitwell would do exactly that — the two ships must be aware of each other, even if they were still miles apart and well out of range of their light main armament. He was vaguely surprised that they hadn't converged already, but both captains seemed content to have *Ludovic* as the rendezvous. By slowing, he'd brought that clash on sooner, and ensured that the Royal Navy cruiser would be on the scene sooner. Then they would have a chance of silencing the German for good.

Baxter clicked his fingers, finally remembering what Andrews had said. *Think of it like a noisy dinner party. You can't really hear what anyone any distance away is saying because there's just so much bloody noise filling the air between you and them. Jamming is like that — you feed the frequencies the other chap uses with rubbish noise so that he can't make out what's being said to him from across the table, or get his point across.*

Baxter didn't know if this was a theory or whether it had actually been tested. Only one way to find out.

"Yates, you have the bridge. I'm going down to the telegraphy room, if you need me."

The telegraphy room was tucked away near the officers' quarters, a reasonably large compartment but one dominated by the complex machinery that was its reason for existence. Like most telegraphy specialists Baxter had encountered in his career, Case was a young man, enthusiastic, and obviously intelligent. The sort of man who'd make an excellent officer, if he'd been born in better circumstances or the Royal Navy hadn't been so hidebound about who received the King's commission.

"I know what you mean, sir," the specialists said, when Baxter described what he wanted doing. "It's been tried before."

"Do you know the German frequencies?" Baxter asked.

"Got them all memorised, sir."

"What do you need to fill them with noise?"

"Might need someone to cover me on the tapper, sir, depending on how long you want me to go for, and some material to use."

"You'll have both." Baxter turned to go.

"When do you want me to start, sir?"

"Right now, Case. Make as much noise as you can."

Baxter headed back to the bridge. Even in the few minutes he'd been belowdecks, they'd closed with the squadron sufficiently that he could just make them out with the naked eye, and the details were quite clear through his field glasses. The two battlecruisers were unmistakable, larger than the ships around them and armed with long 12-inch guns in the modern, turreted manner. Three armoured first-class cruisers and two more modern light cruisers completed the squadron's strength. There was an armed merchant cruiser as well, but she would play no meaningful role in the engagement that would soon come.

Beyond the spread of ships — probably the greatest concentration of military power this part of the world had ever seen — Baxter could make out the low coastline of the Falkland Islands. Hard, rocky and windy, the coaling facility there was the sort of posting any man would dread unless he wanted a quiet, uninteresting life. But it would be welcome shelter for *Ludovic* and a source of supply for the battlecruisers after their month-long voyage.

"They're definitely on a heading to go into Stanley," Yates said. The ships were shouldering aside increasingly heavy seas as they ploughed east and south, aiming to go round the main island and towards the main settlement and the coaling station. "No sign that they've seen us, or if they have, they're not minded to investigate."

Baxter could picture the crews on those ships. The cruisers had been on station here for months, with little rest or resupply, and the battlecruisers had had a gruelling journey. "Well, they've got their orders and we've got ours," he said grimly.

"Sir! The German cruiser — looks like she's breaking off!" a watchman called out.

Both Baxter and Yates moved quickly over to observe the enemy vessel. She was proudly flying the German Imperial ensign. "You're not going to let her get out of sight, are you, sir?" Yates asked.

Baxter's grin was ferocious. "Indeed not, Mr Yates."

He had the liner brought about onto a heading that would, eventually, bring them astern of the cruiser. At the same time, he ordered their speed reduced even further so they didn't get *too* close to the enemy.

The positions and alignments had changed, but the essential problem had not. From the bridge, Baxter could now see both cruisers. *Kassel* was running just south of east now, no doubt trying to reconnoitre the British squadron while remaining out of their reach and indeed sight. *Astute* was now steaming just east of south to try to intercept *Ludovic*.

Baxter could almost feel the tension emanating from the bridge of the German ship. Would the captain abandon his idea of seizing or sinking the liner? It would mean offering battle to *Astute*, which, given their previous encounter, he might have good cause to think he would win. But he now had a more pressing concern — warning von Spee about two battlecruisers in the same waters.

There were too many variables for Baxter to come to any sort of conclusion. He would just have to wait and see which way Neidermeyer jumped, and how Sitwell responded.

He didn't have long to wait. The astute tactical move for the German at this point would have been to turn and run, try to get clear of the jamming so he could signal von Spee. Neidermeyer, Baxter already knew, wasn't the sort to do that. There was an enemy ship nearby, which might have been the source of the jamming, and one that threatened what he still seemed to think was a friendly ship.

As he had anticipated, *Kassel* came about again, flying back towards *Ludovic*.

"Now we've got you!" Baxter said aloud, unable to keep the exultation out of his voice and causing a number of the men to look round.

"Sir, I feel obligated to point out that we're not actually armed," Yates said.

"We're not," Baxter acknowledged, then he pointed to *Astute*, which was coming on in a fine old style and would be on top of them long before the German cruiser had closed to weapons range. "But *she* is. Have Captain Nielsen report to the bridge, Mr Yates, and then start preparing sufficient boats for the able-bodied men."

Baxter remained on the bridge while the two cruisers, both of them no doubt already at action stations, came tearing down on his undefended vessel. He was as certain as he could be that he'd worked out their relative speeds and positions accurately, and also read their intentions, but he knew it would be a close-run thing, and the German cruiser would be almost within weapons range by the time *Astute* reached them — assuming Sitwell didn't adjust course to intercept the German.

For a while, that did seem to be what *Astute* intended, as her course seemed to be aimed at cutting between *Kassel* and the liner. Baxter had their course adjusted onto more of an intercept course with the RN cruiser, but they were now close enough to use signal flags. It would mean that *Kassel* would see them, and a discerning officer would realise they were signalling in English, but Baxter was willing to take the risk if it meant being back aboard an armed vessel. The sixty men he had under his command would also be a welcome addition to the cruiser's crew before they went into action. *Kassel* was almost certainly committed now anyway.

"Signal *Astute* and ask them to come alongside for personnel transfer," Baxter ordered, then turned as Nielsen came onto the bridge, followed by Yates. "Captain, I have a new job for you, and one I think you'll find agreeable."

After days of plain sailing and the unrelenting tension of the two vessels behind them, everything seemed to happen at once. As soon as *Astute* had acknowledged the signal and altered course, Baxter started issuing a string of orders. Men came streaming up from every corner of the ship and made for the boat deck. Baxter couldn't strip everyone from the prize crew — Murphy remained below with the engines and a handful of stokers to supplement the men from Nielsen's crew, and a number of Marines had been detailed to remain behind to keep the German prisoners in line.

The men who had been working in the boiler rooms were filthy as they came, blinking, into the sunlight on deck. It was mid-morning, and the sun was high in a still-cloudless sky. The rising wind had a cutting edge to it, and the men who had come up from the hot gloom of the engineering compartments shivered until they were handed blankets or tunics. While a lot of the men had enjoyed living in the relative comfort of the civilian vessel, there was almost a carnival atmosphere as Pearson and the other petty officers marshalled them to the boats. They were going back to a familiar ship, and a familiar mess, and their mates. In a profession that took them all over the world, the one thing a British tar truly valued was continuity.

Nielsen, portly and weatherbeaten, looked around with a somewhat satisfied expression as he arrived on the bridge, having overseen his people taking over duties around the ship. The signal lamp mounted behind the chartroom was clattering away. *Astute* was now half a mile away, matching speed with *Ludovic*, while the German cruiser was still beyond effective gunnery range. That state wouldn't last long.

"She's all yours, Captain," Baxter said, thrusting out a hand. "Run as fast as you can into Stanley, keep the wireless transmitting on German frequencies, and make a report to the first officer ranked higher than midshipman that you see. Good luck to you."

"It's not us who'll need the luck, Mr Baxter," the merchant captain replied as he shook Baxter's hand firmly.

There was nothing else to say. Baxter looked around the expansive bridge one last time, at the merchant seamen who were now taking up positions at the lookout stations and by the speaking tubes. Then he turned and ran down to the boat deck, Yates on his heels.

"Everything is arranged, sir," the lieutenant reported. "*Astute* will pick us up."

"All right, lads," Baxter called out. "Into the boats, smartly now!"

The men cheered as they scrambled into the lifeboats. They were launching three of the big lifeboats, more than enough space for the men. He couldn't help but notice Hancock was carrying a canvas satchel that clinked slightly as he approached one of the lifeboats. "Not you, Hancock," Baxter said. "I need you to look after the ladies' comfort," he added quickly as the steward's face fell. That restored some of the old man's dignity, and he drew himself up and saluted.

"Very good, sir," he said drily.

Baxter climbed up into the boat, then nodded to the merchant seamen who were waiting to operate the davits. They swung the boat out and lowered away with more enthusiasm than finesse, the boat swinging on its ropes and earning the merchantmen a stream of abuse from their service counterparts.

Then the boat was in the water. "Ship oars!" Baxter barked. "Fend off there!"

A seaman in the bows fended them off from the liner's side far enough for the oars to go into the water. The wind was whipping in now, threatening to drive the boat against the ship's steel sides until the oars bit and gave it enough steerage way for Baxter to turn the tiller and put the bows into the wind and towards *Astute*. The cruiser was coming about in a wide half-circle to come running back in the opposite direction, but much closer this time.

Baxter heard a call from above, and craned his neck. All three boats were in the water now and the bluejackets were managing to pull in unison, driving the lifeboats forward. People were lining the rails, mostly the merchant seamen and some of the crew left behind, all of them cheering and waving their caps as the boats struck out. Baxter was surprised at how pleased he was to see Pippa along with the rest of the family, waving her handkerchief.

The boats were built for stability in heavy seas, which was a blessing, as the waves were taller than he'd appreciated from the stability and vantage point of the big liner. They were not, however, built for speed. "Pull, lads!" he shouted to the men, and the boat lurched forward, the men straining at their oars. The lean, fast cruiser had already completed her turn, close enough that Baxter could see the men at her starboard guns cheering on their shipmates even as the port guns were being trained on the oncoming German cruiser.

"Pull!" he heard Pearson roar at the men in his boat, then the sailor in the third lifeboat picked up the shout. They'd all been lowered more or less at the same time and were rowing in a somewhat staggered line abreast. Baxter rose in the boat, balancing effortlessly despite the rise and fall, and raised his voice. "A bottle of good whisky for the oarsmen of the first boat that makes it to *Astute*!"

The rowing men didn't have the breath to cheer, though he saw one or two grins.

Astute wasn't as tall as the liner, but she still appeared formidable as she cut through the waters, causing the lifeboats to bob dangerously. Baxter ordered the oarsmen forward again, knowing that hooking on to a moving vessel was the most dangerous part of the operation. The bow man managed it without any problem, however, getting his boathook onto the railing. The lifeboat was pulled forward independent of its oars now, several of which went over the side, while ropes and ladders came down to them.

The cruiser was doing less than ten knots — fast enough to cause the lifeboat to heel slightly as it bumped into her side, but not so fast that the boat was upended. The other two lifeboats hooked on, though it took the bowman in Pearson's boat two attempts. The men streamed up the sides, and were greeted with cheerful calls and a bit of mockery as they returned.

"Got tired of the soft beds, did you, mates?" someone asked.

"No mate, we burned them all!" came the response.

Baxter looked up towards the bridge and the tall, spare figure of Lieutenant Commander Sitwell, who beckoned him up. "Cast the boats off when everyone's out," he ordered, then went up the external companionways to make his report.

CHAPTER TWENTY-TWO

HMS *Astute* was already picking up speed by the time Baxter reached the bridge, the empty lifeboats bobbing forlornly in her wake as she came round on a heading to challenge SMS *Kassel*.

"Mr Baxter, good of you to join us," Sitwell said with a thin smile and a hint of warmth. He got right to the point. "Wireless room reports an awful lot of noise on the main German frequency — was that you?"

"I came as soon as I could, sir," Baxter said as he saluted. "And yes, sir — I've had *Ludovic*'s radio room attempting to jam any transmission from *Kassel* since she sighted the squadron. I thought it prudent to stop her getting the word out."

"Good thinking. I assume you've ordered the liner into port?"

"At best possible speed, sir, and to keep transmitting all the way. As well as the telegraphist, I left some engine crew, the surgeon's assistant and some Marines aboard *Ludovic*. Everyone else is back aboard *Astute* and reporting to their duty stations."

Sitwell nodded, taking the information in with the sort of calm assurance that marked him out as a man used to command. "We'll pick up the baton, certainly for as long as we can, but the best way to stop *Kassel* is to sink her."

"Am I back on the forward guns, sir?"

"Starboard battery and the forward guns, if you would?" the acting captain said. It was an order, of course, even if it was phrased as a question. "We'll be in range shortly, so I suggest—"

Sitwell was cut off by the *thud* of a distant gun firing, followed a moment later by the crash of a shell detonating on the water some hundred yards short of its target.

"Well, it seems the gentlemen of Germany have decided to fire first. To your station, Mr Baxter."

Baxter went down the starboard companionway to his new charges. They had a little time yet before they would be properly engaged — the German 4-inch guns had a maximum range of something over seven miles, and the single round that had been fired was short, even if the line had been good. *Astute*'s own guns had a slightly shorter range, which meant she would be subjected to enemy fire before she could return it, even if the enemy would likely find it difficult to land a hit despite their well-drilled gunnery. That would be the true test of the ship's company, both its courage and its discipline.

The men on the starboard guns seemed resolute enough, and as Baxter went from crew to crew he was pleased that he didn't need to give them any sort of encouraging speech or pick up any issues with their preparations. He'd been away from the ship for a good part of his assignment to her and hadn't got to know the men as well as he might have liked. The men seemed calmer and more confident than the last time he'd seen them go to action stations, at least.

"Hiscock, Evans," he greeted the ratings in command of the two forward guns, the men he probably knew best among the crew who had remained aboard *Astute*. "When we engage, it'll be the starboard gun unless we end up in a stern chase. We have to keep up a good rate of fire so, Evans, I want you to assign men from the port gun to support the starboard crew. Particularly when we take casualties."

Both men nodded their understanding. They were veterans, seasoned old salts, who understood that men *were* going to get injured or killed. "Not to worry about the gunnery, sir — Mr Simons has had us on exercises all the bleeding time. Even did some live firing once we'd left Piriápolis."

Baxter was relieved to hear that. Any practice was good practice, even if it wouldn't replace the months of hard drilling a crew needed to become a good crew. "Ammunition supply sorted?"

"Smooth as you like, sir. We're ready for them, this time."

"And we'll thump it into them this time," Baxter replied, finding the men's enthusiasm for the fight surprisingly infectious. It felt good, he had to admit, being back on a warship. *Astute* felt more lively, more responsive under his feet, more solid, even though she was smaller than the civilian ship. Mostly, of course, it was that he was aboard something that could shoot back.

Astute was already back up to speed, making at least fifteen knots by his estimation — one of the benefits of having oil-fired boilers as well as coal-fired, in addition to the relatively new machinery. *Kassel* was still well ahead, steaming on a north-easterly course and clearly intending to run for more open water. Sitwell had brought *Astute* round onto a similar heading but slightly further north, in the hopes of overhauling the German ship to bring his full broadside to bear.

"Is she running, sir?" Hiscock asked, following the direction Baxter was looking.

"Perhaps," Baxter said, then wiped spray from his face as *Astute* went through a taller wave. The seas were getting up, which would make gunnery more of a challenge, and he wondered whether Sitwell would try to close the range before he gave the order. *Astute* had already expended a good amount of ammunition with no chance of a resupply, although the hoist malfunctions had meant she hadn't thrown her entire stock at the enemy cruiser before. "Or he wants us further from the Falklands and Sturdee's ships before he turns and offers battle."

The cruiser's motion was very different to that of the liners, being a smaller, leaner ship not designed for the comfort of paying passengers, but Baxter adapted quickly to it again. He sent a ship's boy down to his cabin to bring up his greatcoat, as the waves were now crashing over the cruiser's sharp bows and sending spray hurling down her length. The men were already bundled against these conditions, a far cry from the almost tropical conditions they were in just a few days ago.

Kassel remained resolutely ahead and with her stern to *Astute*. "She is running, but we're going to catch her!" someone shouted over the noise of the wind and the waves.

Baxter wasn't convinced. Neidermeyer didn't strike him as the type to refuse an engagement, particularly against a similar ship he'd already got the better of once. His only hope, if he did want to escape rather than fight, was to find foul weather and run into it, or manage to stay ahead until nightfall and hope to lose them in the dark, just as Baxter had done off the coast of Uruguay.

It struck him, though, that the German cruiser was perhaps not fleeing, but trying to get clear of the interference. If so, it was a vain hope. *Ludovic*'s wireless set was powerful, but it would be out of range soon. However, there was no escaping *Astute*.

"Here we go, lads," he said, as he saw the twin flash of *Kassel*'s stern guns firing. They threw up splashes two hundred yards ahead of *Astute*'s bows.

"Shall we return fire, sir?" Evans asked.

"Not until we're ordered to." They weren't in range yet, anyway. Simons, as the gunnery officer, would have his eyes glued to a rangefinder in the armoured gunnery control station perched above the bridge, although this sort of stern chase would be making the calculations that bit harder.

As Baxter watched, *Kassel* started to turn, and for a moment it looked like she was ready to fight. The manoeuvre was just to bring one of her stern broadside guns to bear, though. All three guns fired together, a tight grouping not far off *Astute*'s bows, close enough that the wind carried water from the shell splashes back onto Baxter's guns.

Even that slight turn would have lost the German ship ground, which suggested the German captain knew he wasn't going to be able to get clear and was hoping for a lucky hit with the guns he could bring to bear. *Astute* was speeding up again, pressing up towards her maximum speed despite the strain it would be putting on her machinery and fuel stocks, while *Kassel* steadied back on her original course.

They ran on like that for another half an hour, the German ship occasionally turning slightly to bring one or other of her sternmost broadside guns to bare. As the range closed, her shells landed closer and closer, splinters from surface detonations clattering against *Astute*'s bows and causing the men to flinch, though no one showed any sign of ducking or trying to run for cover. There was little to be had on the windswept foredeck.

Baxter was on the verge of going to the speaking tubes mounted behind the gun battery to request permission to try the range, when the messenger boy stationed there dashed forward. "Captain orders independent fire as we bear, sir!" the lad shouted over the sound of another close detonation.

Baxter called Evans and Hiscock over. Both men were grinning, anticipating the chance to return the fire, and they weren't disappointed. "We're not in a rush here," Baxter cautioned them. "Aimed fire, and we'll need to adjust for the closing distance constantly. We'll aim for the aftermast."

The men nodded, though Baxter guessed they'd both rather be trying to hit the guns that were harassing them. The chances of a hit on any part of the enemy ship at this range, still more than five miles, were slim anyway. Killing the enemy cruiser's chance of broadcasting a warning to von Spee was more important than killing her guns, in Baxter's estimation.

He took up his station between and a little behind the two long weapons, ready to receive and pass on orders and targeting information. What he wanted to be doing was getting down behind the sights, ordering fine corrections to the shooting, but it wasn't his role and it would undermine the confidence of the gun crews.

"You may commence when ready!" Baxter shouted when both guns were loaded and laid. "Independent fire!"

The long 4-inch guns slammed back on their mountings almost in unison, muzzle flash bright despite the hour and puffs of foul yellow cordite fumes being ripped away by the wind. Baxter glanced down at his watch to note the time — a quarter past midday — then back up in time to see the shell splashes rise, both of them to port of the target but tightly grouped. Baxter brought his glasses up as the guns were reloaded, first the shell then bagged cordite, both dangerous in their own ways, and watched as *Kassel* turned again, sending three shells hurtling back at her pursuer. The shells straddled the cruiser this time, two bursting to port and one to starboard. Behind him someone screamed in pain, while another voice shouted for stretcher-bearers. Baxter ordered a slight change in the gun's laying. "Wait for it, lads," he said, after watching the other ship for a moment. They were closing all the time, to the extent that Baxter could now make out tiny figures moving around *Kassel*'s exposed stern guns when he looked through the glasses.

The German cruiser adjusted course again, to present the narrowest possible target. "Wait for it," he said again. *Kassel* briefly yawed to port. "Shoot!"

The guns spoke again as the enemy vessel slowed and presented a wider target. One 4-inch shell hit the water just yards from the enemy's stern; the second whipped over the stern gun crews and burst in the water on the far side. The German guns fired, but it seemed at least one of the gun crews had been put off final adjustments by the shell going over their heads, as *Kassel* shot wide.

"That's put the wind up them!" someone shouted.

"Silence on deck!" Baxter snapped. "Reload, smartly now!"

He didn't know if any of the enemy's crew had been hit, but *Astute* had already taken casualties. He'd be damned if she took the first substantive hit, though.

Another correction came from the gunnery post, passed by the signal boy. Bigger ships, Baxter knew, had far better fire control systems, where this information would be fed directly into the well-protected turrets. He felt absurdly exposed, standing tall and ramrod-straight, one of the closest men to the enemy, as he ordered corrections based on the information.

Another turn coming up. Neidermeyer had made the mistake of becoming predictable, twitching his course to port and starboard in order to bring different guns to bear each time. Baxter felt calm as he watched the turn develop. "Shoot!" he ordered.

Hiscock was a second faster this time, his shell splashing into the water within yards of the enemy vessel again. A ragged cheer went up, though, when Evans managed to land a direct hit, the shell bursting on the deck between the aft mast and the stern guns. Baxter let the men cheer a moment longer. "Reload!"

This time, *Kassel* wasn't just turning slightly. She came all the way round in as tight a turn as she could manage onto a southerly heading, bringing her full starboard battery to bear. Four guns fired, a rippling barrage that stopped before the stern gun. *Astute* crashed through the water spouts, splinters ringing against her hull again, but came out unscathed. Baxter expected Sitwell to order a change of course, but he instead held steady, tearing forwards as though he intended to cross *Kassel*'s stern or at least get closer before altering course to bring his full battery to bear.

The German fired again, and again, with the same machine-like precision Baxter had come to respect and fear in equal measures. *Astute* staggered as a shell burst in her upperworks, and again as one hit dangerously close to the waterline. Baxter's mind became detached, clinical almost, as he analysed the situation. The German 4-inch gun fired cased ammunition of a kind he was familiar with from other postings. All the crew had to do was open the breech, throw a complete round in and fire, then swing the breech open to eject the spent cartridge case, slam a new round home and repeat. That meant they could achieve a significantly high rate of fire compared to his own guns, though they didn't seem to be firing with quite the same furious speed as they'd previously encountered.

Baxter's guns were firing without needing orders now. For the next few minutes they would be the only guns that would bear, and his men went about the task with a will and efficiency that made him proud. Sweating despite the chill in the air, they delivered shells and propellant to the guns, and then presented the high-explosive rounds to the German ship. They scored a hit, then another. While they had fewer guns firing, *Kassel* was now an easier target as she lay side-on, showing no sign of completing a turn to come racing down past *Astute* so they would be broadside to broadside. The enemy cruiser was moving almost perpendicular to the line being drawn through the sea by *Astute*, which meant they had to anticipate the amount she would move during the shell's flight, but the RN gun crews finally seemed to have found their rhythm. They weren't hitting every time, and they weren't firing as fast as the Germans, but they *were* hitting the enemy ship.

Yates, who was assigned to damage control, arrived next to Baxter. "Is it me, sir, or is she a bit slow?" he shouted over the noise of the guns.

"I'd say so — her machinery must be pretty worn by now!" he shouted back. "Evans, adjust three degrees starboard!"

"Well, she may not need to be too fast," Yates added, pointing to the south. Baxter, who had been focused on the target, felt his heart lurch as he imagined just for a second that Neidermeyer was running for the protection of von Spee's squadron. Then he saw the mass of storm clouds that were already lashing the sea with rain some distance to the south. "That would be poetic justice, wouldn't it?" said Yates, referring to the squall Baxter had used to extricate them from the last battle between the two ships.

"That rain's going to be colder," Baxter murmured distractedly, then asked the younger lieutenant, "Do you have any damage to control?"

"Everything's under control, and I needed to stretch my legs and see what's going on," came the reply. A moment later, the whole ship rang like a gong as a shell glanced off her bows and exploded thirty yards to port. A gunner went down screaming, his left arm torn off at the elbow. Evans died silently, crumpling at his station with a fragment embedded in his skull.

"Stretcher-bearers!" Baxter roared, while Yates dashed to the fallen man. The stench of burning hair and flesh mingled with cordite fumes, and Baxter realised the heat of the shell fragment had scorched Evans' sandy hair. He stepped forward, placing himself between the dead man and his stunned crew.

"There's nothing you can do for him now, lads," he said, his tone firm and calm. He pointed to a gunner with able seamen insignia. "You're in command of the gun now. Keep up the rate of fire, and keep hitting that bastard."

He had to raise his voice to be heard over the starboard gun firing. The men were clearly rattled, so Baxter led by example. While stretcher-bearers removed the dead and injured, he pushed seamen towards the ammunition hoist and took direct charge of laying the gun. Gradually the men remembered their duty, their training winning out over the shock that had briefly overwhelmed them. Looking across the gun's sights, Baxter was pleased to see *Kassel*'s aft mast was leaning, most of its stay ropes shot away. The two ships had come dangerously close, and Baxter could actually make out the lookouts quickly scurrying down the leaning mast before it went by the board entirely. Grimly, he put a high-explosive shell right into the German cruiser where the aft mast passed through the deck.

The effect was instantaneous and devastating. With a great tear they could hear even across the stretch of shell-torn water, *Kassel*'s mast broke clear and went into the water. It wasn't a clean break, as it was still anchored to the ship by lines, and while that wasn't as devastating as it would have been for a ship under sail, it still served as something of a sea anchor. Men were running with axes to cut away the last of the cables.

"Want us to hit them there again, sir?" the able seaman who now had charge of the gun asked.

"No, concentrate on the forward mast," Baxter ordered, taking in the situation with a sweep of his gaze. The cruisers were hammering each other at close to point-blank range now, through *Kassel* was drawing away and was now almost into the curtain of rain she'd been running for. Their aspects were reversed, *Kassel* now only able to bring her stern guns to bear and those masked by the wreckage of the mast, while *Astute* was able to bring her full broadside into play for the first time.

Baxter went along the starboard guns one by one and exhorted every gun crew to fire as fast and true as they could at the forward sections of the German ship. The men did as they were ordered, hammering shot after shot into the German cruiser as the light dimmed and the first spots of icy-cold rain came down. The sea was becoming properly rough, tall waves starting to roll the cruiser and make the gunners' task harder, but Baxter was gratified to see a number of shells hit home around the forward mast, bast and shrapnel tearing up wire and stays.

Baxter reached the stern guns, which Yates commanded, just as they started losing sight of the cruiser in the worsening weather. Sitwell hadn't ordered a change of course and *Kassel* was pulling away from them, so he knew he had to make these last shots count. Yates was already ordering the crew to aim for the mast, as he understood the need to silence the cruiser if they couldn't sink it. Shells were continuing to pummel the German cruiser, which was rapidly fading from view. She saluted them a final time with the two stern guns just as *Astute* put a last few rounds into her. Baxter thought he caught a flash of something going by the board on the enemy vessel, which might have been her forward mast, but it was impossible to say for sure.

Then the storm was onto them full force, the cruiser pitching so suddenly and violently that Yates lost his footing and went sliding towards the gunwale. Baxter lunged forward, head down into a wall of water and reaching blindly. Somehow he caught a handful of Yates's greatcoat and, straining against the pressure of retreating water that wanted to take the man it had claimed to his grave, he lifted the other officer and deposited him on his feet.

"Grateful to you, Baxter!" Yates shouted over the sudden roar of the wind. He seemed unruffled, even if he'd lost his cap.

Baxter braced himself against the powerful pitching. "Lifelines fore and aft, Mr Yates, and get any man who doesn't need to be on deck below!" he ordered. While it was hard to determine their heading in the sudden tumult of icy rain, he couldn't shake the feeling that Sitwell was turning the ship north, rather than south after their quarry. It wouldn't take them clear of the storm, which was rolling north from the icy wastes of Antarctica, but it would mean they would have no chance of finding *Kassel* again and finally finishing the engagement they'd begun off the coast of Uruguay.

"I'm going to the bridge!" Baxter bellowed in Yates's ear. "See if there are any orders."

CHAPTER TWENTY-THREE

The storm, mercifully, was a short-lived affair. It was intense while it lasted, tossing the cruiser this way and that, as though she was a much smaller vessel. It made damage control that much harder, though there were only two significant holes in the hull to deal with. However, the storm also had the benefit of putting out a couple of fires that had been started by the detonation of German shells.

One of the last two shells that *Kassel* had sent their way had inflicted a terrible blow of a different kind. "There was nothing I could do," Dr Martin, the ship's surgeon, told Baxter quietly as he took a break from his rounds. Baxter had gone to the sickbay to check on the men from his gun crews who had been injured during the engagement and in the subsequent storm. It was calmer by this point, and *Astute* steamed across a relatively placid sea as night drew in. "A shell splinter nicked his carotid artery, and he bled to death on the bridge."

Baxter looked down at Sitwell's lifeless face. The wound near his throat didn't look like much, a small gash really, but the lieutenant commander's life had bled out through it. He and Sitwell had rubbed each other the wrong way from the beginning of their association, but Baxter had come to respect the man, and found him to be a better commander than Gregson had proved himself to be.

"What about Captain Gregson?" he asked, conscious of the fact that he hadn't asked after the ship's actual commander since he'd come back aboard.

"Oh, he went ashore in Uruguay — he was still comatose, and land-based surgeons will be able to do far more for him than I can." Martin paused, looking slightly embarrassed. "I have heard some of the men saying the ship's cursed, but the curse mostly impacts the commanding officers."

Baxter struggled to keep his expression impassive, though there was a superstitious corner of his mind that had started to wonder the same thing. "The bridge is an exposed place, particularly when shells are coming down from above," he said.

"And what does our current commander intend to do?" Martin asked.

"We're making for Stanley, to report in to Admiral Sturdee, resupply and make repairs. We should be in before midnight at the latest."

"Assuming the German ship doesn't find us again."

Baxter snorted contemptuously. "*Kassel* is long gone, either running for Africa in the hopes of finding a friendly port, or south and west to try to find von Spee." Just for a moment, the notion of the battered cruiser wandering the oceans of the world like a modern-day and considerably more lethal *Flying Dutchman* came to his tired brain.

"She might have sunk in the storm, if we're lucky," Martin said, then pulled a sheet reverently over Sitwell's face. "I must tend to my patients who still live."

Baxter thought on the doctor's comment as he made his way back to his quarters. He didn't think they were that lucky, though one of the lookouts had reported seeing flotsam in the wave-tossed aftermath of the storm. That was probably just one of the masts, or something else they'd shot off the cruiser. *Kassel* was either gone, or they would see her again. One last time.

Simons, now the cruiser's second acting captain, clearly thought *Kassel* was long gone. Baxter hadn't had an opportunity to speak to the man aside from a brief, yelled conversation when Simons had effectively rubber-stamped the orders Baxter had already given Yates, and then retreated to the chart room and left Baxter in charge on the bridge. It had been a long and miserable afternoon, the icy storm narrowing their world view down to a wall of battleship-grey rain slashing down from the sky and chilling the men to the bone. The fact the storm had come on the heels of an engagement had left the men deflated and subdued, unable to recover from the adrenalin rush and exhaustion of combat as they fought to keep their ship afloat. When Baxter had tried to propose that they turn once again to the South Atlantic to hunt for *Kassel*, Simons had frostily rejected the suggestion, only unbending slightly to order Baxter to get some rest.

He was a seasoned enough sailor to know when he should rest, and could drop off no matter the conditions. He slept only fitfully, though, and woke after only a few hours in a cold sweat with the image of *Kassel*'s guns blinking at him fresh in his mind.

He swung his feet down onto the cold wood of the deck, then stood, being careful to stoop so he didn't crack his head on the deckhead, and peered in the mirror. He looked haggard, and he knew that was partly because the German cruiser loomed larger in his mind than any previous enemy.

There was something about the stubborn way the enemy ship had dogged him that made it stick in his mind. The next time he crossed paths with her, he would do everything in his power to make sure she was sunk, burned or destroyed.

His cabin smelled of sweat and brine and dampness. Forcing the porthole open, he took a deep breath of clean air. There was a tang of smoke to it, and he realised that his view included a low, dark landmass. They had finally arrived in the Falklands.

Baxter washed and dressed, omitting to shave in the low light, and headed up onto the deck. Ahead, he could see the menacing shapes of the battlecruisers, anchored in the deep water harbour of Port William. The ships were well lit, as this was a friendly harbour and nobody wanted a collision in the darkness, and as *Astute* passed between them he got a good look at the brooding menace contained in the long armoured hulls, the twin 12-inch guns extended from four low armoured turrets. Around the battlecruisers were three armoured cruisers, even more brightly lit and with colliers lashed alongside. Even over the throb of *Astute*'s engines, Baxter could hear the distant shouts of men engaged in the feast of coal.

Astute was exchanging messages via signal lamp with what he assumed was *Invincible*, Vice-Admiral Sir Doveton Sturdee's flagship. The battlecruiser's searchlight briefly illuminated the cruiser, dazzling Baxter. The light went off briefly, having destroyed Baxter's night vision, and *Astute* went on her way, sliding through a narrower channel. The bay beyond was much wider than it was long, stretching for miles to either side of the narrow entry while the town of Stanley itself lay a short distance across from the entry. Looking to one side, Baxter could see the ancient HMS *Canopus*, a relic from the last century, anchored close to the land. She would be far too slow and unreliable for a fight at sea, but her big 12-inch guns would be able to cover the harbour and possibly shell anything approaching from the south.

Stanley itself was much as Baxter remembered it from his previous visit: a collection of white-painted buildings, perhaps more expansive than before, with only municipal buildings and the church built of stone. There were a number of ships in the inner harbour, which wasn't big or deep enough for the heavy ships of the squadron. He saw the two light cruisers in Sturdee's force, and the hulk of an old passenger liner now clearly being used for coal storage. He felt a surprising surge of relief when he saw *Ludovic* there, moored safe at the heart of the docks.

"Well, it seems we made it, old boy," Littleton drawled as he came up alongside Baxter on the afterdeck. "Quite an adventure we've all had. Yates has been regaling me with tales all afternoon. Good job I ordered you to undertake the mission, eh?" Littleton went on, an uncustomary note of caution in his voice.

Baxter glanced at him and saw the officer was looking up at him questioningly. He remembered, in a flash, Sitwell asking him whether Littleton had agreed to the assault on *Ludovic* or whether he had ordered it, and smiled thinly.

"Oh, indeed, Littleton," he said coldly. They both knew the truth of it, but there was little point in Baxter arguing the point publicly. He'd always been an outsider in the RN, not quite the right class to be an officer but too middle-class to have enlisted as a rating. Littleton, on the other hand, was exactly the right sort, and with a feather in his cap from the successful operation he would be able to seek out what his heart desired most — a shore posting, probably at the Admiralty itself. That was his calculation, anyway, though Baxter harboured some doubts that it would shake out the way he thought it would.

"Jolly good, glad we're on the same page. Now, tell me about these two sisters you encountered. Quite a pair of beauties, I gather?"

"Good night, Littleton," Baxter said, and turned away. He walked forward to watch the evolutions as the cruiser was brought into her berth. Her draught was shallow enough for her to tie up alongside the dock rather than anchoring in deeper water.

Those members of the ship's company who had been left on *Ludovic* were paraded on the dock, even the seamen and stokers managing a neat formation next to the impeccable file of Marines. They were all there, even some of the walking wounded, and they raised a cheer as *Astute* tied up. They hurried back aboard as soon as the gangplank was run out, while more than a few men on deck stared at the inviting dockside pubs while their comrades returned.

Baxter knew any hope of shore leave would be futile. The exhausted men were roused from their bunks to begin the necessary repair work, though Simons had sense enough to have the galley fired up so the men could eat first. Littleton was sent ashore to arrange their turn at the coaling hulk and to see if he could scrounge up any more 4-inch ammunition from *Bristol* and *Glasgow*, the two light cruisers moored in the harbour, both of which mounted the same Mk VII gun *Astute* did.

"Well, I expect that's the last we'll see of him tonight," Yates said as he and Baxter set to organising work parties while the now first officer strode confidently down the ramp and then off towards HMS *Glasgow*. "He's been talking about nothing but a run ashore."

Baxter grunted. "As long as he does what he's been sent to do first, I'll be quite happy if he's out from underfoot."

Watching Littleton board the neighbouring vessel, though, Baxter couldn't shake a slight sense of impending disaster.

He shook off that notion and threw himself into the necessary work. *Astute* had damage from both the battle and the storm to repair, and Littleton seemed to be good for something at least as messengers arrived to inform them that work parties would deliver ammunition from the other ships, though not in any great amount, and work parties would be needed to see it safely stowed. Not long after that, a further message arrived to announce that time had been booked alongside the coaling hulk, first thing in the morning.

"Anyone seen Littleton?" Simons demanded testily, an hour after the message had arrived about the coal deliveries. It was going on eleven in the evening, and most of the men were tired to the point of exhaustion.

"Last I saw of him, he was coming off *Great Britain* over there," Yates said, gesturing to the ancient coal hulk that somehow didn't quite suit her name. "I think he might have stopped in at the hotel just along there for a drink."

"Damn him," Simons snapped.

Baxter found himself idly wondering if the Sears party had put up at the hotel, given it was close to where *Ludovic* was tied up. Even with the recent influx of ships, he couldn't imagine the establishment had a lot of guests, and he guessed Mrs Sears at least had had more than enough of sea travel for at least a little while.

His notion was confirmed a few minutes later when Charles Finlay emerged from the hotel and strode along to *Astute*, anxiously scanning the railing for any familiar faces.

"Let him up," Baxter ordered the sentry posted at the bottom of the boarding ramp, and a smile split the young would-be soldier's face as he hurried aboard and shook both Baxter and Yates's hands enthusiastically.

"Bloody happy to see the both of you alive, and Mr Sears sends his compliments," Finlay said, "but I wonder if we might have a quick chat in private, Baxter?"

"There's very little privacy on a warship, Finlay — let's step onto the docks."

They walked a little way from the foot of the ramp in companionable silence. Baxter had to admit, he'd come to like Finlay, even if he was a solicitor and would soon be a soldier.

"This chap Lieutenant Littleton," Finlay said, a little uncertainly. "I think he's in the process of getting you into a spot of bother. He's had a couple of gins in the bar, and is telling everyone who'll listen about how he masterminded getting us out of the pickle we were in, back in Montevideo, and how he ordered you to seize the liner. 'Neutrality and the law be damned!' were the words he used, I believe. He's particularly keen that Pippa knows he ordered the whole thing, though I do have the feeling he may not be telling the whole truth. Us legal types get a nose for that sort of thing…"

He trailed off, and Baxter waited impassively. Littleton's attempt to borrow glory, or what he mistakenly believed was glory, wasn't unexpected, though he was surprised Littleton had taken enough liberty with his permission to go ashore that he was getting very drunk.

"Anyway, the rub of it is, there are some of your chaps in the bar as well. One chap in particular, who everyone refers to as 'Sir Doveton' and who seems to be in a position of authority, was apparently having a drink before returning to his boat, and is now taking quite an interest in what Littleton has to say. He, ah, does not seem particularly happy."

Baxter scratched his cheek, and immediately regretted not having shaved that day. "Sir Doveton Sturdee?" he said. "The vice-admiral in command of this squadron is ashore?"

"Well, yes, I suppose he might be. He seems like a very impressive man."

Baxter wasn't sure which fact concerned him more — that Littleton was running his mouth in front of the most senior officer in these waters, or that said officer was not aboard his command.

"I have to say, I did expect a bit more urgency from your chaps," Finlay was saying. "Everyone's very curious about your ship and the fight you were just in, and the prisoners now on the old ship. But there's also a lot of talk about a shooting expedition tomorrow, and your admiral chap was just saying what a pleasant walk on the beach he had this afternoon."

"Listen, Finlay, I greatly appreciate you coming out to warn me. Is there any way you can get Littleton to shut up? Maybe encourage him to leave?"

"I can go and get my Luger?" Finlay suggested brightly. It seemed he might have developed a taste for shooting people, which was perhaps just as well.

"No, not a good idea," Baxter said. "Probably not, anyway."

He was still thinking about how he might extricate Littleton when a tall, heavyset man with lieutenant commander's stripes on his cuff emerged from the hotel. He paused on the street, slightly taken aback. "You wouldn't be Lieutenant Marcus Baxter by any chance, would you?" he asked, approaching them.

Too late, Baxter thought, as he drew himself up and saluted. "That's me, sir."

"Your colleague Mr Littleton said you were a giant, but we thought he was rather exaggerating. Apparently not."

"Is there something I can do for you, sir?" Baxter asked patiently.

"Admiral Sturdee has asked if you wouldn't mind stepping into the hotel over there and answering some questions about how you came to board and seize that liner."

"Happy to oblige, sir. Finlay, it was good to see you again — please give my regards to your family."

Baxter was acutely conscious that his uniform was disarrayed and he had a couple of days' beard on his jaw as he stepped into the brightly lit interior of the hotel. There was nothing for it but to go full ahead, however.

The bar was slightly disconcerting — despite being thousands of miles from London, it could almost have been transported directly from a more fashionable establishment in the capital. After a moment, though, the illusion wore off and Baxter could see how corners had been cut and the interior simply dolled up to look the part.

There were a number of naval officers sitting on the sofas and chairs arranged around the large room, and every eye turned to him as he entered, followed discreetly by the officer who had summoned him. Littleton was at the bar, giving a blow-by-blow account of the action *Astute* had just fought to a couple of other lieutenants. The only one who mattered was Sir Doveton Sturdee, recently appointed to a seagoing command from a posting at the Admiralty, and a man with a reputation for being firm but fair, and entirely by the book. More problematic for Baxter, however, was that Sturdee was known to be at odds with Jackie Fisher. While that was hardly surprising, as the new First Sea Lord collected enemies with abandon, if Sturdee got wind that Baxter had once served alongside Fisher and might be considered a member of the Fishpond, it may not go well for him.

Sturdee raised a hand to beckon Baxter over. He walked across the room, aware of a falling silence and Littleton's voice trailing off.

"Mr Baxter," Vice-Admiral Sturdee said, in a calm and impassive tone, "I've been listening with rapt attention to what your colleague has been saying about how the service has come to be in possession of such a fine passenger liner. Is there anything you would like to report about the matter or add to what Mr Littleton has said?"

Baxter straightened up, and prepared to do something Ekaterina had always warned him against — tell the truth when a lie would be much better. Before he could speak, however, Littleton stepped up alongside him. "Mr Baxter played his part admirably, sir!" he declared forcefully. Baxter glanced at him, and saw that the other lieutenant, while being a bit tipsy, was clearly not drunk and knew exactly what he was doing. "I only wish I'd been able to go along with him to ensure things went more smoothly. Alas, my duties lay elsewhere."

Baxter clenched his jaw so hard the muscles hurt. It wasn't so much that Littleton was trying to take credit that angered him — he'd never been particularly interested in accolades. It was the way in which he was failing to read the room or the mood of the flag officer he was addressing that put his back up. That and the implication that the overinflated popinjay would have handled the situation better than he did.

"I rather think Mr Baxter can speak for himself, Lieutenant," Sturdee said icily, his gaze never shifting from the subject of his scrutiny.

Ekaterina had always told him he was too honest for the sort of work she did, constitutionally incapable of telling a lie or letting any attempt at dissimulation to show on his face. Littleton made it surprisingly easy for him.

"Nothing to add, sir," he said, managing to keep his voice level. "Mr Littleton ordered me aboard *Ludovic*, and I went."

Sturdee's eyes flashed with anger as he put down his drink to stare imperiously at the two men. "Do you mean to say, Mr Littleton, that you knowingly broke international law and violated the neutrality of a valuable trading partner, in order to seize a paltry *liner*?" he snapped, rising to his feet.

Littleton blanched, realising far too late what Baxter had known all along — that Sturdee was not a receptive audience. He was a sailor of the old school, who had resisted any number of innovations during his time as Third Sea Lord, and who felt the only way to resolve this conflict was an honest, straight-up fight between battlefleets. "Well, we weren't caught sir..." he began weakly. He looked up at Baxter almost beseechingly, and received only a stony glance in return.

"That is entirely beside the point, Lieutenant!" Sturdee barked. "Whether or not your actions caused an international incident is secondary to the fact that neutrality should be considered inviolable. And we cannot know what the long-term ramifications of what you have done will be."

The admiral mastered himself with an effort. "Mr Baxter, I am disappointed with you. An officer should know when the orders he is given are questionable. However, follow orders you did. You will confine yourself to your quarters aboard HMS *Astute* pending disciplinary action."

Sturdee's cold eyes turned towards Littleton. "Mr Littleton, a man of your experience should have known better. I will draft orders to have you removed from your ship and detained ashore until such time as I can decide what to do with you. Dismissed!"

Baxter executed an about-face with parade-ground precision, and forced himself to walk from the hotel with a measured pace. Littleton fled ahead of him, and Baxter braced himself for what he knew was coming.

"You could have said something!" Littleton bleated once they were clear of the hotel. "It was your bloody idea, after all — the whole thing!"

"All that would do is make you look like a liar, Littleton," Baxter said coldly. He knew he could have stepped in, done the honourable thing. He could go back, but he remembered Ekaterina's previous admonitions. *Sometimes, you let a villain hang himself.* "And a braggart."

Littleton flinched. "You have to understand, Baxter. I'm a navy man through and through, of course. But I can't abide being at sea. This was my chance at a plum shore appointment. It doesn't matter to you — you're not a career man —"

Baxter rounded on him. "You know nothing about me," he said in a low growl. "You made this bed, Littleton, and I'm not going to take your place in it."

He left the other officer standing in the cold night and stalked back up the gangplank onto *Astute*, where a furious Simons awaited him. "Just where the devil have you been?" demanded the acting captain. "And where do you think you're going?"

"I've been relieved of duty and confined to quarters." Baxter pointed back to the disconsolate Littleton, who still stood, shoulders slumped, on the dock. "Ask him why."

Baxter brushed past Simons and went up to his tiny cabin. There was a bottle of whisky on the little writing desk, one of those spared when they'd lightened *Ludovic*'s load, and a cut-glass tumbler next to it.

The urge to crack it open and drink the lot was strong, and there was a time he'd have done just that. Instead, Baxter poured himself a stiff measure, corked the bottle and tucked it away in his locker. He managed about half the measure before, still fully clothed, he fell asleep.

CHAPTER TWENTY-FOUR

Dawn the following day was surprisingly clear and calm. The sun shone down from an almost cloudless sky, though the air was cold. Baxter, standing alone on Sapper Hill, relished the peace and quiet after so many fraught days at sea and the pressure of responsibility that had rested on his shoulders. Responsibility he had taken on himself, often against orders — he couldn't deny that. Being shot of it was a welcome relief.

Having been relieved of duty and confined to quarters, he perhaps should not have been out and about, but as an officer he had a certain amount of leeway. Having risen before dawn, he'd felt an overpowering desire to be away from the cruiser that now lay berthed some distance below him.

There were a few people around, despite the early hour. As it was summer at this latitude, the sheep farmers would have been up with the sun a little after four in the morning, and he could see activity on the ships in the bays that glittered in the sunlight. It looked like it was the battlecruisers' turn to coal, and one of the armoured cruisers didn't have steam up, which suggested at least one of her engines was being serviced. Looking through the glasses he'd slung around his neck out of habit, he examined *Astute*. She definitely looked a bit battered, her plating and decks buckled and scorched in places. He wondered why there was no sign of the crew on deck yet, beyond the watchkeepers.

Not my problem, he told himself. Lowering his glasses, Baxter was surprised to see Pippa Sears standing a few feet from him. "There was a time, Miss Sears, when no one would have been able to creep up on me like that," he said.

She was wrapped up warm, in what looked to be locally made clothing, her cheeks red in the chill wind. "I wouldn't say I'd crept up on you, Mr Baxter," she said. "I merely took advantage of your distraction."

"Are you by yourself?"

"I couldn't interest anyone else in an early morning constitutional." She gestured with an expansive arm towards the desolate, rocky landscape around them. "What a wonderful place this is!"

"It has its charm," Baxter admitted. Pippa seemed more relaxed than he'd seen her before, which was perhaps unsurprising.

"And what a collection of warships — surely they must sweep all before them?"

"There're enough to deal with von Spee, without doubt."

"What of that rather odd-looking one, over by the harbour mouth? Will she sail?"

"That's *Canopus*, a battleship. She's too old to steam, but she makes a damn fine battery." Baxter passed her the field glasses and she squinted through them. "See how they've struck her masts and painted the upperworks to match the landscape? With any luck, an approaching raider won't spot her until they're well within range of her heavy guns."

"And the fellows on the hill above will tell her which way to shoot?" she asked, gesturing to one of the watch posts established along the south of the island.

Baxter nodded. "They're connected by telephone to *Canopus*, I gather."

"And your ship, Mr Baxter — *Astute*, was it? Will she be joining the fight?"

His face fell. The thought of the cruiser steaming out to face the enemy without him suddenly seemed utterly … wrong.

She read his expression. "Oh, I do apologise. Henrietta said you'd had a spot of bother."

He waved her apology away. "I made a decision that Sir Doveton disapproves of, and that's the end of it."

"You don't strike me as someone who gives up so easily, Mr Baxter."

He squinted into the wind, trying to find the words for just how tired he was, how frustrated by men like Littleton, how the Saunders and Arbuthnotts of the world tied him up in their schemes. But Pippa was right. He wasn't the sort to give up easily.

He grinned at her. "You're right, of course, Miss Sears."

"Call me Pippa," she said. "Just not when my parents can hear."

He was about to reply, to try out her name, when the *crack* of a gun firing reverberated across the bay. Baxter's head snapped up in time to see the puff of smoke dissipating from *Glasgow*'s signal gun. Both she and *Canopus* were flying the signal any sailor worth his salt would recognise, and *Glasgow* had her searchlight trained on the flagship's bridge, trying to get the crew's attention through the haze of coal dust that surrounded the ship.

Enemy in sight.

Baxter turned on the spot. He could see plumes of smoke to the south, dangerously close to the southern coast of the island. His heart thudded in his chest — had all their efforts of the previous day been in vain? Von Spee, from what Baxter knew of him, was the sort of commander who, if informed his enemy had just arrived in port, might just risk a throw of the dice on surprising a more powerful squadron at anchor. He might try to do as much damage as possible before escaping, rather than giving the islands a wide berth. Torpedoes, in that confined bay, would be devastating. They would have to run the gauntlet of both the piquet ship, the light cruiser HMS *Kent*, and von Spee had to know there would be shore batteries, so any attack would not be a foregone conclusion.

Watching the smoke, however, he realised there were likely only two ships. A scout force, testing the assumed defences? Or had von Spee made a catastrophic error, and thought the islands as yet lightly defended, leading him to send in a raiding force?

The more he watched, the more he started to think it was the latter. That von Spee was planning a hit-and-run raid to burn coal stocks, rather than coming in in full force to attack capital ships.

"Mr Baxter?"

"Marcus," he said, absently. He rarely used his first name or invited others to use it, but somehow it felt natural with Pippa.

"Marcus — what's happening?"

He turned back to her, unable to stop a grim smile spreading over his face. "The German admiral has quite possibly made a terrible mistake, and is attacking Stanley."

His smile faded as he realised that, technically, he should play no part in it — that he had been relieved of duty.

"Well, what are you going to do about it?" Pippa asked, with a hint of her old asperity.

"Get back to my ship and fight the blighters," he said, realising there was no way he was going to sit this one out. "I will see you safely back to your hotel —"

She dismissed the suggestion. "Unless you think the beastly Germans are going to land Marines to carry off sheep and womenfolk, I shall be quite all right. You must hurry."

He hesitated for only a moment longer. "You know, Pippa, whatever else happens, I'm quite glad I met you."

"And you've been tolerably diverting, Marcus," she said, stepping in quickly to kiss him on the cheek. He turned and started back down to the harbour, and HMS *Astute*.

By the time he arrived, the squadron's dispositions had begun to change dramatically. He'd seen a flurry of signals appearing on *Invincible*'s halyards and not long after, the first-class cruiser HMS *Kent* was standing out to sea to cover the armed merchant cruiser on piquet duty. *Glasgow* was getting up steam and appeared to be heading out to join the screen by the time Baxter was running up *Astute*'s gangplank, while *Bristol* was a hive of activity as her crew scrambled to put her engines back into order.

Everything seemed very placid on the scout cruiser, however. The men had gone to breakfast, but now parties of them were standing around watching the flurry of activity with little more than idle curiosity. Baxter cast around, looking for an officer, and saw Yates and Taylor standing on the afterdeck watching *Glasgow* picking up speed.

"Apparently first sighting was by a sheep-farmer's wife — she had her maids running down to telephone in progress reports," Yates was saying. "The ships would have caught us with our trousers down, if not for her."

"What the bloody hell is going on?" Baxter demanded.

"German cruisers, old chap, two of them. *Gneisenau* and *Nürnberg*, apparently. More standing out to sea — looks like the whole shooting match."

"I meant, why the bloody hell aren't we going to stations and getting underway?" Baxter ground out, barely mastering his anger.

"No orders as yet — Simons thinks the flagship's forgotten we're also under orders, and he seems quite happy about it."

"Where is he?"

"Captain's cabin, as he's the acting captain," Taylor said, starting to take umbrage at Baxter's tone. "I don't know why you're behaving as though you're the first officer, old chap — you were relieved of duty, just like Littleton."

"Well, someone needs to take this ruddy ship in hand," Baxter snarled, before turning on his heel and marching up to the captain's cabin located just below the bridge. He fought to master his anger as he went, knowing it wouldn't help in this situation. As Taylor had said, Simons was the captain until relieved of duty or a more senior officer was put in.

He knocked on the door. "Come!" came a snapped response. Baxter stepped through, cap tucked under his arm.

"Ah, Baxter," Simons said, looking suddenly uncertain. "I rather thought it was someone bringing breakfast."

Baxter kept his expression neutral — it was well past nine in the morning, which seemed a little late to be expecting breakfast. Judging by the stack of ledgers and papers on the desk, though, Simons had been up late.

"Sorry to disturb you, sir. I wanted to enquire as to whether there are any orders? The squadron is preparing for battle."

"We have not been included in Sir Doveton's signals, and in all honesty, Mr Baxter, we're not in a fit state to fight."

"With respect, sir, the ship has taken a few knocks, but she's in fighting trim. More to the point, the men are ready and raring to go."

He didn't know that for sure, of course, but nor did Simons.

"What business is it of yours?" Simons snapped, suddenly testy. "You've been relieved of duty, and if it was up to me you'd be off my ship." He glared at Baxter. "I wish to Christ it was you, not Littleton, confined ashore."

"I understand, sir," Baxter said, mastering himself with an effort, though he really couldn't understand anyone wanting Littleton aboard, whether Baxter was in the equation or not.

"Do you? You've been nothing but trouble since you came aboard. You ran from a fight, then sought one out, and now you demand that we inject ourselves into the admiral's calculations!"

Baxter sighed, put his cap down on the stack of ledgers and ran his hand through his hair. He stopped within a hair's breadth of pulling Simons out of his seat by his shirt front, but the anger came through in his voice.

"The next man who accuses me of cowardice," he said, slowly and clearly, "is going to discover exactly why I have survived — and won — more engagements that the rest of the bloody officers on this bloody ship combined."

Simons stared up at him, taken aback by his tone as much as his words. The moment balanced on a knife edge. Would Simons decide to exert his rank, or crumble?

Suddenly the bay was filled with the roar of gunfire. Stepping quickly to the seaward scuttle, Baxter peered out and saw that *Canopus'* forward 12-inch guns were aimed to the southeast, over the little town, and elevated to their maximum. A cloud of dirty yellow cordite smoke drifted away from the old battleship. He glanced at his watch. Nine twenty.

"What do you think we should do?" asked Simons, who had almost jumped out of his chair at the noise of the guns.

"Start raising steam, report our status as fuelled and battle ready to the flag, and ask for orders."

Simons pulled himself out of his chair and reached for his coat and cap. "You're confined to quarters, Baxter," he said as he straightened himself up, then smiled faintly. "But given the circumstances, I'll need you in gunnery control."

Baxter nodded. It wouldn't be the same as being on the bridge, but he'd have a better view of what was going on and at least some influence over events.

"Very good, sir," he said. "Shall I send for Littleton?"

"I doubt very much he will be in a fit state to serve just now," the acting captain said drily.

Canopus' shots, Baxter knew, signalled the start of the battle of the Falkland Islands, but the real fury would still be some time coming. They had certainly galvanised Simons and the rest of *Astute*'s crew, who seemed to have woken up to the fact that they might once again have to face the crucible of battle.

Yates and Taylor were hovering on the companionway that led up to the bridge. Both men appeared relieved that they hadn't had to come into the captain's cabin to intervene.

"What are your orders, sir?" Yates asked.

Simons managed to sound calm and official as he relayed what Baxter had just suggested to him. The two lieutenants snapped to with alacrity. Petty officers were sent down into messes to rouse the men to their duty stations, while Simons ordered Larkin down in the engine room to bring the boilers up to pressure as quickly as possible.

The acting captain looked more confident now that they were actually doing something. He was grinning as he turned from the speaking tubes. "Apparently, Larkin started bringing us up to speed as soon as *Glasgow* signalled," he said, clapping his hands together cheerfully.

At least someone knows their duty, Baxter thought.

Taylor, who was filling in as the signals officer, had a telescope trained on *Invincible*, visible through the narrow entrance to the harbour. "Flag has made our number, sir, and ordered us to follow on as soon as we can make twelve knots."

"I do believe we can do better than that already!" Simons declared, glancing surreptitiously as Baxter, who nodded slightly. "Stations to unmoor, gentlemen. Let's show these luggards how it's done, eh?"

The crew, newly reunited, went to their stations and the operation to cast off and get underway was undertaken with a minimum of fuss. *Bristol*'s crew stared enviously at *Astute* as she eased away from the dock, unable as they were to join the procession of ships, then a few started waving their hats and cheering.

"Mr Yates, you may return the compliment!" Simons called down from the bridge.

"Three cheers for *Bristol* lads!" Yates called out, and *Astute*'s men lined the railing to hail the ship they left behind.

It didn't take long for the scout cruiser to come up to speed, sliding out into Port William. The larger, deeper outer harbour was busy, with colliers and tenders steaming as fast as they could to get clear, and heavily laden smaller boats apparently abandoned by their crews in the rush to get back aboard and prepare their vessels for combat. *Glasgow* was already on her way out into the open sea, to join *Kent* in covering the lightly armed and unarmoured *Macedonia* as she ran for the safety of the harbour.

The battlecruisers, Fisher's greyhounds, were underway as *Astute* cruised towards the open sea. Battle ensigns were starting to appear at every masthead as plumes of smoke belched from *Invincible* and *Inflexible*'s stacks, the first-class cruisers following suit. Simons ordered their own ensigns hoisted. As the cruiser cleared the harbour and went out into the open sea to join the other two ships already at large, Baxter felt the knot of tension in his guts start to ease. He'd been in Zanzibar when *Königsberg*, under an enterprising commander, had managed to catch HMS *Pegasus* and shell her into a blazing hulk before she'd been able to get up steam. That was not going to happen this day. The two German ships that had approached Stanley were at least eight miles away, running for the flimsy safety of the rest of von Spee's squadron, little more than streaks of smoke on a clear and bright horizon.

Simons called the remaining officers of his command to the bridge and then hauled himself up into the wooden chair that had been previously occupied by Gregson and then Sitwell. "Gentlemen, we are reduced to a happy few," he said as they gathered around. "Mr Yates, I must ask you to abandon your torpedoes and manage the gun batteries by yourself. Mr Taylor, damage control — and make no mistake, we *will* take hits. Mr Baxter, gunnery officer's station. Let us all do our duty, and do our best to send the enemy to the bottom."

It was hardly the most rousing of speeches, but at least Simons was trying. "We'll also do our best not to go to the bottom ourselves, sir," Yates said cheerfully.

"That we will. And if we see *Kassel*, let's finish the job we started yesterday."

Baxter stood slightly apart from the other officers, assessing them. Simons, for the moment, seemed confident, but there was a brittleness to his words that gave him pause. Taylor was pale but looked determined. Yates he had complete confidence in, having seen him conduct himself over the previous week in trying circumstances.

"Flagship coming out, sir," a lookout reported, and they turned as one as the rest of the squadron deployed. *Carnarvon*, an older but still powerful armoured cruiser, led the way, Rear Admiral Stoddart's command pennant flying from her masthead. Then the battlecruisers, *Inflexible* leading the flagship, and finally *Cornwall*, even older than *Carnarvon* but still game despite the fact her engines had been taken apart mere hours before. It was nothing compared to the full might of the Grand Fleet back in Scapa, or even the Russian fleet Baxter had sailed with, but it stirred his blood nonetheless.

There were fierce grins on a lot of faces now. *Astute* had had a long, lonely voyage and had twice battled the enemy by herself. Now she was at sea as part of an overwhelming force, ready to bring an end to the depredations of von Spee's squadron and avenge Coronel.

CHAPTER TWENTY-FIVE

Von Spee did the only thing he could, outgunned and outnumbered as he was, and fled south and east as soon as the raiding force had rejoined his line. There was no shame in that, but also little hope of escaping the vengeful squadron that chased him.

As the sun climbed higher in the sky and then inched over to begin its long journey towards the western horizon, the excitement of those moments as the squadron had put to sea settled into tense anticipation of what was to come. Sturdee's ships had slowly but surely closed the range, even though both *Astute* and *Glasgow* had been reined in, so they didn't get too far ahead and risk being overwhelmed if the German line turned. Even in their best condition, the German armoured cruisers were slower, and all von Spee's ships would be long overdue maintenance. He ran for nightfall — but that wouldn't be for hours yet — or in the hope of a fog bank or squall, but the day remained resolutely clear, the sea calm. A perfect gunnery day.

Every man who wasn't on duty crammed the upper decks to enjoy the spectacular view and watch the enemy ships as they grew gradually larger, and something like a carnival atmosphere developed. As the day wore on towards its middle, the spectacle obviously lost its hold on some of the men, and from the bridge Baxter could see a card game developing and knots of men standing around talking as *Invincible* and *Inflexible* gradually edged past the slower cruisers, their powerful engines driving them onwards until only *Astute* and *Glasgow* were ahead. The men were sent to lunch shortly before midday, as it was clear that the battlecruisers at least would be in range soon, though it would take some time for *Astute* to bring her 4-inchers into action. Simons, as the captain, could have dined in splendid isolation but was invited to join the officers for a quick, mostly silent lunch in the wardroom. The room, which normally felt a bit cramped, was oddly spacious with so many officers absent, which made the atmosphere strangely oppressive.

"Thank you for your hospitality, gentlemen," Simons said, with stiff formality, as they finished their meal.

"Shall we go to battle stations, sir?" Baxter asked. He could sense Hancock disapproving of this talk happening at the dining table rather than on the bridge.

Simons didn't seem to care. "Battle stations, Mr Baxter."

The Marine bugler was on hand this time, and when ordered, blew with enthusiasm and plenty of puff, the notes of the call sounding across the ship. There was less of a stampede, as a lot of men were already at their stations in anticipation of the command being given, and everyone seemed to know what they were about.

Baxter and the other officers shook hands, wished each other luck, and went about their business. He climbed into the armoured box of the observation platform and settled in behind the powerful telescopes, field glasses, and a modern rangefinder. He was gratified to discover Pearson assigned to the position, along with a leading seaman he didn't know. The space was cramped with all three of them in it, and horribly exposed despite the thin armoured plate that enclosed it.

It did, however, afford a breathtaking view across the wide sweep of the South Atlantic. Staring through the powerful glasses, Baxter carefully observed von Spee's squadron. The two armoured cruisers, *Gneisenau* and *Scharnhorst*, would be a match for *Kent* or *Carnarvon* but were as outclassed by the

British battlecruisers as they had outclassed Cradock's ships a month ago. The light cruisers, *Leipzig*, *Nürnberg* and *Dresden* were keeping close company with the bigger, slower ships, although they would stand little chance against the big British ships.

"Flagship signalling '*engage the enemy*', sir," Rowe, the leading seaman, said in a soft West Country burr. It was shortly before one, and the double crash of *Invincible*'s forward turret firing at extreme range at a trailing German light cruiser marked the true start of the battle. Baxter watched the waterspouts raised by the heavy shells and felt a measure of sympathy for the cruiser's crew. She was the *Leipzig*, slightly older than *Astute* but not so different, and he shuddered to think what it would be like to receive 12-inch gunfire in a relatively flimsy vessel.

Inflexible fired, then the flagship again. The heavy guns didn't have a high rate of fire, but the battlecruisers' turret crews were doing a fair job of reloading, in his estimation. The shells were falling around or just short of the light cruiser, which had detached from von Spee's line and was manoeuvring independently. Baxter wondered if she would make a suicidal run at the much bigger ships, sacrificing herself to buy time for the rest of the line. *Glasgow* was running in close enough to engage her as well with her forward 6-inch gun. That went on for another few minutes, with no hits being scored, before a hoist of signals broke out on *Scharnhorst*'s signal halyards.

"What's he doing now?" Pearson, who was on the rangefinder, murmured. It became apparent a few minutes later, when the German light cruisers broke away from the line and, led by *Dresden*, started running due south as fast as they could go. At the same time, the two German armoured cruisers, their proud ensigns a splash of colour against the sea and sky, turned onto a course to close with the battlecruisers.

"He must know he can't win, sir," Pearson said, a slight note of wonder in his voice.

"He knows," Baxter said grimly. "He's sacrificing the slow ships in order to buy time for the light cruisers to escape."

He had to admit, it was an admirable move and a magnificent sight as the two cruisers turned, trying to close the distance to bring their 8-inch guns into play and at least give some sort of account of themselves while their compatriots escaped.

Sturdee was having none of it. *Invincible* hoisted a new signal. "*General chase*," Rowe read out, the almost Nelsonian tone of the signal seeming to electrify him. Almost immediately, *Glasgow* came out of the line and turned after the light cruisers. Luce, her captain, was the senior cruiser captain engaged as the elderly *Carnarvon* was lagging some miles behind, and he threw out a flurry of signals that brought *Kent* and *Cornwall* round in pursuit. *Astute*, ordered into line to follow, was beginning her turn when Pearson started to say something.

The battlecruisers opened a proper fire at that moment, firing their four main guns almost together, which drew everyone's attention to the ships. Long plumes of dirty yellow smoke jetted from the massive weapons, mixing with the coal smoke that was starting to hang around the ships as they reduced speed to fight. The shells churned up the water around the German ships, though it was too much to hope for an early victory. Baxter glanced between the big vessels thoughtfully. Sturdee was clearly going to try to keep the enemy at arm's length, close enough for his 12-inchers to hit but far enough that their own more numerous but smaller main guns were out of range. That would be a fine calculation, though, and the lack of wind meant that the battlecruisers were quickly becoming shrouded in their own smoke cloud from their engines and guns.

"Sir?" Pearson said again.

"What is it, Pearson?"

"Smoke to the south-east — looks like one ship."

Baxter swung his glasses round and quickly picked out the ship Pearson had spotted while everyone else was fixated on the developing tableau of the main battle.

"I think it's *Kassel*, sir."

"I think you may be right," Baxter said. He was angry with himself for not having spotted the ship, but kept his tone level. "Range and speed?"

"Nine miles and sixteen knots, sir."

It looked like she was steaming to intercept and join the German cruisers as they attempted to escape, which seemed futile. While Baxter could understand the desire for the support of friendly ships in the vast, lonely expanse of sea, all it would really do was hasten Neidermeyer's own ship's death.

Which was fine by him.

He made a quick calculation in his head and concluded there was still plenty of time before the ships came into long range of each other. "I'm going down to the bridge," he said, before swinging open the hatch in the bottom of the gunnery platform and lowering himself onto the ladder. Even though the enemy was still miles away and it would be at least an hour before they started to exchange fire, he still felt painfully vulnerable as he clattered down the rungs.

"We've seen her, Baxter," Simons said as he arrived on the bridge. The acting captain appeared calm, but his knuckles were white as he held his glasses.

Baxter stepped up next to the chair. "If I might make a suggestion, sir? Given the admiral has indicated a general chase and the three ships in front are already outmatched, we could separate and intercept *Kassel*."

"That would put us one on one," Simons pointed out.

"We're a match for her, and we can outrun everything but *Glasgow* to stop the enemy combining."

"Very well," Simons said. "Taylor, make to *Glasgow* and request permission to detach and engage the enemy ship to the southeast."

Baxter stepped back and waited, taking the opportunity to stretch his legs. The gunnery platform might have provided a superb vantage point, but it wasn't designed for a man of his size. Even the hatch was sufficiently tight to be awkward for him.

The cruisers ran on, *Glasgow* and *Astute* making twenty-three knots to the Germans' twenty-two. Baxter forced himself not to glance at the lead British cruiser but occasionally looked towards *Kassel* to confirm she was still closing.

"*Glasgow* signalling, sir — '*permission granted and good hunting*'," said Taylor.

Simons, to his credit, didn't hesitate and started issuing orders to bring them onto a heading that would run them between the lone German and the ships she was trying to join up with.

"Mr Baxter, you will be needed at your station shortly — we should be in range to salute *Leipzig* as we go by, which should get the gun crews warmed up!"

That would mean, of course, they would be in range of the German cruisers as they went past, though they would open the distance quickly. *Astute* was already at her full operational speed, but somehow Larkin down in the engine room was managing to squeeze at least a half knot more. Baxter raced back up the ladder to the gunnery platform and took a moment to look back towards the clash of the big ships.

As he'd suspected, the British ships were caught in a cloud of their own making, which must have made gunnery direction hellishly difficult. Despite that, it was clear that both German armoured cruisers had been hit, with at least one fire on *Scharnhorst*'s deck. They were surrounded by almost continuous waterspouts now, but had used the battlecruisers' obscured vision to close the range sufficiently to bring their main guns and secondary batteries into play, firing at their tormentors with admirable regularity and accuracy, and landing hits of their own. The 8-inch guns were potent, but would make little impact on the battlecruiser's heavy armour plating. Von Spee might have had a vague hope of scoring a lucky hit, but it was a slim chance indeed.

"Would you look at that," Rowe breathed, just as Baxter caught a flicker of white. Focusing on it, he was surprised to see a three-masted sailing ship, her sails and white steel hull bleached by the high sun as she ran down between the warring ships. By some trick of wind and distance the thunder of artillery was silenced, and for a moment the image of a graceful ship from another age hung there like a mirage.

Then her crew must have realised what they had stumbled into, as her masts suddenly sprouted as much canvas as she could carry. What might have been a Norwegian flag broke out at her masthead as she turned before the wind and ran as fast as she could from the engagement.

"Daft blighters," Pearson said.

"They may not even have known there was a war on," Baxter said, "if they've been at sea for months without a radio."

"Must have been a bit of a surprise, sir."

"Indeed. However, we have more pressing concerns."

There was something slightly surreal about the way the British ships chased the German light cruisers, not yet quite in range, while the bigger ships hammered away at each other. It took almost an hour for *Astute* to overhaul *Leipzig*, at a distinct angle to the latter's direction, for the guns to be brought to bear. The enemy ship was first to fire, landing a neat salvo short. Baxter was feeding information to Yates, increasingly frustrated by the almost non-existent centralised fire control. Their first salvo, though, neatly bracketed the enemy ship, and Baxter was fairly certain at least one shell in their second salvo burst close enough to rattle the enemy crew if nothing else. *Astute*'s gunners were getting the hang of things now, and while they couldn't match the enemy rate of fire, they were getting a good six or seven rounds a minute, hammering fire at the enemy ship as the distance between them widened. *Glasgow*, a little distance behind, was firing with her forward 6-inch gun as well, making life miserable for the German crew.

"Cease shooting!" Baxter called into the speaking tube, once he was certain they were well out of range. While *Astute*'s magazines had been restocked, thanks to the other light cruisers, he was concerned they wouldn't have enough to finish *Kassel*.

The German ship got the last word in with her longer-range guns, most of a hastily aimed flurry of shots landing short but one catching *Astute* in the stern. The ship shook with the impact and men shouted in alarm and pain, but Baxter had other issues to worry about. Taylor was doubling up on damage control and signals, and should be heading towards the impact site to assess damage and clear casualties.

Astute was diverging from the line on which both sets of ships were sailing, keeping her well out of range now. *Dresden* was flying along at the head of the German line, and as he watched, she started to outstrip her compatriots. A few minutes later, the German line scattered in the hopes that at least one of them would escape.

The speaking tube that connected him to the bridge whistled. "Gunnery, bridge," came Simons' tinny voice. "Range to *Dresden*?"

It took a moment to calculate, and Baxter could almost feel the acting captain vibrating with annoyance. "Fifteen thousand yards, sir, and opening," he said after Pearson had supplied the information. He wondered how far he could push it. "We're not going to be able to overhaul her."

There was a long pause. "Agreed," Simons said at last. "Focus on *Kassel*."

Baxter let out a breath that he hadn't realised he'd been holding. If Simons had decided to go after the lead enemy cruiser, as *Astute* was the fastest and furthest forward, they would have spent hours fruitlessly trying to overhaul her. As it was, *Kassel* was coming on regardless of her compatriots starting to scatter. The cruiser that had dogged them for so long was a sorry sight: missing both her masts, a stump of a foremast had been jury-rigged to give her lookouts at least some height, and her battle ensign flew from a pole at her stern. Her guns certainly looked to be crewed, and she showed no indication that she intended to run.

Soon, Baxter thought, then turned his attention back to the battlecruisers very briefly. They clearly had the upper hand now, both German cruisers aflame but continuing to resist, and *Carnarvon* had caught up to the main engagement to add her firepower. One of the enemy ships, which Baxter thought might have been the flagship, appeared to be trying for a ram, even though she was desperately low in the water and sluggish.

Even as he watched, she began to roll in a stately fashion, her screws still thrashing as they came out of the water. It took mere moments for the ship to roll over completely and then disappear.

"Good lord," Rowe said, sounding chilled. "No one could have survived that."

Baxter opened the speaking tube. "Bridge, gunnery. *Scharnhorst* just went down."

It was a quarter past four, he noted, and there were still several hours of good gunnery light left.

It took them another hour to meet *Kassel*. In that time, the battle had degenerated into a number of separate duels. *Glasgow* and *Cornwall* were chasing *Leipzig* somewhere to the south, while somehow the old armoured cruiser *Kent* was slowly overhauling *Nürnberg*, which on paper at least should have been faster. Only *Dresden* seemed to be making good her escape, disappearing to the southwest, while the main engagement was little more than a smudge on the horizon and the very distant rumble of the guns.

Kassel had turned at last, having appeared to be ready to give battle, and tried to move up in support of *Nürnberg*. She was certainly not making the sort of speed they'd seen from her before, no doubt the result of the long stern chase down South America after *Ludovic*, and perhaps damage *Astute* had meted out to her. Simons managed to overhaul her and put his command between her and the other ships just as *Kent* finally closed the range with her quarry far enough to bring her guns into action.

It was beginning to get misty as twilight approached, and a light drizzle was marring what had been an otherwise beautiful day. Baxter watched intently as the two ships gradually closed the distance between them, broadside to broadside. *Kassel* had the range on them, but didn't fire. *She must be low on ammunition,* he thought, *and wants to maximise the chance of hitting us.* He'd had time to consult with the crews in the magazines and shell rooms, and knew they only had enough for a few rounds per gun as well. Then it would come down to the secondary armament of little 3-pounders.

Simons called up from the bridge. "You may fire when ready, Mr Baxter," he said, the tension obvious in his voice despite the distortion of the speaking tubes.

"Thank you, sir — I propose waiting until we're a bit closer. We need to make this count."

"Don't wait too long, if you please."

Simons had matched speed with *Kassel*, which made gunnery easier, and Pearson kept up a steady flow of information as the range crept down. The two ships were steaming on converging courses, eyeing each other warily, almost as though they were daring each other to fire first.

The speaking tube from the bridge whistled. "Baxter —" Simons started.

Baxter cut across him, demanding a course change that would put them exactly parallel to *Kassel*. "Commencing directly, sir," he added by way of explanation.

Looking back through his glasses, the ship was close enough that Baxter could just make out the German sailors busy making last corrections. He leant over to the bouquet of tubes and picked the one that could connect him to Yates, who had been receiving a stream of corrections data from Pearson. "Target on the port beam, all guns — commence, continuous!"

After a brief pause, *Astute*'s six guns fired in a rippling broadside. At that range, they could still quite easily have missed, particularly without previous salvos to work in to the target. At least three shells struck home, however, the guns firing on a relatively flat trajectory and hammering into *Kassel*'s side and conning tower. Vitally, one shell managed to land in one of the barbettes on her broadside, shattering the gun and making a horrific mess of her crew.

Kassel responded, the guns disappearing behind puffs of smoke and long muzzle flashes. She mounted one fewer guns on the broadside and was a mounting down, but one of the four shells she fired detonated against *Astute*'s conning tower. At the same time, much smaller explosions blossomed across water and against her side — the ships were close enough that *Kassel*'s secondary guns, small 2-inch semi-automatic guns, were firing.

It would be a fight to the death, Baxter knew. Without waiting for orders, the crews on *Astute*'s secondary guns, two three-pounders on each broadside, joined their fire to the main guns. The scout cruiser shook as she was hit, but while the German guns had a higher rate of fire, *Astute* was throwing a heavier broadside. There were fires aft on *Kassel* as more and more British shells hit her. The German's light guns were taking a terrible toll on *Astute*'s exposed gun crew, though, while the German guns had at least some protection from light shells and fragments behind their gun shields.

"Bridge, gunnery," Baxter said into the speaking tube. "Request permission to close range and finish the job."

There was no response, but the noise was so great that it was entirely possible that no one had heard him. Baxter didn't know exactly how many rounds they had fired, but they must have been running low.

One of *Kassel*'s secondary guns put a shell into *Astute*'s upperworks just below the gunner platform, shrapnel pinging off the underside. "That seems a bit personal," Rowe said, just before a second round came through the platform's armoured side and detonated over his breastbone. Baxter choked on fumes from the explosion, his ears ringing from the detonation. His left arm stung where shrapnel had peppered him, but it was nothing compared to the awful wound that cratered the leading seaman's chest. Somehow, the Cornishman was still alive, and managed to whisper something about Christ — a prayer or a curse, Baxter couldn't tell — before his brain caught up with his body and died.

CHAPTER TWENTY-SIX

"Out, now!" Baxter shouted to Pearson, who had rocked back on his stool and looked stunned.

The petty officer ducked down to open the hatch, just avoiding having his head torn off as another shell flew over the confined space. "Jammed, sir!" he shouted over the racket.

"Move!" Baxter reached up to the top of the gunnery platform, grabbed on to the spar there and hoisted himself up so he could kick down with both heels and all his weight behind the blow. The hatch splintered, then disintegrated with the second blow. "Go!"

Pearson went out, fast and agile, his training making him well used to navigating the upperworks of a warship. Baxter squeezed out after him, and looking down, saw the ladder had been blown away by a previous hit. "Jump!" he yelled, but Pearson had already swung out onto one of the support stays and was shimmying down.

One of the light gun crews on *Kassel* had definitely decided to make a sport of peppering their gunnery platform. As more shells smacked into it, Baxter swung from the lowest rung that still existed on the torn ladder, then let himself drop the remaining ten feet down onto the chart room's roof. He landed badly, sprawling as he twisted his ankle, but was able to hobble down the companionway to the bridge.

"Keep firing, damn your eyes!" Simons was yelling down to the forward gun crews, a manic note in his voice. While it was good to see he'd finally found his fighting spirit, the last thing the men needed was a madman on the bridge. Baxter limped over to him, put a hand on his shoulder and squeezed until

Simons swivelled round. "Sir, collect yourself," he said, his voice low and hard.

Simons swallowed, taking several deep breaths. "You're covered in blood, man — you look a disgrace!" he said, then took another breath. "Are we winning, Baxter?"

"We will, sir. With your permission, I'd like to take her closer."

"Closer? Are you mad?" Simons screamed. "We should stand off and batter that thing to scrap!"

His voice was rising again. Baxter glanced around to see if anyone was looking. Pearson quickly looked away as Baxter tripped his acting captain and stunned him with a heel to the head on the way down.

"Pearson, the captain has been hit!" Baxter called out. "Take him to the sickbay, would you?"

"Aye, sir," Pearson said punctiliously, stepping forward to support the dazed commander.

Baxter looked around, able to assess the situation better now that he was on the bridge. *Astute* was on fire, though Taylor seemed to have things under control. All the guns that could bear were still firing, although their rate of fire was dropping off as the crews suffered under enemy attack.

The German's rate of fire seemed to be slackening as well, certainly from the main guns, although the secondary guns were still making the scout cruiser's upper deck a miserable place to be, and she had more than a few fires burning on her deck as well. The ships were close enough that he could see men struggling to get hoses on to the flames. As he watched, one fire-fighting party took a direct hit from one of *Astute*'s main guns, the men torn apart and the hose left snaking as it jetted high-pressure water. *Kassel* was slowing down, and although she was a more heavily armed ship, she seemed to be getting the worst of the fight. Her battle ensigns were still flying, though, and she was still shooting.

Baxter moved to the centre of the bridge. He didn't know where the other officers were, and he knew his duty. He ordered a course change to bring *Astute*'s bow round towards the enemy, then moved to the engine telegraph and pushed it to 'ahead full'.

Yates appeared on deck, eyes darting around. "Just saw Simons," he said, stepping closer but still having to shout over the noise. "Muttered something about a shell splinter. Poor chap didn't look at all well. Lucky to be alive, though. That probably makes you senior man, sir."

Baxter nodded, expressionless. They were both tacitly ignoring the fact that, while he was technically fourth lieutenant, he was also relieved of duty.

"What are your orders, sir? We're down to a couple of rounds per gun for the main battery. Are we going to ram?"

Baxter glanced at the other ship. They were closing fast, and while *Kassel* was trying to turn to port, aiming to double back along *Astute*'s course, she seemed to be sluggish on the steering. It was also a mistake, one of Neidermeyer's first.

"Don't be ridiculous," Baxter said cheerfully. "This isn't the Roman navy."

He quickly outlined his intended course, gave Yates his orders and sent him on his way.

This was the most dangerous time. The ships were closing fast, and the light was starting to fail. *Astute*'s speed and the acute angle of approach made her a hard target, but she was still being hit. The angle also meant that only the forward 4-inch guns and the three-pounders mounted above could give fire, although all the crews were giving the enemy everything they had, and had a much easier target to aim for.

Baxter stepped to the rail and leaned forward, trying to take the weight off his sprained ankle but not wanting to show any weakness in front of the bridge crew. The air reeked of smoke, not just from the funnels but also from the wooden deck burning, and of blood and spent explosives. The men were still at their stations, some looking scared, others with a fierce gleam in their eyes as the forward guns put shell after shell into the torn-up aft of the enemy ship. Yates had found Taylor and sent him to the starboard guns, which until now had been unengaged but had been stripped of crew to keep the port guns firing, before disappearing belowdecks.

Baxter forced himself to walk back to the speaking tubes, rather than limp. *Kassel* was still turning, painfully slowly, to bring her broadside to bear again. *Too slow*, Baxter thought with grim satisfaction. Before *Astute* surged across her enemy's foaming wake, Baxter used the telegraph to order a reduction in speed. The way started to come off the cruiser, not by much, but it would give the gunners more time to make their last few shots count.

Baxter selected a speaking tube. "Yates, are you there?" he called into it.

"Waiting for your orders, sir," came the reply.

The ships were barely eight hundred yards apart. If *Kassel* was in a better condition and had more ammunition, she would have torn *Astute* to pieces at this range. Baxter knew in his gut what Neidermeyer planned to do, as he seemingly didn't have the option of drowning his enemy in a torrent of well-aimed shells.

Astute's starboard guns started a steady, considered fire at almost point-blank range, and while some shells went over, most hammered into the enemy ship. One of *Kassel*'s stern guns was hit, tearing clean from its mount. "Just surrender, you bastard," Baxter whispered. They'd come here for vengeance, for Cradock and for the men and ships he'd commanded, and for the blows this ship had struck against them. Baxter found he'd lost his taste for it, watching this fine ship being torn apart. But she kept her colours flying, and over the water he could very faintly hear the German crew singing what sounded like their national anthem.

"Mr Yates, launch!" he snapped into the speaking tube.

A moment later, a line of bubbles shot from the cruiser's side as Yates discharged both portside tubes. The torpedoes ran straight and true as *Kassel* continued her turn, finally bringing her broadside to bear again.

"Hard port!" Baxter ordered the wheelhouse, bringing *Astute* round to run directly away from the enemy. He'd seen the matching trails from the German cruiser as she loosed her own torpedoes. Someone had seen the weapons launched by *Astute*, but it was too late for her to turn to avoid them.

Both British 18-inch torpedoes hit, each one delivering 320 pounds of high explosive below *Kassel*'s waterline. Remarkably, both detonated, enormous plumes of water rising as the weapons ripped out the ship's guts and broke her back. It would be hell in the lower decks, boiler and engine rooms, as tons of water flooded in and anyone who had survived the blasts scrabbled to get out before they were dragged down to a watery grave.

The turn Baxter had ordered had brought *Astute* out of the path of the German torpedoes and he watched their tracks running parallel to and then overtaking the ship. Baxter ordered a course change to bring them back towards the enemy ship, then limped to the captain's chair and pulled himself into it. His ankle was throbbing, and he wasn't entirely sure he hadn't fractured it. *Kassel*, the ship that had hunted them for more than a thousand miles, had broken in two. There was an explosion of steam as one of her boilers went, and her sharp bow was almost pointed skyward. There were men in the frigid water, clinging to bits of flotsam or trying to get damaged boats clear of the wreckage before they were sucked under. *Astute*'s sailors were lining the rail, shouting to them to swim for it or starting work to repair boats and gather rope and anything buoyant to throw to the men as the cruiser returned to the scene of her final victory.

Yates arrived back on the bridge, followed by Taylor.

"Orders, sir?" the latter asked.

"Prepare to recover survivors, and get anything that floats into the water — those men won't last long in these temperatures. And get the galleys going — our men will need food, and the survivors will need a hot drink."

"Aye, sir." Taylor snapped a salute before dashing away.

Yates was staring with a mix of curiosity and apprehension at Baxter. "You did it, sir," he said quietly.

"No, Mr Yates, you and the others did. Even Simons, until his unfortunate wounding. I'm relieved of duty, remember?"

Yates nodded, then glanced out as *Astute* nosed towards the spreading wreckage that was all that marked the passing of another ship. They were alone on the sea, although the horizon flickered with distant gunfire, the noise coming to them faintly. "Any further orders, sir?"

"Yes. Signal the flag — pleased to report enemy cruiser *Kassel* sunk by torpedo and gunfire. We are recovering survivors and proceeding to Port Stanley."

A NOTE TO THE READER

The Battle of Coronel, fought at night and in truly atrocious conditions on 1st November 1914, was the Royal Navy's first major defeat in more than a century. In common with many battles of this period, it was an engagement that happened almost by chance but led to the deaths of 1,660 men. Much has been written about whether Kit Cradock should have taken his outnumbered and outmatched ships against von Spee, and who was ultimately responsible for the British ships being in that position. Suffice to say, the action galvanised the Admiralty and was the first major test of the incoming First Sea Lord, Sir John Arbuthnot Fisher of *Dreadnought* fame. The situation also exemplified a significant challenge for the Royal Navy throughout the war; while it was at the time the largest navy in the world, it also had an enormous sphere of responsibility both to protect British and Allied shipping, and also to strangle Germany's trade. By detaching three battlecruisers from the Grand Fleet, charged as it was with containing the *Kaiserliche Marine's* High Seas Fleet, Fisher was taking a calculated risk to eliminate a significant threat to British trade and avenge a defeat.

The Battle of the Falkland Islands, though it was fought in daylight and in perfect gunnery conditions, was in some ways the mirror image of Coronel. Neither squadron expected to fight — von Spee expected a surprise attack on a lightly defended coaling base, while Sir Doveton Sturdee was anticipating a few days for his ships to be overhauled and resupplied before embarking on an arduous hunt for enemy cruisers raiding the rich shipping waters of South America.

The German squadron fought with skill and determination, demonstrating outstanding gunnery, but could neither outrun nor outfight their pursuers. Von Spee's quality as a man and a commander can be seen in his order for his slower armoured cruisers to turn and fight to try to give the light cruisers a chance to escape, although in the end only one light cruiser remained at large. He comes across in the historical record as a thoroughly decent officer and gentleman, who refused to celebrate his victory over an officer he knew and respected. He was also a realist who knew he was in an impossible position, low on fuel and ammunition and far from a friendly harbour, with little chance of getting home. Refusing a celebratory bouquet of flowers from the German expatriate community in Chile, he is said to have remarked, "These will do nicely for my grave." In the end, both he and his two sons went down with their ships at the Falklands and know no other grave but the sea.

As usual, I have tried to keep as close as possible to the historical events, people and ships. I took a slight liberty by having Jackie Fisher visiting Devonport, allowing Baxter to seize the initiative and wrest himself from the Naval Intelligence Division's influence. Vice-Admiral Sir Doveton Sturdee, who was not as feted or recognised as he deserved due to Fisher's enmity, was a fascinating man, who had indeed taken his ease ashore at Stanley the night before the unanticipated battle, which led to Baxter's almost disastrous encounter with him. HMS *Astute* and her crew are entirely fictitious, although the Fearless-class of scout cruisers (often referred to as light cruisers) I assigned him to were quite real. Fast, lightly armed and armoured, they were intended to be the eyes of the battlefleet and to lead destroyer squadrons, but were already an outdated concept by the start of the war. There have been two HMS *Astutes*, both submarines, and I picked the name in part because it sounded appropriate for a scout vessel and in part due to a long discussion I once had with someone who'd taken exception to the naming of the Astute-class of nuclear submarines.

SMS *Kassel* is an invented member of the Königsberg-class of light cruisers (the namesake of which gave Baxter so much trouble in East Africa). There were, however, German light cruisers in that area and Cradock himself gave chase to one he encountered by chance in the mid-Atlantic while she was transferring guns and men to a passenger liner to convert her into a commerce raider. SS *Ludovic* is fictional, though based as closely as possible on a number of fast German passenger liners that had brief and varied careers as commerce raiders early in the war.

There is evidence that German agents in Montevideo were aware that a powerful British squadron had assembled at the Abrolhos Rocks off Uruguay's coast, but for some reason did not pass the information on as a matter of urgency. There is nothing to say that British intelligence had any hand in preventing it. While 'Blinker' Hall — Director of Naval Intelligence — claimed in later life that von Spee had been lured into attacking the Falklands through false wireless transmissions, this must be taken with a pinch of salt. German agents in various South American countries *had* made arrangements to send out colliers and supply ships to meet the German squadron in the hopes it would make it to the east coast of the continent, so it is not outside the bounds of possibility that a fast ship might have been sent bearing vital supplies and information. This, then, is the gap in which I have written Baxter's most recent adventure.

Towards the end of 1914, the US remained a sleeping giant in world affairs. Woodrow Wilson would become committed to finding peace without territorial changes and with everyone's honour and dignity left intact. There was a strong German immigrant population in the US, however, and it could be quite vocal in support of the Kaiser. *Leutnant* Leiter, one imagines, might be one such man. I doubt we have heard the last of him.

I am greatly indebted to a number of people for helping to bring this novel to fruition. The members of the Edinburgh Schismatics writing group suffered through and helped polish some earlier drafts, and their constructive and fair criticism is always welcome. My good friend Gareth Hunt provided invaluable insight into some technical details around propellant, as well as being my conduit to the incomparable Neil Ferguson, Keeper of Firearms and Artillery at the Royal Armouries in Leeds, his colleagues and his predecessor Peter Smithurst, who gave a complete stranger their time and expertise freely. Any technical errors that have crept into the book are my own. Last but not least, thank you to the editorial team at Sapere Books for their work in preparing this book for publication.

Thank you for taking the time to read this, my fifth historical fiction novel — I hope you enjoyed reading it as much as I enjoyed researching and writing it. If you enjoyed it, it would be great if you could drop a review onto **Amazon** and **Goodreads** — these can be a great help to authors. You can find me on Twitter (**@ReaverRedemptor**) and Facebook (**Tim Chant Author**) for short rambles about my hobbies, other interests and writing. I'm also developing a blog, mostly about naval history and my great-grandfather's career in the Royal Navy, which can be found here: **timchantauthor.com**.

Sapere Books is an exciting new publisher of brilliant fiction and popular history.

To find out more about our latest releases and our monthly bargain books visit our website:
saperebooks.com